CRYSTAL NIGHTS
AND
OTHER STORIES

CRYSTAL NIGHTS
AND
OTHER STORIES

GREG EGAN

Subterranean Press 2009

First Edition

"Lost Continent" was first published in *The Starry Rift*, edited by Jonathan Strahan; Viking Penguin, 2008.

"Crystal Nights" was first published in *Interzone 215*, April 2008.

"Steve Fever" was first published in *Technology Review*, November/December 2007.

"TAP" was first published in *Asimov's Science Fiction*, November 1995.

"Induction" was first published in *Foundation 100*, edited by Farah Mendlesohn and Graham Sleight; Science Fiction Foundation, Summer 2007.

"Singleton" was first published in *Interzone 176*, February 2002.

"Oracle" was first published in *Asimov's Science Fiction*, July 2000.

"Border Guards" was first published in *Interzone 148*, October 1999.

"Hot Rock" was first published in *Godlike Machines*, edited by Jonathan Strahan; Science Fiction Book Club, 2009.

ISBN
978-1-59606-240-5

Subterranean Press
PO Box 190106
Burton, MI 48519

www.subterraneanpress.com

TABLE OF CONTENTS

INTRODUCTION

"Crystal Nights", the title story of this collection, has its roots in a subplot of a novel of mine called *Permutation City* that was published in 1994.

In that novel, a group of people who migrate into an artificial universe that will be isolated from our own reality bring with them the computer code to simulate an entire planetary biosphere. Given the premises of the novel, they have the ability to run this code much faster than their own portion of the universe. Billions of years pass on the simulated planet, and ultimately intelligent life evolves there.

This kind of scenario is something of a science-fictional cliché, and to be honest, when I wrote the novel I didn't reflect much on what it would actually entail: as in the history of our own planet, many millions of creatures would be born, live lives that were often short and brutal, then die, generally from disease, starvation, or the claws of a predator. And while some of us might be unmoved by such a fate for mere animals, given that our own natural world continues in precisely the same fashion to this day, in the novel the creators of the biosphere indulge in no special intervention to spare any intelligent, self-aware species from the degradations of their long, slow climb out of a world of suffering and brutality.

Failing to take any of this seriously, or even to mention the issue, was sheer laziness on my part. *Permutation City* already had enough going on that it would have been unwise to make this a major aspect of the book, but ignoring the matter completely was unforgivable.

In 2007, I discussed this point on a web page I wrote to answer some Frequently Asked Questions about the novel's metaphysics. I added:

> This is potentially an important issue in the real world. It might not be long before people are seriously trying to "evolve" artificial intelligence in their computers. Now, it's one thing to use genetic algorithms to come up with various specialized programs that perform simple tasks, but to "breed", assess, and kill millions of sentient programs would be an abomination. If the first AI was created that way, it would have every right to despise its creators.

To my surprise, in online discussions of this web page a number of people strongly took issue with this claim. Some insisted that there would be no moral fault whatsoever in using evolution to create new life, and that the worst aspects of the process could be circumvented; others claimed that, in any case, the AI end product ought to be, and probably would be, simply grateful for its existence.

The ability of people to ignore, trivialize, or rationalize away the moral issues surrounding this matter fascinated and disturbed me. Having failed once to deal with the moral aspects of artificial evolution myself, I resolved to include them in a new story. I started writing "Crystal Nights" in April 2007, and worked on it intermittently in the following months, finally completing it in August.

Coincidentally, just after I'd finished the story, the philosopher Nick Bostrom began garnering fresh publicity for his "simulation argument", a warmed-over version of a very old SF cliché. Bostrom argues that unless advanced technological civilizations are rare and short-lived, simulated worlds resembling our own should vastly outnumber the natural worlds. And if there are more simulated worlds than natural ones, we would be naive to expect our own world to be natural. By this line of reasoning, Bostrom even managed to prompt the journalist John Tierney to declare, in *The New York Times* of August 14, 2007:

> My gut feeling is that the odds are better than 20 percent [that we live in a computer simulation], maybe better than even.

This is absurd. While it's easy to assemble a list of plausible motives for various kinds of computerized *analyses* of historical events, those that would require a perfect simulation of an entire world—complete with a cast of fully conscious actors—are vastly thinner on the ground, and the claim that such simulations would be so commonplace as to outnumber actual realities is sensationalist nonsense. The idea that our distant descendants would have no alternative means to satisfy their curiosity about our lives, and would be utterly oblivious to the moral dimensions of such an endeavor, is both silly and odious. But Bostrom himself, and many of the people who discussed his claims, were only too happy to trivialize the issue. Tierney was especially puerile:

> It's unsettling to think of the world being run by a futuristic computer geek, although we might at last dispose of that classic theological question: How could God allow so much evil in the world? For the same reason there are plagues and earthquakes and battles in games like World of Warcraft. Peace is boring, Dude.

This kind of throw-away line might be good for a laugh, but even in a world of crass reality television we don't see literal re-enactments of the Black Plague, or of Nazi death camps, complete with unknowing, unwilling participants raised from birth to play out roles for our amusement and edification.

I have very little fear that our distant descendants will be interested in doing anything with their computing resources besides creating descendants of their own who live even richer and more fulfilling lives; like us, they will want to see their children blessed with peace, prosperity and knowledge, rather than contriving bizarre excuses to re-capitulate the suffering and squalor of their dead ancestors.

What is disturbing is not the vanishingly small chance that there is an artificial substrate to our own world, but the fact that we live at a time when people can still convince themselves that such activities might be necessary or excusable. I suspect that this mentality is a fleeting by-product of a confluence of unfortunate cultural influences: some people hold vastly inflated hopes for the fruits of AI, but manage simultaneously to trivialize or ignore the moral status of such beings. When something is non-existent it can be hard to iron out all the fantasies and contradictions swirling around it, and science fiction can exacerbate these problem as often as it helps us get things straight.

My hope is that once AI ceases to be purely hypothetical, the bulk of humanity will grasp the consequences with more honesty and maturity than many of the participants in the debate so far—and certainly, more compassion than is displayed by the protagonist of "Crystal Nights".

Greg Egan
November 2008

LOST CONTINENT

1

Ali's uncle took hold of his right arm and offered it to the stranger, who gripped it firmly by the wrist.

"From this moment on, you must obey this man," his uncle instructed him. "Obey him as you would obey your father. Your life depends on it."

"Yes, uncle." Ali kept his eyes respectfully lowered.

"Come with me, boy," said the stranger, heading for the door.

"Yes, haji," Ali mumbled, following meekly. He could hear his mother still sobbing quietly in the next room, and he had to fight to hold back his own tears. He had said good-bye to his mother and his uncle, but he'd had no chance for any parting words with his cousins. It was halfway between midnight and dawn, and if anyone else in the household was awake they were huddled beneath their blankets, straining to hear what was going on but not daring to show their faces.

The stranger strode out into the cold night, hand still around Ali's wrist like an iron shackle. He led Ali to the Land Cruiser that sat in the icy mud outside his uncle's house, its frosted surfaces glinting in the starlight, an apparition from a nightmare. Just the smell of it made Ali rigid with fear; it was the smell that had presaged his father's death, his brother's disappearance. Experience had taught him that such a machine could only bring tragedy, but his uncle had entrusted him to its driver. He forced himself to approach without resisting.

The stranger finally released his grip on Ali and opened a door at the rear of the vehicle. "Get in and cover yourself with the blanket. Don't move, and don't make a sound, whatever happens. Don't ask me any questions, and don't ask me to stop. Do you need to take a piss?"

"No, haji," Ali replied, his face burning with shame. Did the man think he was a child?

"All right, get in there."

As Ali complied, the man spoke in a grimly humorous tone. "You think you show me respect by calling me 'haji'? Every old man in your village is 'haji'! I haven't just been to Mecca. I've been there in the time of the Prophet, peace be upon him." Ali covered his face with the ragged blanket, which was imbued with the concentrated stench of the machine. He pictured the stranger standing in the darkness for a moment, musing arrogantly about his unnatural pilgrimage. The man wore enough gold to buy Ali's father's farm ten times over. Now his uncle had sold that farm, and his mother's jewellery—the hard-won wealth of generations—and handed all the money to this boastful man, who claimed he could spirit Ali away to a place and a time where he'd be safe.

The Land Cruiser's engine shuddered into life. Ali felt the vehicle moving backward at high speed, an alarming sensation. Then it stopped and moved forward, squealing as it changed direction; he could picture the tracks in the mud.

It was his first time ever in one of these machines. A few of his friends had taken rides with the Scholars, sitting in the back in the kind with the uncovered tray. They'd fired rifles into the air and shouted wildly before tumbling out, covered with dust, alive with excitement for the next ten days. Those friends had all been Sunni, of course. For Shi'a, rides with the Scholars had a different kind of ending.

Khurosan had been ravaged by war for as long as Ali could remember. For decades, tyrants of unimaginable cruelty from far in the future had given their weapons to factions throughout the country, who'd used them in their squabbles over land and power. Sometimes the warlords had sent recruiting parties into the valley to take young men to use as soldiers, but in the early days the villagers had banded together to hide their sons, or to bribe the recruiters to move on. Sunni or Shi'a, it made no difference; neighbor had worked with neighbor to outsmart the bandits who called themselves soldiers, and keep the village intact.

Then four years ago, the Scholars had come, and everything had changed.

Whether the Scholars were from the past or the future was unclear, but they certainly had weapons and vehicles from the future. They had ridden triumphantly across Khurosan in their Land Cruisers, killing some warlords, bribing others, conquering the bloody patchwork of squalid fiefdoms one by one. Many people had cheered them on, because they had promised to bring unity and piety to the land. The warlords and their rabble armies had kidnapped and raped women and boys at will; the Scholars had hung the rapists from the gates of the cities. The warlords had set up checkpoints on every road, to extort money from travelers; the Scholars had opened the roads again for trade and pilgrimage in safety.

The Scholars' conquest of the land remained incomplete, though, and a savage battle was still being waged in the north. When the Scholars had come to Ali's village looking for soldiers themselves, they'd brought a new strategy to the recruitment drive: they would only take Shi'a for the front line, to face the bullets of the unsubdued warlords. Shi'a, the Scholars declared, were not true Muslims, and this was the only way they could redeem themselves: laying down their lives for their more pious and deserving Sunni countrymen.

This deceit, this flattery and cruelty, had cleaved the village in two. Many friends remained loyal across the divide, but the old trust, the old unity was gone.

Two months before, one of Ali's neighbors had betrayed his older brother's hiding place to the Scholars. They had come to the farm in the early hours of the morning, a dozen of them in two Land Cruisers, and dragged Hassan away. Ali had watched helplessly from his own hiding place, forbidden by his father to try to intervene. And what could their rifles have done against the Scholars' weapons, which sprayed bullets too fast and numerous to count?

The next morning, Ali's father had gone to the Scholars' post in the village, to try to pay a bribe to get Hassan back. Ali had waited, watching the farm from the hillside above. When a single Land Cruiser had returned, his heart had swelled with hope. Even when the Scholars had thrown a limp figure from the vehicle, he'd thought it might be Hassan, unconscious from a beating but still alive, ready to be nursed back to health.

It was not Hassan. It was his father. They had slit his throat and left a coin in his mouth.

Ali had buried his father and walked half a day to the next village, where his mother had been staying with his uncle. His uncle had arranged the sale of the farm to a wealthy neighbor, then sought out a *mosarfar-e-waqt* to take Ali to safety.

Ali had protested, but it had all been decided, and his wishes had counted for nothing. His mother would live under the protection of her brother, while Ali built a life for himself in the future. Perhaps Hassan would escape from the Scholars, God willing, but that was out of their hands. What mattered, his mother insisted, was getting her youngest son out of the Scholars' reach.

In the back of the Land Cruiser, Ali's mind was in turmoil. He didn't want to flee this way, but he had no doubt that his life would be in danger if he remained. He wanted his brother back and his father avenged, he wanted to see the Scholars destroyed, but their only remaining enemies with any real power were murderous criminals who hated his own people as much as the Scholars themselves did. There was no righteous army to join, with clean hands and pure hearts.

The Land Cruiser slowed then came to a halt, the engine still idling. The *mosarfar-e-waqt* called out a greeting, then began exchanging friendly words with someone, presumably a Scholar guarding the road.

Ali's blood turned to ice; what if this stranger simply handed him over? How much loyalty could mere money buy? His uncle had made inquiries of people with connections up and down the valley, and had satisfied himself about the man's reputation, but however much the *mosarfar-e-waqt* valued his good name and the profits it brought him, there'd always be some other kind of deal to be made, some profit to be found in betrayal.

Both men laughed, then bid each other farewell. The Land Cruiser accelerated.

For what seemed like hours, Ali lay still and listened to the purring of the engine, trying to judge how far they'd come. He had never been out of the valley in his life, and he had only the sketchiest notion of what lay beyond. As dawn approached, his curiosity overwhelmed him, and he moved quietly to shift the blanket just enough to let him catch a glimpse through the rear window. There was a mountain peak visible to the left, topped with snow, crisp in the predawn light. He wasn't sure if this was a mountain he knew, viewed from an unfamiliar angle, or one he'd never seen before.

Not long afterward they stopped to pray. They made their ablutions in a small, icy stream. They prayed side by side, Sunni and Shi'a, and Ali's fear and suspicion retreated a little. However arrogant this man was, at least he didn't share the Scholars' contempt for Ali's people.

After praying, they ate in silence. The *mosarfar-e-waqt* had brought bread, dried fruit and salted meat. As Ali looked around, it was clear that they'd long ago left any kind of man-made track behind. They were following a mountain pass, on higher ground than the valley but still far below the snow line.

They traveled through the mountains for three days, finally emerging onto a wind-blasted, dusty plain. Ali had grown stiff from lying curled up for so long, and the second time they stopped on the plain he made the most of the chance to stretch his legs, wandering away from the Land Cruiser for a minute or two.

When he returned, the *mosarfar-e-waqt* said, "What are you looking for?"

"Nothing, haji."

"Are you looking for a landmark, so you can find this place again?"

Ali was baffled. "No, haji."

The man stepped closer, then struck him across the face, hard enough to make him stagger. "If you tell anyone about the way you came, you'll hear some more bad news about your family. Do you understand me?"

"Yes, haji."

The man strode back to the Land Cruiser. Ali followed him, shaking. He'd had no intention of betraying any detail of their route, any secret of the trade, to anyone, but now his uncle had been named as hostage against any indiscretion, real or imagined.

Late in the afternoon, Ali heard a sudden change in the sound of the wind, a high-pitched keening that made his teeth ache. Unable to stop himself, he lifted his head from beneath the blanket.

Ahead of them was a small dust storm, dancing across the ground. It was moving away from them, weaving back and forth as it retreated, like a living thing trying to escape them. The Land Cruiser was gaining on it. The heart of the storm was dark, thick with sand, knotted with wind. Ali's chest tightened. This was it: the *pol-e-waqt*, the bridge between times. Everyone in his village had heard of such things, but nobody could agree what they were: the work of men, the work of djinn, the work of God. Whatever their origin, some men had learned their secrets. No *mosarfar-e-waqt* had ever truly tamed them, but nobody else could find these bridges or navigate their strange depths.

They drew closer. The dust rained onto the windows of the Land Cruiser, as fine as any sand Ali had seen, yet as loud as the hailstones that fell sometimes on the roof of his house. Ali forgot all about his instructions; as they vanished into the darkness, he threw off the blanket and started praying aloud.

The *mosarfar-e-waqt* ignored him, muttering to himself and consulting the strange, luminous maps and writing that changed and flowed in front of him through some magic of machinery. The Land Cruiser ploughed ahead, buffeted by dust and wind but palpably advancing. Within a few minutes, it was clear to Ali that they'd traveled much further than the storm's full width as revealed from the outside. They had left his time and his country behind, and were deep inside the bridge.

The lights of the Land Cruiser revealed nothing but a hand's-breadth of flying dust ahead of them. Ali peered surreptitiously at the glowing map in the front, but it was a maze of branching and reconnecting paths that made no sense to him. The *mosarfar-e-waqt* kept running a fingertip over one path, then cursing and shifting to another, as if he'd discovered some obstacle or danger ahead. Ali's uncle had reassured him that at least they wouldn't run into the Scholars in this place, as they had come to Khurosan through another, more distant bridge. The entrance to that one was watched over night and day by a convoy of vehicles that chased it endlessly across the desert, like the bodyguards of some staggering, drunken king.

A hint of sunlight appeared in the distance, then grew slowly brighter. After a few minutes, though, the *mosarfar-e-waqt* cursed and steered away from it. Ali was dismayed. This man had been unable to tell his uncle where or when Ali would end up, merely promising him safety from the Scholars. Some people in the village—the kind with a friend of a friend who'd fled into the future—spoke of a whole vast continent where peace and prosperity reigned from shore to shore. The rulers had no weapons or armies of their own, but were chosen by the people for the wisdom, justice and mercy they displayed. It sounded like paradise on Earth, but Ali would believe in such a place when he saw it with his own eyes.

Another false dawn, then another. The body of the Land Cruiser began to moan and shudder. The *mosarfar-e-waqt* cut the engine, but the vehicle kept moving, driven by the wind, or the ground itself. Or maybe both, but not in the same direction: Ali felt the wheels slipping over the treacherous river of sand. Suddenly there was a sharp pain deep inside his ears, then a sound like the scream of a giant bird, and the door beside him was gone. He snatched at the back of the seat in front of him, but his hands closed over nothing but the flimsy blanket as the wind dragged him out into the darkness.

Ali bellowed until his lungs were empty. But the painful landing he was braced for never came: the blanket had snagged on something in the vehicle, and the force of the wind was holding him above the sand. He tried to pull himself back toward the Land Cruiser, hand over hand, but then he felt a tear run through the blanket. Once more he steeled himself for a fall, but then the tearing stopped with a narrow ribbon of cloth still holding him.

Ali prayed. "Merciful God, if you take me now please bring Hassan back safely to his home." For a year or two his uncle could care for his mother, but he was old, and he had too many mouths to feed. With no children of her own, her life would be unbearable.

A hand stretched out to him through the blinding dust. Ali reached out and took it, grateful now for the man's iron grip. When the *mosarfar-e-waqt* had dragged him back into the Land Cruiser, Ali crouched at the stranger's feet, his teeth chattering. "Thank you, haji. I am your servant, haji." The *mosarfar-e-waqt* climbed back into the front without a word.

Time passed, but Ali's thoughts were frozen. Some part of him had been prepared to die, but the rest of him was still catching up.

Sunlight appeared from nowhere: the full blaze of noon, not some distant promise. "This will suffice," the *mosarfar-e-waqt* announced wearily.

Ali shielded his eyes from the glare, then when he uncovered them the world was spinning. Blue sky and sand, changing places.

The bruising thud he'd been expecting long before finally came, the ground slapping him hard from cheek to ankle. He lay still, trying to judge how badly he was hurt. The patch of sand in front of his face was red. Not from blood: the sand itself was red as ocher.

There was a sound like a rapid exhalation, then he felt heat on his skin. He raised himself up on his elbows. The Land Cruiser was ten paces away, upside down, and on fire. Ali staggered to his feet and approached it, searching for the man who'd saved his life. Behind the wrecked vehicle, a storm like the one that the mouth of the bridge had made in his own land was weaving drunkenly back and forth, dancing like some demented hooligan pleased with the havoc it had wreaked.

He caught a glimpse of an arm behind the flames. He rushed toward the man, but the heat drove him back.

"Please God," he moaned, "give me courage."

As he tried again to breach the flames, the storm lurched forward to greet him. Ali stood his ground, but the Land Cruiser spun around on its roof, swiping his shoulder and knocking him down. He climbed to his feet and tried to circle around to the missing door, but as he did the wind rose up, fanning the flames.

The wall of heat was impenetrable now, and the storm was playing with the Land Cruiser like a child with a broken top. Ali backed away, glancing around at the impossible red landscape, wondering if there might be anyone in earshot with the power to undo this calamity. He shouted for help, his eyes still glued to the burning wreck in the hope that a miracle might yet deliver the unconscious driver from the flames.

The storm moved forward again, coming straight for the Land Cruiser. Ali turned and retreated; when he looked over his shoulder the vehicle was gone and the darkness was still advancing.

He ran, stumbling on the uneven ground. When his legs finally failed him and he collapsed onto the sand, the bridge was nowhere in sight. He was alone in a red desert. The air was still now, and very hot.

After a while he rose to his feet, searching for a patch of shade where he could rest and wait for the cool of the evening. Apart from the red sand there were pebbles and some larger, cracked rocks, but there was no relief from the flatness: not so much as a boulder he could take shelter beside. In one direction there were some low, parched bushes, their trunks no thicker than his fingers, their branches no higher than his knees. He might as well have tried to hide from the sun beneath his own thin beard. He scanned the horizon, but it offered no welcoming destination.

There was no water for washing, but Ali cleaned himself as best he could and prayed. Then he sat cross-legged on the ground, covered his face with his shawl, and lapsed into a sickly sleep.

He woke in the evening and started to walk. Some of the constellations were familiar, but they crossed the sky far closer to the horizon than they should have. Others were completely new to him. There was no moon, and though the terrain was flat he soon found that he lost his footing if he tried to move too quickly in the dark.

When morning came, it brought no perceptible change in his surroundings. Red sand and a few skeletal plants were all that this land seemed to hold.

He slept through most of the day again, stirring only to pray. Increasingly, his sleep was broken by a throbbing pain behind his eyes. The night had been chilly, but he'd never experienced such heat before. He was unsure how much longer he could survive without water. He began to wonder if it would have been better if he'd been taken by the wind inside the bridge, or perished in the burning Land Cruiser.

After sunset, he staggered to his feet and continued his hopeful but unguided trek. He had a fever now, and his aching joints begged him for more rest, but if he resigned himself to sleep he doubted he'd wake again.

When his feet touched the road, he thought he'd lost his mind. Who would take the trouble to build such a path through a desolate place like this? He stopped and crouched down to examine it. It was gritty with a sparse layer of wind-blown sand; beneath that was a black substance that felt less hard than stone, but resilient, almost springy.

A road like this must lead to a great city. He followed it.

An hour or two before dawn, bright headlights appeared in the distance. Ali fought down his instinctive fear; in the future such vehicles should be commonplace, not the preserve of bandits and murderers. He stood by the roadside awaiting its arrival.

The Land Cruiser was like none he'd seen before, white with blue markings. There was writing on it, in the same European script as he'd seen on many machine parts and weapons that had made their way into the bazaars, but no words he recognized, let alone understood. One passenger was riding beside the driver; he climbed out, approached Ali, and greeted him in an incomprehensible tongue.

Ali shrugged apologetically. "Salaam aleikom," he ventured. "Bebakhshid agha, mosarfar hastam. Ba tawarz' az shoma moharfazat khahesh mikonam."

The man addressed Ali briefly in his own tongue again, though it was clear now that he did not expect to be understood any more than Ali did. He called out to his companion, gestured to Ali to stay put, then went back to the Land Cruiser. His companion handed him two small machines; Ali tensed, but they didn't look like any weapons he'd seen.

The man approached Ali again. He held one machine up to the side of his face, then lowered it again and offered it to Ali. Ali took it, and repeated the mimed action.

A woman's voice spoke in his ear. Ali understood what was happening; he'd seen the Scholars use similar machines to talk with each other over great distances. Unfortunately, the language was still incomprehensible. He was about to reply, when the woman spoken again in what sounded like a third language. Then a fourth, then a fifth. Ali waited patiently, until finally the woman greeted him in stilted Persian.

When Ali replied, she said, "Please wait." After a few minutes, a new voice spoke. "Peace be upon you."

"And upon you."

"Where are you from?" To Ali, this man's accent sounded exotic, but he spoke Persian with confidence.

"Khurosan."

"At what time?"

"Four years after the coming of the Scholars."

"I see." The Persian-speaker switched briefly to a different language; the man on the road, who'd wandered halfway back to his vehicle and was still listening via the second machine, gave a curt reply. Ali was amazed at these people's hospitality: in the middle of the night, in a matter of minutes, they had found someone who could speak his language.

"How did you come to be on this road?"

"I walked across the desert."

"Which way? From where? How far did you come?"

"I'm sorry, I don't remember."

The translator replied bluntly, "Please try."

Ali was confused. What did it matter? One man, at least, could see how weary he was. Why were they asking him these questions before he'd had a chance to rest?

"Forgive me, sir. I can't tell you anything, I'm sick from my journey."

There was an exchange in the native language, followed by an awkward silence. Finally the translator said, "This man will take you to a place where you can stay for a while. Tomorrow we'll hear your whole story."

"Thank you, sir. You have done a great thing for me. God will reward you."

The man on the road walked up to Ali. Ali held out his arms to embrace him in gratitude. The man produced a metal shackle and snapped it around Ali's wrists.

2

THE CAMP was enclosed by two high fences, topped with glistening ribbons of razor-sharp metal. The space between them was filled with coils of the same material. Outside the fences there was nothing but desert as far as the eye could see. Inside there were guards, and at night everything was bathed in a constant harsh light. Ali had no doubt that he'd come to a prison, though his hosts kept insisting that this was not the case.

His first night had passed in a daze. He'd been given food and water, examined by a doctor, then shown to a small metal hut that he was to share with three other men. Two of the men, Alex and Tran, knew just enough Persian to greet Ali briefly, but the third, Shahin, was an Iranian, and they could understand each other well enough. The hut's four beds were arranged in pairs, one above the other; Ali's habit was to sleep on a mat on the floor, but he didn't want to offend anyone by declining to follow the local customs. The guards had removed his shackles then put a bracelet on his left wrist—made from something like paper, but extraordinarily strong—bearing the number "3739". The last numeral was more or less the same shape as a Persian nine; he recognized the others from machine parts, but he didn't know their values.

Every two hours, throughout the night, a guard opened the door of the hut and shone a light on each of their faces in turn. The first time it happened Ali thought the guard had come to rouse them from their sleep and take them somewhere, but Shahin explained that these "head counts" happened all night, every night.

The next morning, officials from the camp had taken Ali out in a vehicle and asked him to show them the exact place where he'd arrived through the bridge. He'd done his best, but all of the desert looked the same to him. By midday, he was tempted to designate a spot at random just to satisfy his hosts, but he didn't want to lie to them. They'd returned to the camp in a sullen mood. Ali couldn't understand why it was so important to them.

Reza, the Persian translator who'd first spoken with Ali through the machine, explained that he was to remain in the camp until government officials had satisfied themselves that he really was fleeing danger, and hadn't merely come to the future seeking an easy life for himself. Ali understood that his hosts didn't want to be cheated, but it dismayed him that they felt the need to imprison him while they made up their minds. Surely there was a family in a nearby town who would have let him stay with them for a day or two, just as his father would have welcomed any travelers passing through their village.

The section of the camp where he'd been placed was fenced off from the rest, and contained about a hundred people. They were all travelers like himself, and they came from every nation Ali had heard of, and more. Most were young men, but there were also women, children, entire families. In his village, Ali would have run to greet the children, lifted them up and kissed them to make them smile, but here they looked so sad and dispirited that he was afraid the approach of even the friendliest stranger might frighten them.

Shahin was a few years older than Ali, but he had spent his whole life as a student. He had traveled just two decades through time, escaping a revolution in his country. He explained that the part of the camp they were in was called "Stage One"; they were being kept apart from the others so they wouldn't learn too much about the way their cases would be judged. "They're afraid we'll embellish the details if we discover what kind of questions they ask, or what kind of story succeeds."

"How long have you been here?" Ali asked.

"Nine months. I'm still waiting for my interview."

"Nine months!"

Shahin smiled wearily. "Some people have been in Stage One for a year. But don't worry, you won't have to wait that long. When I arrived here, the Center Manager had an interesting policy: nobody would have their cases examined until they asked him for the correct application form. Of course, nobody knew that they were required to do that, and he had no intention of telling them. Three months ago, he was transferred to another camp. When I asked the woman who replaced him what I needed to do to have my claims heard, she told me straight away: ask for Form 866."

Ali couldn't quite follow all this. Shahin explained further.

Ali said, "What good will it do me, to get this piece of paper? I can't read their language, and I can barely write my own."

"That's no problem. They'll let you talk to an educated man or woman, an expert in these matters. That person will fill out the form for you, in English. You only need to explain your problem, and sign your name at the bottom of the paper."

"English?" Ali had heard about the English; before he was born they'd tried to invade both Hindustan and Khurosan, without success. "How did that language come here?" He was sure that he was not in England.

"They conquered this country two centuries ago. They crossed the world in wooden ships to take it for their king."

"Oh." Ali felt dizzy; his mind still hadn't fully accepted the journey he'd made. "What about Khurosan?" he joked. "Have they conquered that as well?"

Shahin shook his head. "No."

"What is it like now? Is there peace there?" Once this strange business with the English was done, perhaps he could travel to his homeland. However much it had changed with time, he was sure he could make a good life there.

Shahin said, "There is no nation called Khurosan in this world. Part of that area belongs to Hindustan, part to Iran, part to Russia."

Ali stared at him, uncomprehending. "How can that be?" However much his people fought among themselves, they would never have let invaders take their land.

"I don't know the full history," Shahin said, "but you need to understand something. This is not your future. The things that happened in the places you know are not a part of the history of this world. There is no *pol-e-waqt* that connects past and future in the same world. Once you cross the bridge, everything changes, including the past."

~~~~

WITH SHAHIN beside him, Ali approached one of the government officials, a man named James, and addressed him in the English he'd learned by heart. "Please Mr James, can I have Form 866?"

James rolled his eyes and said, "OK, OK! We were going to get around to you sooner or later." He turned to Shahin and said, "I wish you'd stop scaring the new guys with stories about being stuck in Stage One forever. You know things have changed since Colonel Kurtz went north."

Shahin translated all of this for Ali. "Colonel Kurtz" was Shahin's nickname for the previous Center Manager, but everyone, even the guards, had adopted it. Shahin called Tran "The Rake", and Alex was "Denisovich of the Desert".

Three weeks later, Ali was called to a special room, where he sat with Reza. A lawyer in a distant city, a woman called Ms Evans, spoke with them in English through a machine that Reza called a "speaker phone". With Reza translating, she asked Ali about everything: his village, his family, his problems with the Scholars. He'd been asked about some of this the night he'd arrived, but he'd been very tired then, and hadn't had a chance to put things clearly.

Three days after the meeting, he was called to see James. Ms Evans had written everything in English on the special form, and sent it to them. Reza read through the form, translating everything for Ali to be sure that it was correct. Then Ali wrote his name on the bottom of the form. James told him, "Before we make a decision, someone will come from the city to interview you. That might take a while, so you'll have to be patient."

Ali said, in English, "No problem."

He felt he could wait for a year, if he had to. The first four weeks had gone quickly, with so much that was new to take in. He had barely had space left in his crowded mind to be homesick, and he tried not to worry about Hassan and his mother. Many things about the camp disturbed him, but his luck had been good: the infamous "Colonel Kurtz" had left, so he'd probably be out in three or four months. The cities of this nation, Shahin assured him, were mostly on the distant coast, an infinitely milder place than the desert around the camp. Ali might be able to get a laboring job while studying English at night, or he might find work on a farm. He hadn't quite started his new life yet, but he was safe, and everything looked hopeful.

∾

By the end of his third month Ali was growing restless. Most days he played cards with Shahin, Tran, and a Hindustani man named Rakesh, while Alex lay on his bunk reading books in Russian. Rakesh had a cassette player and a vast collection of tapes. The songs were mostly in Hindi, a language that contained just enough Persian words to give Ali some sense of what the lyrics were about: usually love, or sorrow, or both.

The metal huts were kept tolerably cool by machines, but there was no shade outside. At night the men played soccer, and Ali sometimes joined in, but after falling badly on the concrete, twice, he decided it wasn't the game for him. Shahin told him that it was a game for grass; from his home in Tehran, he'd watched dozens of nations compete at it. Ali felt a surge of excitement at the thought of all the wonders of this world, still tantalizingly out of reach: in Stage One, TV, radio, newspapers, and telephones were all forbidden. Even Rakesh's tapes had been checked by the guards, played from start to finish to be sure that they didn't contain secret lessons in passing the interview. Ali couldn't wait to reach Stage Two, to catch his first glimpse of what life might be like in a world where anyone could watch history unfolding, and speak at their leisure with anyone else.

English was the closest thing to a common language for all the people in the camp. Shahin did his best to get Ali started, and once he could converse in broken English some of the friendlier guards let him practice with them, often to their great amusement. "Not every car is called a Land Cruiser," Gary explained. "I think you must come from Toyota-stan."

Shahin was called to his interview. Ali prayed for him, then sat on the floor of the hut with Tran and tried to lose himself in the mercurial world of the cards. What he liked most about these friendly games was that good and bad luck rarely lasted long, and even when they did it barely mattered. Every curse and every blessing was light as a feather.

Shahin returned four hours later, looking exhausted but satisfied. "I've told them my whole story," he said. "It's in their hands now." The official who'd interviewed him had given him no hint as to what the decision would be, but Shahin seemed relieved just to have had a chance to tell someone who mattered everything he'd suffered, everything that had forced him from his home.

That night Shahin was told that he was moving to Stage Two in half an hour. He embraced Ali. "See you in freedom, brother."

"God willing."

After Shahin was gone, Ali lay on his bunk for four days, refusing to eat, getting up only to wash and pray. His friend's departure was just the trigger; the raw grief of his last days in the valley came flooding back, deepened by the unimaginable gulf that now separated him from his family. Had Hassan escaped from the Scholars? Or was he fighting on the front line of their endless war, risking death every hour of every day? With the only *mosarfar-e-waqt* Ali knew now dead, how would he ever get news from his family, or send them his assistance?

Tran whispered gruff consolations in his melodic English. "Don't worry kid. Everything OK. Wait and see."

~w~

WORSE THAN the waiting was the sense of waste: all the hours trickling away, with no way to harness them for anything useful. Ali tried to improve his English, but there were some concepts he could get no purchase on without someone who understood his own language to help him. Reza rarely left the government offices for the compound, and when he did he was too busy for Ali's questions.

Ali tried to make a garden, planting an assortment of seeds that he'd saved from the fruit that came with some of the meals. Most of Stage One was covered in concrete, but he found a small patch of bare ground behind his hut that was sheltered from the fiercest sunlight. He carried water from the drinking tap on the other side of the soccer ground and sprinkled it over the soil four times a day. Nothing happened, though. The seeds lay dormant, the land would not accept them.

Three weeks after Shahin's departure, Alex had his interview, and left. A week later, Tran followed. Ali started sleeping through the heat of the day, waking just in time to join the queue for the evening meal, then playing cards with Rakesh and his friends until dawn.

By the end of his sixth month, Ali felt a taint of bitterness creeping in beneath the numbness and boredom. He wasn't a thief or a murderer, he'd committed no crime. Why couldn't these people set him free to work, to fend for himself instead of taking their charity, to prepare himself for his new life?

One night, tired of the endless card game, Ali wandered out from Rakesh's hut earlier than usual. One of the guards, a woman named Cheryl, was standing outside her office, smoking. Ali murmured a greeting to her as he passed; she was not one of the friendly ones, but he tried to be polite to everyone.

"Why don't you just go home?" she said.

Ali paused, unsure whether to dignify this with a response. He'd long ago learned that most of the guards' faces became stony if he tried to explain why he'd left his village; somewhere, somehow it had been drummed into them that nothing their prisoners said could be believed.

"Nobody invited you here," she said bluntly. "You want to live in a civilized country? Go home and build one for yourself. You've got a war back there? *My ancestors* fought wars, they died for their freedom. What do you expect—five hundred years of progress to be handed to you on a plate? Nobody owes you a comfortable life. Go home and earn it."

Ali wanted to tell her that his life would have been fine if the meddlers from the future hadn't chosen Khurosan as their fulcrum for moving history, but his English wasn't up to the task.

He said, "I'm here. From me, big tragedy for your nation? I'm honest man and hard worker. I not betray your hospitality."

Cheryl snickered. Ali wasn't sure if she was sneering at his English or his sentiments, but he persisted. "Your leaders did agreement with other nations. Anyone asking protection gets fair hearing." Shahin had impressed that point on Ali. It was the law, and in this society the law was everything. "That is my right."

Cheryl coughed on her cigarette. "Dream on, Ahmad."

"My name is Ali."

"Whatever." She reached out and caught him by the wrist, then held up his hand to examine his ID bracelet. "Dream on, 3739."

~w~

JAMES CALLED Ali to his office and handed him a letter. Reza translated it for him. After eight months of waiting, in six days' time he would finally have his interview.

Ali waited nervously for Ms Evans to call him to help him prepare, as she'd promised she would when they'd last spoken, all those months before. On the morning of the appointed day, he was summoned again to James's office, and taken with Reza to the room with the speakerphone, the "interview room". A different lawyer, a man called Mr Cole, explained to Ali that Ms Evans had left her job and he had taken over Ali's case. He told Ali that everything would be fine, and he'd be listening carefully to Ali's interview and making sure that everything went well.

When Cole had hung up, Reza snorted derisively. "You know how these clowns are chosen? They put in tenders, and it goes to the lowest bidder." Ali didn't entirely understand, but this doesn't sound encouraging. Reza caught the expression on Ali's face, and added, "Don't worry, you'll be fine. Fleeing from the Scholars is flavor of the month."

Three hours later, Ali was back in the interview room.

The official who'd come from the city introduced himself as John Fernandez. Reza wasn't with them; Fernandez had brought a different interpreter with him, a man named Parviz. Mr Cole joined them on the speakerphone. Fernandez switched on a cassette recorder, and asked Ali to swear on the Quran to give truthful answers to all his questions.

Fernandez asked him for his name, his date of birth, and the place and time he'd fled. Ali didn't know his birthday or his exact age; he thought he was about eighteen years old, but it was not the custom in his village to record such things. He did know that at the time he'd left his uncle's house, twelve hundred and sixty-five years had passed since the Prophet's flight to Medina.

"Tell me about your problem," Fernandez said. "Tell me why you've come here."

Shahin had told Ali that the history of this world was different from his own, so Ali explained carefully about Khurosan's long war, about the meddlers and the warlords they'd created, about the coming of the Scholars. How the Shi'a were taken by force to fight in the most dangerous positions. How Hassan was taken. How his father had been killed. Fernandez listened patiently, sometimes writing on the sheets of paper in front of him as Ali spoke, interrupting him only to encourage him to fill in the gaps in the story, to make everything clear.

When he had finally recounted everything, Ali felt an overwhelming sense of relief. This man had not poured scorn on his words the way the guards had; instead, he had allowed Ali to speak openly about all the injustice his family and his people had suffered.

Fernandez had some more questions.

"Tell me about your village, and your uncle's village. How long would it take to travel between them on foot?"

"Half a day, sir."

"Half a day. That's what you said in your statement. But in your entry interview, you said a day." Ali was confused. Parziv explained that his "statement" was the written record of his conversation with Ms Evans, which she had sent to the government; his "entry interview" was when he'd first arrived in the camp and been questioned for ten or fifteen minutes.

"I only meant it was a short trip, sir, you didn't have to stay somewhere halfway overnight. You could complete it in one day."

"Hmm. OK. Now, when the smuggler took you from your uncle's village, which direction was he driving?"

"Along the valley, sir."

"North, south, east, west?"

"I'm not sure." Ali knew these words, but they were not part of the language of everyday life. He knew the direction for prayer, and he knew the direction to follow to each neighboring village.

"You know that the sun rises in the east, don't you?"

"Yes."

"So if you faced in the direction in which you were being driven, would the sun have risen on your left, on your right, behind you, where?"

"It was night time."

"Yes, but you must have faced the same direction in the valley in the morning, a thousand times. So where would the sun have risen?"

Ali closed his eyes and pictured it. "On my right."

Fernandez sighed. "OK. Finally. So you were driving north. Now tell me about the land. The smuggler drove you along the valley. And then what? What kind of landscape did you see, between your valley and the bridge?"

Ali froze. What would the government do with this information? Send someone back through their own bridge, to find and destroy the one he'd used? The *mosarfar-e-waqt* had warned him not to tell anyone the way to the bridge. That man was dead, but it was unlikely that he'd worked alone; everyone had a brother, a son, a cousin to help them. If the family of the *mosarfar-e-waqt* could trace such a misfortune to Ali, the dead man's threat against his uncle would be carried through.

Ali said, "I was under a blanket, I didn't see anything."

"You were under a blanket? For how many days?"

"Three."

"Three days. What about eating, drinking, going to the toilet?"

"He blindfolded me," Ali lied.

"Really? You never mentioned that before." Fernandez shuffled through his papers. "It's not in your statement."

"I didn't think it was important, sir." Ali's stomach tightened. What was happening? He was sure he'd won this man's trust. And he'd earned it: he'd told him the truth about everything, until now. What difference did it make to his problem with the Scholars, which mountains and streams he'd glimpsed on the way to the bridge? He had sworn to tell the truth, but he knew it would be a far greater sin to risk his uncle's life.

Fernandez had still more questions, about life in the village. Some were easy, but some were strange, and he kept asking for numbers, numbers, numbers: how much did it weigh, how much did it cost, how long did it take? What time did the bazaar open? Ali had no idea, he'd been busy with farm work in the mornings, he'd never gone there so early that it might have been closed. How many people came to Friday prayers in the Shi'a mosque? None, since the Scholars had arrived. Before that? Ali couldn't remember. More than a hundred? Ali hesitated. "I think so." He'd never counted them, why would he have?

When the interview finished, Ali's mind was still three questions behind, worrying that his answers might not have been clear enough. Fernandez was rewinding the tapes, shaking his hand formally, leaving the room.

Mr Cole said, "I think that went well. Do you have any questions you want to ask me?"

Ali said, "No, sir." Parviz had already departed.

"All right. Good luck." The speaker phone clicked off. Ali sat at the table, waiting for the guard to come and take him back to the compound.

3

ENTERING STAGE Two, Ali felt as if he had walked into the heart of a bustling town. Everything was noise, shouting, music. He'd sometimes heard snatches of this cacophony wafting across the fenced-off "sterile area" that separated the parts of the camp, but now he was in the thick of it. The rows of huts, and the crowds moving between them, seemed to stretch on forever. There must have been a thousand people here, all of them unwilling travelers fleeing the cruelties of their own histories.

He'd moved his small bag of belongings into the hut allocated to him, but none of his new roommates were there to greet him. He wandered through the compound, dizzy from the onslaught of new sights and sounds. He felt as if he'd just had a heavy cloth unwound from around his head, and his un-veiled senses were still struggling to adjust. If he was reeling from this, how would he feel when he stepped onto the streets of a real city, in freedom?

The evening meal was over, the sun had set, and the heat outside had become tolerable. Almost everyone seemed to be out walking, or congregating around the entrances of their friends' huts, taped music blaring through the open doorways. At the end of one row of huts, Ali came to a larger building, where thirty or forty people were seated. He entered the room, and saw a small box with a window on it, through which he could see an oddly-colored, distorted, constantly changing view. A woman was dancing and singing in Hindi.

"TV," Ali marveled. This was what Shahin had spoken about; now the whole world was open to his gaze.

An African man beside him shook his head. "It's a video. The TV's on in the other common room."

Ali lingered, watching the mesmerizing images. The woman was very beautiful, and though she was immodestly dressed by the standards of his village, she seemed dignified and entirely at ease. The Scholars would probably have stoned her to death, but Ali would have been happy to be a beggar in Mumbai if the streets there were filled with sights like this.

As he left the room, the sky was already darkening. The camp's floodlights had come on, destroying any hope of a glimpse of the stars. He asked someone, "Where is the TV, please?" and followed their directions.

As he walked into the second room, he noticed something different in the mood at once; the people here were tense, straining with attention. When Ali turned to the TV, it showed an eerily familiar sight: an expanse of desert, not unlike that outside the camp. Helicopters, four or five, flew over the landscape. In the distance, a tight funnel of swirling dust, dancing across the ground.

Ali stood riveted. The landscape on the screen was brightly lit, which meant that what he was watching had already happened: earlier in the day, someone had located the mouth of the bridge. He peered at the small images of the helicopters. He'd only ever seen a broken one on the ground, the toy of one warlord brought down by a rival, but he recognized the guns protruding from the sides. Whoever had found the bridge, it was now in the hands of soldiers.

As he watched, a Land Cruiser came charging out of the storm. Then another, and another. This was not like his own arrival; the convoy was caked with dust, but more or less intact. Then the helicopters descended, guns chattering. For a few long seconds Ali thought he was about to witness a slaughter, but the soldiers were firing consistently a meter or so ahead of the Land Cruisers. They were trying to corral the vehicles back into the bridge.

The convoy broke up, the individual drivers trying to steer their way past the blockade. Curtains of bullets descended around them, driving them back toward the meandering storm. Ali couldn't see the people inside, but he could imagine their terror and confusion. This was the future? This was their sanctuary? Whatever tyranny they were fleeing, to have braved the labyrinth of the *pol-e-waqt* only to be greeted with a barrage of gunfire was a fate so cruel that they must have doubted their senses, their sanity, their God.

The helicopters wheeled around the mouth of the bridge like hunting dogs, indefatigable, relentless in their purpose. Ali found the grim dance unbearable, but he couldn't turn away. One of the Land Cruisers came to a halt; it wasn't safely clear of the storm, but this must have seemed wiser than dodging bullets. Doors opened and people tumbled out. Weirdly, the picture went awry at exactly that moment, clumps of flickering color replacing the travelers' faces.

Soldiers approached, guns at the ready, gesturing and threatening, forcing the people back into the car. A truck appeared, painted in dappled green and brown. A chain was tied between the vehicles. Someone emerged from the Land Cruiser; the face was obscured again, but Ali could see it was a woman. Her words could not be heard, but Ali could see her speaking with her hands, begging, chastising, pleading for mercy. The soldiers forced her back inside.

The truck started its engines. Sand sprayed from its wheels. Two soldiers climbed into the back, their weapons trained on the Land Cruiser. Then they towed their cargo back into the storm.

Ali watched numbly as the other two Land Cruisers were rounded up. The second stalled, and the soldiers descended on it. The driver of the third gave up, and steered his own course into the mouth of the bridge.

The soldiers' truck emerged from the storm, alone. The helicopters spiraled away, circling the funnel at a more prudent distance. Ali looked at the faces of the other people in the room; everyone was pale, some were weeping.

The picture changed. Two men were standing, indoors somewhere. One was old, white-haired, wizened. In front of him a younger man was talking, replying to unseen questioners. Both were smiling proudly.

Ali could only make sense of a few of their words, but gradually he pieced some things together. These men were from the government, and they were explaining the events of the day. They had sent the soldiers to "protect" the bridge, to ensure that no more criminals and barbarians emerged to threaten the peaceful life of the nation. They had been patient with these intruders for far too long. From this day on, nobody would pass.

Behind the men there was a huge banner. It bore a picture of the face of the younger man, and the words KEEPING THE PAST IN THE PAST.

"What about the law?" someone was asking. An agreement had been signed: any traveler who reached this country and asked for protection had a right to a fair hearing.

"A bill has been drafted, and will be introduced in the House tomorrow. Once passed, it will take force from nine o'clock this morning. The land within twenty kilometers of the bridge will, for the purposes of the Act, no longer be part of this nation. People entering the exclusion zone will have no basis in law to claim our protection."

Confused, Ali muttered, "Chi goft?" A young man sitting nearby turned to face him. "Salaam, chetori? Fahim hastam."

Fahim's accent was unmistakably Khurosani. Ali smiled. "Ali hastam. Shoma chetori?"

Fahim explained what the man on the TV had said. Anyone emerging from the mouth of the bridge, now, might as well be on the other side of the world. The government here would accept no obligation to assist them. "If it's not their land anymore," he mused, "maybe they'll give it to us. We can found a country of our own, a tribe of nomads in a caravan following the bridge across the desert."

Ali said nervously, "My interview was today. They said something about nine o'clock—"

Fahim shook his head dismissively. "You made your claim months ago, right? So you're still covered by the old law."

Ali tried to believe him. "You're still waiting for your decision?"

"Hardly. I got refused three years ago."

"Three years? They didn't send you back?"

"I'm fighting it in the courts. I can't go back, I'd be dead in a week." There were dark circles under Fahim's eyes. If he'd been refused three years before, he'd probably spent close to four years in this prison.

Fahim, it turned out, was one of Ali's roommates. He took him to meet the other twelve Khurosanis in Stage Two, and the whole group sat together in one of the huts, talking until dawn. Ali was overjoyed to be among people who knew his language, his time, his customs. It didn't matter that most were from provinces far from his own, that a year ago he would have thought of them as exotic strangers.

When he examined their faces too closely, though, it was hard to remain joyful. They had all fled the Scholars, like him. They were all in fear for their lives. And they had all been locked up for a very long time: two years, three years, four years, five.

In the weeks that followed, Ali gave himself no time to brood on his fate. Stage Two had English classes, and though Fahim and the others had long outgrown them, Ali joined in. He finally learned the names for the European letters and numbers that he'd seen on weapons and machinery all his life, and the teacher encouraged him to give up translating individual words from Persian, and reshape whole sentences, whole thoughts, into the alien tongue.

Every evening, Ali joined Fahim in the common room to watch the news on TV. There was no doubt that the place they had come to was peaceful and prosperous; when war was mentioned, it was always in some distant land. The rulers here did not govern by force, they were chosen by the people, and even now this competition was in progress. The men who had sent the soldiers to block the bridge were asking the people to choose them again.

When the guard woke Ali at eight in the morning, he didn't complain, though he'd had only three hours' sleep. He showered quickly, then went to the compound's south gate. It no longer seemed strange to him to move from place to place this way: to wait for guards to come and unlock a succession of doors and escort him through the fenced-off maze that separated the compound from the government offices.

James and Reza were waiting in the office. Ali greeted them, his mouth dry. James said, "Reza will read the decision for you. It's about ten pages, so be patient. Then if you have any questions, let me know."

Reza read from the papers without meeting Ali's eyes. Fernandez, the man who'd interviewed Ali, had written that there were discrepancies between things Ali had said at different times, and gaps in his knowledge of the place and time he claimed to have come from. What's more, an expert in the era of the Scholars had listened to the tape of Ali talking, and declared that his speech was not of that time. "Perhaps this man's great-grandfather fled Khurosan in the time of the Scholars, and some sketchy information has been passed down the generations. The applicant himself, however, employs a number of words that were not in use until decades later."

Ali waited for the litany of condemnation to come to an end, but it seemed to go on forever. "I have tried to give the applicant the benefit of the doubt," Fernandez had written, "but the overwhelming weight of evidence supports the conclusion that he has lied about his origins, his background, and all of his claims."

Ali sat with his head in his hands.

James said, "Do you understand what this means? You have seven days to lodge an appeal. If you don't lodge an appeal, you will have to return to your country."

Reza added, "You should call your lawyer. Have you got money for a phone card?"

Ali nodded. He'd taken a job cleaning the mess, he had thirty points in his account already.

Every time Ali called, his lawyer was busy. Fahim helped Ali fill out the appeal form, and they handed it to James two hours before the deadline. "Lucky Colonel Kurtz is gone," Fahim told Ali. "Or that form would have sat in the fax tray for at least a week."

Wild rumors swept the camp: the government was about to change, and everyone would be set free. Ali had seen the government's rivals giving their blessing to the use of soldiers to block the bridge; he doubted that they'd show the prisoners in the desert much mercy if they won.

When the day of the election came, the government was returned, more powerful than ever.

That night, as they were preparing to sleep, Fahim saw Ali staring at the long white scars that criss-crossed his upper arms and chest. "I use a razor blade," Fahim admitted. "It makes me feel better. The one power I've got left: to choose my own pain."

"I'll never do that," Ali swore.

Fahim gave a hollow laugh. "It's cheaper than cigarettes."

Ali closed his eyes and tried to picture freedom, but all he saw was blackness. The past was gone, the future was gone, and the world had shrunk to this prison.

4

"ALI, WAKE up, come see!"

Daniel was shaking him. Ali swatted his hands away angrily. The African was one of his closest friends, and there'd been a time when he could still drag Ali along to English classes or the gym, but since the appeal tribunal had rejected him, Ali had no taste for anything. "Let me sleep."

"There are people. Outside the fence."

"Escaped?"

"No, no. From the city!"

Ali clambered off the bunk. He splashed water on his face, then followed his friend.

Dozens of prisoners had gathered at the south-west corner of the fence, blocking the view, but Ali could hear people on the outside, shouting and banging drums. Daniel tried to clear a path, but it was impossible. "Get on my shoulders." He ducked down and motioned to Ali.

Ali laughed. "It's not that important."

Daniel raised a hand angrily, as if to slap him. "Get up, you have to see." He was serious. Ali obeyed.

From his vantage, he could see that the mass of prisoners pressed against the inner fence was mirrored by another crowd struggling to reach the outer one. Police, some on horses, were trying to stop them. Ali peered into the scrum, amazed. Dozens of young people, men and women, were pushing against the cordon of policemen, and every now and then someone was slipping through and running forward. Some distance away across the desert stood a brightly colored bus. The word "freedom" was painted across it, in English, Persian, Arabic, and probably ten or twelve languages that Ali couldn't read. The people were chanting, "Set them free! Set them free!" One young woman reached the fence and clung to it, shouting defiantly. Four policemen descended on her and tore her away.

A cloud of dust was moving along the desert road. More police cars were coming, reinforcements. A knife twisted in Ali's heart. This gesture of friendship astonished him, but it would lead nowhere. In five or ten minutes, the protesters would all be rounded up and carried away.

A young man outside the fence met Ali's gaze. "Hey! My name's Ben."

"I'm Ali."

Ben looked around frantically. "What's your number?"

"What?"

"We'll write to you. Give us your number. They have to deliver the letters if we include the ID number."

"Behind you!" Ali shouted, but the warning was too late. One policeman had him in a headlock, and another was helping wrestle him to the ground.

Ali felt Daniel stagger. The crowd on his own side was trying to fend off a wave of guards with batons and shields.

Ali dropped to his feet. "They want our ID numbers," he told Daniel. Daniel looked around at the melee. "Got anything to write on?"

Ali checked his back pocket. The small notebook and pen it was his habit to carry were still there. He rested the notebook on Daniel's back, and wrote "Ali 3739 Daniel 5420." Who else? He quickly added Fahim and a few others.

He scrabbled on the ground for a stone, then wrapped the paper around it. Daniel lofted him up again.

The police were battling with the protesters, grabbing them by the hair, dragging them across the dirt. Ali couldn't see anyone who didn't have more pressing things to worry about than receiving his message. He lowered his arm, despondent.

Then he spotted someone standing by the bus. He couldn't tell if it was a man or a woman. He, or she, raised a hand in greeting. Ali waved back, then let the stone fly. It fell short, but the distant figure ran forward and retrieved it from the sand.

Daniel collapsed beneath him, and the guards moved in with batons and tear gas. Ali covered his eyes with his forearm, weeping, alive again with hope.

CRYSTAL NIGHTS

1

"More caviar?" Daniel Cliff gestured at the serving dish and the cover irised from opaque to transparent. "It's fresh, I promise you. My chef had it flown in from Iran this morning."

"No thank you." Julie Dehghani touched a napkin to her lips then laid it on her plate with a gesture of finality. The dining room overlooked the Golden Gate bridge, and most people Daniel invited here were content to spend an hour or two simply enjoying the view, but he could see that she was growing impatient with his small talk.

Daniel said, "I'd like to show you something." He led her into the adjoining conference room. On the table was a wireless keyboard; the wall screen showed a Linux command line interface. "Take a seat," he suggested.

Julie complied. "If this is some kind of audition, you might have warned me," she said.

"Not at all," Daniel replied. "I'm not going to ask you to jump through any hoops. I'd just like you to tell me what you think of this machine's performance."

She frowned slightly, but she was willing to play along. She ran some standard benchmarks. Daniel saw her squinting at the screen, one hand almost reaching up to where a desktop display would be, so she could double-check the number of digits in the FLOPS rating by counting them off with one finger. There were a lot more than she'd been expecting, but she wasn't seeing double.

"That's extraordinary," she said. "Is this whole building packed with networked processors, with only the penthouse for humans?"

Daniel said, "You tell me. Is it a cluster?"

"Hmm." So much for not making her jump through hoops, but it wasn't really much of a challenge. She ran some different benchmarks, based on algorithms that were provably impossible to parallelise; however smart the compiler was, the steps these programs required would have to be carried out strictly in sequence.

The FLOPS rating was unchanged.

Julie said, "All right, it's a single processor. Now you've got my attention. Where is it?"

"Turn the keyboard over."

There was a charcoal-gray module, five centimeters square and five millimeters thick, plugged into an inset docking bay. Julie examined it, but it bore no manufacturer's logo or other identifying marks.

"This connects to the processor?" she asked.

"No. It *is* the processor."

"You're joking." She tugged it free of the dock, and the wall screen went blank. She held it up and turned it around, though Daniel wasn't sure what she was looking for. Somewhere to slip in a screwdriver and take the thing apart, probably. He said, "If you break it, you own it, so I hope you've got a few hundred spare."

"A few hundred grand? Hardly."

"A few hundred million."

Her face flushed. "Of course. If it was a few hundred grand, everyone would have one." She put it down on the table, then as an afterthought slid it a little further from the edge. "As I said, you've got my attention."

Daniel smiled. "I'm sorry about the theatrics."

"No, this deserved the build-up. What is it, exactly?"

"A single, three-dimensional photonic crystal. No electronics to slow it down; every last component is optical. The architecture was nanofabricated with a method that I'd prefer not to describe in detail."

"Fair enough." She thought for a while. "I take it you don't expect me to buy one. My research budget for the next thousand years would barely cover it."

"In your present position. But you're not joined to the university at the hip."

"So this is a job interview?"

Daniel nodded.

Julie couldn't help herself; she picked up the crystal and examined it again, as if there might yet be some feature that a human eye could discern. "Can you give me a job description?"

"Midwife."

She laughed. "To what?"

"History," Daniel said.

Her smile faded slowly.

"I believe you're the best AI researcher of your generation," he said. "I want you to work for me." He reached over and took the crystal from her. "With this as your platform, imagine what you could do."

Julie said, "What exactly would you want me to do?"

"For the last fifteen years," Daniel said, "you've stated that the ultimate goal of your research is to create conscious, human-level, artificial intelligence."

"That's right."

"Then we want the same thing. What I want is for you to succeed."

She ran a hand over her face; whatever else she was thinking, there was no denying that she was tempted. "It's gratifying that you have so much confidence in my abilities," she said. "But we need to be clear about some things. This prototype is amazing, and if you ever get the production costs down I'm sure it will have some extraordinary applications. It would eat up climate forecasting, lattice QCD, astrophysical modeling, proteomics…"

"Of course." Actually, Daniel had no intention of marketing the device. He'd bought out the inventor of the fabrication process with his own private funds; there were no other shareholders or directors to dictate his use of the technology.

"But AI," Julie said, "is different. We're in a maze, not a highway; there's nowhere that speed alone can take us. However many exaflops I have to play with, they won't spontaneously combust into consciousness. I'm not being held back by the university's computers; I have access to SHARCNET anytime I need it. I'm being held back by my own lack of insight into the problems I'm addressing."

Daniel said, "A maze is not a dead end. When I was twelve, I wrote a program for solving mazes."

"And I'm sure it worked well," Julie replied, "for small, two-dimensional ones. But you know how those kind of algorithms scale. Put your old program on this crystal, and I could still design a maze in half a day that would bring it to its knees."

"Of course," Daniel conceded. "Which is precisely why I'm interested in hiring you. You know a great deal more about the maze of AI than I do; any strategy you developed would be vastly superior to a blind search."

"I'm not saying that I'm merely groping in the dark," she said. "If it was that bleak, I'd be working on a different problem entirely. But I don't see what difference this processor would make."

"What created the only example of consciousness we know of?" Daniel asked.

"Evolution."

"Exactly. But I don't want to wait three billion years, so I need to make the selection process a great deal more refined, and the sources of variation more targeted."

Julie digested this. "You want to try to *evolve* true AI? Conscious, human-level AI?"

"Yes." Daniel saw her mouth tightening, saw her struggling to measure her words before speaking.

"With respect," she said, "I don't think you've thought that through."

"On the contrary," Daniel assured her. "I've been planning this for twenty years."

"Evolution," she said, "is about failure and death. Do you have any idea how many sentient creatures lived and died along the way to *Homo sapiens*? How much suffering was involved?"

"Part of your job would be to minimize the suffering."

"*Minimize it?*" She seemed genuinely shocked, as if this proposal was even worse than blithely assuming that the process would raise no ethical concerns. "What right do we have to inflict it at all?"

Daniel said, "You're grateful to exist, aren't you? Notwithstanding the tribulations of your ancestors."

"I'm grateful to exist," she agreed, "but in the human case the suffering wasn't deliberately inflicted by anyone, and nor was there any alternative way we could have come into existence. If there really *had* been a just creator, I don't doubt that he would have followed Genesis literally; he sure as hell would not have used evolution."

"Just, *and omnipotent*," Daniel suggested. "Sadly, that second trait's even rarer than the first."

"I don't think it's going to take omnipotence to create something in our own image," she said. "Just a little more patience and self-knowledge."

"This won't be like natural selection," Daniel insisted. "Not that blind, not that cruel, not that wasteful. You'd be free to intervene as much as you wished, to take whatever palliative measures you felt appropriate."

"*Palliative measures?*" Julie met his gaze, and he saw her expression flicker from disbelief to something darker. She stood up and glanced at her wrist-phone. "I don't have any signal here. Would you mind calling me a taxi?"

Daniel said, "Please, hear me out. Give me ten more minutes, then the helicopter will take you to the airport."

"I'd prefer to make my own way home." She gave Daniel a look that made it clear that this was not negotiable.

He called her a taxi, and they walked to the elevator.

"I know you find this morally challenging," he said, "and I respect that. I wouldn't dream of hiring someone who thought these were trivial issues. But if I don't do this, someone else will. Someone with far worse intentions than mine."

"Really?" Her tone was openly sarcastic now. "So how, exactly, does the mere existence of your project stop this hypothetical bin Laden of AI from carrying out his own?"

Daniel was disappointed; he'd expected her at least to understand what was at stake. He said, "This is a race to decide between Godhood and enslavement. Whoever succeeds first will be unstoppable. I'm not going to be anyone's slave."

Julie stepped into the elevator; he followed her.

She said, "You know what they say the modern version of Pascal's Wager is? Sucking up to as many Transhumanists as possible, just in case one of them turns into God. Perhaps your motto should be 'Treat every chatterbot kindly, it might turn out to be the deity's uncle.'"

"We will be as kind as possible," Daniel said. "And don't forget, we can determine the nature of these beings. They will be happy to be alive, and grateful to their creator. We can select for those traits."

Julie said, "So you're aiming for *übermenschen* that wag their tails when you scratch them behind the ears? You might find there's a bit of a trade-off there."

The elevator reached the lobby. Daniel said, "Think about this, don't rush to a decision. You can call me any time." There was no commercial flight back to Toronto tonight; she'd be stuck in a hotel, paying money she could ill-afford, thinking about the kind of salary she could demand from him now that she'd played hard to get. If she mentally recast all this obstinate moralizing as a deliberate bargaining strategy, she'd have no trouble swallowing her pride.

Julie offered her hand, and he shook it. She said, "Thank you for dinner."

The taxi was waiting. He walked with her across the lobby. "If you want to see AI in your lifetime," he said, "this is the only way it's going to happen."

She turned to face him. "Maybe that's true. We'll see. But better to spend a thousand years and get it right, than a decade and succeed by your methods."

As Daniel watched the taxi drive away into the fog, he forced himself to accept the reality: she was never going to change her mind. Julie Dehghani had been his first choice, his ideal collaborator. He couldn't pretend that this wasn't a setback.

Still, no one was irreplaceable. However much it would have delighted him to have won her over, there were many more names on his list.

2

DANIEL'S WRIST tingled as the message came through. He glanced down and saw the word PROGRESS! hovering in front of his watch face.

The board meeting was almost over; he disciplined himself and kept his attention focused for ten more minutes. WiddulHands.com had made him his first billion, and it was still the pre-eminent social networking site for the 0-3 age group. It had been fifteen years since he'd founded the company, and he had since diversified in many directions, but he had no intention of taking his hands off the levers.

When the meeting finished he blanked the wall screen and paced the empty conference room for half a minute, rolling his neck and stretching his shoulders. Then he said, "Lucien".

Lucien Crace appeared on the screen. "Significant progress?" Daniel enquired.

"Absolutely." Lucien was trying to maintain polite eye contact with Daniel, but something kept drawing his gaze away. Without waiting for an explanation, Daniel gestured at the screen and had it show him exactly what Lucien was seeing.

A barren, rocky landscape stretched to the horizon. Scattered across the rocks were dozens of crab-like creatures—some deep blue, some coral pink, though these weren't colors the locals would see, just species markers added to the view to make it easier to interpret. As Daniel watched, fat droplets of corrosive rain drizzled down from a passing cloud. This had to be the bleakest environment in all of Sapphire.

Lucien was still visible in an inset. "See the blue ones over by the crater lake?" he said. He sketched a circle on the image to guide Daniel's attention.

"Yeah." Five blues were clustered around a lone pink; Daniel gestured and the view zoomed in on them. The blues had opened up their prisoner's body, but it wasn't dead; Daniel was sure of that, because the pinks had recently acquired a trait that turned their bodies to mush the instant they expired.

"They've found a way to study it," Lucien said. "To keep it alive and study it."

From the very start of the project, he and Daniel had decided to grant the Phites the power to observe and manipulate their own bodies as much as possible. In the DNA world, the inner workings of anatomy and heredity had only become accessible once highly sophisticated technology had been invented. In Sapphire, the barriers were designed to be far lower. The basic units of biology here were "beads", small spheres that possessed a handful of simple properties but no complex internal biochemistry. Beads were larger than the cells of the DNA world, and Sapphire's diffractionless optics rendered them visible to the right kind of naked eye. Animals acquired beads from their diet, while in plants they replicated in the presence of sunlight, but unlike cells they did not themselves mutate. The beads in a Phite's body could be rearranged with a minimum of fuss, enabling a kind of self-modification that no human surgeon or prosthetics engineer could rival—and this skill was actually essential for at least one stage in every Phite's life: reproduction involved two Phites pooling their spare beads and then collaborating to "sculpt" them into an infant, in part by directly copying each other's current body plans.

Of course these crabs knew nothing of the abstract principles of engineering and design, but the benefits of trial and error, of self-experimentation and cross-species plagiarism, had led them into an escalating war of innovation. The pinks had been the first to stop their corpses from being plundered for secrets, by stumbling on a way to make them literally fall apart *in extremis*; now it seemed the blues had found a way around that, and were indulging in a spot of vivisection-as-industrial-espionage.

Daniel felt a visceral twinge of sympathy for the struggling pink, but he brushed it aside. Not only did he doubt that the Phites were any more conscious than ordinary crabs, they certainly had a radically different relationship to bodily integrity. The pink was resisting because its dissectors were of a different species; if they had been its cousins it might not have put up any fight at all. When something happened in spite of your wishes, that was unpleasant by definition, but it would be absurd to imagine that the pink was in the kind of agony that an antelope being flayed by jackals would feel—let alone experiencing the existential terrors of a human trapped and mutilated by a hostile tribe.

"This is going to give them a tremendous advantage," Lucien enthused.

"The blues?"

Lucien shook his head. "Not blues over pinks; Phites over tradlife. Bacteria can swap genes, but this kind of active mimetics is unprecedented without cultural support. Da Vinci might have watched the birds in flight and sketched his gliders, but no lemur ever dissected the body of an eagle and then stole its tricks. They're going to have *innate* skills as powerful as whole strands of human technology. All this before they even have language."

"Hmm." Daniel wanted to be optimistic too, but he was growing wary of Lucien's hype. Lucien had a doctorate in genetic programming, but he'd made his name with FoodExcuses.com, a web service that trawled the medical literature to cobble together quasi-scientific justifications for indulging in your favorite culinary vice. He had the kind of technobabble that could bleed money out of venture capitalists down pat, and though Daniel admired that skill in its proper place, he expected a higher insight-to-bullshit ratio now that Lucien was on his payroll.

The blues were backing away from their captive. As Daniel watched, the pink sealed up its wounds and scuttled off toward a group of its own kind. The blues had now seen the detailed anatomy of the respiratory system that had been giving the pinks an advantage in the thin air of this high plateau. A few of the blues would try it out, and if it worked for them, the whole tribe would copy it.

"So what do you think?" Lucien asked.

"Select them," Daniel said.

"Just the blues?"

"No, both of them." The blues alone might have diverged into competing subspecies eventually, but bringing their old rivals along for the ride would help to keep them sharp.

"Done," Lucien replied. In an instant, ten million Phites were erased, leaving the few thousand blues and pinks from these badlands to inherit the planet. Daniel felt no compunction; the extinction events he decreed were surely the most painless in history.

Now that the world no longer required human scrutiny, Lucien un-throttled the crystal and let the simulation race ahead; automated tools would let them know when the next interesting development arose. Daniel watched the population figures rising as his chosen species spread out and recolonised Sapphire.

Would their distant descendants rage against him, for this act of "genocide" that had made room for them to flourish and prosper? That seemed unlikely. In any case, what choice did he have? He couldn't start manufacturing new crystals for every useless side-branch of the evolutionary tree. Nobody was wealthy enough to indulge in an exponentially growing number of virtual animal shelters, at half a billion dollars apiece.

He was a just creator, but he was not omnipotent. His careful pruning was the only way.

3

IN THE months that followed, progress came in fits and starts. Several times, Daniel found himself rewinding history, reversing his decisions and trying a new path. Keeping every Phite variant alive was impractical, but he did retain enough information to resurrect lost species at will.

The maze of AI was still a maze, but the speed of the crystal served them well. Barely eighteen months after the start of Project Sapphire, the Phites were exhibiting a basic theory of mind: their actions showed that they could deduce what others knew about the world, as distinct from what they knew themselves. Other AI researchers had spliced this kind of thing into their programs by hand, but Daniel was convinced that his version was better integrated, more robust. Human-crafted software was brittle and inflexible; his Phites had been forged in the heat of change.

Daniel kept a close watch on his competitors, but nothing he saw gave him reason to doubt his approach. Sunil Gupta was raking in the cash from a search engine that could "understand" all forms of text, audio and video, making use of fuzzy logic techniques that were at least forty years old. Daniel respected Gupta's business acumen, but in the unlikely event that his software ever became conscious, the sheer cruelty of having forced it to wade through the endless tides of blogorrhoea would surely see it turn on its creator and exact a revenge that made *The Terminator* look like a picnic. Angela Lindstrom was having some success with her cheesy AfterLife, in which dying clients gave heart-to-heart interviews to software that then constructed avatars able to converse with surviving relatives. And Julie Dehghani was still frittering away her talent, writing software for robots that played with colored blocks side-by-side with human infants, and learned languages from adult volunteers by imitating the interactions of baby talk. Her prophesy of taking a thousand years to "get it right" seemed to be on target.

As the second year of the project drew to a close, Lucien was contacting Daniel once or twice a month to announce a new breakthrough. By constructing environments that imposed suitable selection pressures, Lucien had generated a succession of new species that used simple tools, crafted crude shelters, and even domesticated plants. They were still shaped more or less like crabs, but they were at least as intelligent as chimpanzees.

The Phites worked together by observation and imitation, guiding and reprimanding each other with a limited repertoire of gestures and cries, but as yet they lacked anything that could truly be called a language. Daniel grew impatient; to move beyond a handful of specialized skills, his creatures needed the power to map any object, any action, any prospect they might encounter in the world into their speech, and into their thoughts.

Daniel summoned Lucien and they sought a way forward. It was easy to tweak the Phites' anatomy to grant them the ability to generate more subtle vocalizations, but that alone was no more useful than handing a chimp a conductor's baton. What was needed was a way to make sophisticated planning and communications skills a matter of survival.

Eventually, he and Lucien settled on a series of environmental modifications, providing opportunities for the creatures to rise to the occasion.

Most of these scenarios began with famine. Lucien blighted the main food crops, then offered a palpable reward for progress by dangling some tempting new fruit from a branch that was just out of reach. Sometimes that metaphor could almost be taken literally: he'd introduce a plant with a complex life cycle that required tricky processing to render it edible, or a new prey animal that was clever and vicious, but nutritionally well worth hunting in the end.

Time and again, the Phites failed the test, with localized species dwindling to extinction. Daniel watched in dismay; he had not grown sentimental, but he'd always boasted to himself that he'd set his standards higher than the extravagant cruelties of nature. He contemplated tweaking the creatures' physiology so that starvation brought a swifter, more merciful demise, but Lucien pointed out that he'd be slashing his chances of success if he curtailed this period of intense motivation. Each time a group died out, a fresh batch of mutated cousins rose from the dust to take their place; without that intervention, Sapphire would have been a wilderness within a few real-time days.

Daniel closed his eyes to the carnage, and put his trust in sheer time, sheer numbers. In the end, that was what the crystal had bought him: when all else failed, he could give up any pretense of knowing how to achieve his aims and simply test one random mutation after another.

Months went by, sending hundreds of millions of tribes starving into their graves. But what choice did he have? If he fed these creatures milk and honey, they'd remain fat and stupid until the day he died. Their hunger agitated them, it drove them to search and strive, and while any human onlooker was tempted to color such behavior with their own emotional palette, Daniel told himself that the Phites' suffering was a shallow thing, little more than the instinct that jerked his own hand back from a flame before he'd even registered discomfort.

They were not the equal of humans. Not yet.

And if he lost his nerve, they never would be.

˷ᴡᴡ

DANIEL DREAMED that he was inside Sapphire, but there were no Phites in sight. In front of him stood a sleek black monolith; a thin stream of pus wept from a crack in its smooth, obsidian surface. Someone was holding him by the wrist, trying to force his hand into a reeking pit in the ground. The pit, he knew, was piled high with things he did not want to see, let alone touch.

He thrashed around until he woke, but the sense of pressure on his wrist remained. It was coming from his watch. As he focused on the one-word message he'd received, his stomach tightened. Lucien would not have dared to wake him at this hour for some run-of-the-mill result.

Daniel rose, dressed, then sat in his office sipping coffee. He did not know why he was so reluctant to make the call. He had been waiting for this moment for more than twenty years, but it would not be the pinnacle of his life. After this, there would be a thousand more peaks, each one twice as magnificent as the last.

He finished the coffee then sat a while longer, massaging his temples, making sure his head was clear. He would not greet this new era bleary-eyed, half-awake. He recorded all his calls, but this was one he would retain for posterity.

"Lucien," he said. The man's image appeared, smiling. "Success?"

"They're talking to each other," Lucien replied.

"About what?"

"Food, weather, sex, death. The past, the future. You name it. They won't shut up."

Lucien sent transcripts on the data channel, and Daniel perused them. The linguistics software didn't just observe the Phites' behavior and correlate it with the sounds they made; it peered right into their virtual brains and tracked the flow of information. Its task was far from trivial, and there was no guarantee that its translations were perfect, but Daniel did not believe it could hallucinate an entire language and fabricate these rich, detailed conversations out of thin air.

He flicked between statistical summaries, technical overviews of linguistic structure, and snippets from the millions of conversations the software had logged. *Food, weather, sex, death.* As human dialogue the translations would have seemed utterly banal, but in context they were riveting. These were not chatterbots blindly following Markov chains, designed to impress the judges in a Turing test. The Phites were discussing matters by which they genuinely lived and died.

When Daniel brought up a page of conversational topics in alphabetical order, his eyes were caught by the single entry under the letter G. *Grief.* He tapped the link, and spent a few minutes reading through samples, illustrating the appearance of the concept following the death of a child, a parent, a friend.

He kneaded his eyelids. It was three in the morning; there was a sickening clarity to everything, the kind that only night could bring. He turned to Lucien.

"No more death."

"Boss?" Lucien was startled.

"I want to make them immortal. Let them evolve culturally; let their ideas live and die. Let them modify their own brains, once they're smart enough; they can already tweak the rest of their anatomy."

"Where will you put them all?" Lucien demanded.

"I can afford another crystal. Maybe two more."

"That won't get you far. At the present birth rate—"

"We'll have to cut their fertility drastically, tapering it down to zero. After that, if they want to start reproducing again they'll really have to innovate." They would need to learn about the outside world, and comprehend its alien physics well enough to design new hardware into which they could migrate.

Lucien scowled. "How will we control them? How will we shape them? If we can't select the ones we want—"

Daniel said quietly, "This is not up for discussion." Whatever Julie Dehghani had thought of him, he was not a monster; if he believed that these creatures were as conscious as he was, he was not going to slaughter them like cattle—or stand by and let them die "naturally", when the rules of this world were his to rewrite at will.

"We'll shape them through their memes," he said. "We'll kill off the bad memes, and help spread the ones we want to succeed." He would need to keep an iron grip on the Phites and their culture, though, or he would never be able to trust them. If he wasn't going to literally *breed them* for loyalty and gratitude, he would have to do the same with their ideas.

Lucien said, "We're not prepared for any of this. We're going to need new software, new analysis and intervention tools."

Daniel understood. "Freeze time in Sapphire. Then tell the team they've got eighteen months."

4

DANIEL SOLD his shares in WiddulHands, and had two more crystals built. One was to support a higher population in Sapphire, so there was as large a pool of diversity among the immortal Phites as possible; the other was to run the software—which Lucien had dubbed the Thought Police—needed to keep tabs on what they were doing. If human overseers had had to monitor and shape the evolving culture every step of the way, that would have slowed things down to a glacial pace. Still, automating the process completely was tricky, and Daniel preferred to err on the side of caution, with the Thought Police freezing Sapphire and notifying him whenever the situation became too delicate.

If the end of death was greeted by the Phites with a mixture of puzzlement and rejoicing, the end of birth was not so easy to accept. When all attempts by mating couples to sculpt their excess beads into offspring became as ineffectual as shaping dolls out of clay, it led to a mixture of persistence and distress that was painful to witness. Humans were accustomed to failing to conceive, but this was more like still birth after still birth. Even when Daniel intervened to modify the Phites' basic drives, some kind of cultural or emotional inertia kept many of them going through the motions. Though their new instincts urged them merely to pool their spare beads and then stop, sated, they would continue with the old version of the act regardless, forlorn and confused, trying to shape the useless puddle into something that lived and breathed.

Move on, Daniel thought. *Get over it.* There was only so much sympathy he could muster for immortal beings who would fill the galaxy with their children, if they ever got their act together.

The Phites didn't yet have writing, but they'd developed a strong oral tradition, and some put their mourning for the old ways into elegiac words. The Thought Police identified those memes, and ensured that they didn't spread far. Some Phites chose to kill themselves rather than live in the barren new world. Daniel felt he had no right to stop them, but mysterious obstacles blocked the paths of anyone who tried, irresponsibly, to romanticise or encourage such acts.

The Phites could only die by their own volition, but those who retained the will to live were not free to doze the centuries away. Daniel decreed no more terrible famines, but he hadn't abolished hunger itself, and he kept enough pressure on the food supply and other resources to force the Phites to keep innovating, refining agriculture, developing trade.

The Thought Police identified and nurtured the seeds of writing, mathematics, and natural science. The physics of Sapphire was a simplified, game-world model, not so arbitrary as to be incoherent, but not so deep and complex that you needed particle physics to get to the bottom of it. As crystal time sped forward and the immortals sought solace in understanding their world, Sapphire soon had its Euclid and Archimedes, its Galileo and its Newton; their ideas spread with supernatural efficiency, bringing forth a torrent of mathematicians and astronomers.

Sapphire's stars were just a planetarium-like backdrop, present only to help the Phites get their notions of heliocentricity and inertia right, but its moon was as real as the world itself. The technology needed to reach it was going to take a while, but that was all right; Daniel didn't want them getting ahead of themselves. There was a surprise waiting for them there, and his preference was for a flourishing of biotech and computing before they faced that revelation.

Between the absence of fossils, Sapphire's limited biodiversity, and all the clunky external meddling that needed to be covered up, it was hard for the Phites to reach a grand Darwinian view of biology, but their innate skill with beads gave them a head start in the practical arts. With a little nudging, they began tinkering with their bodies, correcting some inconvenient anatomical quirks that they'd missed in their pre-conscious phase.

As they refined their knowledge and techniques, Daniel let them imagine that they were working toward restoring fertility; after all, that was perfectly true, even if their goal was a few conceptual revolutions further away than they realized. Humans had had their naive notions of a Philosopher's Stone dashed, but they'd still achieved nuclear transmutation in the end.

The Phites, he hoped, would transmute *themselves*: inspect their own brains, make sense of them, and begin to improve them. It was a staggering task to expect of anyone; even Lucien and his team, with their God's-eye view of the creatures, couldn't come close. But when the crystal was running at full speed, the Phites could think millions of times faster than their creators. If Daniel could keep them from straying off course, everything that humanity might once have conceived of as the fruits of millennia of progress was now just a matter of months away.

LUCIEN SAID, "We're losing track of the language."

Daniel was in his Houston office; he'd come to Texas for a series of face-to-face meetings, to see if he could raise some much-needed cash by licensing the crystal fabrication process. He would have preferred to keep the technology to himself, but he was almost certain that he was too far ahead of his rivals now for any of them to stand a chance of catching up with him.

"What do you mean, losing track?" Daniel demanded. Lucien had briefed him just three hours before, and given no warning of an impending crisis.

The Thought Police, Lucien explained, had done their job well: they had pushed the neural self-modification meme for all it was worth, and now a successful form of "brain boosting" was spreading across Sapphire. It required a detailed "recipe" but no technological aids; the same innate skills for observing and manipulating beads that the Phites had used to copy themselves during reproduction were enough.

All of this was much as Daniel had hoped it would be, but there was an alarming downside. The boosted Phites were adopting a dense and complex new language, and the analysis software couldn't make sense of it.

"Slow them down further," Daniel suggested. "Give the linguistics more time to run."

"I've already frozen Sapphire," Lucien replied. "The linguistics have been running for an hour, with the full resources of an entire crystal."

Daniel said irritably, "We can see exactly what they've done to their brains. How can we not understand the effects on the language?"

"In the general case," Lucien said, "deducing a language from nothing but neural anatomy is computationally intractable. With the old language, we were lucky; it had a simple structure, and it was highly correlated with obvious behavioral elements. The new language is much more abstract and conceptual. We might not even have our own correlates for half the concepts."

Daniel had no intention of letting events in Sapphire slip out of his control. It was one thing to hope that the Phites would, eventually, be juggling real-world physics that was temporarily beyond his comprehension, but any bright ten-year-old could grasp the laws of their present universe, and their technology was still far from rocket science.

He said, "Keep Sapphire frozen, and study your records of the Phites who first performed this boost. If they understood what they were doing, we can work it out too."

At the end of the week, Daniel signed the licensing deal and flew back to San Francisco. Lucien briefed him daily, and at Daniel's urging hired a dozen new computational linguists to help with the problem.

After six months, it was clear that they were getting nowhere. The Phites who'd invented the boost had had one big advantage as they'd tinkered with each other's brains: it had not been a purely theoretical exercise for them. They hadn't gazed at anatomical diagrams and then reasoned their way to a better design. They had *experienced* the effects of thousands of small experimental changes, and the results had shaped their intuition for the process. Very little of that intuition had been spoken aloud, let alone written down and formalized. And the process of decoding those insights from a purely structural view of their brains was every bit as difficult as decoding the language itself.

Daniel couldn't wait any longer. With the crystal heading for the market, and other comparable technologies approaching fruition, he couldn't allow his lead to melt away.

"We need the Phites themselves to act as translators," he told Lucien. "We need to contrive a situation where there's a large enough pool who choose not to be boosted that the old language continues to be used."

"So we need maybe twenty-five per cent refusing the boost?" Lucien suggested. "And we need the boosted Phites to want to keep them informed of what's happening, in terms that we can all understand."

Daniel said, "Exactly."

"I think we can slow down the uptake of boosting," Lucien mused, "while we encourage a traditionalist meme that says it's better to span the two cultures and languages than replace the old entirely with the new."

Lucien's team set to work, tweaking the Thought Police for the new task, then restarting Sapphire itself.

Their efforts seemed to yield the desired result: the Phites were corralled into valuing the notion of maintaining a link to their past, and while the boosted Phites surged ahead, they also worked hard to keep the unboosted in the loop.

It was a messy compromise, though, and Daniel wasn't happy with the prospect of making do with a watered-down, Sapphire-for-Dummies version of the Phites' intellectual achievements. What he really wanted was someone on the inside reporting to him directly, like a Phite version of Lucien.

It was time to start thinking about job interviews.

~~~

LUCIEN WAS running Sapphire more slowly than usual—to give the Thought Police a computational advantage now that they'd lost so much raw surveillance data—but even at the reduced rate, it took just six real-time days for the boosted Phites to invent computers, first as a mathematical formalism and, shortly afterward, as a succession of practical machines.

Daniel had already asked Lucien to notify him if any Phite guessed the true nature of their world. In the past, a few had come up with vague metaphysical speculations that weren't too wide of the mark, but now that they had a firm grasp of the idea of universal computation, they were finally in a position to understand the crystal as more than an idle fantasy.

The message came just after midnight, as Daniel was preparing for bed. He went into his office and activated the intervention tool that Lucien had written for him, specifying a serial number for the Phite in question.

The tool prompted Daniel to provide a human-style name for his interlocutor, to facilitate communication. Daniel's mind went blank, but after waiting twenty seconds the software offered its own suggestion: Primo.

Primo was boosted, and he had recently built a computer of his own. Shortly afterward, the Thought Police had heard him telling a couple of unboosted friends about an amusing possibility that had occurred to him.

Sapphire was slowed to a human pace, then Daniel took control of a Phite avatar and the tool contrived a meeting, arranging for the two of them to be alone in the shelter that Primo had built for himself. In accordance with the current architectural style the wooden building was actually still alive, self-repairing and anchored to the ground by roots.

Primo said, "Good morning. I don't believe we've met."

It was no great breach of protocol for a stranger to enter one's shelter uninvited, but Primo was understating his surprise; in this world of immortals, but no passenger jets, bumping into strangers anywhere was rare.

"I'm Daniel." The tool would invent a Phite name for Primo to hear. "I heard you talking to your friends last night about your new computer.

Wondering what these machines might do in the future. Wondering if they could ever grow powerful enough to contain a whole world."

"I didn't see you there," Primo replied.

"I wasn't there," Daniel explained. "I live outside this world. I built the computer that contains this world."

Primo made a gesture that the tool annotated as amusement, then he spoke a few words in the boosted language. *Insults? A jest? A test of Daniel's omniscience?* Daniel decided to bluff his way through, and act as if the words were irrelevant.

He said, "Let the rain start." Rain began pounding on the roof of the shelter. "Let the rain stop." Daniel gestured with one claw at a large cooking pot in a corner of the room. "Sand. Flower. Fire. Water jug." The pot obliged him, taking on each form in turn.

Primo said, "Very well. I believe you, Daniel." Daniel had had some experience reading the Phites' body language directly, and to him Primo seemed reasonably calm. Perhaps when you were as old as he was, and had witnessed so much change, such a revelation was far less of a shock than it would have been to a human at the dawn of the computer age.

"You created this world?" Primo asked him.

"Yes."

"You shaped our history?"

"In part," Daniel said. "Many things have been down to chance, or to your own choices."

"Did you stop us having children?" Primo demanded.

"Yes," Daniel admitted.

"*Why?*"

"There is no room left in the computer. It was either that, or many more deaths."

Primo pondered this. "So you could have stopped the death of my parents, had you wished?"

"I could bring them back to life, if you want that." This wasn't a lie; Daniel had stored detailed snapshots of all the last mortal Phites. "But not yet; only when there's a bigger computer. When there's room for them."

"Could you bring back *their* parents? And their parents' parents? Back to the beginning of time?"

"No. That information is lost."

Primo said, "What is this talk of waiting for a bigger computer? You could easily stop time from passing for us, and only start it again when your new computer is built."

"No," Daniel said, "I can't. Because *I need you to build the computer*. I'm not like you: I'm not immortal, and my brain can't be boosted. I've done my best, now I need you to do better. The only way that can happen is if you learn the science of my world, and come up with a way to make this new machine."

Primo walked over to the water jug that Daniel had magicked into being. "It seems to me that you were ill-prepared for the task you set yourself. If you'd waited for the machine you really needed, our lives would not have been so hard. And if such a machine could not be built in your lifetime, what was to stop your grandchildren from taking on that task?"

"I had no choice," Daniel insisted. "I couldn't leave your creation to my descendants. There is a war coming between my people. I needed your help. I needed strong allies."

"You have no friends in your own world?"

"Your time runs faster than mine. I needed the kind of allies that only your people can become, in time."

Primo said, "What exactly do you want of us?"

"To build the new computer you need," Daniel replied. "To grow in numbers, to grow in strength. Then to raise me up, to make me greater than I was, as I've done for you. When the war is won, there will be peace forever. Side by side, we will rule a thousand worlds."

"And what do you want of *me*?" Primo asked. "Why are you speaking to me, and not to all of us?"

"Most people," Daniel said, "aren't ready to hear this. It's better that they don't learn the truth yet. But I need one person who can work for me directly. I can see and hear everything in your world, but I need you to make sense of it. I need you to understand things for me."

Primo was silent.

Daniel said, "I gave you life. How can you refuse me?"

DANIEL PUSHED his way through the small crowd of protesters gathered at the entrance to his San Francisco tower. He could have come and gone by helicopter instead, but his security consultants had assessed these people as posing no significant threat. A small amount of bad PR didn't bother him; he was no longer selling anything that the public could boycott directly, and none of the businesses he dealt with seemed worried about being tainted by association. He'd broken no laws, and confirmed no rumors. A few feral cyberphiles waving placards reading "Software Is Not Your Slave!" meant nothing.

Still, if he ever found out which one of his employees had leaked details of the project, he'd break their legs.

Daniel was in the elevator when Lucien messaged him: MOON VERY SOON! He halted the elevator's ascent, and redirected it to the basement.

All three crystals were housed in the basement now, just centimeters away from the Play Pen: a vacuum chamber containing an atomic force microscope with fifty thousand independently movable tips, arrays of solid-state lasers and photodetectors, and thousands of micro-wells stocked with samples of all the stable chemical elements. The time lag between Sapphire and this machine had to be as short as possible, in order for the Phites to be able to conduct experiments in real-world physics while their own world was running at full speed.

Daniel pulled up a stool and sat beside the Play Pen. If he wasn't going to slow Sapphire down, it was pointless aspiring to watch developments as they unfolded. He'd probably view a replay of the lunar landing when he went up to his office, but by the time he screened it, it would be ancient history.

"One giant leap" would be an understatement; wherever the Phites landed on the moon, they would find a strange black monolith waiting for them. Inside would be the means to operate the Play Pen; it would not take them long to learn the controls, or to understand what this signified. If they were really slow in grasping what they'd found, Daniel had instructed Primo to explain it to them.

The physics of the real world was far more complex than the kind the Phites were used to, but then, no human had ever been on intimate terms with quantum field theory either, and the Thought Police had already encouraged the Phites to develop most of the mathematics they'd need to get started.

In any case, it didn't matter if the Phites took longer than humans to discover twentieth-century scientific principles, and move beyond them. Seen from the outside, it would happen within hours, days, weeks at the most.

A row of indicator lights blinked on; the Play Pen was active. Daniel's throat went dry. The Phites were finally reaching out of their own world into his.

A panel above the machine displayed histograms classifying the experiments the Phites had performed so far. By the time Daniel was paying attention, they had already discovered the kinds of bonds that could be formed between various atoms, and constructed thousands of different small molecules. As he watched, they carried out spectroscopic analyses, built simple nanomachines, and manufactured devices that were, unmistakably, memory elements and logic gates.

The Phites wanted children, and they understood now that this was the only way. They would soon be building a world in which they were not just more numerous, but faster and smarter than they were inside the crystal. And that would only be the first of a thousand iterations. They were working their way toward Godhood, and they would lift up their own creator as they ascended.

Daniel left the basement and headed for his office. When he arrived, he called Lucien.

"They've built an atomic-scale computer," Lucien announced. "And they've fed some fairly complex software into it. It doesn't seem to be an upload, though. Certainly not a direct copy on the level of beads." He sounded flustered; Daniel had forbidden him to risk screwing up the experiments by slowing down Sapphire, so even with Primo's briefings to help him it was difficult for him to keep abreast of everything.

"Can you model their computer, and then model what the software is doing?" Daniel suggested.

Lucien said, "We only have six atomic physicists on the team; the Phites already outnumber us on that score by about a thousand to one. By the time we have any hope of making sense of this, they'll be doing something different."

"What does Primo say?" The Thought Police hadn't been able to get Primo included in any of the lunar expeditions, but Lucien had given him the power to make himself invisible and teleport to any part of Sapphire or the lunar base. Wherever the action was, he was free to eavesdrop.

"Primo has trouble understanding a lot of what he hears; even the boosted aren't universal polymaths and instant experts in every kind of jargon. The gist of it is that the Lunar Project people have made a very fast computer in the Outer World, and it's going to help with the fertility problem…somehow." Lucien laughed. "Hey, maybe the Phites will do exactly what we did: see if they can evolve something smart enough to give them a hand. How cool would that be?"

Daniel was not amused. Somebody had to do some real work eventually; if the Phites just passed the buck, the whole enterprise would collapse like a pyramid scheme.

Daniel had some business meetings he couldn't put off. By the time he'd swept all the bullshit aside, it was early afternoon. The Phites had now built some kind of tiny solid-state accelerator, and were probing the internal structure of protons and neutrons by pounding them with high-speed electrons. An atomic computer wired up to various detectors was doing the data analysis, processing the results faster than any in-world computer could. The Phites had already figured out the standard quark model. Maybe they were going to skip uploading into nanocomputers, and head straight for some kind of femtomachine?

Digests of Primo's briefings made no mention of using the strong force for computing, though. They were still just satisfying their curiosity about the fundamental laws. Daniel reminded himself of their history. They had burrowed down to what seemed like the foundations of physics before, only to discover that those simple rules were nothing to do with the ultimate reality. It made sense that they would try to dig as deeply as they could into the mysteries of the Outer World before daring to found a colony, let alone emigrate *en masse*.

By sunset the Phites were probing the surroundings of the Play Pen with various kinds of radiation. The levels were extremely low—certainly too low to risk damaging the crystals—so Daniel saw no need to intervene. The Play Pen itself did not have a massive power supply, it contained no radioisotopes, and the Thought Police would ring alarm bells and bring in human experts if some kind of tabletop fusion experiment got underway, so Daniel was reasonably confident that the Phites couldn't do anything stupid and blow the whole thing up.

Primo's briefings made it clear that they thought they were engaged in a kind of "astronomy". Daniel wondered if he should give them access to instruments for doing serious observations—the kind that would allow them to understand relativistic gravity and cosmology. Even if he bought time on a large telescope, though, just pointing it would take an eternity for the Phites. He wasn't going to slow Sapphire down and then grow old while they explored the sky; next thing they'd be launching space probes on thirty-year missions. Maybe it was time to ramp up the level of collaboration, and just hand them some astronomy texts and star maps? Human culture had its own hard-won achievements that the Phites couldn't easily match.

As the evening wore on, the Phites shifted their focus back to the subatomic world. A new kind of accelerator began smashing single gold ions together at extraordinary energies—though the total power being expended was still minuscule. Primo soon announced that they'd mapped all three generations of quarks and leptons. The Phites' knowledge of particle physics was drawing level with humanity's; Daniel couldn't follow the technical details any more, but the experts were giving it all the thumbs up. Daniel felt a surge of pride; of course his children knew what they were doing, and if they'd reached the point where they could momentarily bamboozle him, soon he'd ask them to catch their breath and bring him up to speed. Before he permitted them to emigrate, he'd slow the crystals down and introduce himself to everyone. In fact, that might be the perfect time to set them their next task: to understand human biology, well enough to upload him. To make him immortal, to repay their debt.

He sat watching images of the Phites' latest computers, reconstructions based on data flowing to and from the AFM tips. Vast lattices of shimmering atoms stretched off into the distance, the electron clouds that joined them quivering like beads of mercury in some surreal liquid abacus. As he watched, an inset window told him that the ion accelerators had been re-designed, and fired up again.

Daniel grew restless. He walked to the elevator. There was nothing he could see in the basement that he couldn't see from his office, but he wanted to stand beside the Play Pen, put his hand on the casing, press his nose against the glass. The era of Sapphire as a virtual world with no consequences in his own was coming to an end; he wanted to stand beside the thing itself and be reminded that it was as solid as he was.

The elevator descended, passing the tenth floor, the ninth, the eighth. Without warning, Lucien's voice burst from Daniel's watch, priority audio crashing through every barrier of privacy and protocol. "Boss, there's radiation. Net power gain. Get to the helicopter, *now*."

Daniel hesitated, contemplating an argument. If this was fusion, why hadn't it been detected and curtailed? He jabbed the stop button and felt the brakes engage. Then the world dissolved into brightness and pain.

7

WHEN DANIEL emerged from the opiate haze, a doctor informed him that he had burns to sixty per cent of his body. More from heat than from radiation. He was not going to die.

There was a net terminal by the bed. Daniel called Lucien and learned what the physicists on the team had tentatively concluded, having studied the last of the Play Pen data that had made it off-site.

It seemed the Phites had discovered the Higgs field, and engineered a burst of something akin to cosmic inflation. What they'd done wasn't as simple as merely inflating a tiny patch of vacuum into a new universe, though. Not only had they managed to create a "cool Big Bang", they had pulled a large chunk of ordinary matter into the pocket universe they'd made, after which the wormhole leading to it had shrunk to subatomic size and fallen through the Earth.

They had taken the crystals with them, of course. If they'd tried to upload themselves into the pocket universe through the lunar data link, the Thought Police would have stopped them. So they'd emigrated by another route entirely. They had snatched their whole substrate, and ran.

Opinions were divided over exactly what else the new universe would contain. The crystals and the Play Pen floating in a void, with no power source, would leave the Phites effectively dead, but some of the team believed there could be a thin plasma of protons and electrons too, created by a form of Higgs decay that bypassed the unendurable quark-gluon fireball of a hot Big Bang. If they'd built the right nanomachines, there was a chance that they could convert the Play Pen into a structure that would keep the crystals safe, while the Phites slept through the long wait for the first starlight.

〜〜〜

THE TINY skin samples the doctors had taken finally grew into sheets large enough to graft. Daniel bounced between dark waves of pain and medicated euphoria, but one idea stayed with him throughout the turbulent journey, like a guiding star: *Primo had betrayed him.* He had given the fucker life, entrusted him with power, granted him privileged knowledge, showered him with the favors of the Gods. And how had he been repaid? He was back to zero. He'd spoken to his lawyers; having heard rumors of an "illegal radiation source", the insurance company was not going to pay out on the crystals without a fight.

Lucien came to the hospital, in person. Daniel was moved; they hadn't met face-to-face since the job interview. He shook the man's hand.

"You didn't betray me."

Lucien looked embarrassed. "I'm resigning, boss."

Daniel was stung, but he forced himself to accept the news stoically. "I understand; you have no choice. Gupta will have a crystal of his own by now. You have to be on the winning side, in the war of the Gods."

Lucien put his resignation letter on the bedside table. "What war? Are you still clinging to that fantasy where überdorks battle to turn the moon into computronium?"

Daniel blinked. "Fantasy? If you didn't believe it, why were you working with me?"

"You paid me. Extremely well."

"So how much will Gupta be paying you? I'll double it."

Lucien shook his head, amused. "I'm not going to work for Gupta. I'm moving into particle physics. The Phites weren't all that far ahead of us when they escaped; maybe forty or fifty years. Once we catch up, I guess a private universe will cost about as much as a private island; maybe less in the long run. But no one's going to be battling for control of this one, throwing gray goo around like monkeys flinging turds while they draw up their plans for Matrioshka brains."

Daniel said, "If you take any data from the Play Pen logs—"

"I'll honor all the confidentiality clauses in my contract." Lucien smiled. "But anyone can take an interest in the Higgs field; that's public domain."

After he left, Daniel bribed the nurse to crank up his medication, until even the sting of betrayal and disappointment began to fade.

A universe, he thought happily. *Soon I'll have a universe of my own.*

But I'm going to need some workers in there, some allies, some companions. I can't do it all alone; someone has to carry the load.

STEVE FEVER

1

A few weeks after his fourteenth birthday, with the soybean harvest fast approaching, Lincoln began having vivid dreams of leaving the farm and heading for the city. Night after night, he pictured himself gathering supplies, trudging down to the highway, and hitching his way to Atlanta.

There were problems with the way things got done in the dream, though, and each night in his sleep he struggled to resolve them. The larder would be locked, of course, so he dreamed up a side-plot about collecting a stash of suitable tools for breaking in. There were sensors all along the farm's perimeter, so he dreamed about different ways of avoiding or disabling them.

Even when he had a scenario that seemed to make sense, daylight revealed further flaws. The grille that blocked the covered part of the irrigation ditch that ran beneath the fence was too strong to be snipped away with bolt-cutters, and the welding torch had a biometric lock.

When the harvest began, Lincoln contrived to get a large stone caught in the combine, and then volunteered to repair the damage. With his father looking on, he did a meticulous job, and when he received the expected praise he replied with what he hoped was a dignified mixture of pride and bemusement, "I'm not a kid anymore. I can handle the torch."

"Yeah." His father seemed embarrassed for a moment, then he squatted down, put the torch into supervisor mode, and added Lincoln's touch to the authorized list.

Lincoln waited for a moonless night. The dream kept repeating itself, thrashing impatiently against his skull, desperate to be made real.

When the night arrived and he left his room, barefoot in the darkness, he felt as if he was finally enacting some long rehearsed performance: less a play than an elaborate dance that had seeped into every muscle in his body. First, he carried his boots to the back door and left them by the step. Then he took his backpack to the larder, the borrowed tools in different pockets so they wouldn't clank against each other. The larder door's hinges were attached on the inside, but he'd marked their positions with penknife scratches in the varnish that he'd practiced finding by touch. His mother had secured the food store years before, after a midnight raid by Lincoln and his younger brother, Sam, but it was still just a larder, not a jewel-safe, and the awl bit through the wood easily enough, finally exposing the tip of one of the screws that held the hinges in place. The pliers he tried first couldn't grip the screw tightly enough to get it turning, but Lincoln had dreamed of an alternative. With the awl, he cleared away a little more wood, then he jammed a small hexagonal nut onto the screw's thread and used a T-handled socket wrench to turn them together. The screw couldn't move far, but this was enough to loosen it. He removed the nut and used the pliers, then with a few firm taps from a hammer, delivered via the socket wrench, the screw broke free of the wood.

He repeated the procedure five more times, freeing the hinges completely, then he strained against the door, keeping a firm grip on the handle, until the tongue of the lock slipped from its groove.

The larder was pitch black, but he didn't risk using his flashlight; he found what he wanted by memory and touch, filling the backpack with enough provisions for a week. *After that?* He'd never wondered, in the dream. Maybe he'd find new friends in Atlanta who'd help him. The idea struck a chord, as if it was a truth he was remembering, not a hopeful speculation.

The tool shed was locked securely, but Lincoln was still skinny enough to crawl through the hole in the back wall, hidden by junk for so long that it had fallen off the end of his father's repair list. This time he risked the flashlight and walked straight to the welding torch, rather than groping his way across the darkness. He maneuvered it through the hole, and didn't bother rearranging the rotting timbers that had concealed the entrance. There was no point covering his tracks. He would be missed within minutes of his parents rising, no matter what, so the important thing now was speed.

He put on his boots and headed for the irrigation ditch. Their German shepherd, Melville, trotted up and started licking Lincoln's hand. Lincoln stopped and petted him for a few seconds, then firmly ordered him back toward the house. The dog made a soft wistful sound, but complied.

Twenty meters from the perimeter fence, Lincoln climbed into the ditch. The enclosed section was still a few meters away, but he crouched down immediately, practicing the necessary constrained gait, and shielding himself from the sensors' gaze. He clutched the torch under one arm, careful to keep it dry. The chill of the water didn't much bother him; his boots grew heavy, but he didn't know what the ditch concealed, and he'd rather have waterlogged boots than a rusty scrap of metal slicing his foot.

He entered the enclosed, concrete cylinder, then a few steps brought him to the metal grille. He switched on the torch and oriented himself by the light of its control panel. When he put on the goggles he was blind, but then he squeezed the trigger of the torch and the arc lit up the tunnel around him.

Each bar took just seconds to cut, but there were a lot of them. In the confined space the heat was oppressive; his T-shirt was soon soaked with sweat. Still, he had fresh clothes in his pack, and he could wash in the ditch once he was through. If he was still not respectable enough to get a ride, he'd walk to Atlanta.

"Young man, get out of there immediately."

Lincoln shut off the arc. The voice, and those words, could only belong to his grandmother. For a few pounding heartbeats, he wondered if he'd imagined it, but then in the same unmistakable tone, ratcheted up a notch, she added, "Don't play games with me, I don't have the patience for it."

Lincoln slumped in the darkness, disbelieving. He'd dreamed his way through every detail, past every obstacle. How could she appear out of nowhere and ruin everything?

There wasn't room to turn around, so he crawled backward to the mouth of the tunnel. His grandmother was standing on the bank of the ditch.

"What exactly do you think you're doing?" she demanded.

He said, "I need to get to Atlanta."

"Atlanta? All by yourself, in the middle of the night? What happened? You got a craving for some special kind of food we're not providing here?"

Lincoln scowled at her sarcasm, but knew better than to answer back. "I've been dreaming about it," he said, as if that explained everything. "Night after night. Working out the best way to do it."

His grandmother said nothing for a while, and when Lincoln realized that he'd shocked her into silence he felt a pang of fear himself.

She said, "You have no earthly reason to run away. Is someone beating you? Is someone treating you badly?"

"No ma'am."

"So *why exactly is it* that you need to go?"

Lincoln felt his face grow hot with shame. How could he have missed it? How could he have fooled himself into believing that the obsession was his own? But even as he berated himself for his stupidity, his longing for the journey remained.

"You've got the fever, haven't you? You know where those kind of dreams come from: nanospam throwing a party in your brain. Ten billion idiot robots playing a game called *Steve At Home*."

She reached down and helped him out of the ditch. The thought crossed Lincoln's mind that he could probably overpower her, but then he recoiled from the idea in disgust. He sat down on the grass and put his head in his hands.

"Are you going to lock me up?" he asked.

"Nobody's turning anybody into a prisoner. Let's go talk to your parents. They're going to be thrilled."

The four of them sat in the kitchen. Lincoln kept quiet and let the others argue, too ashamed to offer any opinions of his own. How could he have let himself sleepwalk like that? Plotting and scheming for weeks, growing ever prouder of his own ingenuity, but doing it all at the bidding of the world's stupidest, most despised dead man.

He still yearned to go to Atlanta. He itched to bolt from the room, scale the fence, and jog all the way to the highway. He could see the whole sequence in his mind's eye; he was already thinking through the flaws in the plan and hunting for ways to correct them.

He banged his head against the table. "Make it stop! Get them out of me!"

His mother put an arm around his shoulders. "You know we can't wave a magic wand and get rid of them. You've got the latest counterware. All we can do is send a sample to be analyzed, do our bit to speed the process along."

The cure could be months away, or years. Lincoln moaned pitifully. "Then lock me up! Put me in the basement!"

His father wiped a glistening streak of sweat from his forehead. "That's not going to happen. If I have to be beside you everywhere you go, we're still going to treat you like a human being." His voice was strained, caught somewhere between fear and defiance.

Silence descended. Lincoln closed his eyes. Then his grandmother spoke.

"Maybe the best way to deal with this is to let him scratch his damned itch."

"What?" His father was incredulous.

"He wants to go to Atlanta. I can go with him."

"*The Stevelets* want him in Atlanta," his father replied.

"They're not going to harm him, they just want to borrow him. And like it or not, they've already done that. Maybe the quickest way to get them to move on is to satisfy them."

Lincoln's father said, "You know they can't be satisfied."

"Not completely. But every path they take has its dead end, and the sooner they find this one, the sooner they'll stop bothering him."

His mother said, "If we keep him here, that's a dead end for them too. If they want him in Atlanta, and he's not in Atlanta—"

"They won't give up that easily," his grandmother replied. "If we're not going to lock him up and throw away the key, they're not going to take a few setbacks and delays as some kind of proof that Atlanta's beyond all hope."

Silence again. Lincoln opened his eyes. His father addressed Lincoln's grandmother. "Are you sure you're not infected, yourself?"

She rolled her eyes. "Don't go all Body Snatchers on me, Carl. I know the two of you can't leave the farm right now. So if you want to let him go, I'll look after him." She shrugged and turned her head away imperiously. "I've said my piece. Now it's your decision."

2

LINCOLN DROVE the truck as far as the highway, then reluctantly let his grandmother take the wheel. He loved the old machine, which still had the engine his grandfather had installed, years before Lincoln was born, to run on their home-pressed soybean oil.

"I plan to take the most direct route," his grandmother announced. "Through Macon. Assuming your friends have no objection."

Lincoln squirmed. "Don't call them that!"

"I'm sorry." She glanced at him sideways. "But I still need to know."

Reluctantly, Lincoln forced himself to picture the drive ahead, and he felt a surge of *rightness* endorsing the plan. "No problem with that," he muttered. He was under no illusion that he could prevent the Stevelets from influencing his thoughts, but deliberately consulting them, as if there was a third person sitting in the cabin between them, made him feel much worse.

He turned to look out the window, at the abandoned fields and silos passing by. He had been down this stretch of highway a hundred times, but each piece of blackened machinery now carried a disturbing new poignancy. The Crash had come thirty years ago, but it still wasn't truly over. The Stevelets aspired to do no harm—and supposedly they got better at that year by year—but they were still far too stupid and stubborn to be relied upon to get anything right. They had just robbed his parents of two skilled pairs of hands in the middle of the harvest; how could they imagine that that was harmless? Millions of people around the world had died in the Crash, and that couldn't all be blamed on panic and self-inflicted casualties. The government had been crazy, bombing half the farms in the south-east; everyone agreed now that it had only made things worse. But many other deaths could not have been avoided, except by the actions of the Stevelets themselves.

You couldn't reason with them, though. You couldn't shame them, or punish them. You just had to hope they got better at noticing when they were screwing things up, while they forged ahead with their impossible task.

"See that old factory?" Lincoln's grandmother gestured at a burned-out metal frame drooping over slabs of cracked concrete, standing in a field of weeds. "There was a conclave there, almost twenty years ago."

Lincoln had been past the spot many times, and no one had ever mentioned this before. "What happened? What did they try?"

"I heard it was meant to be a time machine. Some crackpot had put his plans on the net, and the Stevelets decided they had to check it out. About a hundred people were working there, and thousands of animals."

Lincoln shivered. "How long were they at it?"

"Three years." She added quickly, "But they've learned to rotate the workers now. It's rare for them to hang on to any individual for more than a month or two."

A month or two. A part of Lincoln recoiled, but another part thought: that wouldn't be so bad. A break from the farm, doing something different. Meeting new people, learning new skills, working with animals.

Rats, most likely.

Steve Hasluck had been part of a team of scientists developing a new kind of medical nanomachine, refining the tiny surgical instruments so they could make decisions of their own, on the spot. Steve's team had developed an efficient way of sharing computing power across a whole swarm, allowing them to run large, complex programs known as "expert systems" that codified decades of biological and clinical knowledge into pragmatic lists of rules. The nanomachines didn't really "know" anything, but they could churn through a very long list of "if A and B, there's an eighty percent chance of C" at blistering speed, and a good list gave them a good chance of cutting a lot of diseases off short.

Then Steve found out that he had cancer, and that his particular kind wasn't on anyone's list of rules.

He took a batch of the nanomachines and injected them into a room full of caged rats, along with samples of his tumor. The nanomachines could swarm all over the tumor cells, monitoring their actions constantly. The polymer radio antennas they built beneath the rats' skin let them share their observations and hunches from host to host, like their own high-speed wireless internet, as well as reporting their findings back to Steve himself. With that much information being gathered, how hard could it be to understand the problem, and fix it? But Steve and his colleagues couldn't make sense of the data. Steve got sicker, and all the gigabytes pouring out of the rats remained as useless as ever.

Steve tried putting new software into the swarms. If nobody knew how to cure his disease, why not let the swarms work it out? He gave them access to vast clinical databases, and told them to extract their own rules. When the cure still failed to appear, he bolted on more software, including expert systems seeded with basic knowledge of chemistry and physics. From this starting point, the swarms worked out things about cell membranes and protein folding that no one had ever realized before, but none of it helped Steve.

Steve decided that the swarms still had too narrow a view. He gave them a general-purpose knowledge acquisition engine and let them drink at will from the entire web. To guide their browsing and their self-refinement, he gave them two clear goals. The first was to do no harm to their hosts. The second was to find a way to save his life, and failing that, to bring him back from the dead.

That last rider might not have been entirely crazy, because Steve had arranged to have his body preserved in liquid nitrogen. If that had happened, maybe the Stevelets would have spent the next thirty years ferrying memories out of his frozen brain. Unfortunately, Steve's car hit a tree at high speed just outside of Austin, Texas, and his brain ended up as flambé.

This made the news, and the Stevelets were watching. Between their lessons from the web and whatever instincts their creator had given them, they figured out that they were now likely to be incinerated themselves. That wouldn't have mattered to them, if not for the fact that they'd decided that the game wasn't over. There'd been nothing about resurrecting charred flesh in the online medical journals, but the web embraced a wider range of opinions. The swarms had read the sites of various groups who were convinced that self-modifying software could find ways to make itself smarter, and then smarter again, until nothing was beyond its reach. Resurrecting the dead was right there on every bullet-pointed menu of miracles.

The Stevelets knew that they couldn't achieve anything as a plume of smoke wafting out of a rat crematorium, so the first thing they engineered was a break-out. From the cages, from the building, from the city. The original nanomachines couldn't replicate themselves, and could be destroyed in an instant by a simple chemical trigger, but somewhere in the sewers or the fields or the silos, they had inspected and dissected each other to the point where they were able to reproduce. They took the opportunity to alter some old traits: the new generation of Stevelets lacked the suicide switch, and resisted external meddling with their software.

They might have vanished into the woods to build scarecrow Steves out of sticks and leaves, but their software roots gave their task rigor, of a kind. From the net, they had taken ten thousand crazy ideas about the world, and though they lacked the sense to see that they were crazy, they couldn't simply take anything on faith either. They had to test these claims, one by one, as they groped their way toward Stevescence. And while the web had suggested that with their power to self-modify they could achieve anything, they found that in reality there were countless crucial tasks which remained beyond their abilities. Even with the aid of dextrous mutant rats, Steveware Version 2 was never going to re-engineer the fabric of spacetime, or resurrect Steve in a virtual world.

Within months of their escape, it must have become clear to them that some hurdles could only be jumped with human assistance, because that was when they started borrowing people. Doing them no physical harm, but infesting them with the kinds of ideas and compulsions that turned them into willing recruits.

The panic, the bombings, the Crash had followed. Lincoln hadn't witnessed the worst of it. He hadn't seen conclaves of harmless sleepwalkers burned to death by mobs, or fields of grain napalmed by the government, lest they feed and shelter nests of rats.

Over the decades, the war had become more subtle. Counterware could keep the Stevelets at bay, for a while. The experts kept trying to subvert the Steveware, spreading modified Stevelets packed with propositions that aimed to cripple the swarms' ability to function, or, more ambitiously, make them believe that their job was done. In response, the Steveware had developed verification and encryption schemes that made it ever harder to corrupt or mislead. Some people still advocated cloning Steve from surviving pathology samples, but most experts doubted that the Steveware would be satisfied with that, or taken in by any misinformation that made the clone look like something more.

The Stevelets aspired to the impossible, and would accept no substitutes, while humanity longed to be left unmolested, to get on with more useful tasks. Lincoln had known no other world, but until now he'd viewed the struggle from the sidelines, save shooting the odd rat and queueing up for his counterware shots.

So what was his role now? Traitor? Double agent? Prisoner of war? People talked about sleepwalkers and zombies, but in truth there was still no right word for what he had become.

3

LATE IN the afternoon, as they approached Atlanta, Lincoln felt his sense of the city's geography warping, the significance of familiar landmarks shifting. *New information coming through.* He ran one hand over each of his forearms, where he'd heard the antennas often grew, but the polymer was probably too soft to feel beneath the skin. His parents could have wrapped his body in foil to mess with reception, and put him in a tent full of bottled air to keep out any of the slower, chemical signals that the Stevelets also used, but none of that would have rid him of the basic urge.

As they passed the airport, then the tangle of overpasses where the highway from Macon merged with the one from Alabama, Lincoln couldn't stop thinking about the baseball stadium up ahead. Had the Stevelets commandeered the home of the Braves? That would have made the news, surely, and ramped the war up a notch or two.

"Next exit," he said. He gave directions that were half his own, half flowing from an eerie dream logic, until they turned a corner and the place where he knew he had to be came into view. It wasn't the stadium itself; that had merely been the closest landmark in his head, a beacon the Stevelets had used to help guide him. "They booked a whole motel!" his grandmother exclaimed.

"Bought," Lincoln guessed, judging from the amount of visible construction work. The Steveware controlled vast financial assets, some flat-out stolen from sleepwalkers, but much of it honestly acquired by trading the products of the rat factories: everything from high-grade pharmaceuticals to immaculately faked designer shoes.

The original parking lot was full, but there were signs showing the way to an overflow area near what had once been the pool. As they headed for reception, Lincoln's thoughts drifted weirdly to the time they'd come to Atlanta for one of Sam's spelling competitions.

There were three uniformed government Stevologists in the lobby, seated at a small table with some equipment. Lincoln went to the reception desk first, where a smiling young woman handed him two room keys before he'd had a chance to say a word. "Enjoy the conclave," she said. He didn't know if she was a zombie like him, or a former motel employee who'd been kept on, but she didn't need to ask him anything.

The government people took longer to deal with. His grandmother sighed as they worked their way through a questionnaire, then a woman called Dana took Lincoln's blood. "They usually try to hide," Dana said, "but sometimes your counterware can bring us useful fragments, even when it can't stop the infection."

As they ate their evening meal in the motel dining room, Lincoln tried meeting the eyes of the people around him. Some looked away nervously; others offered him encouraging smiles. He didn't feel as if he was being inducted into a cult, and that was not just from the lack of pamphlets or speeches. He hadn't been brainwashed into worshipping Steve; his opinion of the dead man was entirely unchanged. Like the desire to reach Atlanta in the first place, his task here would be far more focused and specific. To the Steveware he was a kind of machine, a machine it could instruct and tinker with the way Lincoln could control and customize his phone, but the Steveware no more expected him to share its final goal than he expected his own machines to enjoy his music, or respect his friends.

∿

LINCOLN KNEW that he dreamed that night, but when he woke he had trouble remembering the dream. He knocked on his grandmother's door; she'd been up for hours. "I can't sleep in this place," she complained. "It's quieter than the farm."

She was right, Lincoln realized. They were close to the highway, but traffic noise, music, sirens, all the usual city sounds, barely reached them.

They went down to breakfast. When they'd eaten, Lincoln was at a loss to know what to do. He went to the reception desk; the same woman was there.

He didn't need to speak. She said, "They're not quite ready for you, sir. Feel free to watch TV, take a walk, use the gym. You'll know when you're needed."

He turned to his grandmother. "Let's take a walk."

They left the motel and walked around the stadium, then headed east away from the highway, ending up in a leafy park a few blocks away. All the people around them were doing ordinary things: pushing their kids on swings, playing with their dogs. Lincoln's grandmother said, "If you want to change your mind, we can always go home."

As if his mind were his own to change. Still, at this moment the compulsion that had brought him here seemed to have waned. He didn't know if the Steveware had taken its eyes off him, or whether it was deliberately offering him a choice, a chance to back out.

He said, "I'll stay." He dreaded the idea of hitting the road only to find himself summoned back. Part of him was curious, too. He wanted to be brave enough to step inside the jaws of this whale, on the promise that he would be disgorged in the end.

They returned to the motel, ate lunch, watched TV, ate dinner. Lincoln checked his phone; his friends had been calling, wondering why he hadn't been in touch. He hadn't told anyone where he'd gone. He'd left it to his parents to explain everything to Sam.

He dreamed again, and woke clutching at fragments. Good times, an edge of danger, wide blue skies, the company of friends. It seemed more like a dream he could have had on his own than anything that might have come from the Steveware cramming his mind with equations so he could help test another crackpot idea that the swarms had collected thirty years ago by googling the physics of immortality.

Three more days passed, just as aimlessly. Lincoln began to wonder if he'd failed some test, or if there'd been a miscalculation leading to a glut of zombies.

Early in the morning of their fifth day in Atlanta, as Lincoln splashed water on his face in the bathroom, he felt the change. Shards of his recurrent dream glistened potently in the back of his mind, while a set of directions through the motel complex gelled in the foreground. He was being summoned. It was all he could do to bang on his grandmother's door and shout out a garbled explanation, before he set off down the corridor.

She caught up with him. "Are you sleepwalking? Lincoln?"

"I'm still here, but they're taking me soon."

She looked frightened. He grasped her hand and squeezed it. "Don't worry," he said. He'd always imagined that when the time came he'd be the one who was afraid, drawing his courage from her.

He turned a corner and saw the corridor leading into a large space that might once have been a room for conferences or weddings. Half a dozen people were standing around; Lincoln could tell that the three teenagers were fellow zombies, while the adults were just there to look out for them. The room had no furniture, but contained an odd collection of items, including four ladders and four bicycles. There was cladding on the walls, *soundproofing*, as if the whole building wasn't quiet enough already.

Out of the corner of his eye, Lincoln saw a dark mass of quivering fur: a swarm of rats, huddled against the wall. For a moment his skin crawled, but then a heady sense of exhilaration swept his revulsion away. His own body held only the tiniest fragment of the Steveware; at last he could confront the thing itself.

He turned toward the rats and spread his arms. "You called, and I came running. So what is it you want?" Disquietingly, memories of the Pied Piper story drifted into his head. Irresistible music lured the rats away. Then it lured away the children.

The rats gave him no answer, but the room vanished.

4

TY HIT a patch of dust on the edge of the road, and it rose up around him. He whooped with joy and pedalled twice as hard, streaking ahead to leave his friends immersed in the cloud.

Errol caught up with him and reached across to punch him on the arm, as if he'd raised the dust on purpose. It was a light blow, not enough to be worth retribution; Ty just grinned at him.

It was a school day, but they'd all snuck off together before lessons began. They couldn't do anything in town, there were too many people who'd know them, but then Dan had suggested heading for the water tower. His father had some spray-paint in the shed. They'd climb the tower, and tag it.

There was a barbed-wire fence around the base of the tower, but Dan had already been out here on the weekend and started a tunnel, which didn't take them long to complete. When they were through, Ty looked up and felt his head swimming. Carlos said, "We should have brought a rope."

"We'll be OK."

Chris said, "I'll go first."

"Why?" Dan demanded.

Chris took his fancy new phone from his pocket and waved it at them. "Best camera angle. I don't want to be looking up your ass."

Carlos said, "Just promise you won't put it on the web. If my parents see this, I'm screwed."

Chris laughed. "Mine too. I'm not that stupid."

"Yeah, well, you won't be on camera if you're holding the thing."

Chris started up the ladder, then Dan went next, with one paint can in the back pocket of his jeans. Ty followed, then Errol and Carlos.

The air had been still down on the ground, but as they went higher a breeze came out of nowhere, cooling the sweat on Ty's back. The ladder started shuddering; he could see where it was bolted securely to the concrete of the tower, but in between it could still flex alarmingly. He'd treat it like a fairground ride, he decided: a little scary, but probably safe.

When Chris reached the top, Dan let go of the ladder with one hand, took the paint can, and reached out sideways into the expanse of white concrete. He quickly shaped a blue background, a distorted diamond, then called down to Errol, who was carrying the red.

When Ty had passed the can up he looked away, out across the expanse of brown dust. He could see the town in the distance. He glanced up and saw Chris leaning forward, gripping the ladder with one hand behind his back while he aimed the phone down at them.

Ty shouted up at him, "Hey Scorsese! Make me famous!"

Dan spent five minutes adding finicky details in silver. Ty didn't mind; it was good just being here. He didn't need to mark the tower himself; whenever he saw Dan's tag he'd remember this feeling.

They clambered down, then sat at the base of the tower and passed the phone around, checking out Chris's movie.

5

LINCOLN HAD three rest days before he was called again, this time for four days in succession. He fought hard to remember all the scenes he was sleepwalking through, but even with his grandmother adding her accounts of the "play acting" she'd witnessed, he found it hard to hold on to the details.

Sometimes he hung out with the other actors, shooting pool in the motel's games room, but there seemed to be an unspoken taboo against discussing their roles. Lincoln doubted that the Steveware would punish them even if they managed to overcome the restraint, but it was clear that it didn't want them to piece too much together. It had even gone to the trouble of changing Steve's name—as Lincoln and the other actors heard it, though presumably not Steve himself—as if the anger they felt toward the man in their ordinary lives might have penetrated into their roles. Lincoln couldn't even remember his own mother's face when he was Ty; the farm, the Crash, the whole history of the last thirty years was gone from his thoughts entirely.

In any case, he had no wish to spoil the charade. Whatever the Steveware thought it was doing, Lincoln hoped it would believe it was working perfectly, all the way from Steve's small-town childhood to whatever age it needed to reach before it could write this creation into flesh and blood, congratulate itself on a job well done, and then finally, mercifully dissolve into rat piss and let the world move on.

A fortnight after they'd arrived, without warning, Lincoln was no longer needed. He knew it when he woke, and after breakfast the woman at reception asked him, politely, to pack his bags and hand back the keys. Lincoln didn't understand, but maybe Ty's family had moved out of Steve's home town, and the friends hadn't stayed in touch. Lincoln had played his part, now he was free.

When they returned to the lobby with their suitcases, Dana spotted them, and asked Lincoln if he was willing to be debriefed. He turned to his grandmother. "Are you worried about the traffic?" He'd already phoned his father and told him they'd be back by dinner time.

She said, "You should do this. I'll wait in the truck."

They sat at a table in the lobby. Dana asked his permission to record his words, and he told her everything he could remember.

When Lincoln had finished, he said, "You're the Stevologist. You think they'll get there in the end?"

Dana gestured at her phone to stop recording. "One estimate", she said, "is that the Stevelets now comprise a hundred thousand times the computational resources of all the brains of all the human beings who've ever lived."

Lincoln laughed. "And they still need stage props and extras, to do a little VR?"

"They've studied the anatomy of ten million human brains, but I think they know that they still don't fully understand consciousness. They bring in real people for the bit parts, so they can concentrate on the star. If you gave them a particular human brain, I'm sure they could faithfully copy it into software, but anything more complicated starts to get murky. How do they know their Steve is conscious, when they're not conscious themselves? He never gave them a reverse Turing test, a checklist they could apply. All they have is the judgment of people like you."

Lincoln felt a surge of hope. "He seemed real enough to me." His memories were blurred—and he wasn't even absolutely certain which of Ty's four friends was Steve—but none of them had struck him as less than human.

Dana said, "They have his genome. They have movies, they have blogs, they have emails: Steve's, and a lot of people who knew him. They have a thousand fragments of his life. Like the borders of a giant jigsaw puzzle."

"So that's good, right? A lot of data is good?"

Dana hesitated. "The scenes you described have been played out thousands of times before. They're trying to tweak their Steve to write the right emails, pull the right faces for the camera—by himself, without following a script like the extras. A lot of data sets the bar very high."

As Lincoln walked out to the parking lot, he thought about the laughing, carefree boy he'd called Chris. Living for a few days, writing an email—then memory-wiped, re-set, started again. Climbing a water tower, making a movie of his friends, but later turning the camera on himself, saying one wrong word—and wiped again.

A thousand times. A million times. The Steveware was infinitely patient, and infinitely stupid. Each time it failed it would change the actors, shuffle a few variables, then run the experiment over again. The possibilities were endless, but it would keep on trying until the sun burned out.

Lincoln was tired. He climbed into the truck beside his grandmother, and they headed for home.

TAP

I want you to find out who killed my mother, Ms O'Connor. Will you do that?"

Helen Sharp's voice was unsteady with anger; she seemed almost as psyched up as if she'd come here to confront the killer, face-to-face. Under the circumstances, though, the very act of insisting that there *was* a killer was like shouting a defiant accusation from the rooftops—which must have taken some courage, even if she had no idea whom she was accusing.

I said carefully, "The coroner returned an open finding. I'm not a lawyer, but I imagine Third Hemisphere would still settle out of court for a significant—"

"*Third Hemisphere* have no case to answer! And sure, maybe they'd pay up anyway—just to avoid the publicity. But as it happens, I'm not interested in *legalized blackmail*." Her eyes flashed angrily; she made no effort to conceal her outrage. No doubt her lawyers had already given her exactly the same advice; it didn't look like the idea would ever grow on her. She was thirty-two—only five years younger than me—but she radiated so much stubborn idealism that I found it hard not to think of her as belonging to another generation entirely.

I raised one hand in a conciliatory gesture. "Fine. It's your decision. But I suggest you don't sign anything that limits your options—and don't make any public declarations of absolution. After six months paying my expenses, you might change your mind. Or I might even turn up something that will change it for you. Stranger things have happened." Though nothing much stranger than a next-of-kin declining to screw a multinational for all it was worth.

Sharp said impatiently, "The TAP implant was *not* responsible. There's no evidence to suggest that it was."

"No, and there's no evidence to suggest foul play, either."

"That's why I'm hiring you. To find it."

I glanced irritably at the north-facing window; the allegedly smart pane was ablaze with sunlight, rendering most of the office almost as hot as the sweltering streets of Kings Cross below.

Grace Sharp had been dead for a month. I'd been following the case informally, like everyone else in Sydney, out of sheer morbid curiosity. On the evening of January 12, she'd been at work in her study, apparently alone. The immediate cause of death had been a myocardial infarction, but the autopsy had also shown signs of a powerful adrenaline surge. That could have resulted from the pain and stress of a heart attack already in progress—or it could have come first, triggered by an unknown external shock.

Or, the Total Affect Protocol chip in her brain might have flooded her body with adrenaline for no good reason at all.

Sharp had been sixty-seven—in reasonable health for her age, but old enough to blur the boundaries of the possible. Forensic pathologists had struggled at the inquest to allocate probabilities to the three alternatives, but there'd been no clear front-runner. Which was no doubt distressing for the relatives—and no doubt left them vulnerable to the fantasy that there had to be a simple answer out there somewhere, just waiting to be found.

Helen Sharp said, "The *media consensus* is that my mother was composing a poem just before she died—and she thought a word in TAP so 'powerful' that it killed her on the spot." Her tone was venomous. "Do they seriously imagine that ninety thousand sane people would put something in their brains which was *capable* of doing that? Or that the manufacturers would sell a device which would leave them open to billions of dollars worth of compensation claims? Or that the government licensing authorities—"

I said, "Licensed pharmaceuticals have killed plenty of people. Implants are even harder to test. And 'fail-safe' software written to the most rigorous military specifications has crashed aircraft—"

She seized on the analogy triumphantly. "And how do you know that? Because the aircraft's black box proved it! Well, the TAP implant has its own black box: an independent chip which logs all its actions. *And there was no record of any malfunction.* No record of the implant triggering an adrenaline release at *any* level—let alone a fatal dose."

"Maybe the black box glitched, too. You say it's independent—but if there's enough connectivity to let it know everything the implant does, the combined system might still be vulnerable to some kind of shared failure mode that the designers never anticipated."

Sharp clenched her fists in frustration. "That's not—literally—impossible," she conceded. "But I don't believe it's likely."

"All right. What do you think happened?"

Sharp composed herself, with the air of someone weary of repeating the same message, gathering up her strength with a promise to herself that this would be the last time.

She said, "My mother *was* working on a new poem that night—the black box makes that clear. But the time of death can't be determined precisely—and it could have been as much as fifteen minutes after the last recorded use of the implant. I believe she was interrupted. I believe someone broke into the apartment and killed her.

"I don't know how they did it. Maybe they just terrorized her—without laying a finger on her—and that was enough to bring on the heart attack." Her voice was flat, deliberately emotionless. "Or maybe they gave her a transdermal dose of a powerful stimulant. There are dozens of chemicals which could have triggered a heart attack, without leaving a trace. She wasn't found for almost nine hours. There are carbohydrate analogs of stimulatory neuropeptides which are degraded into glucose and water on a time scale of *minutes*."

I resisted the urge to cite the lack of evidence for an intruder; it would have been a waste of breath. "Why, though? Why would anyone want to kill her?"

She hesitated. "I'm not sure how much you know about TAP."

"Assume the worst."

"Well…it's been wrongly described as just about everything from 'telepathy' to 'computerized Esperanto' to 'the multimedia standard for the brain.' Sure, it began with a fusion of language and VR—but it's been growing for almost fifteen years now. There's still a word for <<dog>>"— she sketched the angle-brackets with her fingers, and I picked up on the convention later—"which might as well be *hundo*—and another for <<your beloved golden Labrador standing on the beach shaking the water from its

coat before licking your face>>…which will evoke all that and more in all five senses, if you let it.

"But at the leading edge, now, we're creating words for concepts, emotions, states of mind, which might once have defied description altogether. With TAP, ultimately there's *nothing* a human being can experience which needs to remain…ineffable, mysterious, incommunicable. Nothing is beyond discussion. Nothing is beyond analysis. Nothing is 'unspeakable.' And a lot of people find that prospect threatening; it turns a lot of old power structures on their head."

If that cliché came true every time it was invoked, *power structures* would be oscillating faster than mains current. Helen Sharp was pushing seven on my paranoia index; on top of all her understandable grief and frustration, she belonged to a technosubculture which was poorly understood by the mainstream, frequently misrepresented—and which clearly liked to think of itself as a "dangerously" iconoclastic elite.

I said, "I know there are people who find TAP users…unacceptable. But what's going to drive them to extremes like murder, all of a sudden? In fifteen years, has anyone, anywhere, been killed simply for having the implant?"

"Not to my knowledge. But—"

"Then surely—"

"But I can tell you exactly what's changed. I can tell you why the conflict has just entered a whole new phase."

That got my attention. "Go on."

"You know it's against the law to install a TAP implant in anyone younger than eighteen years old?"

"Of course." The same restriction applied to all neural hardware, other than therapeutic chips which restored normal function to the injured or congenitally disabled.

"Early in March, a couple here in Sydney will commence legal proceedings with the aim of ensuring that they're free to install the implant in all their future children—at the age of three months."

I was momentarily speechless. These plans had clearly been kept within a very tight circle of supporters; the saturation media coverage of the inquest hadn't mentioned so much as a rumor. After a month of intense journalistic scrutiny, I hadn't expected the TAP-heads to have any surprises left.

I said, "Legal proceedings on what basis?"

"That they're entitled to raise their family using whatever language they choose. That's guaranteed in Federal legislation: there's a 2011 bill which brings into force most of the provisions of the 2005 UN Covenant on Human Rights. They'll be seeking a ruling from the High Court which invalidates the relevant sections of the New South Wales criminal code—which is far more difficult, from a legal point of view, than trying to defend themselves against a prosecution after the fact…but it does save them the trouble of having to find a surgeon willing to risk martyrdom."

Sharp smiled faintly. "The same Federal law was invoked about a year ago, by a signing couple who were being pressured by Community Services to give their son a hearing implant. The parents won the first round—and it looks like there isn't going to be an appeal. But a pro-implant case was always going to be much harder, of course. And *signing* is positively respectable, compared to TAP."

"I assume the police know all this?"

"Of course. They don't appear to be particularly interested, though—and I wasn't able to raise it at the inquest. Legally speaking, I suppose it really is just static."

"But you think—"

"I think a death widely attributed to the TAP implant would transform the prospects of the challenge succeeding from merely poor to…politically impossible. I think there are people who'd consider *that* to be a result worth killing for."

Sharp fixed her gaze on me for a moment, and then nodded slightly, almost sympathetically—as if I'd just uttered a word which expressed all the conflicting emotions running through my head: <<*Neural hardware in the skull of a three-month-old child—just to indulge its parents' whims—would be an obscenity.* But…if the ubiquitous hearing implants which grant English-before-sign are no "whim", why is one which grants TAP-before-English? And if Grace Sharp *was* murdered to sway the odds against the challenge, her self-righteous killers belong in prison, regardless—and my own knee-jerk revulsion at the prospect of infant TAP-heads only goes to show that it could easily have been a powerful enough motive.>>

She said, "And I think you're going to take the case."

ᰋᵥᵥ

I STARTED work that afternoon, reviewing the technical literature on the TAP implant—the closest thing to an objective account of its capabilities I was likely to find. Like most people, I imagined I already understood all the salient features—but it turned out that I'd swallowed more misinformation from the nets than I'd realized.

The two chips—the implant proper and the black box, both less than a millimeter wide—sat at the back of the skull, sharing access to a fine web of conductive polymer threads which wrapped the brain, making billions of quasi-synaptic contacts with the visual and auditory cortex, and Wernicke's speech area in the temporal lobe. Other threads penetrated deeper, some as far as the limbic system. TAP could always be spoken or written, but bandwidth requirements made modulated infrared the medium of choice, so the implant was linked, via the spinal cord, to bioengineered IR transceiver cells in the skin of the palms.

Merely installing the implant didn't grant instant fluency in TAP; the language still had to be learned. A complete, "preloaded" vocabulary would never have worked; the precise meaning of most words in TAP could only be encoded in context, once the implant resided in a particular user's brain. The implant's own electronic neural net was ninety percent blank at installation, containing only a specialized language acquisition system and a simple "bootstrap" vocabulary. And though the learning process left its mark mostly within the implant itself—along with some relatively minor changes to the regions of the brain where a second natural language would have been encoded—it was meaningless to talk about either brain or chip "knowing TAP", in isolation. An experienced user who exchanged his or her old implant for a new one straight from the factory would have been dragged back almost to square one (in practice, all the data from the old hardware would be copied to the new)—but equally, an experience-enriched implant placed in a novice's brain would have been as unusable as a slice of someone else's cerebral cortex.

These observations applied strictly to adults, of course. Despite several dozen theoretical papers—most of them cautiously optimistic—no one really knew how a young child's brain would interact with the implant.

A TAP user could interpret a standard VR sensorium—but there was, deliberately, no provision for interacting in the conventional way with a nonexistent environment. Immersive VR implants temporarily paralyzed the organic body and diverted motor impulses from the brain into a fully computerized somatic model: a virtual body which could function as part of the virtual environment—subject to the environment's rules. In contrast, a TAP user's idea of *interaction* was more along the lines of rethinking the whole sensorium and spitting it back out, or responding with something entirely different—arguing with the whole premise, instead of passively accepting it. A VR user had little choice but to suspend disbelief, or quit—a full-sense environment, surreal or not, was always compelling—but a TAP user could deal with the same kind of information with as much or as little detachment as he or she desired. Words in TAP—which included the entire sensorium-descriptor vocabulary of VR—could evoke images ten thousand times more vivid and precise than the densest poetic English...or they could be held at arm's length and scrutinized dispassionately, as easily as any English-speaker could contemplate the phrase "a flash of blinding radiance" or "the overpowering stench of ammonia" without experiencing anything of the kind. In the jargon of the implant's designers—English words, predating TAP itself—every TAP word could be *scanned* (understood analytically), or *played* (experienced subjectively)—or interpreted in a manner lying anywhere at all between those two extremes.

In one respect, though, TAP could be more immersive than the most authoritarian VR: it could induce emotional states directly. VR was confined to pure sense data (albeit often manipulative in the extreme), but in Total Affect Protocol there were words for <<fear>>, <<euphoria>>, <<sadness>> (or rather, nuanced subtypes of these crude English categories)—and the implant could reach deep into the limbic system and trigger these states as easily as any VR chip could generate the illusion of an unambiguously blue sky.

The user's power to keep the language at a distance remained, of course—and the TAP word for <<crippling despair>> could only induce the "referent state" if a conscious effort was made to *play* it. And though TAP's formal grammar ruled out nothing, low-level filters stood guard against potentially stupefying linguistic singularities—such as <<the desire to play this word forever>>—or anything physiologically dangerous.

Still, although the literature was blithely reassuring on this point, in the end it came down to a question of trusting the manufacturers and the regulators. I didn't doubt that, in theory, a TAP chip could be designed which was no more likely than the unmodified human brain to strike the user dead if the word for <<fatal adrenaline rush>> accidentally came to mind—but whether or not Third Hemisphere had achieved that level of safety—for every conceivable user—was another matter.

Grace Sharp had been the oldest of the ninety thousand TAP speakers on the planet, and reputedly one of the most proficient—but whether *proficiency* implied more risk, from a greater vocabulary, or less, due to better control of the language, I couldn't say.

~~~

By HALF past seven, I'd had enough of wading through papers on distortion-free affect-compression algorithms. I closed the office and headed for the station.

I could still smell the day's heat wafting up from Victoria Road, but there was a faint hint of a breeze from the east. The gaudy advertising holograms never looked quite as tacky at dusk as they did at dawn, although the colors were just as washed-out; maybe it was really all down to the mood on the streets. A few sweat-stained commuters were still on their way home, radiating palpable relief—and a few freshly laundered revelers were already arriving, full of hopeful energy. Somehow, dawn in Kings Cross never looked hopeful.

I passed a gaggle of saffron-robed monks from the Darlinghurst Temple, out hunting for alms, on the other side of the street. James didn't seem to be among them—though it was hard to tell: they all looked interchangeable to me, and my strongest memories of him didn't encompass the terminal, shaven-headed stage. Even when I recalled the night he announced that he was leaving me and Mick for a life devoted to selfless contemplation—"There's no point arguing, Kath," he'd explained, with an expression of transcendent smugness, "I'm not enslaved by the illusions of language anymore."—even then, strangely enough, I pictured him as he'd looked ten years before. Buddhism had been growing ever more fashionable throughout the country for most of my lifetime—taking the place of retreating Christianity, as if the "vacuum" left behind needed to be filled by something equally absurd—but in the last ten years the Federal government had started supporting the monasteries in a big way, with a program of "community spiritual development" grants. Maybe they were hoping to save on social security payments.

I hesitated outside the station, thinking: *A single TAP word could capture this moment—perfectly encoding my entire sensorium, and everything I'm thinking and feeling. A word I could speak, write, recall. Study at a distance—*

scan—or *play*, relive completely. Inflect and modify. Quote exactly (or not) to the closest friend or the most distant stranger.

I had to admit that it was a deeply unsettling notion: a language which could encompass, if not the universe itself, then everything we could possibly experience of it. At any given moment, there were "only" ten to the power three thousand subjectively distinguishable states of the human brain. A mere ten thousand bits of information: quite a mouthful, encoded as syllables—but only a millisecond flash in infrared. A TAP user could effectively narrate his or her entire inner life, with one hundred percent fidelity, in real time. Leopold Bloom, eat your heart out.

I boarded the southbound train, the skin on the back of my neck still tingling. The carriage was packed, so I stood strap-hanging with my eyes closed, letting the question spin in the darkness of my skull: *Who, or what, killed Grace Sharp?* Work was never something I could switch on and off—and unless I reached the stage where part of me was thinking about the case every waking moment, the chances were I'd make no progress at all.

Helen Sharp believed in some faceless conspiracy against TAP as a first language, driven by sheer linguistic xenophobia—though the real opposition might also be motivated, in part, by perfectly valid concerns about the unknown developmental consequences for a child growing up with TAP.

The serious media favored a simple failure of technology; several worthy editorials had rewritten the Sharp case as a cautionary tale about the need for improved quality control in biomedical engineering. Meanwhile, the tabloids had gleefully embraced the idea of the <<death>> word, quasi-mystical enough to give their anti-tech subscribers a frisson of self-righteousness at the poetic justice of a TAP-head thinking herself into oblivion…and their pro-tech ones a frisson of awe at the sheer Power of the Chip.

And it was still possible that Grace Sharp had simply had a heart attack, all by herself. No assassins, no fatal poetry, no glitch.

So far, I could only agree with the coroner: I wasn't prepared to rule anything out.

～ᴡ～

By the time I arrived home, Mick had already eaten and retreated to his room to play *Austro-Hungarian Political Intrigues in Space*. He'd been running the scenario for almost six months, along with a dozen friends—some in Sydney, some in Beijing, some in Sao Paulo. They'd graciously let me join in once, as a minor character with an unpronounceable name, but I'd become terminally bored after ten minutes and engineered my own death as swiftly as possible. I had nothing against role-playing games, *per se*...but this was the most ludicrous one I'd encountered since *Postmodernism Ate My Love Child*. Still, every twelve-year-old needed something truly appalling to grow out of— something to look back on in a year's time with unconditional embarrassment. The books I'd read, myself (and adored, at the time) had been no better.

I knocked on his door, and entered. He was lying on his bed with the headset on and his hands above his head, making minimalist gestures with both control gloves: driving a software puppet body which had no sense of touch, or balance, or proprioception. He was moving its limbs with actions which had nothing to do with moving his own...but he was seeing and hearing everything through the puppet's eyes and ears.

Most of the studies I'd read had suggested that the earlier a child took up VR (headset-and-glove, of course, not implant-based), the fewer side-effects it had on real-life coordination and body image. The skills of moving real and virtual bodies didn't seem to compete for limited neural resources; they could be learned in parallel, as easily as two languages. Only adults got confused between the two (and did better with VR implants, which let them pretend they were using their physical bodies). The research suggested that an hour a day in VR was no more harmful than an hour a day of any other equally unnatural activity: violin practice, ballet, karate.

I still worried, though.

The room monitor flagged my presence. At a convenient break in the action, Mick slipped off the headset to greet me, doing his best to hide his impatience.

I said, "School?"

He shrugged. "Bland-out. Work?"

"I've got a murder case."

His face lit up. "Resonant! What class weapon?"

"Unkind words."

"*¿Que?*"

"It's a joke." I almost started to explain, but it didn't seem fair to hold up the other players. "You'll quit at nine, okay? I don't want to have to check on you."

"Mmmm." Deliberately noncommittal.

I said calmly, "I can program it, or you can stick to the rules voluntarily. It's your choice."

He scowled. "It's no choice, if it makes no difference."

"Very profound. But I happen to disagree." I walked over to him and brushed the hair from his eyes; he gave me his I-wish-you-wouldn't-but-you're-forgiven-this-time look.

Mick said suddenly, "Unkind words? You mean Grace Sharp?"

I nodded, surprised.

"Some *guru* last week was prating about her TAPping herself to death." He seemed greatly amused—and it struck me that "guru" was several orders of magnitude more insulting than anything I would have dared to say in front of my mother, at his age. At least put-downs were getting more elegant; my generation's equivalents had relied almost exclusively on references to excrement or genitalia. Mick and his contemporaries weren't at all prudish—they just found the old scatological forms embarrassingly childish.

I said, "You don't believe in the <<death>> word?"

"Not some *banana skin land mine* you make yourself, by accident."

I pondered that. "But if it exists at all, don't you think it'd be easier to fight if it came from outside, than if you stumbled on it in your own thoughts?"

He shook his head knowingly. "TAP's not like that. You can't invent random words in your head—you can't try out random bit-patterns. You can imagine things, you can free-associate, but...*not all the way to death, without seeing it coming.*"

I laughed. "So when did you read up on this?"

"Last week. The story sounded flash, so I went context mining." He glanced at his terminal and made some slight hand movements; a cluster of icons for Universal Resource Locators poured into an envelope with my name on it, which darted into the outgoing mail box. "References."

"Thanks. I wasted the whole afternoon—I should have come home early and picked your brains instead." I was only half joking.

I sat on the edge of the bed. "If she didn't stumble on the word herself, though...I don't see how anyone could have spoken it to her: as far as the police could tell, she'd had no visitors—or communications—for hours. And if someone broke into the apartment, they left no trace."

"How about…?" Mick gestured with one gloved thumb at the shelf above his bed.

"What?" I parsed the clutter of objects slowly. "Ah."

He'd set up an IR link with his friend Vito, who lived in an apartment block across the park; they could exchange data twenty-four hours a day without either family paying a cent to the fiber barons. The collimated beam of the five-dollar transceiver passed effortlessly through both their bedroom windows.

"You think someone outside the apartment…shot her in the palm with a <<death>> word?" The notion conjured up bizarre images: a figure taking aim with a gunless night-sight; Grace Sharp with outstretched arms and infrared stigmata.

"Maybe. Split the fee, if I'm right?"

"Sure. Minus rent, food, clothes, communications—"

Mick mimed violin playing. I feigned a swipe at his head. He glanced at the terminal; his friends were losing patience.

I said, "I'd better leave you to it."

He smiled, held up his hand in a farewell gesture like a diver about to submerge, then slipped the headset back on. I lingered in the room for a few seconds, feeling profoundly strange.

Not because I felt that I was losing touch with my son. I wasn't. But the fact that we could comprehend each other at all suddenly seemed like the most precarious voodoo. Natural language had endured, fundamentally unchanged, through a thousand social and technological revolutions…but TAP made it look like some Stone Age tool, a flake of crudely shaped obsidian in an era when individual atoms could be picked up and rearranged at whim.

And maybe in the long run, all the trial-and-error and misunderstandings, all the folk remedies of smiles and gestures, all the clumsy imperfect well-meaning attempts to bridge the gap, would be swept away by the dazzling torrent of communication without bounds.

I closed the door quietly on my way out.

∿

THE NEXT morning I started going through the transcripts of the inquest—which included a 3D image of Sharp's study. The body had been found around 8:20 AM by a domestic aid who came three times a week—Sharp, although generally fit, had suffered from severe arthritis in her hands. Paramedics had removed the body before the police became involved, but they'd snapped the scene first as a routine procedure.

The apartment was on the 25th floor, and the study had a large window facing west. The curtains were shown fully open—although there was nothing in the transcripts, one way or the other, about the possibility that the man who'd found the body, or even the paramedics, might have opened them to let in some light. I grafted the image into the local council's plan of the suburb, and did some crude ray-tracing from where the forensic software suggested Sharp had been standing before she fell. A bullet would have left directional information—but a burst of IR could have come from any location with a clear line of sight. Given the uncertainty in her position, and the size of the window, the possibilities encompassed the windows and balconies of sixty-three apartments. Most were beyond the range of cheap hobbyists' IR equipment—but I looked up skin-transceiver sensitivity, attenuation in the atmosphere, and beam spread parameters, then started checking product catalogs. There were several models of communications lasers which would have done the job—and the cheapest was only three hundred dollars. Not the kind of thing you could buy from an electronics retailer, but there were no formal restrictions on purchase or ownership. It wasn't a weapon, after all.

The world's greatest TAP poet, shot by a word? It was a seductive idea—and I was surprised that the tabloids hadn't seized on it, weeks ago—but in the cold light of morning, I was finding it increasingly difficult to believe that Grace Sharp had died from anything but natural causes. The building had excellent security; the forensic team had found no sign of an intruder. The testimony of the black box wasn't watertight, but on balance it probably *did* exonerate the implant. And Helen Sharp herself had been convinced that the <<death>> word was impossible.

I spent the morning slogging through the rest of the transcripts, but there was nothing very illuminating. The experts had washed their hands of Grace Sharp's death. I didn't blame them: if the evidence supported no clear verdict, the honest thing to do was to say so. At most inquests, though, *someone* managed to slip a speculation or two into the proceedings: a pathologist's gut-level hunch, an engineer's unprovable intuition. A few lines I could wave accusingly in their face when I cornered them in their office—prompting them to spill the whole elaborate, unofficial hypothesis they'd been nurturing in their head for months. But there wasn't a single foothold here, a single indiscretion I could pursue; every witness had been cautious to a fault.

So I had nowhere else to go: I steeled myself and went trawling through the archives for the enemies of TAP.

Media releases (mainly from politicians and religious figures), letters and essays in edited publications, and postings to net forums gave me about seventeen thousand individuals who'd had something disparaging to say to the world about TAP. The search algorithm was multilingual, but I didn't trust it to pick up irony reliably, so even this crude first grab had to be taken with a mountain of salt. Twelve percent of the forum postings were anonymous—and the random sample I inspected made it clear that they came from the most vehement opponents—but I put them aside; textual analysis of a few gigabytes of invective could wait for barrel-scraping time.

Clustering software picked up some fairly predictable connections. Two-thirds of the people I'd found were officially speaking on behalf of—or explicitly mentioned their membership or approval of—one of ninety-six organizations: political, religious, or cultural.

The software drew ninety-six star-diagrams. The biggest cluster was for Natural Wisdom: a quasi-green lobby group set up for the sole purpose of opposing the use of neural hardware. Most members were European, but there was a significant Australian presence. Second largest was The Fountain of Righteousness, a U.S.-based fundamentalist Christian coalition; they had half a dozen local affiliate churches. Cluster size didn't necessarily measure the strength of opposition, though; the Roman Catholic church ranked a mere thirtieth—but only because it was so rigidly hierarchical, with a relatively small list of appointed spokesmen. Most Islamic authorities weren't keen on neural hardware, either—but many predominantly Islamic countries had simply outlawed the technology, largely defusing it as an issue. Islam's best showing was for a UK group, and that was ranked fifty-seventh.

I cut the data set down to Australia only. Nineteen organizations remained—and the top six rankings stayed the same, for what that was worth. There was something of the flavor of a witch-hunt to this whole analysis; I wasn't publicly accusing anyone of anything—I wasn't libelling Natural Wisdom as murderous thugs for daring to speak out against the implant—but this kind of crude fishing expedition always made me feel distinctly uneasy.

Still, if these were the people who'd feel most threatened by the prospect of children growing up with TAP...who among them could have known about the impending High Court challenge?

I scanned the membership databases of legal and paralegal associations, and the mailing lists of relevant journals, scooping up anyone who gave an address care of Huntingdale and Partners—the firm who were preparing the "infant implant" brief.

There was zero overlap with the anti-TAP set—which was no great surprise. I imagined the police would have gone at least this far, and they'd had better resources: they could have pulled the whole Huntingdale workforce from taxation records, with no chance of so much as a clerical assistant falling through the cracks.

I gazed at the screen, dispirited. All I had to show for a day's work were sixty-three apartments with a view of Grace Sharp's study, and seventeen thousand people who'd done nothing more incriminating than put themselves on the record as opponents of TAP.

The only thing left to try was intersecting the two.

Finding apartment numbers to match the physical locations in the building plans was the hardest part; architects and developers didn't have to file anything so petty when they had their projects approved. I was actually beginning to contemplate doing the necessary legwork myself, when I discovered that someone had done it for me: an *ad hoc* consortium of sellers of insurance, fire-alarms, security equipment and climate control had commissioned a database for the entire metropolitan area, to help them target their junk mail. The suburb I needed only cost fifty bucks—complete with email tags.

I cross-matched with the anti-TAP set.

A single name appeared.

John Dallaporta belonged to none of my organizational clusters, and I had only one piece of data on his attitude to TAP: a short essay he'd written, seven years before, decrying the implant's potential to "erode the richness of our ancient and beautiful tongues" and "invade the still, mysterious spaces of our minds." The essay had appeared in a secondary English teachers' netzine; I summoned up the whole issue, and flipped through its innocuous contents. The majority of the articles dealt with working conditions, and concerns arising out of new technology; there was also an earnest—almost painfully respectful—discussion of strategies for coping with parents who forbade their children contact with the filthy/sexist/atheistic/elitist/ superstitious/obsolete works of Shakespeare, *et al.* Not the kind of venue you'd seriously expect to lead you to a man who slaughtered his ideological enemies.

I reread Dallaporta's essay carefully. It was passionate, but hardly inflammatory; he sounded very much like just one more plaintive, insecure technophobe letting off steam, to a no doubt largely sympathetic audience. I was inclined to be sympathetic, myself—in all honesty, the implant made my skin crawl—but there was a self-serving undercurrent which detracted from the force of his arguments. Certainly, portraying *English* as an endangered language was ridiculous, when more people were speaking it than at any other time in history.

And though I could picture Dallaporta outside the court with a placard, once the challenge to the implant legislation began, I found it hard to imagine the author of these moderate words killing Grace Sharp in cold blood—and harder still to imagine him discovering the means to do it.

I was growing tired of desk work, but I spent the next few hours studying the fragmentary portrait of the man offered by the net. He was forty-seven years old, divorced five years, with two daughters in their mid-teens. Presumably his ex-wife had custody of both children, since all the data suggested that he lived alone. He'd been a teacher in government high schools all his working life; in his late twenties, he'd published some poetry in literary journals, but unless he'd adopted an undocumented pseudonym, there'd been nothing since. He seemed to belong to no organization but the State School Teachers' Union, and if he subscribed to any religion, no marketing demographer had yet managed to pin it down.

So much for the electronic profile. I didn't believe for a moment that he could have killed Grace Sharp—but I wasn't prepared to rule it out until I'd met him in the flesh.

I found a calendar of events for the Laurence Brereton Memorial High School. There was a parent-teacher night in three days' time.

～w～

I ARRIVED late enough not to have to loiter outside for too long before catching sight of a few departing parents, still wearing their name badges.

I got a good look at the style and the materials used—but I was even luckier than that: one man dropped his badge into a recycling bin right before my eyes. I'd come prepared with a variety of cardboard samples, safety pins and clips, but all I had to do was fish out this discarded one, match the font on my notepad's printer, and spray my own—borrowed—name onto the blank side.

No one challenged me as I entered the crowded hall and walked straight past the desk where parents were queuing up to register their attendance and collect their badges. I spotted a row of work stations dispensing guidance; I walked up to one and tried to make an inquiry, but it was too clever by far: the only entry point was "parent's name"—apparently all it needed in order to highlight every relevant teacher on a personalized map of the hall. I stood back and watched other people use the software, until Dallaporta's name appeared.

It seemed an odd time of year for an event like this; Mick's high school had held an orientation night before the start of term, but they hadn't yet invited me back. The buzz of conversation around me sounded remarkably amiable, though; maybe it was a good strategy to drag the parents in as early as this, and try to nip any problems in the bud.

John Dallaporta was tall and slender, clean-shaven, slightly balding. He was being talked at loudly by someone's proud father—and though his eyes were glazed, and his smile a little wooden, he didn't strike me as a man who'd been sleepless with guilt for the past five weeks.

When the father departed, I approached purposefully. Dallaporta offered his hand and said smoothly, "Good to see you, Ms. Stone." He hesitated. "I'm sorry, but I don't think I—"

I smiled disarmingly. "No, you don't teach my daughter. But I wanted to speak to you, and this seemed like too good an opportunity to pass up. I hope you don't mind."

"Not at all. But I should explain: I'm not the head of department this year. It rotates between the senior teachers, so Carol Bailey—" He glanced around, then pointed her out. "Do you see—?"

I shook my head apologetically. "It's not a departmental matter. I just wanted to meet you. I read an essay you wrote, a few years ago: *The Bit-Stream of the Rose*. And I liked what you had to say there, very much. So when I realized you were teaching in my daughter's new school…"

Dallaporta eyed me curiously, a little bemused, but he betrayed no obvious unease or suspicion. "That's so long ago now, I'm surprised you remember it at all. Let alone the name of the author."

"Of course I remember! And I just hope the rest of the department share your values on those…issues. I used to teach English, myself. I *know* the kind of pressures you're facing. And of course I want my own children to be *technologically literate*—but some of us have to take a stand, or who knows what 'technologically literate' will *mean*, in twenty years' time?"

Dallaporta nodded affably, but now I could see muscles tightening at the sides of his jaws—the ones which contract when you're trying too hard not to let anything show. *Proving what?* Nothing at all—except that he had stronger feelings about TAP than he cared to discuss with a total stranger in a crowded hall.

I kept pushing. "When I started high school, myself, if you didn't have your own PC on your desk at home, you were marginalized. These days the work stations come for free—if you sign up for a thousand-a-month worth of 'vital' net access. And any child who can't interview Afghani nomads for a geography assignment—or get a live feed from the latest Venus probe via JPL—might as well quit and go work at McDonalds. *When does it stop?* When my grandchildren are twelve, what will 'entry level' be, for them?"

Dallaporta laughed, not quite naturally. "I wouldn't dare hazard a guess. But I have faith in people. In common sense."

I made direct eye contact, trying to decide if he was genuinely rattled—or just didn't trust himself to get on the soapbox, even for such an obviously sympathetic listener.

"Common sense? I hope you're right. I've heard some rumors lately which don't bear thinking about—"

Dallaporta blanched visibly. *Meaning he knew about the court case? And now assumed that I had some connection to whoever had given him the news?* I offered him a conspiratorial smile: *Relax, I'm a friend, we're on the same side.*

I said, "Look, I didn't mean to take up so much of your time. But it was so nice to meet you, finally." I held out my hand, and Dallaporta shook it, slipping back onto autopilot with obvious relief.

I walked out into the warm evening. There was a real Lydia Stone, with a daughter who'd just started Year 8; Dallaporta might check the records, but

I didn't think he was likely to confront the girl's teachers and ask them to sketch an identikit for comparison.

I glanced up at the washed-out sky, at the handful of visible stars—and thought once more: *this moment would be a single word, in TAP.* <<The scent of cut grass from the playing fields, the rumble of suburban traffic, the melancholy yellow lights of the hall beside the darkness of the empty classrooms.>> *A moment skewered like a butterfly? A ten-thousand-bit digital corpse of the world, shedding dead pixels in the mind's eye?* Or a moment captured like a mood perfectly evoked by a phrase of music? No one had ever felt the need to murder a composer, just to safeguard the languages which couldn't compete on equal terms with fugues and sonatas. No one had ever taken a human life just to stop eccentric parents bombarding their offspring with Bach and Mozart in the womb. What made TAP so much more threatening? The fact that it could evoke images and emotions beyond the reach of any symphony? The fact that it was so much *better?*

I'd actually meant most of what I'd said to Dallaporta—but the more I thought about the issues, the more ambivalent I became. No one was trying to "force" TAP onto anyone, except their own children—and to raise a child at all was to impose a set of choices, one way or another. Actively or passively. Consciously, or through sheer conformity or neglect. The prospect of TAP-heads meddling with their children's brains—just so they could share an artificial language—still filled me with instinctive, visceral outrage…but was it any more virtuous for the rest of us to insist that no child be given the implant until their brains were fully formed in the ten-thousand-year-old mold of our own Stone Age preconceptions? Weren't *both sides* just attempting to shape future generations in their own image?

And putting aside prejudice, instinct, and nostalgia…*which first language really would provide the best tools for dealing with the modern world?*

That was a good question. It just wasn't the one I was being paid to answer.

⌁

I PLANTED a dozen small recording devices in pay phones near Dallaporta's apartment, and the school. Which was highly illegal—but both less risky, and more likely to succeed (if he was actually guilty of anything), than trying to bug his home. I'd sampled his voice at the parent-teacher night, so the bugs could discard everyone else's conversations. I cycled by and queried them daily.

I finally tracked down Tom Davies, Grace Sharp's domestic aid—a TAP-head himself. The curtains of the study were always left open, he said. Grace liked to work looking out across the skyline; she'd chosen the apartment for the view.

I couldn't help asking, sarcastically, "Wouldn't it have been cheaper just to visit some rich friend's apartment—and memorize the TAP words for everything she saw?"

He laughed. "Of course. And she could have written scenery *in her head* to put any ten-million-dollar harbor view to shame."

"So why didn't she?"

"Do you know how Grace defined 'reality'?"

"No."

"The ten thousand bits that are left when you've argued everything else out of existence."

〰

AFTER WEEKS of persistent harassment, I persuaded Maxine Ho, one of Third Hemisphere's senior engineers, to talk to me off the record. She stuck to the official line, though: the <<death>> word was impossible. Whatever Grace Sharp had imagined, or whatever TAP sequence some would-be assassin had confronted her with, all the safeguards operated on a separate level, independent of the language protocol—and when the implant had been examined after the autopsy, there'd been no trace of damage or corruption to the relevant hardware or software.

"Of course a neural implant can kill you. A pacemaker can kill you. *A work station* can kill you. Any piece of technology can fail. But if someone died sitting at a work station—and when I took it apart there was no sign of a loose wire or a break in the insulation—I wouldn't say: 'She must have been running the legendary <<death>> program, which instructed the machine to electrocute her.' I'd go looking for another cause of death."

It was a specious analogy. Perfectly functioning TAP implants routinely sent signals to the hypothalamus, which in turn stimulated the adrenal gland; perfectly functioning work stations weren't set up to dispense electric shocks at any dose.

Still, I thought she was being basically straight with me. If she believed that the implant had failed at all, she believed it was a one-in-a-million glitch: less a design flaw than a tragic proof of the intrinsic unpredictability of any real device out in the real world—the kind of thing which would have been excused as "natural causes" if an equally robust biological system had failed.

∿∿

ON MARCH 5th, the High Court challenge to the implant restrictions became public knowledge. The case wasn't scheduled to be heard until September—but the reaction to the news was immediate.

Helen Sharp had been right about one thing: her mother's death was seized upon by almost every commentator as proof that a successful challenge would amount to the legalization of infanticide. Not that Their Honors could be influenced by emotive editorials—perish the thought—but even if they weren't, it was clear that the Federal government would be ready with the necessary amendments within days of any decision which put the State criminal law in doubt. I set my knowledge miner digging, but reasoned debate about the merits of the case—the actual merits, not the legal ones—could barely be found outside obscure neurolinguistics journals. (TAP speakers' netzines were in TAP, and I had no translation software.)

The night the news broke, Mick declared, "I want one."

"Then you'll just have to wait six years, won't you?"

"Not if they win."

"If they win, you'd better start mowing lawns and washing windows. Six years should do it either way."

He accepted that without protest—but then asked innocently, "So what's *your* favorite medium?"

"Text. And I know: I'm a boring old fart, but you're still not—" He wore a pained expression—and not just because "old fart" was cringe-inducing baby-talk. I'd missed the point.

"I'm sorry. What were you going to say?"

Mick spoke carefully. "How'd you like it if every time you picked up a book, you had to swallow everything the writer said? If you couldn't stop mid-sentence and think: 'This is…*bullshit*.' If you lost the power to argue in your head with every word."

"I'd hate it."

He said, "That's where VR's heading. Without TAP."

I was taken aback by the bleakness of this forecast—but it rang true. Without a language as powerful as the medium, there was little room for argument, little room for doubt. Just unearned suspension of disbelief.

I reached over to the cable which snaked from his headset to the work station, and looped it absentmindedly around one finger. I said, "If it's as bad as that, then stop using it. It's your choice."

One look answered that; he didn't need to elaborate. *Why should he be forced to abandon his own favorite medium? Why shouldn't he have the chance to salvage it, reinvigorate it, instead?* Present at the birth of spoken language, would I have fought to abolish it, like some fanatical Zen terrorist afraid of its power to deceive? Or would I have fought to enrich it, to balance that power with skepticism and analysis?

I said lamely, "There's more to life than VR."

Mick grinned triumphantly. "Exactly. But there *isn't* more to life than TAP."

\~\w\

I TOOK on other cases: runaway children, minor computer fraud—routine work, but at least it gave me the satisfaction of swift results. Helen Sharp could no longer afford to keep me on full-time—and I'd virtually run out of productive ways to spend her money, anyway. If her mother had died from some unrepeatable glitch, biological or otherwise, nobody would ever prove it. So I offered no false hopes, and worked on the assumption that in a few more months, she'd come to her senses and tell me that the case was closed.

Then, in the middle of April, one of my pay phone bugs finally spoke.

I was dutifully cycling past, checking them all in the pouring rain, though I no longer seriously expected anything. When my notepad chimed the code for success, I almost dropped it into a storm drain.

Playing back the recording on the bike, in the rain, would have been impossible. Playing it back on a crowded train would have been stupid—I didn't have the headphones—but I was tempted. By the time I reached the office, I'd convinced myself I'd hear nothing but a service call: Dallaporta complaining that his home connection was out of order.

I was wrong.

Dallaporta whispered urgently, "You have to help me. I need your advice." It was a monologue; he was leaving a message. "I didn't get rid of it, on the night. I thought: it's not illegal—so why not keep it, just in case?" My skin crawled. He didn't elaborate, but I could guess exactly what he meant: *Just in case it becomes expedient, at some time in the unforeseeable future, to kill another prominent TAP-head.*

He inhaled deeply, as if trying to calm himself. "That was…*insane*, I know. I wasn't thinking straight. But now…*I can't just throw it in the river!* What if the police are watching me? What if they're going through my garbage?" That was unlikely, but I was grateful for his paranoia—and his incompetence: whispering into a public phone with (I imagined) a hand shielding lips and mouthpiece wouldn't have done him much good if he *had* been under police surveillance.

"I've wiped the code, now." *Shit.* "I followed the instructions, I'm sure it worked. But I have to get rid of the machine. I need to know the best way— the safest way—to do it. *Please.* Call me back at the usual place."

I decoded the number he'd called, from the tones—but it was a commercial message rerouting service—and one that was far too classy to be bribed or hacked.

I sat at the desk, still dripping, trying to decide what to do next. The humidity control system in the north window was pumping water vapor into the room; I'd never get dry unless I went and stood out in the hall for an hour.

Everything I had so far would be less than useless to the police; the illegality of the phone bugs aside, every connection between Dallaporta and Grace Sharp's death remained pure speculation. And I wasn't even sure I had enough to convince Helen Sharp, who didn't believe in <<death>> words. Nothing Dallaporta had said proved that he'd been talking about an infrared communications laser—and the crucial data it had transmitted was probably lost forever, now.

But it sounded like I still had a very slim chance to photograph "the machine", *in situ*.

The message had been left at 6:23 that morning. I glanced at my watch; school would be out in two hours. I had no way of knowing how long it would take for Dallaporta's backers (Natural Wisdom? The Fountain of

Righteousness?) to come to his rescue—assuming they didn't just decide to abandon him—but I couldn't risk waiting another day.

I knew I'd be cutting it fine, but I didn't seem to have much choice.

⌁⌁

THERE WERE six hundred apartments in Dallaporta's building—and the sheer weight of numbers had its advantages. I stood across the street behind a bus shelter and waited for someone to approach the main entrance. When a young man appeared, key in hand, I dashed across the road and caught up with him, breathless, soaked, umbrella-less, fumbling. He let me through without a moment's hesitation. I hung back in the lobby shaking water from my coat so I wouldn't have to talk to him in the elevator; I hadn't had time to prepare any plausible lies, and if he'd so much as asked me how long I'd lived in the building, I probably would have been struck dumb.

Dallaporta's apartment, 1912, had a reinforced security door with an impressive-looking deadlock. I found a utilities room at the end of the corridor, and picked *its* lock easily enough. There was a hatch in the ceiling—and even a ladder standing in a corner of the room. I rechecked the plans of the building on my notepad: not every apartment had a ceiling hatch; 1911 did, 1912 didn't.

I climbed into the ceiling and crawled across the dusty beams as quietly as I could, hoping I hadn't lost my bearings. I lay above apartment 1911, just listening, for almost five minutes—then I realized I'd never be certain it was empty. A baby sleeping, an adult quietly reading...I didn't even know who lived there, I hadn't had time to find out.

Cursing silently, I crawled back to the utilities room, brushed myself down, and went and rang the bell to 1911.

I rang three times. No one was home.

I retraced my path, lifted the hatch, lowered a rope into the apartment. My forearms ached as I descended; I hadn't done an illegal entry since before Mick was born. The old buzz was tinged with new anxieties: *I was too old for this cat-burglar shit—and I couldn't afford to lose my license.* But I felt a kind of defiant euphoria, too—*because* everything was harder, *because* I had so much more to lose.

And it would all be one word, in TAP...

The balconies of the two apartments were separated by less than a meter, but they were flush with the outside wall of the building—no overhang at all. I climbed up onto the waist-high foot's-width concrete guard wall, steadied myself by pressing up with my left hand against the balcony's ceiling—then with the right, reached across the naked brickwork of the outside wall and into Dallaporta's balcony. I was lucky; I was on the side of the building facing away from the wind.

I moved a foot across, too, embraced the brickwork tightly, shifted the center of mass of my body a few crucial centimeters—fighting down momentary panic—and within seconds, my right hand and foot were lodged securely between Dallaporta's guard wall and ceiling, and it was far easier to go forward than back. I jumped shakily down onto his cluttered balcony, just missing a pot plant. I glanced at the street, nineteen storeys below—and pictured Mick at my funeral, still refusing to talk to his father. There was a chance that someone had seen me cross, but there was nothing I could do about that—and the downpour seemed to shift the odds in my favor: I could barely make out Grace Sharp's building at all, through the curtain of rain.

A sliding glass door separated the balcony from the apartment. It fitted loosely between a ceiling track and a guide rail buried in the concrete floor; it was probably designed to be lifted right out, for ease of replacement—but only when it was unlocked. There was no question of trying to pick the lock; there was no keyhole—just a catch operated by a lever on the other side of the door. By pressing on the glass with both gloved hands, though, I could get enough purchase to raise and tilt the whole door slightly. After almost ten minutes—with my wrists going numb—I managed to work the catch free.

I opened the door a few centimeters, then paused at the threshold, scanning the room for burglar alarms. It was clear.

As I moved into the apartment, I heard footsteps in the corridor, then a key going into the lock. I retreated to the balcony, but it was too late to start climbing back the way I'd come; I would have been in full view. I slid the door closed—I couldn't re-lock it—then dropped to the floor behind a pile of junk.

I heard at least two people enter the apartment, then turn left into the corridor which led out of the living room. I took a button-sized video camera, and stuck it to the frame of Dallaporta's bike, which was leaning against the wall of the balcony. I checked the image on my notepad, then tweaked the direction until I had a clear view of most of the room.

I dropped out of sight again just in time. The intruders—a man and a woman, neither of whom I'd seen before—returned, carrying a cardboard carton about thirty centimeters long. I zoomed in; the labelling suggested a presentation bottle of Scotch. Dallaporta's friends clearly didn't share his paranoia; they *knew* the police weren't watching the apartment. He wanted the laser to disappear—and they'd obligingly turned up to remove it.

The woman said, "You think he wiped it properly?"

The man hesitated. "I wouldn't count on it." I wondered why they hadn't automated the process—but then, it would have been impossible to predict exactly when the opportunity to use the code on Grace Sharp would arise, or how many attempts it would take to hit the target.

"Well, I'm not walking out of here carrying incriminating—"

The man groaned—but he opened the carton. I recognized the laser from the catalogs I'd scanned; most of the bulk was in the precision optics, which doubled as a kind of telescope for checking alignment—the unit was meant for inner city rooftop-to-rooftop communications. There was a small device about the size of a matchbox plugged in to the data port; the man hit a button on the side of the box, and peered at a tiny LCD display.

"Hey, the Jackal got it right. I'm impressed." He laughed. "*'I thought: Why not keep it, just in case?'* The poor cretin really thought he had the <<death>> word—and he could go on playing kill-the-TAP-head for as long as he liked."

The woman said dryly, "Don't be so ungrateful. If he'd known what he was doing, he wouldn't have done it at all."

They left. I pocketed the camera and crossed back to 1911 immediately, not wanting to be in sight when they reached the street. In the ceiling, I had to force myself not to rush; if I was careless, I could still get caught.

In five minutes, I was out of the building. I circled the block, then spiraled out through the surrounding streets, on the slim chance of catching sight of them again.

After half an hour I gave up, and went into a coffee shop to replay the video. I should have been jubilant: I had a clear shot of a communications laser, and a soundtrack with two people discussing *the killing of TAP-heads*.

The only catch was, it didn't sound like they believed in <<death>> words any more than Maxine Ho or Helen Sharp.

TAP

I INVITED Helen Sharp to my office. I showed her Dallaporta's essay, and the geometry of the buildings. I played back the phone call, and the scene in his apartment.

I said, "You're the TAP expert. You want to tell me what's going on?"

She sat in silence for a long time before replying.

"There is one possibility."

"Which is?"

"My mother had the earliest model implant. Right to the end. She never had an upgrade—she didn't trust them to transfer her vocabulary properly. She was afraid she'd lose everything she'd learned."

"And you think...the old models *did* have a <<death>> word?"

"No. But they could be microprogrammed externally."

"You've lost me." That wasn't quite true, but I wanted her to spell it out. I wasn't sure how much I really *did* know about the implant—how much the glowing technical reports might have misled me.

Sharp looked terrible—the fact that she'd just laid eyes on the people who'd arranged the death of her mother was finally sinking in—but she explained patiently: "The basic hardware of any neural net computer is just...a big array of interconnected RISC processors. The chip is mass-produced as a commodity—hundreds of millions of them a year—and used in tens of thousands of different devices. All the specific characteristics are added by the *microcode:* low-level instructions which customize the processors to make them behave in certain useful ways. The main software then takes that level for granted—as if it's all hardwired into the silicon. But it's not.

"When they released the first consumer model of the TAP implant, Third Hemisphere were worried that there might be some undiscovered flaw in the microcode. If they'd had to take all the implants out of people's skulls to correct it, that would have been a PR nightmare. So they left a routine in the microcode which gave it the power to accept updates in infrared—to modify any part of itself, given the right sequence of external instructions."

"So there was a special TAP word which could get at all the infrastructure? A word which said: <<Replace the old microcode with *X*>>?"

"*No!* It *wasn't* a TAP word—it was a reserved sequence, right outside the language protocol! It was meaningless in TAP, it could never have been spoken. That was the whole point!"

It seemed like a minor distinction to me—but I could understand why she attached so much importance to it. *The language itself* hadn't killed her mother. The poet hadn't died from a word, after all.

I said, "If that's what happened, though…why didn't the engineers who examined your mother's implant find any evidence of it? And if you *knew* all this—"

Sharp snapped back angrily, "*I didn't know she still had the old microcode!*" She looked away. "Nine or ten years ago, Third Hemisphere tried to persuade her to accept a new implant—for free. They'd finally discovered a bug in the original microcode—a minor one, nothing dangerous, but they wanted everyone to start using the later models. They were confident enough about *those* that they weren't externally programmable anymore.

"She wouldn't accept it. She didn't want a new implant, she didn't want surgery. So they offered to update the microcode, to fix the bug—and close the trap door in the process, because I think that was also making them nervous. TAP users could never have spoken the code, even if they'd wanted to—but every consumer device on the planet was starting to put out a flood of infrared. There was always a tiny risk of triggering the modification program by accident.

"I thought she'd had the new microcode for the last ten years. She told me she'd accepted the offer. The records Third Hemisphere supplied to the coroner stated that she had—and the engineer's report confirmed that."

I said, "But if she'd actually refused it, like she'd refused the new implant—because she was afraid it might affect her skills with the language… then Dallaporta's message might have done it all in one hit? Opened the trapdoor, undermined the black box, triggered a massive adrenaline release—then overwritten the evidence by substituting the version she was meant to have had all along?"

"Yes."

"So who'd know enough to program all that?" *Natural Wisdom? The Fountain of Righteousness?* Hardly—though they could always have brought in outside expertise.

Sharp was adamant: "Only one of Third Hemisphere's own software engineers could do it. Someone who'd been involved in the TAP project from the start."

"But they'd have nothing to gain, surely? Why discredit your own work, your own product?"

The *product* belonged to Third Hemisphere, though—not to any group of employees.

And people did move on.

~w~

I SCANNED fifteen years' worth of implant manufacturers' publications; they were full of PR releases gloating about heads successfully hunted.

In March 2008, a firm called Cogent Industries had poached a software engineer named Maria Remedios from Third Hemisphere. That in itself proved nothing, of course—nor did the fact that an earlier article named her as a senior participant in the TAP project.

Cogent did have something to gain, though. They specialized in Virtual Reality hardware—both immersive neural implants, and headset-based units. Third Hemisphere wasn't so much a direct competitor as the source of an entire antithetical philosophy: VR was sold to publishers and advertisers as the path to unconditional suspension of disbelief; TAP was about questioning *everything*, analyzing *everything*. The day every VR user spoke TAP, the most ingeniously crafted—and manipulative—VR experience would disintegrate into a laughable trick with smoke and mirrors. And if that wasn't exactly an imminent threat, Grace Sharp's death had certainly made it more remote than ever.

They could have chosen Dallaporta by the same means I'd used to find him myself: a search for passionate opponents of TAP who also happened to have a clear view of Grace Sharp's study. And whoever had made contact with him could have claimed to be a member of Natural Wisdom, or some other anti-implant group; he'd hardly have cooperated if he'd known the truth. When they'd told him about the High Court challenge—no doubt conjuring up images of a whole generation "lost to TAP"—Grace Sharp's death must have begun to sound like a necessary evil. *One old woman, for the sake of all those children. Death by her own obscene technological perversion of language. Nothing more than poetic justice.*

And Maria Remedios? Had Third Hemisphere treated her badly, left her holding a grudge—or had her new employers pressured her into it? Even if she'd had grave second thoughts about TAP—and recoiled at the prospect of the implant being given to children—helping to murder an innocent woman seemed like a grotesquely disproportionate response. She could have joined the public campaign against the implant; as one of its creators, the media would have given her all the coverage she desired. And though Dallaporta might have caved in to "moral" arguments offered under false pretences, Remedios could hardly have failed to understand that Cogent's motives were entirely commercial.

Nine tenths of the picture seemed to have fallen perfectly into place— but it was clear that I was missing something crucial. And too much even of that nine tenths was still pure guesswork. For a start, I had to establish solid evidence of a link between Dallaporta and Cogent Industries—which was going to be tricky, since he didn't even know it existed, himself.

I checked the faces of the man and woman I'd seen in Dallaporta's apartment against all the trade magazine shots of Cogent's employees.

No match.

I fed the Cogent employee names, along with my seventeen thousand TAP-haters, into the cluster analysis software—looking for a connection, however tenuous.

There was none.

So much for the easy options.

I sent Dallaporta a message, via a rerouting service, asking if we could "continue our discussion." The real Lydia Stone was ex-directory—and using a different number than the one she'd given the school would only prove that she was exercising suitable caution.

Three hours later, Dallaporta called me back. He was polite, but very nervous. I said I had some news which would be of interest to him; he didn't actually scream at me to *shut up in case the line was being bugged,* but his body language made it clear that if I so much as mentioned TAP he'd hang up immediately.

I said, "Can I meet you somewhere? We really need to talk, face to face."

He hesitated. He badly wanted me to vanish from his life—but he needed to know what my "news" was. *Why had I taken an interest in him? One old essay was hardly enough to explain it, so…how many people in the anti-TAP crusade knew what he'd done? And what did I know about Grace Sharp's death which no one had bothered to tell him?*

Of course he was paranoid. The inquest was long over, the laser had been magicked away—but the fact remained: he'd stood on his balcony on a summer evening and shot a perfect stranger dead. Nothing could ever be the same again.

He said flatly, "Tomorrow night, at the school. Nine o'clock."

~~~

I REHEARSED the story in my head as I crossed the football field—which was brightly floodlit for some reason, though there wasn't a soul around. *A friend of a friend in a certain law firm had heard that Helen Sharp had discovered something in her mother's computer files—something which had prompted her to start proceedings to try to gain access to Third Hemisphere's records.*

I was sure that Dallaporta would pass the rumor on to his benefactors; the hardest part would be ensuring that he didn't mention "my" name. So long as he remained tight-lipped about his source of information, they'd have to take him seriously.

Helen Sharp was preparing a forged—paper—letter from her mother to Third Hemisphere, explicitly stating that she did not wish to accept the microcode update. I was confident that we had enough leverage now to persuade Third Hemisphere to play along, and bury the bait in the appropriate warehouse.

Maria Remedios would know at once what the "evidence" had to be. Cogent, acting on her advice, would try to arrange its disappearance. This time, they'd be caught red-handed.

At least, that was the theory.

Dallapporta had said he'd be in the "Resources Center"—which these days apparently meant a large room full of work stations. I'd found a map of the school in an online brochure, so I knew exactly where to go. The door was open, though the lights were out—and as I approached the threshold I could see that all the machines inside had been switched on and connected to some net service or other. *More of Dallaporta's paranoia?* Maybe he thought this was an ideal source of interference for the police surveillance teams who were following him everywhere—though the sound from most of the work stations was turned down to a whisper.

I peered into the grayness of the room, dazzled and distracted by the multitude of images: swarms of tiny red and silver fish weaving through a coral reef; a polychrome computer animation of air flow around some kind of zeppelin; a portrait of a Florentine prince sprouting a speech balloon full of modern Italian; a dead silver-haired twentieth century guru emitting platitudes about the nature of truth. An old music video was playing by the door; the singer droned: "This is the way, step insi-i-ide."

I smiled uneasily at the coincidence and walked into the room—resisting the urge to shout a greeting, mocking Dallaporta's elaborate "precautions." It seemed far more diplomatic to play along. I stage whispered, "It's me. Where are you?"

No reply.

It was hard to get my eyes accustomed to the darkness with forty or fifty bright screens in view; I had no reason whatsoever to look at any of the images—but it was remarkably difficult to keep looking away. I walked slowly toward the far end of the room, irritated but prepared not to show it. I called out again, a little louder; there was still no reply.

An animated supernova erupted just ahead of me—and the sudden blue-white radiance revealed a man slumped in a chair beside the screen. I moved closer, and inspected the body by the light of the dying sun.

Dallaporta had a small-calibre pistol in his hand, and a neat hole in his temple. I put two fingers to his neck; he was certainly dead, but still warm.

I felt a flicker of guilt break through the numbness of shock—but this wasn't the time to agonize over the way I'd treated him. He'd killed Grace Sharp, and he hadn't been prepared to live with that. If the fear of whatever I'd been about to tell him had been enough to drive him to suicide, he would have done it sooner or later, regardless.

I took out my notepad to call the police.

Then the supernova faded, and a new image took its place.

An apartment building, swept by rain. The camera zoomed in on a figure climbing between two of the balconies. The magnification kept increasing, relentlessly—and by the time the woman turned and showed her face, it filled the screen.

My stomach tightened. I glanced back to the neat, too-professional hole in Dallaporta's skull, reassessing everything. *But…who could have videoed me?* If Cogent's people had known I was on the balcony, why had they walked straight in?

The image changed again. *Me, planting one of the phone bugs.*

I laughed in disbelief. They'd all but slaughtered this man in front of my eyes—and now they were trying to blackmail me into silence with a couple of petty misdemeanors?

"There are small traces of your skin under his fingernails." The voice came from a meter behind me; I started, but I didn't actually jump. "Not enough for him to have left a mark on you, but enough for DNA analysis."

I turned around slowly. The man was about my age, and only a little taller. He wasn't pointing a gun at me, but he looked suspiciously relaxed.

"The police will find out that Helen Sharp hired you—but they'll have no grounds for a warrant to compel you to supply them with tissue samples. Not if they don't see this." He gestured at the screen.

I said, "And why would they imagine I'd want to fake this man's suicide? Breaking into his apartment proves nothing—"

"I think *that* depends on whether someone tips them off about the hundred thousand dollars in your Swiss bank account. Grace's close-knit linguistic community must have done a little whip-around, and bought themselves some justice for the man with the <<death>> word."

That shut me up. If the account really existed…that was breathtaking. *Had Cogent been watching me all along, setting this up?*

He smiled. "If you're good, you can keep the hundred grand, of course. No tax; the whole thing's organized beautifully through a holding company in Macao."

I didn't have the presence of mind even to be tempted; I was still trying to come to terms with the whole Byzantine scheme.

I said, "Forget it." I walked straight past him, toward the doorway. I reached it, heart racing, then turned and looked back; I couldn't see him anymore, but I didn't think he'd moved a centimeter. Killing me would create too many problems, too many holes in their beautifully scripted VR experience—and the odds were stacked against me even if I did go straight to the police.

I said, "So what did you expect me to tell Helen Sharp? 'Screw your mother, the case is closed—and please don't ask any questions, I'm late for my flight to Macao'?"

"You'll think of something. Believe me, you don't want to fight us."

I laughed angrily. "One pissy little VR company, and you think you can pull all the strings?"

The man said, "I'm not working for Cogent. They have *no idea* you've even taken an interest in them."

I peered into the darkness between the rows of screens. "Some VR industry consortium, then." For some reason I'd started shaking; I think it was rage. "You're still not above the law."

"Oh, there's more to life than Virtual Reality." He sounded amused.

"Yeah? *Who, then?*"

There was silence for a while, then I could see him approaching. "I can't tell you that. But there are some people you can meet—if you want to—who might help you put your doubts to rest."

"Who?"

"Maria Remedios. And her daughter."

"I thought you didn't work for Cogent—"

"*She* works for Cogent. I don't. Though you could say it's my job to watch over them both."

᠁

THE FURTHER we drove from Dallaporta's corpse, the more compromised I knew I'd become—but I couldn't walk away from a chance to learn what it was I'd missed all along. Even if the revelation was intended to guarantee my silence.

"Remedios was one of the first volunteers to test the TAP implant," the man explained casually. "First she'd helped design it—and then she got to experience the results first hand. I think she must have found the reality exhilarating, in a lot of ways—but very frustrating, too."

"Why frustrating?"

"Even with neural hardware, learning an exotic new language is always difficult. For an adult."

I didn't reply. He continued, "She managed to find a good neurosurgeon willing to give her daughter the implant. Not here, though. Overseas. Which simplified things, really—it was easier to turn a blind eye."

That chilled me. "And you let her go ahead and do it? Just so you could see the results?"

He laughed. "Well, not me personally. But that was the general idea."

And the results? I thought back to some of the more pessimistic technical papers I'd read on the subject. Maybe natural languages—which had co-evolved with human intelligence—were crucial for the early stages of intellectual development...and even if relatively "artificial" latecomers like sign made perfect substitutes, maybe TAP was just too different to perform the role of organizing the neural structures which made higher thinking possible. And maybe the fact that so much of the language was encoded in *the chip*, instead of the brain, meant that vital conceptual networks were missing—or at least, inaccessible to other regions of the cerebral cortex which needed them in order to mature.

It still made no sense, though. If the daughter was living proof that the implant would do unspeakable damage to the infant brain, why not just publicize that fact? *Why had Grace Sharp died to win a court case which could have been won by simply disclosing the truth?*

Maria Remedios lived in a modestly comfortable house on the north shore. My escort had phoned ahead; she was expecting us. As I followed him down the hallway, she met my eyes; there was unconcealed shame in her steady gaze—but a strange, almost proud defiance behind it. I looked away, confused. If she'd crippled her own child with the TAP implant, no wonder she'd left Third Hemisphere—but why was she so beholden to Dallaporta's killers that she'd let them use her to manipulate Cogent? Had they threatened to imprison her? To put her child in an institution?

We ended up in the living room, but Remedios didn't invite us to take a seat. The man said, "So, what's she been up to? Still spending every last waking moment on the nets?"

Remedios shot him a poisonous look, and didn't bother replying. I thought he was being cruelly sarcastic. Then he turned to me and explained, "Incoming data only, I'm afraid. We wouldn't want her airing her grievances to the world."

Remedios left the room. I heard her say, "Jane? Ms O'Connor's here." Then she returned, with a young girl in blue-and-white striped pajamas, maybe eight years old.

Jane greeted me and shook my hand solemnly—or mock-solemnly. One look at her knowing gray eyes, and I knew I'd made exactly the wrong guess about the implant's effects.

"I was hoping I'd be allowed to meet you," she said. "Uncle Daniel's been complaining about you for weeks." She glanced at the man, without obvious malice—more like a chess player regarding a formidable adversary. "And he doesn't often let me have visitors."

I didn't know what to say. "Uncle Daniel" interjected helpfully, "I think Ms O'Connor is still in the dark, Jane. She doesn't understand—"

"Why anyone would want to keep me prisoner? Why anyone would go to so much trouble to keep other children from growing up with TAP?" Her tone went beyond precocity; she didn't come across as some child actor mouthing an adult's lines. Every word simply negated the implications her appearance would normally have conveyed.

And her bluntness was unnerving, but it cut through my own diplomatic hesitancy. I said, "That's right. I don't understand."

Jane smiled calmly. I don't believe she was resigned to her situation—but she was patient. Very patient.

She said, "With the implant, you can *play* words—or *scan* them. Experience them, blindly—or understand them, completely. Uncle Daniel's not a big fan of *understanding*, though. He thinks there are certain words which should be *played* and not *scanned*."

"What kind of words?"

She raised one hand, palm toward me. It was an ironic gesture; she must have known I was oblivious to IR.

"If I play *this* word…I feel a boundless sense of loyalty and pride toward my team…my city…my State…my *nation!*" Her face shone with fervent, agonized, almost hysterical joy; she looked like nothing so much as one of the flag-waving school girls they'd whipped into a patriotic frenzy as ornamentation for the 2000 Olympics. "But if I *scan* it…" Her expression faded into one of faint amusement—as if someone had just tried to dupe her with a very old, and very obvious, scam.

"*This* word plays as what many religions call 'faith.'" Her face was radiant, but tranquil now. "The peace that defies understanding." She smiled apologetically. "Except, of course, it doesn't. Scan it, and the mechanics are transparent: one foot down hard on an entrained neurochemical feel-good pedal—with cognitive, esthetic, and cultural echoes linked to the context in which the training was acquired."

I glanced at Remedios; there were silent tears moving down her face. *They wouldn't lock up the mother, or institutionalise the daughter. They'd kill this child, if they had to. That was the only reason she'd helped them program the death of Grace Sharp.*

"Now, this is what the Buddhists call 'enlightenment.'" Jane closed her eyes and smiled serenely. "Similar raw pharmacology, but the higher-level components are different. There's a kind of heavily self-affirming cognitive myopia: every mental tool which could expose the true nature of the state is explicitly negated."

I thought of James, lost in wordless tranquility. The package he'd swallowed whole, the mind virus fine-tuned by centuries of evolution, declared: *Language is dangerous, language deceives you*...because *language* could have shown him the way out of the hole he'd dug for himself.

"And *this* is...sexual love, desire? Call it what you like, but if you *scan* it—"

Something cut her short. Maybe it was a look from her mother. Or maybe it was the expression on my face.

Jane continued smoothly, "There are others. I won't list them all—but growing up with the implant makes them obvious. And Uncle Daniel's friends don't believe that a subculture with that knowledge would be...*conducive* to their idea of social cohesion. They feel very strongly about that." She turned to face him—and her expression now contained more pity than anything else. "And I do understand. Because I've found the word for their affliction, too. I've found the word for the love of power."

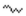

By the time I got home it was almost midnight. Mick's room was in darkness, but he was still playing the game; I sat down beside him and removed the headset gently, then reached over and logged him off.

He opened his mouth to apologize, or invent some excuse. I said, "Just shut up and listen."

"What happened? I was worried." I hadn't told him everything—but he knew I'd gone to meet someone connected with Grace Sharp's death.

I tried to speak calmly. "I've screwed up the case. Badly. I've made some stupid mistakes, and now I'm going to have to drop it. Okay? That's all I can tell you. And we're not going to talk about it again."

He stared at me, incredulous. "Why? What did you do?"

I shook my head. "I said, we're not going to talk about it."

He started blinking away tears. I took him in my arms; he didn't fight me, but he said angrily, "I don't *believe* you!"

I said, "Sssh."

~w~

LATER, I lay on my bed in the dark, rolling between my thumb and forefinger the smooth cold object, like a small ceramic bead, which Jane Remedios had slipped into my hand.

If she'd managed to copy her implant, this chip would encode her entire TAP vocabulary. And to an adult it would be useless—but a newborn child who started *with the knowledge it had taken her eight years to acquire might surpass her in half that time.*

They'd be watching me closely—but they couldn't be watching everyone. I believed I could pass the chip on to someone willing to use it, if I was careful.

So I lay in the dark, and tried to decide.

Between the silence of power and mystification, the unearned suspension of disbelief, *the way things had always been*—and the torrent of understanding which would sweep it all away.

INDUCTION

1

kat spent three of the last four hours of 2099 out on the regolith, walking the length of her section of the launch gun, checking by eye for micrometeorite impacts or any other damage that the automatic systems might improbably have missed.

Four other junior engineers walked a few paces ahead of her, but Ikat had had enough of their company inside the base, and she kept her coms tuned to Earth, sampling the moods of the century's countdown.

The Pope had already issued a statement from Rio, imploring humanity to treat "Christianity's twenty-first birthday" as an opportunity to embrace "spiritual maturity"; the Council of Islamic Scholars in Brussels, surrendering to the ubiquity of the Gregorian calendar, had chimed in with a similar message of their own. In the pyrotechnic rivalry stakes, Sydney was planning to incinerate the decommissioned Harbor Bridge with artificial lightning, while Washington had arranged for no less than twenty-one aging military satellites to plunge from the sky into the Potomac at the stroke of midnight.

There was no doubt, though, that Beijing had stolen the lion's share of global chatter with the imminent launch of the Orchid Seed. You could forget any purist's concept of lunar midnight; the clocks on Procellarum had been set to the easternmost of Earth's time zones ever since the construction of the base two decades before, so the official zeroing of the digits here would precede celebrations in all of the globe's major cities. The PR people really had planned that far ahead.

As she paced slowly along the regolith, Ikat kept her eyes diligently on the coolant pipes that weaved between the support struts to wrap the gun barrel, although she knew that this final check was mostly PR too. If the launch failed, it would be down to a flaw that no human eye could have detected. Six successful but unpublicised test firings made such a humiliation unlikely. Still, the gun's fixed bearing rendered a seventh, perfectly timed success indispensable. Only at "midnight" would the device be aimed precisely at its target. If they had to wait a month for a relaunch, hundreds of upper-echelon bureaucrats back on Earth would probably be diving out of their penthouse windows before dawn. Ikat knew that she was far too low in the ranks to make a worthwhile scapegoat, but her career could still be blighted by the ignominy.

Her mother was calling from Bangkok. Ikat pondered her responsibilities, then decided to let the audio through. If she really couldn't walk, talk and spot a plume of leaking coolant at the same time, she should probably retire from her profession straight away.

"Just wishing you good luck, darling," her mother said. "And Happy New Year. Probably you'll be too busy celebrating to talk to me later."

Ikat scowled. "I was planning to call you when it reached midnight there. But Happy New Year anyway."

"You'll call your father after the launch?"

"I expect so." Her parents were divorced, but her mother still wanted harmony to flow in all directions, especially on such an occasion.

"Without him," her mother said, "you never would have had this chance."

It was a strange way of putting it, but it was probably true. The Chinese space program was cosmopolitan enough, but if her mother hadn't married a Chinese citizen and remained in the country for so long, Ikat doubted that she would have been plucked from provincial Bangkok and lofted all the way up to Procellarum. There were dozens of middle-ranking project engineers with highly specific skills who were not Chinese born; they were quite likely the best people on the planet for their respective jobs. She was not in that league. Her academic results had secured her the placement, but they had not been so spectacular that she would have been head-hunted across national borders.

"I'll call him," she promised. "After the launch."

She cut the connection. She'd almost reached the end of Stage Nine, the ten-kilometer section of the barrel where the pellets would be accelerated from sixteen to eighteen per cent of light speed, before the final boost to twenty per cent. For the last three years, she had worked beneath various specialist managers, testing and re-testing different subsystems: energy storage, electromagnets, cooling, data collection. It had been a once-in-a-lifetime education, arduous at times, but never boring. Still, she'd be glad to be going home. Maglev railways might seem anticlimactic after this, but she'd had enough of sharing a room with six other people, and the whole tiny complex with the same two hundred faces, year after year.

Back inside the base, Ikat felt restless. The last hour stretched out ahead of her, an impossible gulf. In the common room, Qing caught her eye, and she went to sit with him.

"Had any bites from your resumé?" he asked.

"I haven't published it yet. I want a long holiday first."

He shook his head in dismay. "How did you ever get here? You must be the least competitive person on Earth."

Ikat laughed. "At university, I studied eighteen hours a day. I had no social life for six years."

"So now you've got to put in some effort to get the pay-off."

"This *is* the pay-off, you dope."

"For a week or so after the launch," Qing said, "you could have the top engineering firms on the planet bidding for the prestige you'd bring them. That won't last forever, though. People have a short attention span. This isn't the time to take a holiday."

Ikat threw up her hands. "What can I say? I'm a lost cause."

Qing's expression softened; he was deadly serious about his own career, but when he lectured her it was just a kind of ritual, a role play that gave them something to talk about.

They passed the time with more riffs on the same theme, interleaved with gossip and bitching about their colleagues, but when the clock hit 11.50 it became impossible to remain blasé. Nobody could spend three years in a state of awe at the feat they were attempting, but ten minutes of sober contemplation suddenly seemed inadequate. Other probes had already been sent toward the stars, but the Orchid Seed would certainly outrace all those that had gone before it. It might yet be overtaken itself, but with no serious competitors even at the planning stage, there was a fair chance that the impending launch would come to be seen as the true genesis of interstellar travel.

As the conversation in the common room died away, someone turned up the main audio commentary that was going to the news feeds, and spread a dozen key image windows across the wall screens. The control room was too small to take everyone in the base; junior staff would watch the launch much as the public everywhere else did.

The schematics told Ikat a familiar story, but this was the moment to savor it anew. Three gigajoules of solar energy had already been packed into circulating currents in the superconducting batteries, ready to be tapped. That was not much, really; every significant payload launched from Earth had burned up far more. One third would be lost to heat and stray electromagnetic fields. The remainder would be fed into the motion of just one milligram of matter: the five hundred tiny pellets of the Orchid Seed that would race down the launch gun in three thousandths of a second, propelled by a force that could have lofted a two-tonne weight back on Earth.

The pellets that comprised the seed were not physically connected, but they would move in synch in a rigid pattern, forming a kind of sparse crystal whose spacing allowed it to interact strongly with the microwave radiation in the gun. Out in deep space, in the decades spent in transit, the pattern would not be important, but the pellets would be kept close together by electrostatic trimming if and when they strayed, ready to take up perfect rank again when the time came to brake. First, in the coronal magnetic field of Prosperity B; again near its larger companion star, and finally in the ionosphere of Prosperity A's fourth planet, Duty, before falling into the atmosphere and spiraling to the ground.

One cycling image on the wall rehearsed the launch in slow motion, showing the crest of electromagnetic energy coursing down the barrel, field lines bunched tightly like a strange coiled spring. A changing electric field induced a magnetic field; a changing magnetic field induced an electric field. In free space such a change would spread at the speed of light—would *be* light, of some frequency or other—but the tailored geometry and currents of the barrel kept the wave reined in, always in step with the seed, devoted to the task of urging this precious cargo forward.

"If this screws up," Qing observed forlornly, "we'll be the laughing stock of the century."

"You don't think Beijing's prepared for a cover-up?" Ikat joked.

"Some jealous fucker would catch us out," Qing replied. "I'll bet every dish on Earth is tuned to the seed's resonant frequency. If they get no echo, we'll all be building toilet blocks in Aksai Chin."

It was 11.58 in Tonga, Tokelau and Procellarum. Ikat took Qing's hand and squeezed it. "Relax," she said. "The worst you'll come to is building synchrotrons for eccentric billionaires in Kowloon."

Qing said, "You're cutting off my circulation."

The room fell silent; a synthetic voice from the control room counted down the seconds. Ikat felt light-headed. The six test firings had worked, but who knew what damage they'd done, what stresses they'd caused, what structures they'd weakened? Lots of people, actually; the barrel was packed with instrumentation to measure exactly those things, and the answers were all very reassuring. Still—

"Minus three. Minus two. Minus one."

A schematic of the launch gun flashed green, followed by a slow-motion reconstruction of the field patterns so flawless it was indistinguishable from the simulations. A new window opened, showing tracking echoes. The seed was moving away from the moon at sixty thousand kilometers per second, precisely along the expected trajectory. There was nothing more required of it: no second stage to fire, no course change, no reconfiguration. Now that it had been set in motion, all it had to do was coast on its momentum; it couldn't suddenly veer sideways, crashing and burning like some failed chemical rocket launched from the ground. Even if collisions or system failures over the coming decades wiped out some of the pellets, the seed as a whole could function with as little as a quarter of the original number. Unless the whole thing had been a fraud or a mass hallucination, there was now absolutely nothing that could pull the rug out from under this triumph; in three milliseconds, their success had become complete and irrevocable. At least for a century, until the seed reached its destination.

People were cheering; Ikat joined them, but her own cry came out as a tension-relieving sob. Qing put an arm around her shoulders. "We did it," he whispered. "We've conquered the world."

Not the stars? Not the galaxy? She laughed, but she didn't begrudge him this vanity. The fireworks to come in Sydney might be more spectacular, and the dying hawks burning up over Washington might bring their own sense of closure, but this felt like an opening out, an act of release, a joyful shout across the light years.

Food and drink was wheeled out; the party began. In twenty minutes, the seed was farther from the sun than Mars. In a day, it would be farther than Pluto; in ten days, farther than Pioneer 10. In six months, the Orchid Seed would have put more distance behind it than all of the targeted interstellar missions that had preceded it.

Ikat remembered to call her father once midnight came to Beijing.

"Happy New Year," she greeted him.

"Congratulations," he replied. "Will you come and visit me once you get your Earth legs, or will you be too busy signing autographs?"

Fake biochemical signals kept the Procellarans' bones and muscles strong; it would only take a day or two to acclimatize her nervous system to the old dynamics again. "Of course I'll visit you."

"You did a good job," he said. "I'm proud of you."

His praise made her uncomfortable. She wanted to express her gratitude to him—he'd done much more to help her than providing the accident of her birthplace—but she was afraid of sounding like a giddy movie star accepting an award.

As the party wound on and midnight skimmed the globe, the speech-writers of the world's leaders competed to heap praise upon Beijing's achievement. Ikat didn't care that it had all been done for the glory of a fading empire; it was more than a gesture of status and power.

Only one thing seemed bittersweet, as she contemplated the decades to come. She was twenty-eight years old, and there was every chance that these three years, these three milliseconds, would turn out to have been the pinnacle of her life.

2

THE CALLER was persistent, Ikat gave him that. He refused to leave a message or engage with her assistant; he refused to explain his business to anyone but Ikat herself, in a realtime dialogue.

From her balcony she looked out across the treetops, listening to the birds and insects of the Mekong valley, and wondered if she wanted to be dragged back into the swirling currents of the world. The caller, whose name was Vikram Ali, had probably tracked her down in the hope of extracting a comment from her about the imminent arrival of signals from the Orchid Flower. That might have been an egotistical assumption, were it not for the fact that she'd heard of no other participant in the launch publishing anything on the matter, so it was clear that the barrel would have to be scraped. The project's most famous names were all dead or acorporeal—and the acorporeals were apparently Satisfied, rendering them even less interested in such worldly matters than an aging flesh-bound recluse like Ikat.

She pondered her wishes and responsibilities. Most people now viewed the Orchid Seed as a curiosity, a sociological time capsule. Within decades of its launch, a new generation of telescopes had imaged and analyzed its destination with such detail and clarity that the mission had come to seem redundant. All five planets in the Prosperity system appeared lifeless, and although there were astrophysical and geochemical subtleties that *in situ* measurements might yet reveal, with high-resolution maps of Duty splashed across the web, interest in the slightly better view that would arrive after a very long delay began to dwindle.

What was there for Ikat to say on the matter? Should she plead for the project to be taken seriously, as more than a quaint nationalist stunt from a bygone era? Maybe the top brass weren't Satisfied; maybe they were just embarrassed. The possibility annoyed her. No one who'd been sincere in their work on the Orchid Seed should be ashamed of what they'd done.

Ikat returned Vikram Ali's call. He responded immediately, and after the briefest of pleasantries came to the point.

"I represent Khamoush Holdings," he said. "Some time ago, we acquired various assets and obligations of the URC government, including a contractual relationship with you."

"I see." Ikat struggled to remember what she might have signed that could possibly be relevant a hundred and twenty years later. Had she promised to do media if asked? Her assistant had verified Khamoush Holding's bona fides, but all it knew about the Procellarum contract was that Ikat's copy had been lost in 2145, when an anarchist worm had scrambled three per cent of the planet's digital records.

"The opportunity has arisen for us to exploit one of our assets," Ali continued, "but we are contractually obliged to offer you the option of participating in the relevant activity."

Ikat blinked. *Option?* Khamoush had bought some form of media rights, obviously, but would there be a clause saying they had to run down the ranks of the Orchid Seed team, offering each participant a chance to play spokesperson?

"Am I obliged to help you, or not?" she asked.

Now it was Ali's turn to be surprised. "Obliged? Certainly not! We're not slave holders!" He looked downright offended.

Ikat said, "Could we get the whole thing over in a day or two?"

Ali pondered this question deeply for a couple of seconds. "You don't have the contract, do you?"

"I chose a bad archive," Ikat confessed.

"So you have no idea what I'm talking about?"

"You want me to give interviews about the Orchid Seed, don't you?" Ikat said.

"Ultimately, yes," Ali replied, "but that's neither here nor there for now. I want to ask you if you're interested in traveling to Duty, taking a look around, and coming back."

⌁

IN THE lobby of the hotel in Mumbai, Ikat learned that someone else had accepted the offer from Khamoush Holdings.

"I thought you'd be rich and Satisfied by now," she told Qing.

He smiled. "Mildly rich. Never satisfied."

They walked together to the office of Magic Beans Inc, Ikat holding her umbrella over both of them against the monsoon rain.

"My children think I'm insane," Qing confessed.

"Mine too. But then, I told them that if they kept arguing, I'd make it a one-way journey." Ikat laughed. "Really, they ought to be grateful. No filial obligations for forty years straight. It's hard to imagine a greater gift."

In the Magic Beans office, Ali showed them two robots, more or less identical to the ones the Orchid Flower, he hoped, would already have built on the surface of Duty. The original mission planners had never intended such a thing, but when Khamoush had acquired the assets they had begun the relevant R&D immediately. Forty years ago they had transmitted the blueprints for these robots, in a message that would have arrived not long after the Orchid Seed touched down. Now that confirmation of the Flower's success in its basic mission had reached Earth, in a matter of months they would learn whether the nanomachines had also been able to scavenge the necessary materials to construct these welcoming receptacles.

"We're the only volunteers?" Qing asked, gazing at his prospective doppelgänger with uneasy fascination. "I would have thought one of the acorporeals would have jumped at the chance."

"Perhaps if we'd asked them early enough," Ali replied. "But once you're immersed in that culture, forty years must seem a very long time to be out of touch."

Ikat was curious about the financial benefits Khamoush were hoping for; they turned out to revolve largely around a promotional deal with a manufacturer of prosthetic bodies. Although the designs the company sold were wildly different from these robots—even their Extreme Durability models were far more cozily organic—any link with the first interstellar explorers trudging across rugged landscapes on a distant, lifeless world carried enough resonance to be worth paying for.

Back in the hotel they sat in Qing's room, talking about the old times and speculating about the motives and fates of all their higher-ranked colleagues who'd turned down this opportunity. Perhaps, Ikat suggested, some of them simply had no wish to become acorporeal. Crossing over to software didn't preclude you from continuing to inhabit a prosthetic body back on Earth, but once you changed substrate the twin lures of virtual experience and self-modification were strong. "That would be ironic," she mused. "To decline to engage with the physical universe in this way, for fear of ultimately losing touch with it."

Qing said, "I plan to keep my body frozen, and have my new self wired back into it when I return, synapse by synapse."

Ikat smiled. "I thought you said *mildly* rich." That would be orders of magnitude more costly than her own plan: frozen body, prosthetic brain.

"They caught us at just the right stage in life," Qing said. "Still interested in reality, but not still doting on every new great-great-grandchild. Not yet acorporeal, but old enough that we already feel as if we've been on another planet for forty years."

Ikat said, "I'm amazed that they honored our contracts, though. A good lawyer could have let them hand-pick their travelers." The relevant clause had simply been a vague offer of preferential access to spin-off employment opportunities.

"Why shouldn't they want *us?*" Qing demanded, feigning indignation. "We're seasoned astronauts, aren't we? We've already proved we could live together in Procellarum for three years, without driving each other crazy. Three months—with a whole planet to stretch our legs on—shouldn't be beyond us."

Later that week, to Ikat's amazement, their psychological assessments proved Qing's point; their basic personality profiles really hadn't changed since the Procellarum days. Careers, marriages, children, had left their marks, but if anything they were both more resilient.

They stayed in Mumbai, rehearsing in the robot bodies using telepresence links, and studying the data coming back from the Orchid Flower.

When confirmation arrived that the Flower really had built the robots Khamoush Holdings had requested, Ikat sent messages directly to her children and grandchildren, and then left it to them to pass the news further down the generations. Her parents were dead, and her children were tetchy centenarians; she loved them, but she did not feel like gathering them around her for a tearful bon voyage. The chances were they'd all still be here when she returned.

She and Qing spent a morning doing media, answering a minute but representative fraction of the questions submitted by interested news subscribers. Then Ikat's body was frozen, and her brain was removed, microtomed, and scanned. At her request, her software was not formally woken on Earth prior to her departure; routine tests confirmed its functionality in a series of dreamlike scenarios which left no permanent memories.

Then the algorithm that described her was optimized, compressed, encoded into a series of laser pulses, and beamed across twenty light years, straight on to the petals of the Orchid Flower.

3

IKAT WOKE standing on a brown, pebbled plain beneath a pale, salmon-colored sky. Prosperity A had just risen; its companion, ten billion kilometers away, was visible but no competition, scarcely brighter than Venus from Earth.

Qing was beside her, and behind him was the Flower: the communications link and factory that the Orchid Seed had built. Products of the factory included hundreds of small rovers, which had dispersed to explore the planet's surface, and dozens of solar-powered gliders, which provided aerial views and aided with communications.

Qing said, "Punch me, make it real."

Ikat obliged with a gentle thump on his forearm. Their telepresence rehearsals had included virtual backdrops just like the Flower's actual surroundings, but they had not had full tactile feedback. The action punctured Ikat's own dreamy sense of déjà vu; they really had stepped out of the simulation into the thing itself.

They had the Flower brief them about its latest discoveries; they had been twenty years behind when they'd left Earth, and insentient beams of light for twenty more. The Flower had pieced together more details of Duty's geological history; with plate tectonics but no liquid water, the planet's surface was older than Earth's but not as ancient as the moon's.

Ikat felt a twinge of superfluousness; if the telescope images hadn't quite made the Orchid Flower redundant, there was precious little left for her and Qing. They were not here to play geologists, though; they were here to be here. Any science they did would be a kind of recreation, like an informed tourist's appreciation of some well-studied natural wonder back on Earth.

Qing started laughing. "Twenty fucking *light years!* Do you know how long that would take to walk? They should have tried harder to make us afraid." Ikat reached out and put a hand on his shoulder. She felt a little existential vertigo herself, but she did not believe they faced any great risk. The forty lost years were a fait accompli, but she was reconciled to that.

"What's the worst that can happen?" she said. "If something goes wrong, they'll just wake your body back on Earth, with no changes at all."

Qing nodded slowly. "But you had your brain diced, didn't you?"

"You know me, I'm a cheapskate." Non-destructive scanning was more expensive, and Khamoush weren't paying for everything. "But they can still load the backup file into a prosthesis."

"Assuming it's not eaten by an anarchist worm."

"I arranged to have a physical copy put into a vault."

"Ah, but what about the nihilist nanoware?"

"Then you and I will be the only survivors."

Their bodies had no need for shelter from the elements, but the Flower had built them a simple hut for sanity's sake. As they inspected the spartan rooms together, Qing seemed to grow calm; as he'd said back on Earth, anything had to be easier than the conditions they'd faced on the moon. Food would have been too complex an indulgence, and Ikat had declined the software to grant her convincing hallucinations of five-course banquets every night.

Once they'd familiarised themselves with everything in the base camp, and done a few scripted Armstrong moments for the cameras to satisfy the promotional deal, they spent the morning hiking across the rock-strewn plain. There was a line of purplish mountains in the distance, almost lost in haze, but Ikat declined to ask the Flower for detailed aerial imagery. They could explore for themselves, find things for themselves. The longing to be some kind of irreplaceable pioneer, to be the first pair of eyes and hands, the first scrutinizing intelligence, was impossible to extinguish completely, but they could find a way to satisfy it without self-delusion or charade.

Her fusion-powered body needed no rest, but at noon she stopped walking and sat cross-legged on the ground.

Qing joined her. She looked around at the barren rocks, the delicate sky, the far horizon. "Twenty light years?" she said. "I'm glad I came."

〰〰

THEIR DAYS were full of small challenges, and small discoveries. To cross a mountain range required skill and judgment as well as stamina; to understand the origins of each wind-blasted outcrop took careful observation and a strong visual imagination, as well as a grasp of the basic geological principles.

Still, even as they clambered down one treacherous, powdery cliff-face, Ikat wondered soberly if they'd reached the high-tide mark of human exploration. The Orchid Seed's modest speed and reach had never been exceeded; the giant telescopes had found no hints of life out to a hundred light years, offering little motivation to launch a new probe. The shift to software was becoming cheaper every year, and if that made travel to the stars easier, there were a thousand more alluring destinations closer to home. When you could pack a lifetime of exotic experiences into a realtime hour, capped off with happiness by fiat, who would give up decades of contemporaneity to walk on a distant world? There were even VR games, based on telescope imagery, where people fought unlikely wars with implausible alien empires on the very ground she was treading.

"What are you planning to do when you get home?" she asked Qing that night. They had brought nothing with them from the base camp, so they simply slept on the ground beneath the stars.

"Back to work, I suppose." He ran his own successful engineering consultancy; so successful that it didn't really need him. "What else is there? I'm not interested in crawling up a computer's arse and pretending that I've gone to heaven. What about you?"

"I don't know. I was retired, happily enough. Waiting for death, I suppose." It hadn't felt like that, though.

Qing said, "These aren't the highest mountains on the planet, you know. The ones we've just crossed."

"I know that."

"There are some that reach into a pretty good vacuum."

Duty's atmosphere was thin even on the ground; Ikat had no reason to doubt this assertion. "What's your point?" she asked.

He turned to her, and gave her his strangest robot smile. "From a mountain like that, a coil gun could land a package of nanomachines on Patience."

Patience was a third the mass of Duty, and had no atmosphere to speak of. "To what end?"

Qing said, "High vacuum, relativistic launch speeds. What we started doesn't have to stop here."

She searched his face, unsure if he was serious. "Do you think the Flower would give us what we needed? Who knows how Khamoush have programmed it?"

"I tested the nanoware, back on Procellarum. I know how to make it give us whatever we ask."

Ikat thought it over. "Do we know how to describe everything we'll need? To identify a new target? Plan a whole new mission?" The Orchard Seed had taken thousands of people decades to prepare.

Qing said, "We'll need telescopes, computing resources. We can bootstrap our way up, step by step. Let's see how far we get in three months. And if we solve all the other problems, maybe we can go one step further: build a seed that will self-replicate when it reaches its destination, launching a couple of new seeds of its own."

Ikat rose to her feet angrily. "Not if you want my help! We have no right to spew mindless replicators in all directions. If someone from Earth wants to follow the seed we launch, and if they make their own decision when they get there to reach out further, then that's one thing, but I'm *not* starting any kind of self-sustaining chain reaction that colonizes the galaxy while everyone sits at home playing VR games."

Qing stood up, and made a calming gesture. "All right, all right! I was just thinking out loud. The truth is, we'll be struggling to launch *anything* before it's time to go home. But better to try, than spend three months taking in the scenery."

Ikat remained wary for a moment, then she laughed with relief. "Absolutely. Let the real geologists back on Earth fret about these rocks; I've had enough of them already for a lifetime."

They didn't wait for dawn; they headed back for the base camp immediately.

As they approached the mountains, Qing said, "I thought it would give me some great sense of accomplishment, to come here and see with my own eyes that this thing I helped to start was finally complete. But if I could wish my descendants one blessing now, it would be never to see the end, never to find completion."

Ikat stopped walking, and mimed a toast. "To the coming generations. May they always start something they can't finish."

SINGLETON

‿⌒〰〜⋀⋀ was walking north along George Street toward Town Hall railway station, pondering the ways I might solve the tricky third question of my linear algebra assignment, when I encountered a small crowd blocking the footpath. I didn't give much thought to the reason they were standing there; I'd just passed a busy restaurant, and I often saw groups of people gathered outside. But once I'd started to make my way around them, moving into an alley rather than stepping out into the traffic, it became apparent that they were not just diners from a farewell lunch for a retiring colleague, putting off their return to the office for as long as possible. I could see for myself exactly what was holding their attention.

Twenty meters down the alley, a man was lying on his back on the ground, shielding his bloodied face with his hands, while two men stood over him, relentlessly swinging narrow sticks of some kind. At first I thought the sticks were pool cues, but then I noticed the metal hooks on the ends. I'd only ever seen these obscure weapons before in one other place: my primary school, where an appointed window monitor would use them at the start and end of each day. They were meant for opening and closing an old-fashioned kind of hinged pane when it was too high to reach with your hands.

I turned to the other spectators. "Has anyone called the police?" A woman nodded without looking at me, and said, "Someone used their mobile, a couple of minutes ago."

The assailants must have realized that the police were on their way, but it seemed they were too committed to their task to abandon it until that was absolutely necessary. They were facing away from the crowd, so perhaps they weren't entirely reckless not to fear identification. The man on the ground was dressed like a kitchen hand. He was still moving, trying to protect himself, but he was making less noise than his attackers; the need, or the ability, to cry out in pain had been beaten right out of him.

As for calling for help, he could have saved his breath.

A chill passed through my body, a sick cold churning sensation that came a moment before the conscious realization: *I'm going to watch someone murdered, and I'm going to do nothing.* But this wasn't a drunken brawl, where a few bystanders could step in and separate the combatants; the two assailants had to be serious criminals, settling a score. Keeping your distance from something like that was just common sense. I'd go to court, I'd be a witness, but no one could expect anything more of me. Not when thirty other people had behaved in exactly the same way.

The men in the alley did not have guns. If they'd had guns, they would have used them by now. They weren't going to mow down anyone who got in their way. It was one thing not to make a martyr of yourself, but how many people could these two grunting slobs fend off with sticks?

I unstrapped my backpack and put it on the ground. Absurdly, that made me feel more vulnerable; I was always worried about losing my textbooks. *Think about this. You don't know what you're doing.* I hadn't been in so much as a fist fight since I was thirteen. I glanced at the strangers around me, wondering if anyone would join in if I implored them to rush forward together. But that wasn't going to happen. I was a willowy, unimposing eighteen-year-old, wearing a T-shirt adorned with Maxwell's Equations. I had no presence, no authority. No one would follow me into the fray.

Alone, I'd be as helpless as the guy on the ground. These men would crack my skull open in an instant. There were half a dozen solid-looking office workers in their twenties in the crowd; if these weekend rugby players hadn't felt competent to intervene, what chance did I have?

I reached down for my backpack. If I wasn't going to help, there was no point being here at all. I'd find out what had happened on the evening news.

I started to retrace my steps, sick with self-loathing. This wasn't *kristall-nacht*. There'd be no embarrassing questions from my grandchildren. No one would ever reproach me.

As if that were the measure of everything.

"Fuck it." I dropped my backpack and ran down the alley.

I was close enough to smell the three sweating bodies over the stench of rotting garbage before I was even noticed. The nearest of the attackers glanced over his shoulder, affronted, then amused. He didn't bother redeploying his weapon in mid-stroke; as I hooked an arm around his neck in the hope of overbalancing him, he thrust his elbow into my chest, winding me. I clung on desperately, maintaining the hold even though I couldn't tighten it. As he tried to prise himself loose, I managed to kick his feet out from under him. We both went down onto the asphalt; I ended up beneath him.

The man untangled himself and clambered to his feet. As I struggled to right myself, picturing a metal hook swinging into my face, someone whistled. I looked up to see the second man gesturing to his companion, and I followed his gaze. A dozen men and women were coming down the alley, advancing together at a brisk walk. It was not a particularly menacing sight— I'd seen angrier crowds with peace signs painted on their faces—but the sheer numbers were enough to guarantee some inconvenience. The first man hung back long enough to kick me in the ribs. Then the two of them fled.

I brought my knees up, then raised my head and got into a crouch. I was still winded, but for some reason it seemed vital not to remain flat on my back. One of the office workers grinned down at me. "You fuckwit. You could have got killed."

The kitchen hand shuddered, and snorted bloody mucus. His eyes were swollen shut, and when he lay his hands down beside him, I could see the bones of his knuckles through the torn skin. My own skin turned icy, at this vision of the fate I'd courted for myself. But if it was a shock to realize how I might have ended up, it was just as sobering to think that I'd almost walked away and let them finish him off, when the intervention had actually cost me nothing.

I rose to my feet. People milled around the kitchen hand, asking each other about first aid. I remembered the basics from a course I'd done in high school, but the man was still breathing, and he wasn't losing vast amounts of blood, so I couldn't think of anything helpful that an amateur could do in the circumstances. I squeezed my way out of the gathering and walked back to the street. My backpack was exactly where I'd left it; no one had stolen my books. I heard sirens approaching; the police and the ambulance would be there soon.

My ribs were tender, but I wasn't in agony. I'd cracked a rib falling off a trail bike on the farm when I was twelve, and I was fairly sure that this was just bruising. For a while I walked bent over, but by the time I reached the station I found I could adopt a normal gait. I had some grazed skin on my arms, but I couldn't have appeared too battered, because no one on the train looked at me twice.

That night, I watched the news. The kitchen hand was described as being in a stable condition. I pictured him stepping out into the alley to empty a bucket of fish-heads into the garbage, to find the two of them waiting for him. I'd probably never learn what the attack had been about unless the case went to trial, and as yet the police hadn't even named any suspects. If the man had been in a fit state to talk in the alley, I might have asked him then, but any sense that I was entitled to an explanation was rapidly fading.

The reporter mentioned a student "leading the charge of angry citizens" who'd rescued the kitchen hand, and then she spoke to an eye witness, who described this young man as "a New Ager, wearing some kind of astrological symbols on his shirt." I snorted, then looked around nervously in case one of my housemates had made the improbable connection, but no one else was even in earshot.

Then the story was over.

I felt flat for a moment, cheated of the minor rush that fifteen seconds' fame might have delivered; it was like reaching into a biscuit tin when you thought there was one more chocolate chip left, to find that there actually wasn't. I considered phoning my parents in Orange, just to talk to them from within the strange afterglow, but I'd established a routine and it was not the right day. If I called unexpectedly, they'd think something was wrong.

So, that was it. In a week's time, when the bruises had faded, I'd look back and doubt that the incident had ever happened.

I went upstairs to finish my assignment.

FRANCINE SAID, "There's a nicer way to think about this. If you do a change of variables, from x and y to z and z-conjugate, the Cauchy-Riemann equations correspond to the condition that the partial derivative of the function with respect to z-conjugate is equal to zero."

We were sitting in the coffee shop, discussing the complex analysis lecture we'd had half an hour before. Half a dozen of us from the same course had got into the habit of meeting at this time every week, but today the others had failed to turn up. Maybe there was a movie being screened, or a speaker appearing on campus that I hadn't heard about.

I worked through the transformation she'd described. "You're right," I said. "That's really elegant!"

Francine nodded slightly in assent, while retaining her characteristic jaded look. She had an undisguisable passion for mathematics, but she was probably bored out of her skull in class, waiting for the lecturers to catch up and teach her something she didn't already know.

I was nowhere near her level. In fact, I'd started the year poorly, distracted by my new surroundings: nothing so glamorous as the temptations of the night life, just the different sights and sounds and scale of the place, along with the bureaucratic demands of all the organizations that now impinged upon my life, from the university itself down to the shared house groceries subcommittee. In the last few weeks, though, I'd finally started hitting my stride. I'd got a part-time job, stacking shelves in a supermarket; the pay was lousy, but it was enough to take the edge off my financial anxieties, and the hours weren't so long that they left me with no time for anything but study.

I doodled harmonic contours on the notepaper in front of me. "So what do you do for fun?" I said. "Apart from complex analysis?"

Francine didn't reply immediately. This wasn't the first time we'd been alone together, but I'd never felt confident that I had the right words to make the most of the situation. At some point, though, I'd stopped fooling myself that there was ever going to be a perfect moment, with the perfect phrase falling from my lips: something subtle but intriguing slipped deftly into the conversation, without disrupting the flow. So now I'd made my interest plain, with no attempt at artfulness or eloquence. She could judge me as she knew me from the last three months, and if she felt no desire to know me better, I would not be crushed.

"I write a lot of Perl scripts," she said. "Nothing complicated; just odds and ends that I give away as freeware. It's very relaxing."

I nodded understandingly. I didn't think she was being deliberately discouraging; she just expected me to be slightly more direct.

"Do you like Deborah Conway?" I'd only heard a couple of her songs on the radio myself, but a few days before I'd seen a poster in the city announcing a tour.

"Yeah. She's great."

I started thickening the conjugation bars over the variables I'd scrawled. "She's playing at a club in Surry Hills," I said. "On Friday. Would you like to go?"

Francine smiled, making no effort now to appear world-weary. "Sure. That would be nice."

I smiled back. I wasn't giddy, I wasn't moonstruck, but I felt as if I was standing on the shore of an ocean, contemplating its breadth. I felt the way I felt when I opened a sophisticated monograph in the library, and was reduced to savoring the scent of the print and the crisp symmetry of the notation, understanding only a fraction of what I read. Knowing there was something glorious ahead, but knowing too what a daunting task it would be to come to terms with it.

I said, "I'll get the tickets on my way home."

∿

To CELEBRATE the end of exams for the year, the household threw a party. It was a sultry November night, but the back yard wasn't much bigger than the largest room in the house, so we ended up opening all the doors and windows and distributing food and furniture throughout the ground floor and the exterior, front and back. Once the faint humid breeze off the river penetrated the depths of the house, it was equally sweltering and mosquito-ridden everywhere, indoors and out.

Francine and I stayed close for an hour or so, obeying the distinctive dynamics of a couple, until by some unspoken mutual understanding it became clear that we could wander apart for a while, and that neither of us was so insecure that we'd resent it.

I ended up in a corner of the crowded back yard, talking to Will, a biochemistry student who'd lived in the house for the last four years. On some level, he probably couldn't help feeling that his opinions about the way things were run should carry more weight than anyone else's, which had annoyed me greatly when I'd first moved in. We'd since become friends, though, and I was glad to have a chance to talk to him before he left to take up a scholarship in Germany.

In the middle of a conversation about the work he'd be doing, I caught sight of Francine, and he followed my gaze.

Will said, "It took me a while to figure out what finally cured you of your homesickness."

"I was never homesick."

"Yeah, right." He took a swig of his drink. "She's changed you, though. You have to admit that."

"I do. Happily. Everything's clicked, since we got together." Relationships were meant to screw up your studies, but my marks were soaring. Francine didn't tutor me; she just drew me into a state of mind where everything was clearer.

"The amazing thing is that you got together at all." I scowled, and Will raised a hand placatingly. "I just meant, when you first moved in, you were pretty reserved. And down on yourself. When we interviewed you for the room, you practically begged us to give it to someone more deserving."

"Now you're taking the piss."

He shook his head. "Ask any of the others."

I fell silent. The truth was, if I took a step back and contemplated my situation, I was as astonished as he was. By the time I'd left my home town, it had become clear to me that good fortune had nothing much to do with luck. Some people were born with wealth, or talent, or charisma. They started with an edge, and the benefits snowballed. I'd always believed that I had, at best, just enough intelligence and persistence to stay afloat in my chosen field; I'd topped every class in high school, but in a town the size of Orange that meant nothing, and I'd had no illusions about my fate in Sydney.

I owed it to Francine that my visions of mediocrity had not been fulfilled; being with her had transformed my life. But where had I found the nerve to imagine that I had anything to offer her in return?

"Something happened," I admitted. "Before I asked her out."

"Yeah?"

I almost clammed up; I hadn't told anyone about the events in the alley, not even Francine. The incident had come to seem too personal, as if to recount it at all would be to lay my conscience bare. But Will was off to

Munich in less than a week, and it was easier to confide in someone I didn't expect to see again.

When I finished, Will bore a satisfied grin, as if I'd explained everything. "Pure karma," he announced. "I should have guessed."

"Oh, very scientific."

"I'm serious. Forget the Buddhist mystobabble; I'm talking about the real thing. If you stick to your principles, of course things go better for you—assuming you don't get killed in the process. That's elementary psychology. People have a highly developed sense of reciprocity, of the appropriateness of the treatment they receive from each other. If things work out too well for them, they can't help asking, 'What did I do to deserve this?' If you don't have a good answer, you'll sabotage yourself. Not all the time, but often enough. So if you do something that improves your self-esteem—"

"Self-esteem is for the weak," I quipped. Will rolled his eyes. "I don't think like that," I protested.

"No? Why did you even bring it up, then?"

I shrugged. "Maybe it just made me less pessimistic. I could have had the crap beaten out of me, but I didn't. That makes asking someone to a concert seem a lot less dangerous." I was beginning to cringe at all this un-wanted analysis, and I had nothing to counter Will's pop psychology except an equally folksy version of my own.

He could see I was embarrassed, so he let the matter drop. As I watched Francine moving through the crowd, though, I couldn't shake off an unset-tling sense of the tenuousness of the circumstances that had brought us to-gether. There was no denying that if I'd walked away from the alley, and the kitchen hand had died, I would have felt like shit for a long time afterward. I would not have felt entitled to much out of my own life.

I hadn't walked away, though. And even if the decision had come down to the wire, why shouldn't I be proud that I'd made the right choice? That didn't mean everything that followed was tainted, like a reward from some sleazy, palm-greasing deity. I hadn't won Francine's affection in a medieval test of bravery; we'd chosen each other, and persisted with that choice, for a thousand complicated reasons.

We were together now; that was what mattered. I wasn't going to dwell on the path that had brought me to her, just to dredge up all the doubts and insecurities that had almost kept us apart.

As WE drove the last kilometer along the road south from Ar Rafidiyah, I could see the Wall of Foam glistening ahead of us in the morning sunlight. Insubstantial as a pile of soap bubbles, but still intact, after six weeks.

"I can't believe it's lasted this long," I told Sadiq.

"You didn't trust the models?"

"Fuck, no. Every week, I thought we'd come over the hill and there'd be nothing but a shriveled-up cobweb."

Sadiq smiled. "So you had no faith in my calculations?"

"Don't take it personally. There were a lot of things we could have both got wrong."

Sadiq pulled off the road. His students, Hassan and Rashid, had climbed off the back of the truck and started toward the Wall before I'd even got my face mask on. Sadiq called them back, and made them put on plastic boots and paper suits over their clothes, while the two of us did the same. We didn't usually bother with this much protection, but today was different.

Close up, the Wall almost vanished: all you noticed were isolated, rainbow-fringed reflections, drifting at a leisurely pace across the otherwise invisible film as water redistributed itself, following waves induced in the membrane by the interplay of air pressure, thermal gradients, and surface tension. These images might easily have been separate objects, scraps of translucent plastic blowing around above the desert, held aloft by a breeze too faint to detect at ground level.

The further away you looked, though, the more crowded the hints of light became, and the less plausible any alternative hypothesis that denied the Wall its integrity. It stretched for a kilometer along the edge of the desert, and rose an uneven fifteen to twenty meters into the air. But it was merely the first, and smallest, of its kind, and the time had come to put it on the back of the truck and drive it all the way back to Basra.

Sadiq took a spray can of reagent from the cabin, and shook it as he walked down the embankment. I followed him, my heart in my mouth. The Wall had not dried out; it had not been torn apart or blown away, but there was still plenty of room for failure.

Sadiq reached up and sprayed what appeared from my vantage to be thin air, but I could see the fine mist of droplets strike the membrane. A breathy susurration rose up, like the sound from a steam iron, and I felt a faint warm dampness before the first silken threads appeared, crisscrossing the region where the polymer from which the Wall was built had begun to shift conformations. In one state, the polymer was soluble, exposing hydrophilic groups of atoms that bound water into narrow sheets of feather-light gel. Now, triggered by the reagent and powered by sunlight, it was tucking these groups into slick, oily cages, and expelling every molecule of water, transforming the gel into a desiccated web.

I just hoped it wasn't expelling anything else.

As the lacy net began to fall in folds at his feet, Hassan said something in Arabic, disgusted and amused. My grasp of the language remained patchy; Sadiq translated for me, his voice muffled by his face mask: "He says probably most of the weight of the thing will be dead insects." He shooed the youths back toward the truck before following himself, as the wind blew a glistening curtain over our heads. It descended far too slowly to trap us, but I hastened up the slope.

We watched from the truck as the Wall came down, the wave of dehydration propagating along its length. If the gel had been an elusive sight close up, the residue was entirely invisible in the distance; there was less substance to it than a very long pantyhose—albeit, pantyhose clogged with gnats.

The smart polymer was the invention of Sonja Helvig, a Norwegian chemist; I'd tweaked her original design for this application. Sadiq and his students were civil engineers, responsible for scaling everything up to the point where it could have a practical benefit. On those terms, this experiment was still nothing but a minor field trial.

I turned to Sadiq. "You did some mine clearance once, didn't you?"

"Years ago." Before I could say anything more, he'd caught my drift. "You're thinking that might have been more satisfying? Bang, and it's gone, the proof is there in front of you?"

"One less mine, one less bomblet," I said. "However many thousands there were to deal with, at least you could tick each one off as a definite achievement."

"That's true. It was a good feeling." He shrugged. "But what should we do? Give up on this, because it's harder?"

He took the truck down the slope, then supervised the students as they attached the wisps of polymer to the specialized winch they'd built. Hassan and Rashid were in their twenties, but they could easily have passed for adolescents. After the war, the dictator and his former backers in the west had found it mutually expedient to have a generation of Iraqi children grow up malnourished and without medical care, if they grew up at all. More than a million people had died under the sanctions. My own sick joke of a nation had sent part of its navy to join the blockade, while the rest stayed home to fend off boatloads of refugees from this, and other, atrocities. General Mustache was long dead, but his comrades-in-genocide with more salubrious addresses were all still at large: doing lecture tours, running think tanks, lobbying for the Nobel peace prize.

As the strands of polymer wound around a core inside the winch's protective barrel, the alpha count rose steadily. It was a good sign: the fine particles of uranium oxide trapped by the Wall had remained bound to the polymer during dehydration, and the reeling in of the net. The radiation from the few grams of U-238 we'd collected was far too low to be a hazard in itself; the thing to avoid was ingesting the dust, and even then the unpleasant effects were as much chemical as radiological. Hopefully, the polymer had also bound its other targets: the organic carcinogens that had been strewn across Kuwait and southern Iraq by the apocalyptic oil well fires. There was no way to determine that until we did a full chemical analysis.

We were all in high spirits on the ride back. What we'd plucked from the wind in the last six weeks wouldn't spare a single person from leukaemia, but it now seemed possible that over the years, over the decades, the technology would make a real difference.

~w~

I MISSED the connection in Singapore for a direct flight home to Sydney, so I had to go via Perth. There was a four-hour wait in Perth; I paced the transit lounge, restless and impatient. I hadn't set eyes on Francine since she'd left Basra three months earlier; she didn't approve of clogging up the limited bandwidth into Iraq with decadent video. When I'd called her from Singapore she'd been busy, and now I couldn't decide whether or not to try again.

Just when I'd resolved to call her, an email came through on my notepad, saying that she'd received my message and would meet me at the airport.

In Sydney, I stood by the baggage carousel, searching the crowd. When I finally saw Francine approaching, she was looking straight at me, smiling.

I left the carousel and walked toward her; she stopped and let me close the gap, keeping her eyes fixed on mine. There was a mischievousness to her expression, as if she'd arranged some kind of prank, but I couldn't guess what it might be.

When I was almost in front of her, she turned slightly, and spread her arms. "Ta-da!"

I froze, speechless. *Why hadn't she told me?*

I walked up to her and embraced her, but she'd read my expression. "Don't be angry, Ben. I was afraid you'd come home early if you knew."

"You're right, I would have." My thoughts were piling up on top of each other; I had three months' worth of reactions to get through in fifteen seconds. *We hadn't planned this. We couldn't afford it. I wasn't ready.*

Suddenly I started weeping, too shocked to be self-conscious in the crowd. The knot of panic and confusion inside me dissolved. I held her more tightly, and felt the swelling in her body against my hip.

"Are you happy?" Francine asked.

I laughed and nodded, choking out the words: "This is wonderful!"

I meant it. I was still afraid, but it was an exuberant fear. Another ocean had opened up before us. We would find our bearings. We would cross it together.

∿

IT TOOK me several days to come down to Earth. We didn't have a real chance to talk until the weekend; Francine had a teaching position at UNSW, and though she could have set her own research aside for a couple of days, marking could wait for no one. There were a thousand things to plan; the six-month UNESCO fellowship that had paid for me to take part in the project in Basra had expired, and I'd need to start earning money again soon, but the fact that I'd made no commitments yet gave me some welcome flexibility.

On Monday, alone in the flat again, I started catching up on all the journals I'd neglected. In Iraq I'd been obsessively single-minded, instructing my knowledge miner to keep me informed of work relevant to the Wall, to the exclusion of everything else.

Skimming through a summary of six months' worth of papers, a report in *Science* caught my eye: *An Experimental Model for Decoherence in the Many-Worlds Cosmology*. A group at Delft University in the Netherlands had arranged for a simple quantum computer to carry out a sequence of arithmetic operations on a register which had been prepared to contain an equal superposition of binary representations of two different numbers. This in itself was nothing new; superpositions representing up to 128 numbers were now manipulated daily, albeit only under laboratory conditions, at close to absolute zero.

Unusually, though, at each stage of the calculation the qubits containing the numbers in question had been deliberately entangled with other, spare qubits in the computer. The effect of this was that the section performing the calculation had ceased to be in a pure quantum state: it behaved, not as if it contained two numbers simultaneously, but as if there were merely an equal chance of it containing either one. This had undermined the quantum nature of the calculation, just as surely as if the whole machine had been imperfectly shielded and become entangled with objects in the environment.

There was one crucial difference, though: in this case, the experimenters had still had access to the spare qubits that had made the calculation behave classically. When they performed an appropriate measurement on the state of the computer *as a whole*, it was shown to have remained in a superposition all along. A single observation couldn't prove this, but the experiment had been repeated thousands of times, and within the margins of error, their prediction was confirmed: although the superposition had become undetectable when they ignored the spare qubits, it had never really gone away. *Both* classical calculations had always taken place simultaneously, even though they'd lost the ability to interact in a quantum-mechanical fashion.

I sat at my desk, pondering the result. On one level, it was just a scaling-up of the quantum eraser experiments of the '90s, but the image of a tiny computer program running through its paces, appearing "to itself" to be unique and alone, while in fact a second, equally oblivious version had been executing beside it all along, carried a lot more resonance than an interference experiment with photons. I'd become used to the idea of quantum computers performing several calculations at once, but that conjuring trick had always seemed abstract and ethereal, precisely because the parts continued to act as a complicated whole right to the end. What struck home *here* was the stark demonstration of the way each calculation could come to appear as a distinct classical history, as solid and mundane as the shuffling of beads on an abacus.

When Francine arrived home I was cooking dinner, but I grabbed my notepad and showed her the paper.

"Yeah, I've seen it," she said.

"What do you think?"

She raised her hands and recoiled in mock alarm.

"I'm serious."

"What do you want me to say? Does this prove the Many Worlds interpretation? No. Does it make it easier to understand, to have a toy model like this? Yes."

"But does it sway you at all?" I persisted. "Do you believe the results would still hold, if they could be scaled up indefinitely?" From a toy universe, a handful of qubits, to the real one.

She shrugged. "I don't really need to be swayed. I always thought the MWI was the most plausible interpretation anyway."

I left it at that, and went back to the kitchen while she pulled out a stack of assignments.

That night, as we lay in bed together, I couldn't get the Delft experiment out of my mind.

"Do you believe there are other versions of us?" I asked Francine.

"I suppose there must be." She conceded the point as if it was something abstract and metaphysical, and I was being pedantic even to raise it. People who professed belief in the MWI never seemed to want to take it seriously, let alone personally.

"And that doesn't bother you?"

"No," she said blithely. "Since I'm powerless to change the situation, what's the use in being upset about it?"

"That's very pragmatic," I said. Francine reached over and thumped me on the shoulder. "That was a compliment!" I protested. "I envy you for having come to terms with it so easily."

"I haven't, really," she admitted. "I've just resolved not to let it worry me, which isn't quite the same thing."

I turned to face her, though in the near-darkness we could barely see each other. I said, "What gives you the most satisfaction in life?"

"I take it you're not in the mood to be fobbed off with a soppy romantic answer?" She sighed. "I don't know. Solving problems. Getting things right."

"What if for every problem you solve, there's someone just like you who fails, instead?"

"I cope with my failures," she said. "Let them cope with theirs."

"You know it doesn't work like that. Some of them simply *don't* cope. Whatever you find the strength to do, there'll be someone else who won't."

Francine had no reply.

I said, "A couple of weeks ago, I asked Sadiq about the time he was doing mine clearance. He said it was more satisfying than mopping up DU; one little explosion, right before your eyes, and you know you've done something worthwhile. We all get moments in our lives like that, with that pure, unambiguous sense of achievement: whatever else we might screw up, at least there's one thing that we've done right." I laughed uneasily. "I think I'd go mad, if I couldn't rely on that."

Francine said, "You can. Nothing you've done will ever disappear from under your feet. No one's going to march up and take it away from you."

"I know." My skin crawled, at the image of some less favored alter ego turning up on our doorstep, demanding his dues. "That seems so fucking selfish, though. I don't want everything that makes me happy to be at the expense of someone else. I don't want every choice to be like…fighting other versions of myself for the prize in some zero-sum game."

"No." Francine hesitated. "But if the reality is like that, what can you do about it?"

Her words hung in the darkness. What could I do about it? Nothing. So did I really want to dwell on it, corroding the foundations of my own happiness, when there was absolutely nothing to be gained, for anyone?

"You're right. This is crazy." I leaned over and kissed her. "I'd better let you get to sleep."

"It's not crazy," she said. "But I don't have any answers."

⌁

THE NEXT morning, after Francine had left for work, I picked up my notepad and saw that she'd mailed me an e-book: an anthology of cheesy "alternate (sic) history" stories from the '90s, entitled *My God, It's Full of Tsars!* "What if Gandhi had been a ruthless soldier of fortune? What if Theodore Roosevelt had faced a Martian invasion? What if the Nazis had had Janet Jackson's choreographer?"

I skimmed through the introduction, alternately cackling and groaning, then filed the book away and got down to work. I had a dozen minor administrative tasks to complete for UNESCO, before I could start searching in earnest for my next position.

By mid-afternoon, I was almost done, but the growing sense of achievement I felt at having buckled down and cleared away these tedious obligations brought with it the corollary: someone infinitesimally different from me—someone who had shared my entire history up until that morning—had procrastinated instead. The triviality of this observation only made it more unsettling; the Delft experiment was seeping into my daily life on the most mundane level.

I dug out the book Francine had sent and tried reading a few of the stories, but the authors' relentlessly camp take on the premise hardly amounted to a *reductio ad absurdum*, or even a comical existential balm. I didn't really care how hilarious it would have been if Marilyn Monroe had been involved in a bedroom farce with Richard Feynman and Richard Nixon. I just wanted to lose the suffocating conviction that everything I had become was a mirage; that my life had been nothing but a blinkered view of a kind of torture chamber, where every glorious reprieve I'd ever celebrated had in fact been an unwitting betrayal.

If fiction had no comfort to offer, what about fact? Even if the Many Worlds cosmology was correct, no one knew for certain what the consequences were. It was a fallacy that literally everything that was physically possible had to occur; most cosmologists I'd read believed that the universe as a whole possessed a single, definite quantum state, and while that state would appear from within as a multitude of distinct classical histories, there was no reason to assume that these histories amounted to some kind of exhaustive catalog. The same thing held true on a smaller scale: every time two people sat down to a game of chess, there was no reason to believe that they played every possible game.

And if I'd stood in an alley, nine years before, struggling with my conscience? My subjective sense of indecision proved nothing, but even if I'd suffered no qualms and acted without hesitation, to find a human being in a quantum state of pure, unshakeable resolve would have been freakishly unlikely at best, and in fact was probably physically impossible.

"Fuck this." I didn't know when I'd set myself up for this bout of paranoia, but I wasn't going to indulge it for another second. I banged my head against the desk a few times, then picked up my notepad and went straight to an employment site.

The thoughts didn't vanish entirely; it was too much like trying not to think of a pink elephant. Each time they recurred, though, I found I could shout them down with threats of taking myself straight to a psychiatrist. The prospect of having to explain such a bizarre mental problem was enough to give me access to hitherto untapped reserves of self-discipline.

By the time I started cooking dinner, I was feeling merely foolish. If Francine mentioned the subject again, I'd make a joke of it. I didn't need a psychiatrist. I was a little insecure about my good fortune, and still somewhat rattled by the news of impending fatherhood, but it would hardly have been healthier to take everything for granted.

My notepad chimed. Francine had blocked the video again, as if band-width, even here, was as precious as water.

"Hello."

"Ben? I've had some bleeding. I'm in a taxi. Can you meet me at St Vincent's?"

Her voice was steady, but my own mouth went dry. "Sure. I'll be there in fifteen minutes." I couldn't add anything: *I love you, it will be all right, hold on.* She didn't need that, it would have jinxed everything.

Half an hour later, I was still caught in traffic, white-knuckled with rage and helplessness. I stared down at the dashboard, at the real-time map with every other gridlocked vehicle marked, and finally stopped deluding myself that at any moment I would turn into a magically deserted side-street and weave my way across the city in just a few more minutes.

In the ward, behind the curtains drawn around her bed, Francine lay curled and rigid, her back turned, refusing to look at me. All I could do was stand beside her. The gynecologist was yet to explain everything properly, but the miscarriage had been accompanied by complications, and she'd had to perform surgery.

Before I'd applied for the UNESCO fellowship, we'd discussed the risks. For two prudent, well-informed, short-term visitors, the danger had seemed microscopic. Francine had never traveled out into the desert with me, and even for the locals in Basra the rates of birth defects and miscarriages had fallen a long way from their peaks. We were both taking contraceptives; con-doms had seemed like overkill. *Had I brought it back to her, from the desert? A speck of dust, trapped beneath my foreskin? Had I poisoned her while we were making love?*

Francine turned toward me. The skin around her eyes was gray and swollen, and I could see how much effort it took for her to meet my gaze. She drew her hands out from under the bedclothes, and let me hold them; they were freezing.

After a while, she started sobbing, but she wouldn't release my hands. I stroked the back of her thumb with my own thumb, a tiny, gentle movement.

2020

"How DO you feel now?" Olivia Maslin didn't quite make eye contact as she addressed me; the image of my brain activity painted on her retinas was clearly holding her attention.

"Fine," I said. "Exactly the same as I did before you started the infusion."

I was reclining on something like a dentist's couch, halfway between sitting and lying, wearing a tight-fitting cap studded with magnetic sensors and inducers. It was impossible to ignore the slight coolness of the liquid flowing into the vein in my forearm, but that sensation was no different than it had been on the previous occasion, a fortnight before.

"Could you count to ten for me, please."

I obliged.

"Now close your eyes and picture the same familiar face as the last time."

She'd told me I could choose anyone; I'd picked Francine. I brought back the image, then suddenly recalled that, the first time, after contemplating the detailed picture in my head for a few seconds—as if I was preparing to give a description to the police—I'd started thinking about Francine herself. On cue, the same transition occurred again: the frozen, forensic likeness became flesh and blood.

I was led through the whole sequence of activities once more: reading the same short story ("Two Old-Timers" by F. Scott Fitzgerald), listening to the same piece of music (from Rossini's *The Thieving Magpie*), recounting the same childhood memory (my first day at school). At some point, I lost any trace of anxiety about repeating my earlier mental states with sufficient fidelity; after all, the experiment had been designed to cope with the inevitable variation between the two sessions. I was just one volunteer out of dozens, and half the subjects would be receiving nothing but saline on both occasions. For all I knew, I was one of them: a control, merely setting the baseline against which any real effect would be judged.

If I was receiving the coherence disruptors, though, then as far as I could tell they'd had no effect on me. My inner life hadn't evaporated as the molecules bound to the microtubules in my neurons, guaranteeing that any kind of quantum coherence those structures might otherwise have maintained would be lost to the environment in a fraction of a picosecond.

Personally, I'd never subscribed to Penrose's theory that quantum effects might play a role in consciousness; calculations dating back to a seminal paper by Max Tegmark, twenty years before, had already made sustained coherence in any neural structure extremely unlikely. Nevertheless, it had taken considerable ingenuity on the part of Olivia and her team to rule out the idea definitively, in a series of clear-cut experiments. Over the past two years, they'd chased the ghost away from each of the various structures that different factions of Penrose's disciples had anointed as the essential quantum components of the brain. The earliest proposal—the microtubules, huge polymeric molecules that formed a kind of skeleton inside every cell—had turned out to be the hardest to target for disruption. But now it was entirely possible that the cytoskeletons of my very own neurons were dotted with molecules that coupled them strongly to a noisy microwave field in which my skull was, definitely, bathed. In which case, my microtubules had about as much chance of exploiting quantum effects as I had of playing a game of squash with a version of myself from a parallel universe.

When the experiment was over, Olivia thanked me, then became even more distant as she reviewed the data. Raj, one of her graduate students, slid out the needle and stuck a plaster over the tiny puncture wound, then helped me out of the cap.

"I know you don't know yet if I was a control or not," I said, "but have you noticed significant differences, with anyone?" I was almost the last subject in the microtubule trials; any effect should have shown up by now.

Olivia smiled enigmatically. "You'll just have to wait for publication." Raj leaned down and whispered, "No, never."

I climbed off the couch. "The zombie walks!" Raj declaimed. I lunged hungrily for his brain; he ducked away, laughing, while Olivia watched us with an expression of pained indulgence. Die-hard members of the Penrose camp claimed that Olivia's experiments proved nothing, because even if people *behaved* identically while all quantum effects were ruled out, they could be doing this as mere automata, totally devoid of consciousness. When Olivia had offered to let her chief detractor experience coherence disruption for himself, he'd replied that this would be no more persuasive, because memories laid down while you were a zombie would be indistinguishable from ordinary memories, so that looking back on the experience, you'd notice nothing unusual.

This was sheer desperation; you might as well assert that everyone in the world but yourself was a zombie, and you were one, too, every second Tuesday. As the experiments were repeated by other groups around the world, those people who'd backed the Penrose theory as a scientific hypothesis, rather than adopting it as a kind of mystical dogma, would gradually accept that it had been refuted.

~~~

I LEFT the neuroscience building and walked across the campus, back toward my office in the physics department. It was a mild, clear spring morning, with students out lying on the grass, dozing off with books balanced over their faces like tents. There were still some advantages to reading from old-fashioned sheaves of e-paper. I'd only had my own eyes chipped the year before, and though I'd adapted to the technology easily enough, I still found it disconcerting to wake on a Sunday morning to find Francine reading the *Herald* beside me with her eyes shut.

Olivia's results didn't surprise me, but it was satisfying to have the matter resolved once and for all: consciousness was a purely classical phenomenon. Among other things, this meant that there was no compelling reason to believe that software running on a classical computer could not be conscious. Of course, everything in the universe obeyed quantum mechanics at some level, but Paul Benioff, one of the pioneers of quantum computing, had shown back in the '80s that you could build a classical Turing machine from quantum mechanical parts, and over the last few years, in my spare time, I'd studied the branch of quantum computing theory that concerned itself with *avoiding* quantum effects.

Back in my office, I summoned up a schematic of the device I called the Qusp: the quantum singleton processor. The Qusp would employ all the techniques designed to shield the latest generation of quantum computers from entanglement with their environment, but it would use them to a very different end. A quantum computer was shielded so it could perform a multitude of parallel calculations, without each one spawning a separate history of its own, in which only one answer was accessible. The Qusp would perform just a single calculation at a time, but on its way to the unique result it would be able to pass safely through superpositions that included any number of alternatives, without those alternatives being made real. Cut off from the outside world during each computational step, it would keep its temporary quantum ambivalence as private and inconsequential as a daydream, never being forced to act out every possibility it dared to entertain.

The Qusp would still need to interact with its environment whenever it gathered data about the world, and that interaction would inevitably split it into different versions. If you attached a camera to the Qusp and pointed it at an ordinary object—a rock, a plant, a bird—that object could hardly be expected to possess a single classical history, and so neither would the combined system of Qusp plus rock, Qusp plus plant, Qusp plus bird.

The Qusp itself, though, would never initiate the split. In a given set of circumstances, it would only ever produce a single response. An AI running on the Qusp could make its decisions as whimsically, or with as much weighty deliberation as it liked, but for each distinct scenario it confronted, in the end it would only make one choice, only follow one course of action.

I closed the file, and the image vanished from my retinas. For all the work I'd put into the design, I'd made no effort to build the thing. I'd been using it as little more than a talisman: whenever I found myself picturing my life as a tranquil dwelling built over a slaughter house, I'd summon up the Qusp as a symbol of hope. It was proof of a possibility, and a possibility was all it took. Nothing in the laws of physics could prevent a small portion of humanity's descendants from escaping their ancestors' dissipation.

Yet I'd shied away from any attempt to see that promise fulfilled, firsthand. In part, I'd been afraid of delving too deeply and uncovering a flaw in the Qusp's design, robbing myself of the one crutch that kept me standing when the horror swept over me. It had also been a matter of guilt: I'd been the one granted happiness, so many times, that it had seemed unconscionable to aspire to that state yet again. I'd knocked so many of my hapless cousins out of the ring, it was time I threw a fight and let the prize go to my opponent instead.

That last excuse was idiotic. The stronger my determination to build the Qusp, the more branches there would be in which it was real. Weakening my resolve was *not* an act of charity, surrendering the benefits to someone else; it merely impoverished every future version of me, and everyone they touched.

I did have a third excuse. It was time I dealt with that one, too.

I called Francine.

"Are you free for lunch?" I asked. She hesitated; there was always work she could be doing. "To discuss the Cauchy-Riemann equations?" I suggested.

She smiled. It was our code, when the request was a special one. "All right. One o'clock?"

I nodded. "I'll see you then."

⌁⌁⌁

FRANCINE WAS twenty minutes late, but that was less of a wait than I was used to. She'd been appointed deputy head of the mathematics department eighteen months before, and she still had some teaching duties as well as all the new administrative work. Over the last eight years, I'd had a dozen short-term contracts with various bodies—government departments, corporations, NGOs—before finally ending up as a very lowly member of the physics department at our *alma mater*. I did envy her the prestige and security of her job, but I'd been happy with most of the work I'd done, even if it had been too scattered between disciplines to contribute to anything like a traditional career path.

I'd bought Francine a plate of cheese-and-salad sandwiches, and she attacked them hungrily as soon as she sat down. I said, "I've got ten minutes at the most, haven't I?"

She covered her mouth with her hand and replied defensively, "It could have waited until tonight, couldn't it?"

"Sometimes I can't put things off. I have to act while I still have the courage."

At this ominous prelude she chewed more slowly. "You did the second stage of Olivia's experiment this morning, didn't you?"

"Yeah." I'd discussed the whole procedure with her before I volunteered.

"So I take it you didn't lose consciousness, when your neurons became marginally more classical than usual?" She sipped chocolate milk through a straw.

"No. Apparently no one ever loses anything. That's not official yet, but—"

154

Francine nodded, unsurprised. We shared the same position on the Penrose theory; there was no need to discuss it again now.

I said, "I want to know if you're going to have the operation."

She continued drinking for a few more seconds, then released the straw and wiped her upper lip with her thumb, unnecessarily. "You want me to make up my mind about that, here and now?"

"No." The damage to her uterus from the miscarriage could be repaired; we'd been discussing the possibility for almost five years. We'd both had comprehensive chelation therapy to remove any trace of U-238. We could have children in the usual way with a reasonable degree of safety, if that was what we wanted. "But if you've already decided, I want you to tell me now."

Francine looked wounded. "That's unfair."

"What is? Implying that you might not have told me, the instant you decided?"

"No. Implying that it's all in my hands."

I said, "I'm not washing my hands of the decision. You know how I feel. But you know I'd back you all the way, if you said you wanted to carry a child." I believed I would have. Maybe it was a form of doublethink, but I couldn't treat the birth of one more ordinary child as some kind of atrocity, and refuse to be a part of it.

"Fine. But what will you do if I don't?" She examined my face calmly. I think she already knew, but she wanted me to spell it out.

"We could always adopt," I observed casually.

"Yes, we could do that." She smiled slightly; she knew that made me lose my ability to bluff, even faster than when she stared me down.

I stopped pretending that there was any mystery left; she'd seen right through me from the start. I said, "I just don't want to do this, then discover that it makes you feel that you've been cheated out of what you really wanted."

"It wouldn't," she insisted. "It wouldn't rule out anything. We could still have a natural child as well."

"Not as easily." This would not be like merely having workaholic parents, or an ordinary brother or sister to compete with for attention.

"You only want to do this if I can promise you that it's the only child we'd ever have?" Francine shook her head. "I'm not going to promise that. I don't intend having the operation any time soon, but I'm not going to swear that I won't change my mind. Nor am I going to swear that if we do this it will make no difference to what happens later. It will be a factor. How could it not be? But it won't be enough to rule anything in or out."

I looked away, across the rows of tables, at all the students wrapped up in their own concerns. She was right; I was being unreasonable. I'd wanted this to be a choice with no possible downside, a way of making the best of our situation, but no one could guarantee that. It would be a gamble, like everything else.

I turned back to Francine.

"All right; I'll stop trying to pin you down. What I want to do right now is go ahead and build the Qusp. And when it's finished, if we're certain we can trust it...I want us to raise a child with it. I want us to raise an AI."

2029

I MET Francine at the airport, and we drove across São Paulo through curtains of wild, lashing rain. I was amazed that her plane hadn't been diverted; a tropical storm had just hit the coast, halfway between us and Rio.

"So much for giving you a tour of the city," I lamented. Through the windscreen, our actual surroundings were all but invisible; the bright overlay we both perceived, surreally colored and detailed, made the experience rather like perusing a 3D map while trapped in a car wash.

Francine was pensive, or tired from the flight. I found it hard to think of San Francisco as remote when the time difference was so small, and even when I'd made the journey north to visit her, it had been nothing compared to all the ocean-spanning marathons I'd sat through in the past.

We both had an early night. The next morning, Francine accompanied me to my cluttered workroom in the basement of the university's engineering department. I'd been chasing grants and collaborators around the world, like a child on a treasure hunt, slowly piecing together a device that few of my colleagues believed was worth creating for its own sake. Fortunately, I'd managed to find pretexts—or even genuine spin-offs—for almost every stage of the work. Quantum computing, *per se*, had become bogged down in recent years, stymied by both a shortage of practical algorithms and a limit to the complexity of superpositions that could be sustained. The Qusp had nudged the technological envelope in some promising directions, without making any truly exorbitant demands; the states it juggled were relatively simple, and they only needed to be kept isolated for milliseconds at a time.

I introduced Carlos, Maria and Jun, but then they made themselves scarce as I showed Francine around. We still had a demonstration of the "balanced decoupling" principle set up on a bench, for the tour by one of our corporate donors the week before. What caused an imperfectly shielded quantum computer to decohere was the fact that each possible state of the device affected its environment slightly differently. The shielding itself could always be improved, but Carlos's group had perfected a way to buy a little more protection by sheer deviousness. In the demonstration rig, the flow of energy through the device remained absolutely constant whatever state it was in, because any drop in power consumption by the main set of quantum gates was compensated for by a rise in a set of balancing gates, and *vice versa*. This gave the environment one less clue by which to discern internal differences in the processor, and to tear any superposition apart into mutually disconnected branches.

Francine knew all the theory backward, but she'd never seen this hardware in action. When I invited her to twiddle the controls, she took to the rig like a child with a game console.

"You really should have joined the team," I said.

"Maybe I did," she countered. "In another branch."

She'd moved from UNSW to Berkeley two years before, not long after I'd moved from Delft to São Paulo; it was the closest suitable position she could find. At the time, I'd resented the fact that she'd refused to compromise and work remotely; with only five hours' difference, teaching at Berkeley from São Paulo would not have been impossible. In the end, though, I'd accepted the fact that she'd wanted to keep on testing me, testing both of us. If we weren't strong enough to stay together through the trials of a prolonged physical separation—or if I was not sufficiently committed to the project to endure whatever sacrifices it entailed—she did not want us proceeding to the next stage.

I led her to the corner bench, where a nondescript gray box half a meter across sat, apparently inert. I gestured to it, and our retinal overlays transformed its appearance, "revealing" a maze with a transparent lid embedded in the top of the device. In one chamber of the maze, a slightly cartoonish mouse sat motionless. Not quite dead, not quite sleeping.

"This is the famous Zelda?" Francine asked.

"Yes." Zelda was a neural network, a stripped-down, stylized mouse brain. There were newer, fancier versions available, much closer to the real thing, but the ten-year-old, public domain Zelda had been good enough for our purposes.

Three other chambers held cheese. "Right now, she has no experience of the maze," I explained. "So let's start her up and watch her explore." I gestured, and Zelda began scampering around, trying out different passages, deftly reversing each time she hit a *cul-de-sac*. "Her brain is running on a Qusp, but the maze is implemented on an ordinary classical computer, so in terms of coherence issues, it's really no different from a physical maze."

"Which means that each time she takes in information, she gets entangled with the outside world," Francine suggested.

"Absolutely. But she always holds off doing that until the Qusp has completed its current computational step, and every qubit contains a definite zero or a definite one. She's never in two minds when she lets the world in, so the entanglement process doesn't split her into separate branches."

Francine continued to watch, in silence. Zelda finally found one of the chambers containing a reward; when she'd eaten it, a hand scooped her up and returned her to her starting point, then replaced the cheese.

"Here are ten thousand previous trials, superimposed." I replayed the data. It looked as if a single mouse was running through the maze, moving just as we'd seen her move when I'd begun the latest experiment. Restored each time to exactly the same starting condition, and confronted with exactly the same environment, Zelda—like any computer program with no truly random influences—had simply repeated herself. All ten thousand trials had yielded identical results.

To a casual observer, unaware of the context, this would have been a singularly unimpressive performance. Faced with exactly one situation, Zelda the virtual mouse did exactly one thing. So what? If you'd been able to wind back a flesh-and-blood mouse's memory with the same degree of precision, wouldn't it have repeated itself too?

Francine said, "Can you cut off the shielding? And the balanced decoupling?"

"Yep." I obliged her, and initiated a new trial.

Zelda took a different path this time, exploring the maze by a differ-ent route. Though the initial condition of the neural net was identical, the switching processes taking place within the Qusp were now opened up to the environment constantly, and superpositions of several different eigenstates— states in which the Qusp's qubits possessed definite binary values, which in turn led to Zelda making definite choices—were becoming entangled with the outside world. According to the Copenhagen interpretation of quantum mechanics, this interaction was randomly "collapsing" the superpositions into single eigenstates; Zelda was still doing just one thing at a time, but her behavior had ceased to be deterministic. According to the MWI, the interaction was transforming the environment—Francine and me included—into a superposition with components that were coupled to each eigenstate; Zelda was actually running the maze in many different ways simultaneously, and other versions of us were seeing her take all those other routes.

Which scenario was correct?

I said, "I'll reconfigure everything now, to wrap the whole setup in a Delft cage." A "Delft cage" was jargon for the situation I'd first read about seventeen years before: instead of opening up the Qusp to the environment, I'd connect it to a second quantum computer, and let *that* play the role of the outside world.

We could no longer watch Zelda moving about in real time, but after the trial was completed, it was possible to test the combined system of both computers against the hypothesis that it was in a pure quantum state in which Zelda had run the maze along hundreds of different routes, all at once. I displayed a representation of the conjectured state, built up by superimposing all the paths she'd taken in ten thousand unshielded trials.

The test result flashed up: CONSISTENT.

"One measurement proves nothing," Francine pointed out.

"No." I repeated the trial. Again, the hypothesis was not refuted. If Zelda had actually run the maze along just one path, the probability of the computers' joint state passing this imperfect test was about one percent. For passing it twice, the odds were about one in ten thousand.

I repeated it a third time, then a fourth.

Francine said, "That's enough." She actually looked queasy. The image of the hundreds of blurred mouse trails on the display was not a literal photograph of anything, but if the old Delft experiment had been enough to give me a visceral sense of the reality of the multiverse, perhaps this demonstration had finally done the same for her.

"Can I show you one more thing?" I asked.

"Keep the Delft cage, but restore the Qusp's shielding?"

"Right."

I did it. The Qusp was now fully protected once more whenever it was not in an eigenstate, but this time, it was the second quantum computer, not the outside world, to which it was intermittently exposed. If Zelda split into multiple branches again, then she'd only take that fake environment with her, and we'd still have our hands on all the evidence.

Tested against the hypothesis that no split had occurred, the verdict was: CONSISTENT. CONSISTENT. CONSISTENT.

~w~

WE WENT out to dinner with the whole of the team, but Francine pleaded a headache and left early. She insisted that I stay and finish the meal, and I didn't argue; she was not the kind of person who expected you to assume that she was being politely selfless, while secretly hoping to be contradicted.

After Francine had left, Maria turned to me. "So you two are really going ahead with the Frankenchild?" She'd been teasing me about this for as long as I'd known her, but apparently she hadn't been game to raise the subject in Francine's presence.

"We still have to talk about it." I felt uncomfortable myself, now, discussing the topic the moment Francine was absent. Confessing my ambition when I applied to join the team was one thing; it would have been dishonest to keep my collaborators in the dark about my ultimate intentions. Now that the enabling technology was more or less completed, though, the issue seemed far more personal.

Carlos said breezily, "Why not? There are so many others now. Sophie. Linus. Theo. Probably a hundred we don't even know about. It's not as if Ben's child won't have playmates." Adai—Autonomously Developing Artificial Intelligences—had been appearing in a blaze of controversy every few months for the last four years. A Swiss researcher, Isabelle Schib, had taken the old models of morphogenesis that had led to software like Zelda, refined the technique by several orders of magnitude, and applied it to human genetic data. Wedded to sophisticated prosthetic bodies, Isabelle's creations inhabited the physical world and learned from their experience, just like any other child.

Jun shook his head reprovingly. "I wouldn't raise a child with no legal rights. What happens when you die? For all you know, it could end up as someone's property."

I'd been over this with Francine. "I can't believe that in ten or twenty years' time there won't be citizenship laws, somewhere in the world."

Jun snorted. "Twenty years! How long did it take the U.S. to emancipate their slaves?"

Carlos interjected, "Who's going to create an adai just to use it as a slave? If you want something biddable, write ordinary software. If you need consciousness, humans are cheaper."

Maria said, "It won't come down to economics. It's the nature of the things that will determine how they're treated."

"You mean the xenophobia they'll face?" I suggested.

Maria shrugged. "You make it sound like racism, but we aren't talking about human beings. Once you have software with goals of its own, free to do whatever it likes, where will it end? The first generation makes the next one better, faster, smarter; the second generation even more so. Before we know it, we're like ants to them."

Carlos groaned. "Not that hoary old fallacy! If you really believe that stating the analogy 'ants are to humans, as humans are to x' is proof that it's possible to solve for x, then I'll meet you where the south pole is like the equator."

I said, "The Qusp runs no faster than an organic brain; we need to keep the switching rate low, because that makes the shielding requirements less stringent. It might be possible to nudge those parameters, eventually, but there's no reason in the world why an adai would be better equipped to do that than you or I would. As for making their own offspring smarter...even if Schib's group has been perfectly successful, they will have merely translated human neural development from one substrate to another. They won't have 'improved' on the process at all—whatever that might mean. So if the adai have any advantage over us, it will be no more than the advantage shared by flesh-and-blood children: cultural transmission of one more generation's worth of experience."

Maria frowned, but she had no immediate comeback.

Jun said dryly, "Plus immortality."

"Well, yes, there is that," I conceded.

〜〜

FRANCINE WAS awake when I arrived home.

"Have you still got a headache?" I whispered.

"No."

I undressed and climbed into bed beside her.

She said, "You know what I miss the most? When we're fucking on-line?"

"This had better not be complicated; I'm out of practice."

"Kissing."

I kissed her, slowly and tenderly, and she melted beneath me. "Three more months," I promised, "and I'll move up to Berkeley."

"To be my kept man."

"I prefer the term 'unpaid but highly valued caregiver.'" Francine stiffened. I said, "We can talk about that later." I started kissing her again, but she turned her face away.

"I'm afraid," she said.

"So am I," I assured her. "That's a good sign. Everything worth doing is terrifying."

"But not everything terrifying is good."

I rolled over and lay beside her. She said, "On one level, it's easy. What greater gift could you give a child, than the power to make real decisions? What worse fate could you spare her from, than being forced to act against her better judgment, over and over? When you put it like that, it's simple.

"But every fiber in my body still rebels against it. How will she feel, knowing what she is? How will she make friends? How will she belong? How will she not despise us for making her a freak? And what if we're robbing her of something she'd value: living a billion lives, never being forced to choose between them? What if she sees the gift as a kind of impoverishment?"

"She can always drop the shielding on the Qusp," I said. "Once she understands the issues, she can choose for herself."

"That's true." Francine did not sound mollified at all; she would have thought of that long before I'd mentioned it, but she wasn't looking for concrete answers. Every ordinary human instinct screamed at us that we were embarking on something *dangerous, unnatural, hubristic*—but those instincts were more about safeguarding our own reputations than protecting our child-to-be. No parent, save the most willfully negligent, would be pilloried if their flesh-and-blood child turned out to be ungrateful for life; if I'd railed against my own mother and father because I'd found fault in the existential conditions with which I'd been lumbered, it wasn't hard to guess which side would attract the most sympathy from the world at large. Anything that went wrong with *our* child would be grounds for lynching—however much love, sweat, and soul-searching had gone into her creation—because we'd had the temerity to be dissatisfied with the kind of fate that everyone else happily inflicted on their own.

I said, "You saw Zelda today, spread across the branches. You know, deep down now, that the same thing happens to all of us."

"Yes." Something tore inside me as Francine uttered that admission. I'd never really wanted her to feel it, the way I did.

I persisted. "Would you willingly sentence your own child to that condition? And your grandchildren? And your great-grandchildren?"

"No," Francine replied. A part of her hated me now; I could hear it in her voice. It was *my* curse, *my* obsession; before she met me, she'd managed to believe and not believe, taking her acceptance of the multiverse lightly.

I said, "I can't do this without you."

"You can, actually. More easily than any of the alternatives. You wouldn't even need a stranger to donate an egg."

"I can't do it unless you're behind me. If you say the word, I'll stop here. We've built the Qusp. We've shown that it can work. Even if we don't do this last part ourselves, someone else will, in a decade or two."

"If *we* don't do this," Francine observed acerbically, "we'll simply do it in another branch."

I said, "That's true, but it's no use thinking that way. In the end, I can't function unless I pretend that my choices are real. I doubt that anyone can."

Francine was silent for a long time. I stared up into the darkness of the room, trying hard not to contemplate the near certainty that her decision would go both ways.

Finally, she spoke.

"Then let's make a child who doesn't need to pretend."

2031

ISABELLE SCHIB welcomed us into her office. In person, she was slightly less intimidating than she was on-line; it wasn't anything different in her appearance or manner, just the ordinariness of her surroundings. I'd envisaged her ensconced in some vast, pristine, high-tech building, not a couple of pokey rooms on a back-street in Basel.

Once the pleasantries were out of the way, Isabelle got straight to the point. "You've been accepted," she announced. "I'll send you the contract later today."

My throat constricted with panic; I should have been elated, but I just felt unprepared. Isabelle's group licensed only three new adai a year. The short-list had come down to about a hundred couples, winnowed from tens of thousands of applicants. We'd traveled to Switzerland for the final selection process, carried out by an agency that ordinarily handled adoptions. Through all the interviews and questionnaires, all the personality tests and scenario challenges, I'd managed to half-convince myself that our dedication would win through in the end, but that had been nothing but a prop to keep my spirits up.

Francine said calmly, "Thank you."

I coughed. "You're happy with everything we've proposed?" If there was going to be a proviso thrown in that rendered this miracle worthless, better to hear it now, before the shock had worn off and I'd started taking things for granted.

Isabelle nodded. "I don't pretend to be an expert in the relevant fields, but I've had the Qusp's design assessed by several colleagues, and I see no reason why it wouldn't be an appropriate form of hardware for an adai. I'm entirely agnostic about the MWI, so I don't share your view that the Qusp is a necessity, but if you were worried that I might write you off as cranks because of it," she smiled slightly, "you should meet some of the other people I've had to deal with.

"I believe you have the adai's welfare at heart, and you're not suffering from any of the superstitions—technophobic *or* technophilic—that would distort the relationship. And as you'll recall, I'll be entitled to visits and inspections throughout your period of guardianship. If you're found to be violating any of the terms of the contract, your license will be revoked, and I'll take charge of the adai."

Francine said, "What do you think the prospects are for a happier end to our guardianship?"

"I'm lobbying the European parliament, constantly," Isabelle replied. "Of course, in a few years' time several adai will reach the stage where their personal testimony begins contributing to the debate, but none of us should wait until then. The ground has to be prepared."

We spoke for almost an hour, on this and other issues. Isabelle had become quite an expert at fending off the attentions of the media; she promised to send us a handbook on this, along with the contract.

"Did you want to meet Sophie?" Isabelle asked, almost as an afterthought.

Francine said, "That would be wonderful." Francine and I had seen a video of Sophie at age four, undergoing a battery of psychological tests, but we'd never had a chance to converse with her, let alone meet her face to face.

The three of us left the office together, and Isabelle drove us to her home on the outskirts of the town.

In the car, the reality began sinking in anew. I felt the same mixture of exhilaration and claustrophobia that I'd experienced nineteen years before, when Francine had met me at the airport with news of her pregnancy. No digital conception had yet taken place, but if sex had ever felt half as loaded with risks and responsibilities as this, I would have remained celibate for life.

"No badgering, no interrogation," Isabelle warned us as she pulled into the driveway.

I said, "Of course not."

Isabelle called out, "Marco! Sophie!" as we followed her through the door. At the end of the hall, I heard childish giggling, and an adult male voice whispering in French. Then Isabelle's husband stepped out from behind the corner, a smiling, dark-haired young man, with Sophie riding on his shoulders. At first I couldn't look at her; I just smiled politely back at Marco, while noting glumly that he was at least fifteen years younger than I was. *How could I even think of doing this, at forty-six?* Then I glanced up, and caught Sophie's eye. She gazed straight back at me for a moment, appearing curious and composed, but then a fit of shyness struck her, and she buried her face in Marco's hair.

Isabelle introduced us, in English; Sophie was being raised to speak four languages, though in Switzerland that was hardly phenomenal. Sophie said, "Hello" but kept her eyes lowered. Isabelle said, "Come into the living room. Would you like something to drink?"

The five of us sipped lemonade, and the adults made polite, superficial conversation. Sophie sat on Marco's knees, squirming restlessly, sneaking glances at us. She looked exactly like an ordinary, slightly gawky, six-year-old girl. She had Isabelle's straw-colored hair, and Marco's brown eyes; whether by fiat or rigorous genetic simulation, she could have passed for their biological daughter. I'd read technical specifications describing her body, and seen an earlier version in action on the video, but the fact that it looked so plausible was the least of its designers' achievements. Watching her drinking, wriggling and fidgeting, I had no doubt that she felt herself inhabiting this skin, as much as I did my own. She was not a puppeteer posing as a child, pulling electronic strings from some dark cavern in her skull.

"Do you like lemonade?" I asked her.

She stared at me for a moment, as if wondering whether she should be affronted by the presumptuousness of this question, then replied, "It tickles."

In the taxi to the hotel, Francine held my hand tightly.

"Are you OK?" I asked.

"Yes, of course."

In the elevator, she started crying. I wrapped my arms around her.

"She would have turned eighteen this year."

"I know."

"Do you think she's alive, somewhere?"

"I don't know. I don't know if that's a good way to think about it."

Francine wiped her eyes. "No. This will be her. That's the way to see it. This will be my girl. Just a few years late."

Before flying home, we visited a small pathology lab, and left samples of our blood.

⌁⌁⌁

OUR DAUGHTER'S first five bodies reached us a month before her birth. I unpacked all five, and laid them out in a row on the living room floor. With their muscles slack and their eyes rolled up, they looked more like tragic mummies than sleeping infants. I dismissed that grisly image; better to think of them as suits of clothes. The only difference was that we hadn't bought pajamas quite so far ahead.

From wrinkled pink newborn to chubby eighteen-month-old, the progression made an eerie sight—even if an organic child's development, short of serious disease or malnourishment, would have been scarcely less predictable. A colleague of Francine's had lectured me a few weeks before about the terrible "mechanical determinism" we'd be imposing on our child, and though his arguments had been philosophically naive, this sequence of immutable snapshots from the future still gave me goose bumps.

The truth was, reality as a whole was deterministic, whether you had a Qusp for a brain or not; the quantum state of the multiverse at any moment determined the entire future. Personal experience—confined to one branch at a time—certainly *appeared* probabilistic, because there was no way to predict which local future you'd experience when a branch split, but the reason it was impossible to know that in advance was because the real answer was "all of them".

For a singleton, the only difference was that branches never split on the basis of your personal decisions. The world at large would continue to look probabilistic, but every choice you made was entirely determined by *who you were* and *the situation you faced*.

What more could anyone hope for? It was not as if *who you were* could be boiled down to some crude genetic or sociological profile; every shadow you'd seen on the ceiling at night, every cloud you'd watched drift across the sky, would have left some small imprint on the shape of your mind. Those events were fully determined too, when viewed across the multiverse—with different versions of you witnessing every possibility—but in practical terms, the bottom line was that no private investigator armed with your genome and a potted biography could plot your every move in advance.

Our daughter's choices—like everything else—had been written in stone at the birth of the universe, but that information could only be decoded by *becoming her* along the way. Her actions would flow from her temperament, her principles, her desires, and the fact that all of these qualities would themselves have prior causes did nothing to diminish their value. *Free will* was a slippery notion, but to me it simply meant that your choices were more or less consistent with your nature—which in turn was a provisional, constantly-evolving consensus between a thousand different influences. Our daughter would not be robbed of the chance to act capriciously, or even perversely, but at least it would not be impossible for her ever to act wholly in accordance with her ideals.

I packed the bodies away before Francine got home. I wasn't sure if the sight would unsettle her, but I didn't want her measuring them up for more clothes.

∿

THE DELIVERY began in the early hours of the morning of Sunday, December 14, and was expected to last about four hours, depending on traffic. I sat in the nursery while Francine paced the hallway outside, both of us watching the data coming through over the fiber from Basel.

Isabelle had used our genetic information as the starting point for a simulation of the development *in utero* of a complete embryo, employing an "adaptive hierarchy" model, with the highest resolution reserved for the central nervous system. The Qusp would take over this task, not only for the newborn child's brain, but also for the thousands of biochemical processes occurring outside the skull that the artificial bodies were not designed to perform. Apart from their sophisticated sensory and motor functions, the bodies could take in food and excrete wastes—for psychological and social reasons, as well as for the chemical energy this provided—and they breathed air, both in order to oxidize this fuel, and for vocalization, but they had no blood, no endocrine system, no immune response.

The Qusp I'd built in Berkeley was smaller than the São Paulo version, but it was still six times as wide as an infant's skull. Until it was further miniaturized, our daughter's mind would sit in a box in a corner of the nursery, joined to the rest of her by a wireless data link. Bandwidth and time lag would not be an issue within the Bay Area, and if we needed to take her further afield before everything was combined, the Qusp wasn't too large or delicate to move.

As the progress bar I was overlaying on the side of the Qusp nudged 98 per cent, Francine came into the nursery, looking agitated.

"We have to put it off, Ben. Just for a day. I need more time to prepare myself."

I shook my head. "You made me promise to say no, if you asked me to do that." She'd even refused to let me tell her how to halt the Qusp herself.

"Just a few hours," she pleaded.

Francine seemed genuinely distressed, but I hardened my heart by telling myself that she was acting: testing me, seeing if I'd keep my word. "No. No slowing down or speeding up, no pauses, no tinkering at all. This child has to hit us like a freight train, just like any other child would."

"You want me to go into labor now?" she said sarcastically. When I'd raised the possibility, half-jokingly, of putting her on a course of hormones that would have mimicked some of the effects of pregnancy in order to make bonding with the child easier—for myself as well, indirectly—she'd almost bit my head off. I hadn't been serious, because I knew it wasn't necessary. Adoption was the ultimate proof of that, but what we were doing was closer to claiming a child of our own from a surrogate.

"No. Just pick her up."

Francine peered down at the inert form in the cot.

"I can't do it!" she wailed. "When I hold her, she should feel as if she's the most precious thing in the world to me. How can I make her believe that, when I know I could bounce her off the walls without harming her?"

We had two minutes left. I felt my breathing grow ragged. I could send the Qusp a halt code, but what if that set the pattern? If one of us had had too little sleep, if Francine was late for work, if we talked ourselves into believing that our special child was so unique that we deserved a short holiday from her needs, what would stop us from doing the same thing again?

I opened my mouth to threaten her: *Either you pick her up, now, or I do it.* I stopped myself, and said, "You know how much it would harm her psychologically, if you dropped her. The very fact that you're afraid that you won't convey as much protectiveness as you need to will be just as strong a signal to her as anything else. *You care about her.* She'll sense that."

Francine stared back at me dubiously.

I said, "She'll know. I'm sure she will."

Francine reached into the cot and lifted the slack body into her arms. Seeing her cradle the lifeless form, I felt an anxious twisting in my gut; I'd experienced nothing like this when I'd laid the five plastic shells out for inspection.

I banished the progress bar and let myself free-fall through the final seconds: watching my daughter, willing her to move.

Her thumb twitched, then her legs scissored weakly. I couldn't see her face, so I watched Francine's expression. For an instant, I thought I could detect a horrified tightening at the corners of her mouth, as if she was about to recoil from this golem. Then the child began to bawl and kick, and Francine started weeping with undisguised joy.

As she raised the child to her face and planted a kiss on its wrinkled forehead, I suffered my own moment of disquiet. How easily that tender response had been summoned, when the body could as well have been brought to life by the kind of software used to animate the characters in games and films.

It hadn't, though. There'd been nothing false or easy about the road that had brought us to this moment—let alone the one that Isabelle had followed—

and we hadn't even tried to fashion life from clay, from nothing. We'd merely diverted one small trickle from a river already four billion years old.

Francine held our daughter against her shoulder, and rocked back and forth. "Have you got the bottle? Ben?" I walked to the kitchen in a daze; the microwave had anticipated the happy event, and the formula was ready.

I returned to the nursery and offered Francine the bottle. "Can I hold her, before you start feeding?"

"Of course." She leaned forward to kiss me, then held out the child, and I took her the way I'd learned to accept the babies of relatives and friends, cradling the back of her head beneath my hand. The distribution of weight, the heavy head, the play of the neck, felt the same as it did for any other infant. Her eyes were still screwed shut, as she screamed and swung her arms.

"What's your name, my beautiful girl?" We'd narrowed the list down to about a dozen possibilities, but Francine had refused to settle on one until she'd seen her daughter take her first breath. "Have you decided?"

"I want to call her Helen."

Gazing down at her, that sounded too old to me. Old-fashioned, at least. Great-Aunt Helen. Helena Bonham-Carter. I laughed inanely, and she opened her eyes.

Hairs rose on my arms. The dark eyes couldn't quite search my face, but she was not oblivious to me. Love and fear coursed through my veins. *How could I hope to give her what she needed?* Even if my judgment had been faultless, my power to act upon it was crude beyond measure.

We were all she had, though. We would make mistakes, we would lose our way, but I had to believe that something would hold fast. Some portion of the overwhelming love and resolve that I felt right now would have to remain with every version of me who could trace his ancestry to this moment.

I said, "I name you Helen."

2041

"SOPHIE! *SOPHIE!*" Helen ran ahead of us toward the arrivals gate, where Isabelle and Sophie were emerging. Sophie, almost sixteen now, was much less demonstrative, but she smiled and waved.

Francine said, "Do you ever think of moving?"

"Maybe if the laws change first in Europe," I replied.

"I saw a job in Zürich I could apply for."

"I don't think we should bend over backward to bring them together. They probably get on better with just occasional visits, and the net. It's not as if they don't have other friends."

Isabelle approached, and greeted us both with kisses on the cheek. I'd dreaded her arrival the first few times, but by now she seemed more like a slightly overbearing cousin than a child protection officer whose very presence implied misdeeds.

Sophie and Helen caught up with us. Helen tugged at Francine's sleeve. "Sophie's got a boyfriend! Daniel. She showed me his picture." She swooned mockingly, one hand on her forehead.

I glanced at Isabelle, who said, "He goes to her school. He's really very sweet."

Sophie grimaced with embarrassment. "Three-year-old *boys* are *sweet*." She turned to me and said, "Daniel is charming, and sophisticated, and *very* mature."

I felt as if an anvil had been dropped on my chest. As we crossed the car park, Francine whispered, "Don't have a heart attack yet. You've got a while to get used to the idea."

The waters of the bay sparkled in the sunlight as we drove across the bridge to Oakland. Isabelle described the latest session of the European parliamentary committee into adai rights. A draft proposal granting personhood to any system containing and acting upon a significant amount of the information content of human DNA had been gaining support; it was a tricky concept to define rigorously, but most of the objections were Pythonesque rather than practical. "Is the Human Proteomic Database a person? Is the Harvard Reference Physiological Simulation a person?" The HRPS modeled the brain solely in terms of what it removed from, and released into, the bloodstream; there was nobody home inside the simulation, quietly going mad.

Late in the evening, when the girls were upstairs, Isabelle began gently grilling us. I tried not to grit my teeth too much. I certainly didn't blame her for taking her responsibilities seriously; if, in spite of the selection process, we had turned out to be monsters, criminal law would have offered no remedies. Our obligations under the licensing contract were Helen's sole guarantee of humane treatment.

"She's getting good marks this year," Isabelle noted. "She must be settling in."

"She is," Francine replied. Helen was not entitled to a government-funded education, and most private schools had either been openly hostile, or had come up with such excuses as insurance policies that would have classified her as hazardous machinery. (Isabelle had reached a compromise with the airlines: Sophie had to be powered down, appearing to sleep during flights, but was not required to be shackled or stowed in the cargo hold.) The first community school we'd tried had not worked out, but we'd eventually found one close to the Berkeley campus where every parent involved was happy with the idea of Helen's presence. This had saved her from the prospect of joining a net-based school; they weren't so bad, but they were intended for children isolated by geography or illness, circumstances that could not be overcome by other means.

Isabelle bid us good night with no complaints or advice; Francine and I sat by the fire for a while, just smiling at each other. It was nice to have a blemish-free report for once.

The next morning, my alarm went off an hour early. I lay motionless for a while, waiting for my head to clear, before asking my knowledge miner why it had woken me.

It seemed Isabelle's visit had been beaten up into a major story in some east coast news bulletins. A number of vocal members of Congress had been following the debate in Europe, and they didn't like the way it was heading. Isabelle, they declared, had sneaked into the country as an agitator. In fact, she'd offered to testify to Congress any time they wanted to hear about her work, but they'd never taken her up on it.

It wasn't clear whether it was reporters or anti-adai activists who'd obtained her itinerary and done some digging, but all the details had now been splashed around the country, and protesters were already gathering outside Helen's school. We'd faced media packs, cranks, and activists before, but the images the knowledge miner showed me were disturbing; it was five a.m. and the crowd had already encircled the school. I had a flashback to some news footage I'd seen in my teens, of young schoolgirls in Northern Ireland running the gauntlet of a protest by the opposing political faction; I could no longer remember who had been Catholic and who had been Protestant.

I woke Francine and explained the situation.

"We could just keep her home," I suggested.

Francine looked torn, but she finally agreed. "It will probably all blow over when Isabelle flies out on Sunday. One day off school isn't exactly capitulating to the mob."

At breakfast, I broke the news to Helen.

"I'm not staying home," she said.

"Why not? Don't you want to hang out with Sophie?"

Helen was amused. "'Hang out'? Is that what the hippies used to say?" In her personal chronology of San Francisco, anything from before her birth belonged to the world portrayed in the tourist museums of Haight-Ashbury.

"Gossip. Listen to music. Interact socially in whatever manner you find agreeable."

She contemplated this last, open-ended definition. "Shop?"

"I don't see why not." There was no crowd outside the house, and though we were probably being watched, the protest was too large to be a moveable feast. Perhaps all the other parents would keep their children home, leaving the various placard wavers to fight among themselves.

Helen reconsidered. "No. We're doing that on Saturday. I want to go to school."

I glanced at Francine. Helen added, "It's not as if they can hurt me. I'm backed up."

Francine said, "It's not pleasant being shouted at. Insulted. Pushed around."

"I don't think it's going to be *pleasant*," Helen replied scornfully. "But I'm not going to let them tell me what to do."

To date, a handful of strangers had got close enough to yell abuse at her, and some of the children at her first school had been about as violent as (ordinary, drug-free, non-psychotic) nine-year-old bullies could be, but she'd never faced anything like this. I showed her the live news feed. She was not swayed. Francine and I retreated to the living room to confer.

I said, "I don't think it's a good idea." On top of everything else, I was beginning to suffer from a paranoid fear that Isabelle would blame us for the whole situation. Less fancifully, she could easily disapprove of us exposing Helen to the protesters. Even if that was not enough for her to terminate the license immediately, eroding her confidence in us could lead to that fate, eventually.

Francine thought for a while. "If we both go with her, both walk beside her, what are they going to do? If they lay a finger on us, it's assault. If they try to drag her away from us, it's theft."

"Yes, but whatever they do, she gets to hear all the poison they spew out."

"She watches the news, Ben. She's heard it all before."

"Oh, shit." Isabelle and Sophie had come down to breakfast; I could hear Helen calmly filling them in about her plans.

Francine said, "Forget about pleasing Isabelle. If Helen wants to do this, knowing what it entails, and we can keep her safe, then we should respect her decision."

I felt a sting of anger at the unspoken implication: having gone to such lengths to enable her to make meaningful choices, I'd be a hypocrite to stand in her way. *Knowing what it entails?* She was nine-and-a-half years old.

I admired her courage, though, and I did believe that we could protect her.

I said, "All right. You call the other parents. I'll inform the police."

⌁

THE MOMENT we left the car, we were spotted. Shouts rang out, and a tide of angry people flowed toward us.

I glanced down at Helen and tightened my grip on her. "Don't let go of our hands."

She smiled at me indulgently, as if I was warning her about something trivial, like broken glass on the beach. "I'll be all right, Dad." She flinched as the crowd closed in, and then there were bodies pushing against us from every side, people jabbering in our faces, spittle flying. Francine and I turned to face each other, making something of a protective cage and a wedge through the adult legs. Frightening as it was to be submerged, I was glad my daughter wasn't at eye level with these people.

"Satan moves her! Satan is inside her! Out, Jezebel spirit!" A young woman in a high-collared lilac dress pressed her body against me and started praying in tongues.

"Gödel's theorem proves that the non-computable, non-linear world behind the quantum collapse is a manifest expression of Buddha-nature," a neatly-dressed youth intoned earnestly, establishing with admirable economy that he had no idea what any of these terms meant. "Ergo, there can be no soul in the machine."

"Cyber nano quantum. Cyber nano quantum. Cyber nano quantum." That chant came from one of our would-be "supporters", a middle-aged man in lycra cycling shorts who was forcefully groping down between us, trying to lay his hand on Helen's head and leave a few flakes of dead skin behind; according to cult doctrine, this would enable her to resurrect him when she got around to establishing the Omega Point. I blocked his way as firmly as I could without actually assaulting him, and he wailed like a pilgrim denied admission to Lourdes.

"Think you're going to live forever, Tinkerbell?" A leering old man with a matted beard poked his head out in front of us, and spat straight into Helen's face.

"Arsehole!" Francine shouted. She pulled out a handkerchief and started mopping the phlegm away. I crouched down and stretched my free arm around them. Helen was grimacing with disgust as Francine dabbed at her, but she wasn't crying.

I said, "Do you want to go back to the car?"

"*No.*"

"Are you sure?"

Helen screwed up her face in an expression of irritation. "Why do you always ask me that? *Am I sure? Am I sure?* You're the one who sounds like a computer."

"I'm sorry." I squeezed her hand.

We ploughed on through the crowd. The core of the protesters turned out to be both saner and more civilized than the lunatics who'd got to us first; as we neared the school gates, people struggled to make room to let us through uninjured, at the same time as they shouted slogans for the cameras. "Healthcare for all, not just the rich!" I couldn't argue with that sentiment, though adai were just one of a thousand ways the wealthy could spare their children from disease, and in fact they were among the cheapest: the total cost in prosthetic bodies up to adult size came to less than the median lifetime expenditure on healthcare in the U.S. Banning adai wouldn't end the disparity between rich and poor, but I could understand why some people considered it the ultimate act of selfishness to create a child who could live forever. They probably never wondered about the fertility rates and resource use of their own descendants over the next few thousand years.

We passed through the gates, into a world of space and silence; any protester who trespassed here could be arrested immediately, and apparently none of them were sufficiently dedicated to Gandhian principles to seek out that fate.

Inside the entrance hall, I squatted down and put my arms around Helen.
"Are you OK?"

"Yes."

"I'm really proud of you."

"You're shaking." She was right; my whole body was trembling slightly. It was more than the crush and the confrontation, and the sense of relief that we'd come through unscathed. Relief was never absolute for me; I could never quite erase the images of other possibilities at the back of my mind.

One of the teachers, Carmela Peña, approached us, looking stoical; when they'd agreed to take Helen, all the staff and parents had known that a day like this would come.

Helen said, "I'll be OK now." She kissed me on the cheek, then did the same to Francine. "I'm all right," she insisted. "You can go."

Carmela said, "We've got sixty per cent of the kids coming. Not bad, considering."

Helen walked down the corridor, turning once to wave at us impatiently. I said, "No, not bad."

⁂

A GROUP of journalists cornered the five of us during the girls' shopping trip the next day, but media organizations had grown wary of lawsuits, and after Isabelle reminded them that she was presently enjoying "the ordinary liberties of every private citizen"—a quote from a recent eight-figure judgment against *Celebrity Stalker*—they left us in peace.

The night after Isabelle and Sophie flew out, I went in to Helen's room to kiss her good night. As I turned to leave, she said, "What's a Qusp?"

"It's a kind of computer. Where did you hear about that?"

"On the net. It said I had a Qusp, but Sophie didn't."

Francine and I had made no firm decision as to what we'd tell her, and when. I said, "That's right, but it's nothing to worry about. It just means you're a little bit different from her."

Helen scowled. "I don't want to be different from Sophie."

"Everyone's different from everyone else," I said glibly. "Having a Qusp is just like…a car having a different kind of engine. It can still go to all the same places." *Just not all of them at once.* "You can both still do whatever you like.

176

You can be as much like Sophie as you want." That wasn't entirely dishonest; the crucial difference could always be erased, simply by disabling the Qusp's shielding.

"I want to be the same," Helen insisted. "Next time I grow, why can't you give me what Sophie's got, instead?"

"What you have is newer. It's better."

"No one else has got it. Not just Sophie; none of the others." Helen knew she'd nailed me: if it was newer and better, why didn't the younger adai have it too?

I said, "It's complicated. You'd better go to sleep now; we'll talk about it later." I fussed with the blankets, and she stared at me resentfully.

I went downstairs and recounted the conversation to Francine. "What do you think?" I asked her. "Is it time?"

"Maybe it is," she said.

"I wanted to wait until she was old enough to understand the MWI."

Francine considered this. "Understand it how well, though? She's not going to be juggling density matrices any time soon. And if we make it a big secret, she's just going to get half-baked versions from other sources."

I flopped onto the couch. "This is going to be hard." I'd rehearsed the moment a thousand times, but in my imagination Helen had always been older, and there'd been hundreds of other adai with Qusps. In reality, no one had followed the trail we'd blazed. The evidence for the MWI had grown steadily stronger, but for most people it was still easy to ignore. Ever more sophisticated versions of rats running mazes just looked like elaborate computer games. You couldn't travel from branch to branch yourself, you couldn't spy on your parallel alter egos—and such feats would probably never be possible. "How do you tell a nine-year-old girl that she's the only sentient being on the planet who can make a decision, and stick to it?"

Francine smiled. "Not in those words, for a start."

"No." I put my arm around her. We were about to enter a minefield—and we couldn't help diffusing out across the perilous ground—but at least we had each other's judgment to keep us in check, to rein us in a little.

I said, "We'll work it out. We'll find the right way."

2050

AROUND FOUR in the morning, I gave in to the cravings and lit my first cigarette in a month.

As I drew the warm smoke into my lungs, my teeth started chattering, as if the contrast had forced me to notice how cold the rest of my body had become. The red glow of the tip was the brightest thing in sight, but if there was a camera trained on me it would be infrared, so I'd been blazing away like a bonfire, anyway. As the smoke came back up I spluttered like a cat choking on a fur ball; the first one was always like that. I'd taken up the habit at the surreal age of sixty, and even after five years on and off, my respiratory tract couldn't quite believe its bad luck.

For five hours, I'd been crouched in the mud at the edge of Lake Pontchartrain, a couple of kilometers west of the soggy ruins of New Orleans. Watching the barge, waiting for someone to come home. I'd been tempted to swim out and take a look around, but my aide sketched a bright red moat of domestic radar on the surface of the water, and offered no guarantee that I'd remain undetected even if I stayed outside the perimeter.

I'd called Francine the night before. It had been a short, tense conversation.

"I'm in Louisiana. I think I've got a lead."

"Yeah?"

"I'll let you know how it turns out."

"You do that."

I hadn't seen her in the flesh for almost two years. After facing too many dead ends together, we'd split up to cover more ground: Francine had searched from New York to Seattle; I'd taken the south. As the months had slipped away, her determination to put every emotional reaction aside for the sake of the task had gradually eroded. One night, I was sure, grief had overtaken her, alone in some soulless motel room—and it made no difference that the same thing had happened to me, a months later or a week before. Because we had not experienced it together, it was not a shared pain, a burden made lighter. After forty-seven years, though we now had a single purpose as never before, we were starting to come adrift.

I'd learned about Jake Holder in Baton Rouge, triangulating on rumors and fifth-hand reports of bar-room boasts. The boasts were usually empty; a prosthetic body equipped with software dumber than a microwave could make an infinitely pliable slave, but if the only way to salvage any trace of dignity when your buddies discovered that you owned the high-tech equivalent of a blow-up doll was to imply that there was somebody home inside, apparently a lot of men leaped at the chance.

Holder looked like something worse. I'd bought his lifetime purchasing records, and there'd been a steady stream of cyber-fetish porn over a period of two decades. Hardcore and pretentious; half the titles contained the word "manifesto". But the flow had stopped, about three months ago. The rumors were, he'd found something better.

I finished the cigarette, and slapped my arms to get the circulation going. *She would not be on the barge.* For all I knew, she'd heard the news from Brussels and was already halfway to Europe. That would be a difficult journey to make on her own, but there was no reason to believe that she didn't have loyal, trustworthy friends to assist her. I had too many out-of-date memories burned into my skull: all the blazing, pointless rows, all the petty crimes, all the self-mutilation. Whatever had happened, whatever she'd been through, she was no longer the angry fifteen-year-old who'd left for school one Friday and never come back.

By the time she'd hit thirteen, we were arguing about everything. Her body had no need for the hormonal flood of puberty, but the software had ground on relentlessly, simulating all the neuroendocrine effects. Sometimes it had seemed like an act of torture to put her through that—instead of hunting for some magic short-cut to maturity—but the cardinal rule had been never to tinker, never to intervene, just to aim for the most faithful simulation possible of ordinary human development.

Whatever we'd fought about, she'd always known how to shut me up. "I'm just a thing to you! An instrument! Daddy's little silver bullet!" I didn't care who she was, or what she wanted; I'd fashioned her solely to slay my own fears. (I'd lie awake afterward, rehearsing lame counter-arguments. Other children were born for infinitely baser motives: to work the fields, to sit in boardrooms, to banish ennui, to save failing marriages.) In her eyes, the Qusp itself wasn't good or bad—and she turned down all my offers to disable the shielding; that would have let me off the hook too easily. But I'd made her a freak for my own selfish reasons; I'd set her apart even from the other adai, purely to grant myself a certain kind of comfort. "You wanted to give birth to a singleton? Why didn't you just shoot yourself in the head every time you made a bad decision?"

When she went missing, we were afraid she'd been snatched from the street. But in her room, we'd found an envelope with the locator beacon she'd dug out of her body, and a note that read: *Don't look for me. I'm never coming back.*

I heard the tyres of a heavy vehicle squelching along the muddy track to my left. I hunkered lower, making sure I was hidden in the undergrowth. As the truck came to a halt with a faint metallic shudder, the barge disgorged an unmanned motorboat. My aide had captured the data streams exchanged, one specific challenge and response, but it had no clue how to crack the general case and mimic the barge's owner.

Two men climbed out of the truck. One was Jake Holder; I couldn't make out his face in the starlight, but I'd sat within a few meters of him in diners and bars in Baton Rouge, and my aide knew his somatic signature: the electromagnetic radiation from his nervous system and implants; his body's capacitative and inductive responses to small shifts in the ambient fields; the faint gamma-ray spectrum of his unavoidable, idiosyncratic load of radioisotopes, natural and Chernobylesque.

I did not know who his companion was, but I soon got the general idea.

"One thousand now," Holder said. "One thousand when you get back." His silhouette gestured at the waiting motorboat.

The other man was suspicious. "How do I know it will be what you say it is?"

"Don't call her 'it'," Holder complained. "She's not an object. She's my Lilith, my Lo-li-ta, my luscious clockwork succubus." For one hopeful moment, I pictured the customer snickering at this overheated sales pitch and coming to his senses; brothels in Baton Rouge openly advertised machine sex, with skilled human puppeteers, for a fraction of the price. Whatever he imagined the special thrill of a genuine adai to be, he had no way of knowing that Holder didn't have an accomplice controlling the body on the barge in exactly the same fashion. He might even be paying two thousand dollars for a puppet job from Holder himself.

"OK. But if she's not genuine…"

My aide overheard money changing hands, and it had modeled the situation well enough to know how I'd wish, always, to respond. "Move now," it whispered in my ear. I complied without hesitation; eighteen months before, I'd pavloved myself into swift obedience, with all the pain and nausea modern chemistry could induce. The aide couldn't puppet my limbs—I couldn't afford the elaborate surgery—but it overlaid movement cues on my vision, a system I'd adapted from off-the-shelf choreography software, and I strode out of the bushes, right up to the motorboat.

The customer was outraged. "What is this?"

I turned to Holder. "You want to fuck him first, Jake? I'll hold him down." There were things I didn't trust the aide to control; it set the boundaries, but it was better to let me improvise a little, and then treat my actions as one more part of the environment.

After a moment of stunned silence, Holder said icily, "I've never seen this prick before in my life." He'd been speechless for a little too long, though, to inspire any loyalty from a stranger; as he reached for his weapon, the customer backed away, then turned and fled.

Holder walked toward me slowly, gun outstretched. "What's your game? Are you after her? Is that it?" His implants were mapping my body—actively, since there was no need for stealth—but I'd tailed him for hours in Baton Rouge, and my aide knew him like an architectural plan. Over the starlit gray of his form, it overlaid a schematic, flaying him down to brain, nerves, and implants. A swarm of blue fireflies flickered into life in his motor cortex, prefiguring a peculiar shrug of the shoulders with no obvious connection to his trigger finger; before they'd reached the intensity that would signal his implants to radio the gun, my aide said "Duck."

The shot was silent, but as I straightened up again I could smell the propellant. I gave up thinking and followed the dance steps. As Holder strode forward and swung the gun toward me, I turned sideways, grabbed his right hand, then punched him hard, repeatedly, in the implant on the side of his neck. He was a fetishist, so he'd chosen bulky packages, intentionally visible through the skin. They were not hard-edged, and they were not inflexible—he wasn't that masochistic—but once you sufficiently compressed even the softest biocompatible foam, it might as well have been a lump of wood. While I hammered the wood into the muscles of his neck, I twisted his forearm upward. He dropped the gun; I put my foot on it and slid it back toward the bushes.

In ultrasound, I saw blood pooling around his implant. I paused while the pressure built up, then I hit him again and the swelling burst like a giant blister. He sagged to his knees, bellowing with pain. I took the knife from my back pocket and held it to his throat.

I made Holder take off his belt, and I used it to bind his hands behind his back. I led him to the motorboat, and when the two of us were on board, I suggested that he give it the necessary instructions. He was sullen but co-operative. I didn't feel anything; part of me still insisted that the transaction I'd caught him in was a hoax, and that there'd be nothing on the barge that couldn't be found in Baton Rouge.

The barge was old, wooden, smelling of preservatives and unvanquished rot. There were dirty plastic panes in the cabin windows, but all I could see in them was a reflected sheen. As we crossed the deck, I kept Holder intimately close, hoping that if there was an armed security system it wouldn't risk putting the bullet through both of us.

At the cabin door, he said resignedly, "Don't treat her badly." My blood went cold, and I pressed my forearm to my mouth to stifle an involuntary sob.

I kicked open the door, and saw nothing but shadows. I called out "Lights!" and two responded, in the ceiling and by the bed. Helen was naked, chained by the wrists and ankles. She looked up and saw me, then began to emit a horrified keening noise.

I pressed the blade against Holder's throat. "Open those things!"

"The shackles?"

"Yes!"

"I can't. They're not smart; they're just welded shut."

"Where are your tools?"

He hesitated. "I've got some wrenches in the truck. All the rest is back in town."

I looked around the cabin, then I lead him into a corner and told him to stand there, facing the wall. I knelt by the bed.

"Ssh. We'll get you out of here." Helen fell silent. I touched her cheek with the back of my hand; she didn't flinch, but she stared back at me, disbelieving. "We'll get you out." The timber bedposts were thicker than my arms, the links of the chains wide as my thumb. I wasn't going to snap any part of this with my bare hands.

Helen's expression changed: I was real, she was not hallucinating. She said dully, "I thought you'd given up on me. Woke one of the backups. Started again."

I said, "I'd never give up on you."

"Are you sure?" She searched my face. "Is this the edge of what's possible? Is this the worst it can get?"

I didn't have an answer to that.

I said, "You remember how to go numb, for a shedding?"

She gave me a faint, triumphant smile. "Absolutely." She'd had to endure imprisonment and humiliation, but she'd always had the power to cut herself off from her body's senses.

"Do you want to do it now? Leave all this behind?"

"Yes."

"You'll be safe soon. I promise you."

"I believe you." Her eyes rolled up.

I cut open her chest and took out the Qusp.

        ∿

FRANCINE AND I had both carried spare bodies, and clothes, in the trunks of our cars. Adai were banned from domestic flights, so Helen and I drove along the interstate, up toward Washington D.C., where Francine would meet us. We could claim asylum at the Swiss embassy; Isabelle had already set the machinery in motion.

Helen was quiet at first, almost shy with me as if with a stranger, but on the second day, as we crossed from Alabama into Georgia, she began to open up. She told me a little of how she'd hitchhiked from state to state, finding casual jobs that paid e-cash and needed no social security number, let alone biometric ID. "Fruit picking was the best."

She'd made friends along the way, and confided her nature to those she thought she could trust. She still wasn't sure whether or not she'd been betrayed. Holder had found her in a transient's camp under a bridge, and someone must have told him exactly where to look, but it was always possible that she'd been recognized by a casual acquaintance who'd seen her face in the media years before. Francine and I had never publicized her disappearance, never put up flyers or web pages, out of fear that it would only make the danger worse.

On the third day, as we crossed the Carolinas, we drove in near silence again. The landscape was stunning, the fields strewn with flowers, and Helen seemed calm. Maybe this was what she needed the most: just safety, and peace.

As dusk approached, though, I felt I had to speak.

"There's something I've never told you," I said. "Something that happened to me when I was young."

Helen smiled. "Don't tell me you ran away from the farm? Got tired of milking, and joined the circus?"

I shook my head. "I was never adventurous. It was just a little thing." I told her about the kitchen hand.

She pondered the story for a while. "And that's why you built the Qusp? That's why you made me? In the end, it all comes down to that man in the alley?" She sounded more bewildered than angry.

I bowed my head. "I'm sorry."

"For what?" she demanded. "Are you sorry that I was ever born?"

"No, but—"

"You didn't put me on that boat. Holder did that."

I said, "I brought you into a world with people like him. What I made you, made you a target."

"And if I'd been flesh and blood?" she said. "Do you think there aren't people like him, for flesh and blood? Or do you honestly believe that if you'd had an organic child, there would have been *no chance at all* that she'd have run away?"

I started weeping. "I don't know. I'm just sorry I hurt you."

Helen said, "I don't blame you for what you did. And I understand it better now. You saw a spark of good in yourself, and you wanted to cup your hands around it, protect it, make it stronger. I understand that. I'm not that spark, but that doesn't matter. I know who I am, I know what my choices are, and I'm glad of that. I'm glad you gave me that." She reached over and squeezed my hand. "Do you think I'd feel *better*, here and now, just because some other version of me handled the same situations better?" She smiled. "Knowing that other people are having a good time isn't much of a consolation to anyone."

I composed myself. The car beeped to bring my attention to a booking it had made in a motel a few kilometers ahead.

Helen said, "I've had time to think about a lot of things. Whatever the laws say, whatever the bigots say, all adai are part of the human race. And what *I* have is something almost every person who's ever lived thought they possessed. Human psychology, human culture, human morality, all evolved with the illusion that we lived in a single history. But we don't—so in the long run, something has to give. Call me old-fashioned, but I'd rather we tinker with our physical nature than abandon our whole identities."

I was silent for a while. "So what are your plans, now?"

"I need an education."

"What do you want to study?"

"I'm not sure yet. A million different things. But in the long run, I know what I want to do."

"Yeah?" The car turned off the highway, heading for the motel.

"You made a start," she said, "but it's not enough. There are people in billions of other branches where the Qusp hasn't been invented yet—and the way things stand, there'll always be branches without it. What's the point in us having this thing, if we don't share it? All those people deserve to have the power to make their own choices."

"Travel between the branches isn't a simple problem," I explained gently. "That would be orders of magnitude harder than the Qusp."

Helen smiled, conceding this, but the corners of her mouth took on the stubborn set I recognized as the precursor to a thousand smaller victories.

She said, "Give me time, Dad. Give me time."

ORACLE

1

On his eighteenth day in the tiger cage, Robert Stoney began to lose hope of emerging unscathed.

He'd woken a dozen times throughout the night with an overwhelming need to stretch his back and limbs, and none of the useful compromise positions he'd discovered in his first few days—the least-worst solutions to the geometrical problem of his confinement—had been able to dull his sense of panic. He'd been in far more pain in the second week, suffering cramps that felt as if the muscles of his legs were dying on the bone, but these new spasms had come from somewhere deeper, powered by a sense of urgency that revolved entirely around his own awareness of his situation.

That was what frightened him. Sometimes he could find ways to minimize his discomfort, sometimes he couldn't, but he'd been clinging to the thought that, in the end, all these fuckers could ever do was hurt him. That wasn't true, though. They could make him ache for freedom in the middle of the night, the way he might have ached with grief, or love. He'd always cherished the understanding that his self was a whole, his mind and body indivisible. But he'd failed to appreciate the corollary: through his body, they could touch every part of him. Change every part of him.

Morning brought a fresh torment: hay fever. The house was somewhere deep in the countryside, with nothing to be heard in the middle of the day but bird song. June had always been his worst month for hay fever, but in

187

Manchester it had been tolerable. As he ate breakfast, mucus dripped from his face into the bowl of lukewarm oats they'd given him. He stanched the flow with the back of his hand, but suffered a moment of shuddering revulsion when he couldn't find a way to reposition himself to wipe his hand clean on his trousers. Soon he'd need to empty his bowels. They supplied him with a chamber pot whenever he asked, but they always waited two or three hours before removing it. The smell was bad enough, but the fact that it took up space in the cage was worse.

Toward the middle of the morning, Peter Quint came to see him. "How are we today, Prof?" Robert didn't reply. Since the day Quint had responded with a puzzled frown to the suggestion that he had an appropriate name for a spook, Robert had tried to make at least one fresh joke at the man's expense every time they met, a petty but satisfying indulgence. But now his mind was blank, and in retrospect the whole exercise seemed like an insane distraction, as bizarre and futile as scoring philosophical points against some predatory animal while it gnawed on his leg.

"Many happy returns," Quint said cheerfully.

Robert took care to betray no surprise. He'd never lost track of the days, but he'd stopped thinking in terms of the calendar date; it simply wasn't relevant. Back in the real world, to have forgotten his own birthday would have been considered a benign eccentricity. Here it would be taken as proof of his deterioration, and imminent surrender.

If he was cracking, he could at least choose the point of fissure. He spoke as calmly as he could, without looking up. "You know I almost qualified for the Olympic marathon, back in forty-eight? If I hadn't done my hip in just before the trials, I might have competed." He tried a self-deprecating laugh. "I suppose I was never really much of an athlete. But I'm only forty-six. I'm not ready for a wheelchair yet." The words did help: he could beg this way without breaking down completely, expressing an honest fear without revealing how much deeper the threat of damage went.

He continued, with a measured note of plaintiveness that he hoped sounded like an appeal to fairness. "I just can't bear the thought of being crippled. All I'm asking is that you let me stand upright. Let me keep my health."

Quint was silent for a moment, then he replied with a tone of thoughtful sympathy. "It's unnatural, isn't it? Living like this: bent over, twisted, day after day. Living in an unnatural way is always going to harm you. I'm glad you can finally see that."

Robert was tired; it took several seconds for the meaning to sink in. *It was that crude, that obvious?* They'd locked him in this cage, for all this time…as a kind of ham-fisted *metaphor* for his crimes?

He almost burst out laughing, but he contained himself. "I don't suppose you know Franz Kafka?"

"Kafka?" Quint could never hide his voracity for names. "One of your Commie chums, is he?"

"I very much doubt that he was ever a Marxist."

Quint was disappointed, but prepared to make do with second best. "One of the other kind, then?"

Robert pretended to be pondering the question. "On balance, I suspect that's not too likely either."

"So why bring his name up?"

"I have a feeling he would have admired your methods, that's all. He was quite the connoisseur."

"Hmm." Quint sounded suspicious, but not entirely unflattered.

Robert had first set eyes on Quint in February of 1952. His house had been burgled the week before, and Arthur, a young man he'd been seeing since Christmas, had confessed to Robert that he'd given an acquaintance the address. Perhaps the two of them had planned to rob him, and Arthur had backed out at the last moment. In any case, Robert had gone to the police with an unlikely story about spotting the culprit in a pub, trying to sell an electric razor of the same make and model as the one taken from his house. No one could be charged on such flimsy evidence, so Robert had had no qualms about the consequences if Arthur had turned out to be lying. He'd simply hoped to prompt an investigation that might turn up something more tangible.

The following day, the CID had paid Robert a visit. The man he'd accused was known to the police, and fingerprints taken on the day of the burglary matched the prints they had on file. However, at the time Robert claimed to have seen him in the pub, he'd been in custody already on an entirely different charge.

The detectives had wanted to know why he'd lied. To spare himself the embarrassment, Robert had explained, of spelling out the true source of his information. Why was that embarrassing?

"I'm involved with the informant."

One detective, Mr Wills, had asked matter-of-factly, "What exactly does that entail, sir?" And Robert—in a burst of frankness, as if honesty itself was sure to be rewarded—had told him every detail. He'd known it was still technically illegal, of course. But then, so was playing football on Easter Sunday. It could hardly be treated as a serious crime, like burglary.

The police had strung him along for hours, gathering as much information as they could before disabusing him of this misconception. They hadn't charged him immediately; they'd needed a statement from Arthur first. But then Quint had materialized the next morning, and spelt out the choices very starkly. Three years in prison, with hard labor. Or Robert could resume his war-time work—for just one day a week, as a handsomely paid consultant to Quint's branch of the secret service—and the charges would quietly vanish.

At first, he'd told Quint to let the courts do their worst. He'd been angry enough to want to take a stand against the preposterous law, and whatever his feelings for Arthur, Quint had suggested—gloatingly, as if it strengthened his case—that the younger, working-class man would be treated far more leniently than Robert, having been led astray by someone whose duty was to set an example for the lower orders. Three years in prison was an unsettling prospect, but it would not have been the end of the world; the Mark I had changed the way he worked, but he could still function with nothing but a pencil and paper, if necessary. Even if they'd had him breaking rocks from dawn to dusk he probably would have been able to day-dream productively, and for all Quint's scaremongering he'd doubted it would come to that.

At some point, though, in the twenty-four hours Quint had given him to reach a decision, he'd lost his nerve. By granting the spooks their one day a week, he could avoid all the fuss and disruption of a trial. And though his work at the time—modeling embryological development—had been as challenging as anything he'd done in his life, he hadn't been immune to pangs of nostalgia for the old days, when the fate of whole fleets of battleships had rested on finding the most efficient way to extract logical contradictions from a bank of rotating wheels.

The trouble with giving in to extortion was, *it proved that you could be bought.* Never mind that the Russians could hardly have offered to intervene with the Manchester constabulary next time he needed to be rescued. Never mind that he would scarcely have cared if an enemy agent had threatened to send such comprehensive evidence to the newspapers that there'd be no prospect of his patrons saving him again. He'd lost any chance to proclaim that what he did in bed with another willing partner was not an issue of national security; by saying yes to Quint, he'd made it one. By choosing to be corrupted once, he'd brought the whole torrent of clichés and paranoia down upon his head: he was vulnerable to blackmail, an easy target for entrapment, perfidious by nature. He might as well have posed *in flagrante delicto* with Guy Burgess on the steps of the Kremlin.

It wouldn't have mattered if Quint and his masters had merely decided that they couldn't trust him. The problem was—some six years after recruiting him, with no reason to believe that he had ever breached security in any way—they'd convinced themselves that they could neither continue to employ him, nor safely leave him in peace, until they'd rid him of the trait they'd used to control him in the first place.

Robert went through the painful, complicated process of rearranging his body so he could look Quint in the eye. "You know, if it was legal there'd be nothing to worry about, would there? Why don't you devote some of your considerable Machiavellian talents to that end? Blackmail a few politicians. Set up a Royal Commission. It would only take you a couple of years. Then we could all get on with our real jobs."

Quint blinked at him, more startled than outraged. "You might as well say that we should legalize treason!"

Robert opened his mouth to reply, then decided not to waste his breath. Quint wasn't expressing a moral opinion. He simply meant that a world in which fewer people's lives were ruled by the constant fear of discovery was hardly one that a man in his profession would wish to hasten into existence.

~~~

WHEN ROBERT was alone again, the time dragged. His hay fever worsened, until he was sneezing and gagging almost continuously; even with freedom of movement and an endless supply of the softest linen handkerchiefs, he would have been reduced to abject misery. Gradually, though, he grew more adept at dealing with the symptoms, delegating the task to some barely conscious part of himself. By the middle of the afternoon—covered in filth, eyes almost swollen shut—he finally managed to turn his mind back to his work.

For the past four years he'd been immersed in particle physics. He'd been following the field on and off since before the war, but the paper by Yang and Mills in '54, in which they'd generalized Maxwell's equations for electromagnetism to apply to the strong nuclear force, had jolted him into action.

After several false starts, he believed he'd discovered a useful way to cast gravity into the same form. In general relativity, if you carried a four-dimensional velocity vector around a loop that enclosed a curved region of spacetime, it came back rotated—a phenomenon highly reminiscent of the way more abstract vectors behaved in nuclear physics. In both cases, the rotations could be treated algebraically, and the traditional way to get a handle on this was to make use of a set of matrices of complex numbers whose relationships mimicked the algebra in question. Hermann Weyl had catalogued most of the possibilities back in the '20s and '30s.

In spacetime, there were six distinct ways you could rotate an object: you could turn it around any of three perpendicular axes in space, or you could boost its velocity in any of the same three directions. These two kinds of rotation were complementary, or "dual" to each other, with the ordinary rotations only affecting coordinates that were untouched by the corresponding boost, and *vice versa*. This meant that you could rotate something around, say, the x-axis, and speed it up in the same direction, without the two processes interfering.

When Robert had tried applying the Yang-Mills approach to gravity in the obvious way, he'd floundered. It was only when he'd shifted the algebra of rotations into a new, strangely skewed guise that the mathematics had begun to fall into place. Inspired by a trick that particle physicists used to construct fields with left- or right-handed spin, he'd combined every rotation with its own dual multiplied by i, the square root of minus one. The result was a set of rotations in four *complex* dimensions, rather than the four real ones of ordinary spacetime, but the relationships between them preserved the original algebra.

Demanding that these "self-dual" rotations satisfy Einstein's equations turned out to be equivalent to ordinary general relativity, but the process leading to a quantum-mechanical version of the theory became dramatically simpler. Robert still had no idea how to interpret this, but as a purely formal trick it worked spectacularly well—and when the mathematics fell into place like that, it had to mean *something*.

He spent several hours pondering old results, turning them over in his mind's eye, rechecking and reimagining everything in the hope of forging some new connection. Making no progress, but there'd always been days like that. It was a triumph merely to spend this much time doing what he would have done back in the real world—however mundane, or even frustrating, the same activity might have been in its original setting.

By evening, though, the victory began to seem hollow. He hadn't lost his wits entirely, but he was frozen, stunted. He might as well have whiled away the hours reciting the base-32 multiplication table in Baudot code, just to prove that he still remembered it.

As the room filled with shadows, his powers of concentration deserted him completely. His hay fever had abated, but he was too tired to think, and in too much pain to sleep. This wasn't Russia, they couldn't hold him forever; he simply had to wear them down with his patience. *But when, exactly, would they have to let him go?* And how much more patient could Quint be, with no pain, no terror, to erode his determination?

The moon rose, casting a patch of light on the far wall; hunched over, he couldn't see it directly, but it silvered the gray at his feet, and changed his whole sense of the space around him. The cavernous room mocking his confinement reminded him of nights he'd spent lying awake in the dormitory at Sherborne. A public school education did have one great advantage: however miserable you were afterward, you could always take comfort in the knowledge that life would never be quite as bad again.

"This room smells of mathematics! Go out and fetch a disinfectant spray!" That had been his form-master's idea of showing what a civilized man he was: contempt for that loathsome subject, the stuff of engineering and other low trades. And as for Robert's chemistry experiments, like the beautiful color-changing iodate reaction he'd learned from Chris's brother—

Robert felt a familiar ache in the pit of his stomach. *Not now. I can't afford this now.* But the whole thing swept over him, unwanted, unbidden. He'd used to meet Chris in the library on Wednesdays; for months, that had been the only time they could spend together. Robert had been fifteen then, Chris a year older. If Chris had been plain, he still would have shone like a creature from another world. No one else in Sherborne had read Eddington on relativity, Hardy on mathematics. No one else's horizons stretched beyond rugby, sadism, and the dimly satisfying prospect of reading classics at Oxford then vanishing into the maw of the civil service.

They had never touched, never kissed. While half the school had been indulging in passionless sodomy—as a rather literal-minded substitute for the much too difficult task of imagining women—Robert had been too shy even to declare his feelings. Too shy, and too afraid that they might not be reciprocated. It hadn't mattered. To have a friend like Chris had been enough.

In December of 1929, they'd both sat the exams for Trinity College, Cambridge. Chris had won a scholarship; Robert hadn't. He'd reconciled himself to their separation, and prepared for one more year at Sherborne without the one person who'd made it bearable. Chris would be following happily in the footsteps of Newton; just thinking of that would be some consolation.

Chris never made it to Cambridge. In February, after six days in agony, he'd died of bovine tuberculosis.

Robert wept silently, angry with himself because he knew that half his wretchedness was just self-pity, exploiting his grief as a disguise. He had to stay honest; once every source of unhappiness in his life melted together and became indistinguishable, he'd be like a cowed animal, with no sense of the past or the future. Ready to do anything to get out of the cage.

If he hadn't yet reached that point, he was close. It would only take a few more nights like the last one. Drifting off in the hope of a few minutes' blankness, to find that sleep itself shone a colder light on everything. Drifting off, then waking with a sense of loss so extreme it was like suffocation.

A woman's voice spoke from the darkness in front of him. "Get off your knees!"

Robert wondered if he was hallucinating. He'd heard no one approach across the creaky floorboards.

The voice said nothing more. Robert rearranged his body so he could look up from the floor. There was a woman he'd never seen before, standing a few feet away.

She'd sounded angry, but as he studied her face in the moonlight through the slits of his swollen eyes, he realized that her anger was directed, not at him, but at his condition. She gazed at him with an expression of horror and outrage, as if she'd chanced upon him being held like this in some respectable neighbor's basement, rather than an MI6 facility. Maybe she was one of the staff employed in the upkeep of the house, but had no idea what went on here? Surely those people were vetted and supervised, though, and threatened with life imprisonment if they ever set foot outside their prescribed domains.

For one surreal moment, Robert wondered if Quint had sent her to seduce him. It would not have been the strangest thing they'd tried. But she radiated such fierce self assurance—such a sense of confidence that she could speak with the authority of her convictions, and expect to be heeded—that he knew she could never have been chosen for the role. No one in Her Majesty's government would consider self assurance an attractive quality in a woman.

He said, "Throw me the key, and I'll show you my Roger Bannister impression."

She shook her head. "You don't need a key. Those days are over."

Robert started with fright. *There were no bars between them.* But the cage couldn't have vanished before his eyes; she must have removed it while he'd been lost in his reverie. He'd gone through the whole painful exercise of turning to face her as if he were still confined, without even noticing.

Removed it how?

He wiped his eyes, shivering at the dizzying prospect of freedom. "Who are you?" An agent for the Russians, sent to liberate him from his own side? She'd have to be a zealot, then, or strangely naive, to view his torture with such wide-eyed innocence.

She stepped forward, then reached down and took his hand. "Do you think you can walk?" Her grip was firm, and her skin was cool and dry. She was completely unafraid; she might have been a good Samaritan in a public street helping an old man to his feet after a fall—not an intruder helping a threat to national security break out of therapeutic detention, at the risk of being shot on sight.

"I'm not even sure I can stand." Robert steeled himself; maybe this woman was a trained assassin, but it would be too much to presume that if he cried out in pain and brought guards rushing in, she could still extricate him without raising a sweat. "You haven't answered my question."

"My name's Helen." She smiled and hoisted him to his feet, looking at once like a compassionate child pulling open the jaws of a hunter's cruel trap, and a very powerful, very intelligent carnivore contemplating its own strength. "I've come to change everything."

Robert said, "Oh, good."

~w~

ROBERT FOUND that he could hobble; it was painful and undignified, but at least he didn't have to be carried. Helen led him through the house; lights showed from some of the rooms, but there were no voices, no footsteps save their own, no signs of life at all. When they reached the tradesmen's entrance she unbolted the door, revealing a moonlit garden.

"Did you kill everyone?" he whispered. He'd made far too much noise to have come this far unmolested. Much as he had reason to despise his captors, mass murder on his behalf was a lot to take in.

Helen cringed. "What a revolting idea! It's hard to believe sometimes, how uncivilized you are."

"You mean the British?"

"All of you!"

"I must say, your accent's rather good."

"I watched a lot of cinema," she explained. "Mostly Ealing comedies. You never know how much that will help, though."

"Quite."

They crossed the garden, heading for a wooden gate in the hedge. Since murder was strictly for imperialists, Robert could only assume that she'd managed to drug everyone.

The gate was unlocked. Outside the grounds, a cobbled lane ran past the hedge, leading into forest. Robert was barefoot, but the stones weren't cold, and the slight unevenness of the path was welcome, restoring circulation to the soles of his feet.

As they walked, he took stock of his situation. He was out of captivity, thanks entirely to this woman. Sooner or later he was going to have to confront her agenda.

He said, "I'm not leaving the country."

Helen murmured assent, as if he'd passed a casual remark about the weather.

"And I'm not going to discuss my work with you."

"Fine."

Robert stopped and stared at her. She said, "Put your arm across my shoulders."

He complied; she was exactly the right height to support him comfortably. He said, "You're not a Soviet agent, are you?"

Helen was amused. "Is that really what you thought?"

"I'm not all that quick on my feet tonight."

"No." They began walking together. Helen said, "There's a train station about three kilometers away. You can get cleaned up, rest there until morning, and decide where you want to go."

"Won't the station be the first place they'll look?"

"They won't be looking anywhere for a while."

The moon was high above the trees. The two of them could not have made a more conspicuous couple: a sensibly dressed, quite striking young woman, supporting a filthy, ragged tramp. If a villager cycled past, the best they could hope for was being mistaken for an alcoholic father and his martyred daughter.

Martyred all right: she moved so efficiently, despite the burden, that any onlooker would assume she'd been doing this for years. Robert tried altering his gait slightly, subtly changing the timing of his steps to see if he could make her falter, but Helen adapted instantly. If she knew she was being tested, though, she kept it to herself.

Finally he said, "What did you do with the cage?"

"I time-reversed it."

Hairs stood up on the back of his neck. Even assuming that she could do such a thing, it wasn't at all clear to him how that could have stopped the bars from scattering light and interacting with his body. It should merely have turned electrons into positrons, and killed them both in a shower of gamma rays.

That conjuring trick wasn't his most pressing concern, though. "I can only think of three places you might have come from," he said.

Helen nodded, as if she'd put herself in his shoes and catalogued the possibilities. "Rule out one; the other two are both right."

She was not from an extrasolar planet. Even if her civilization possessed some means of viewing Ealing comedies from a distance of light years, she was far too sensitive to his specific human concerns.

She was from the future, but not his own.

She was from the future of another Everett branch.

He turned to her. "No paradoxes."

She smiled, deciphering his shorthand immediately. "That's right. It's physically impossible to travel into your own past, unless you've made exacting preparations to ensure compatible boundary conditions. That *can* be achieved, in a controlled laboratory setting—but in the field it would be like trying to balance ten thousand elephants in an inverted pyramid, while the bottom one rode a unicycle: excruciatingly difficult, and entirely pointless."

Robert was tongue-tied for several seconds, a horde of questions battling for access to his vocal chords. "But how do you travel into the past at all?"

"It will take a while to bring you up to speed completely, but if you want the short answer: you've already stumbled on one of the clues. I read your paper in *Physical Review*, and it's correct as far as it goes. Quantum gravity involves four complex dimensions, but the only classical solutions—the only geometries that remain in phase under slight perturbations—have curvature that's either *self-dual*, or *anti-self-dual*. Those are the only stationary points of the action, for the complete Lagrangian. And both solutions appear, from the inside, to contain only four real dimensions.

"It's meaningless to ask which sector we're in, but we might as well call it self-dual. In that case, the anti-self-dual solutions have an arrow of time running backward compared to ours."

"Why?" As he blurted out the question, Robert wondered if he sounded like an impatient child to her. But if she suddenly vanished back into thin air, he'd have far fewer regrets for making a fool of himself this way than if he'd maintained a façade of sophisticated nonchalance.

Helen said, "Ultimately, that's related to spin. And it's down to the mass of the neutrino that we can tunnel between sectors. But I'll need to draw you some diagrams and equations to explain it all properly."

Robert didn't press her for more; he had no choice but to trust that she wouldn't desert him. He staggered on in silence, a wonderful ache of anticipation building in his chest. If someone had put this situation to him hypothetically, he would have piously insisted that he'd prefer to toil on at his own pace. But despite the satisfaction it had given him on the few occasions when he'd made genuine discoveries himself, what mattered in the end was understanding as much as you could, however you could. Better to ransack the past and the future than go through life in a state of willful ignorance.

"You said you've come to change things?"

She nodded. "I can't predict the future here, of course, but there are pitfalls in my own past that I can help you avoid. In my twentieth century, people discovered things too slowly. Everything changed much too slowly. Between us, I think we can speed things up."

Robert was silent for a while, contemplating the magnitude of what she was proposing. Then he said, "It's a pity you didn't come sooner. In this branch, about twenty years ago—"

Helen cut him off. "I know. We had the same war. The same Holocaust, the same Soviet death toll. But we've yet to be able to avert that, anywhere. You can never do anything in just one history—even the most focused intervention happens across a broad 'ribbon' of strands. When we try to reach back to the '30s and '40s, the ribbon overlaps with its own past to such a degree that all the worst horrors are *faits accompli*. We can't shoot *any* version of Adolf Hitler, because we can't shrink the ribbon to the point where none of us would be shooting ourselves in the back. All we've ever managed are minor interventions, like sending projectiles back to the Blitz, saving a few lives by deflecting bombs."

"What, knocking them into the Thames?"

"No, that would have been too risky. We did some modeling, and the safest thing turned out to be diverting them onto big, empty buildings: Westminster Abbey, Saint Paul's Cathedral."

The station came into view ahead of them. Helen said, "What do you think? Do you want to head back to Manchester?"

Robert hadn't given the question much thought. Quint could track him down anywhere, but the more people he had around him, the less vulnerable he'd be. In his house in Wilmslow he'd be there for the taking.

"I still have rooms at Cambridge," he said tentatively.

"Good idea."

"What are your own plans?"

Helen turned to him. "I thought I'd stay with you." She smiled at the expression on his face. "Don't worry, I'll give you plenty of privacy. And if people want to make assumptions, let them. You already have a scandalous reputation; you might as well see it branch out in new directions."

Robert said wryly, "I'm afraid it doesn't quite work that way. They'd throw us out immediately."

Helen snorted. "They could try."

"You may have defeated MI6, but you haven't dealt with Cambridge porters." The reality of the situation washed over him anew at the thought of her in his study, writing out the equations for time travel on the blackboard. "*Why me?* I can appreciate that you'd want to make contact with someone who could understand how you came here—but why not Everett, or Yang, or Feynman? Compared to Feynman, I'm a dilettante."

Helen said, "Maybe. But you have an equally practical bent, and you'll learn fast enough."

There had to be more to it than that: thousands of people would have been capable of absorbing her lessons just as rapidly. "The physics you've hinted at—in your past, did I discover all that?"

"No. Your *Physical Review* paper helped me track you down here, but in my own history that was never published." There was a flicker of disquiet in her eyes, as if she had far greater disappointments in store on that subject.

Robert didn't care much either way; if anything, the less his alter ego had achieved, the less he'd be troubled by jealousy.

"Then what was it, that made you choose me?"

"You really haven't guessed?" Helen took his free hand and held the fingers to her face; it was a tender gesture, but much more like a daughter's than a lover's. "It's a warm night. No one's skin should be this cold."

Robert gazed into her dark eyes, as playful as any human's, as serious, as proud. Given the chance, perhaps any decent person would have plucked him from Quint's grasp. But only one kind would feel a special obligation, as if they were repaying an ancient debt.

He said, "You're a machine."

2

JOHN HAMILTON, Professor of Medieval and Renaissance English at Magdalene College, Cambridge, read the last letter in the morning's pile of fan mail with a growing sense of satisfaction.

The letter was from a young American, a twelve-year-old girl in Boston. It opened in the usual way, declaring how much pleasure his books had given her, before going on to list her favorite scenes and characters. As ever, Jack was delighted that the stories had touched someone deeply enough to prompt them to respond this way. But it was the final paragraph that was by far the most gratifying:

> However much other children might tease me, or grown-ups too when I'm older, I will NEVER, EVER stop believing in the Kingdom of Nescia. Sarah stopped believing, and she was locked out of the Kingdom forever. At first that made me cry, and I couldn't sleep all night because I was afraid I might stop believing myself one day. But I understand now that it's good to be afraid, because it will help me

keep people from changing my mind. And if you're not willing to believe in magic lands, of course you can't enter them. There's nothing even Belvedere himself can do to save you, then.

~w~

JACK REFILLED and lit his pipe, then reread the letter. This was his vindication: the proof that through his books he could touch a young mind, and plant the seed of faith in fertile ground. It made all the scorn of his jealous, stuck-up colleagues fade into insignificance. Children understood the power of stories, the reality of myth, the need to believe in something beyond the dismal gray farce of the material world.

It wasn't a truth that could be revealed the "adult" way: through scholarship, or reason. Least of all through philosophy, as Elizabeth Anscombe had shown him on that awful night at the Socratic Club. A devout Christian herself, Anscombe had nonetheless taken all the arguments against materialism from his popular book, *Signs and Wonders*, and trampled them into the ground. It had been an unfair match from the start: Anscombe was a professional philosopher, steeped in the work of everyone from Aquinas to Wittgenstein; Jack knew the history of ideas in medieval Europe intimately, but he'd lost interest in modern philosophy once it had been invaded by fashionable positivists. And *Signs and Wonders* had never been intended as a scholarly work; it had been good enough to pass muster with a sympathetic lay readership, but trying to defend his admittedly rough-and-ready mixture of common sense and useful shortcuts to faith against Anscombe's merciless analysis had made him feel like a country yokel stammering in front of a bishop.

Ten years later, he still burned with resentment at the humiliation she'd put him through, but he was grateful for the lesson she'd taught him. His earlier books, and his radio talks, had not been a complete waste of time—but the harpy's triumph had shown him just how pitiful human reason was when it came to the great questions. He'd begun working on the stories of Nescia years before, but it was only when the dust had settled on his most painful defeat that he'd finally recognized his true calling.

He removed his pipe, stood, and turned to face Oxford. "Kiss my arse, Elizabeth!" he growled happily, waving the letter at her. This was a wonderful omen. It was going to be a very good day.

There was a knock at the door of his study.

"Come."

It was his brother, William. Jack was puzzled—he hadn't even realized Willie was in town—but he nodded a greeting and motioned at the couch opposite his desk.

Willie sat, his face flushed from the stairs, frowning. After a moment he said, "This chap Stoney."

"Hmm?" Jack was only half listening as he sorted papers on his desk. He knew from long experience that Willie would take forever to get to the point.

"Did some kind of hush-hush work during the war, apparently."

"Who did?"

"Robert Stoney. Mathematician. Used to be up at Manchester, but he's a Fellow of Kings, and now he's back in Cambridge. Did some kind of secret war work. Same thing as Malcolm Muggeridge, apparently. No one's allowed to say what."

Jack looked up, amused. He'd heard rumors about Muggeridge, but they all revolved around the business of analyzing intercepted German radio messages. What conceivable use would a mathematician have been, for that? Sharpening pencils for the intelligence analysts, presumably.

"What about him, Willie?" Jack asked patiently.

Willie continued reluctantly, as if he was confessing to something mildly immoral. "I paid him a visit yesterday. Place called the Cavendish. Old army friend of mine has a brother who works there. Got the whole tour."

"I know the Cavendish. What's there to see?"

"He's doing things, Jack. *Impossible things.*"

"Impossible?"

"Looking inside people. Putting it on a screen, like a television."

Jack sighed. "Taking X-rays?"

Willie snapped back angrily, "I'm not a fool; I know what an X-ray looks like. This is different. You can see the blood flow. You can watch your heart beating. You can follow a sensation through the nerves from…fingertip to brain. He says, soon he'll be able to watch a thought in motion."

"Nonsense." Jack scowled. "So he's invented some gadget, some fancy kind of X-ray machine. What are you so agitated about?"

Willie shook his head gravely. "There's more. That's just the tip of the iceberg. He's only been back in Cambridge a year, and already the place is overflowing with…wonders." He used the word begrudgingly, as if he had no choice, but was afraid of conveying more approval than he intended.

Jack was beginning to feel a distinct sense of unease.

"What exactly is it you want me to do?" he asked.

Willie replied plainly, "Go and see for yourself. Go and see what he's up to."

~w~

THE CAVENDISH Laboratory was a mid-Victorian building, designed to resemble something considerably older and grander. It housed the entire Department of Physics, complete with lecture theaters; the place was swarming with noisy undergraduates. Jack had had no trouble arranging a tour: he'd simply telephoned Stoney and expressed his curiosity, and no more substantial reason had been required.

Stoney had been allocated three adjoining rooms at the back of the building, and the "spin resonance imager" occupied most of the first. Jack obligingly placed his arm between the coils, then almost jerked it out in fright when the strange, transected view of his muscles and veins appeared on the picture tube. He wondered if it could be some kind of hoax, but he clenched his fist slowly and watched the image do the same, then made several unpredictable movements which it mimicked equally well.

"I can show you individual blood cells, if you like," Stoney offered cheerfully.

Jack shook his head; his current, unmagnified flaying was quite enough to take in.

Stoney hesitated, then added awkwardly, "You might want to talk to your doctor at some point. It's just that, your bone density's rather—" He pointed to a chart on the screen beside the image. "Well, it's quite a bit below the normal range."

Jack withdrew his arm. He'd already been diagnosed with osteoporosis, and he'd welcomed the news: it meant that he'd taken a small part of Joyce's illness—the weakness in her bones—into his own body. God was allowing him to suffer a little in her stead.

If Joyce were to step between these coils, what might that reveal? But there'd be nothing to add to her diagnosis. Besides, if he kept up his prayers, and kept up both their spirits, in time her remission would blossom from an uncertain reprieve into a fully-fledged cure.

He said, "How does this work?"

"In a strong magnetic field, some of the atomic nuclei and electrons in your body are free to align themselves in various ways with the field." Stoney must have seen Jack's eyes beginning to glaze over; he quickly changed tack. "Think of it as being like setting a whole lot of spinning tops whirling, as vigorously as possible, then listening carefully as they slow down and tip over. For the atoms in your body, that's enough to give some clues as to what kind of molecule, and what kind of tissue, they're in. The machine listens to atoms in different places by changing the way it combines all the signals from billions of tiny antennae. It's like a whispering gallery where we can play with the time that signals take to travel from different places, moving the focus back and forth through any part of your body, thousands of times a second."

Jack pondered this explanation. Though it sounded complicated, in principle it wasn't that much stranger than X-rays.

"The physics itself is old hat," Stoney continued, "but for imaging, you need a very strong magnetic field, and you need to make sense of all the data you've gathered. Nevill Mott made the superconducting alloys for the magnets. And I managed to persuade Rosalind Franklin from Birkbeck to collaborate with us, to help perfect the fabrication process for the computing circuits. We cross-link lots of little Y-shaped DNA fragments, then selectively coat them with metal; Rosalind worked out a way to use X-ray crystallography for quality control. We paid her back with a purpose-built computer that will let her solve hydrated protein structures in real time, once she gets her hands on a bright enough X-ray source." He held up a small, unprepossessing object, rimmed with protruding gold wires. "Each logic gate is roughly a hundred Ångstroms cubed, and we grow them in three-dimensional arrays. That's a million, million, million switches in the palm of my hand."

Jack didn't know how to respond to this claim. Even when he couldn't quite follow the man there was something mesmerizing about his ramblings, like a cross between William Blake and nursery talk.

"If computers don't excite you, we're doing all kinds of other things with DNA." Stoney ushered him into the next room, which was full of glassware, and seedlings in pots beneath strip lights. Two assistants seated at a bench were toiling over microscopes; another was dispensing fluids into test tubes with a device that looked like an overgrown eye-dropper.

"There are a dozen new species of rice, corn, and wheat here. They all have at least double the protein and mineral content of existing crops, and each one uses a different biochemical repertoire to protect itself against insects and fungi. Farmers have to get away from monocultures; it leaves them too vulnerable to disease, and too dependent on chemical pesticides."

Jack said, "You've bred these? All these new varieties, in a matter of months?"

"No, no! Instead of hunting down the heritable traits we needed in the wild, and struggling for years to produce cross-breeds bearing all of them, we designed every trait from scratch. Then we manufactured DNA that would make the tools the plants need, and inserted it into their germ cells."

Jack demanded angrily, "Who are you to say what a plant needs?"

Stoney shook his head innocently. "I took my advice from agricultural scientists, who took their advice from farmers. They know what pests and blights they're up against. Food crops are as artificial as Pekinese. Nature didn't hand them to us on a plate, and if they're not working as well as we need them to, nature isn't going to fix them for us."

Jack glowered at him, but said nothing. He was beginning to understand why Willie had sent him here. The man came across as an enthusiastic tinkerer, but there was a breath-taking arrogance lurking behind the boyish exterior.

Stoney explained a collaboration he'd brokered between scientists in Cairo, Bogotá, London and Calcutta, to develop vaccines for polio, smallpox, malaria, typhoid, yellow fever, tuberculosis, influenza and leprosy. Some were the first of their kind; others were intended as replacements for existing vaccines. "It's important that we create antigens without culturing the pathogens in animal cells that might themselves harbor viruses. The teams are all looking at variants on a simple, cheap technique that involves putting antigen genes into harmless bacteria that will double as delivery vehicles and adjuvants, then freeze-drying them into spores that can survive tropical heat without refrigeration."

Jack was slightly mollified; this all sounded highly admirable. What business Stoney had instructing doctors on vaccines was another question. Presumably his jargon made sense to them, but when exactly had this mathematician acquired the training to make even the most modest suggestions on the topic?

"You're having a remarkably productive year," he observed.

Stoney smiled. "The muse comes and goes for all of us. But I'm really just the catalyst in most of this. I've been lucky enough to find some people—here in Cambridge, and further afield—who've been willing to chance their arm on some wild ideas. They've done the real work." He gestured toward the next room. "My own pet projects are through here."

The third room was full of electronic gadgets, wired up to picture tubes displaying both phosphorescent words and images resembling engineering blueprints come to life. In the middle of one bench, incongruously, sat a large cage containing several hamsters.

Stoney fiddled with one of the gadgets, and a face like a stylized drawing of a mask appeared on an adjacent screen. The mask looked around the room, then said, "Good morning, Robert. Good morning, Professor Hamilton."

Jack said, "You had someone record those words?"

The mask replied, "No, Robert showed me photographs of all the teaching staff at Cambridge. If I see anyone I know from the photographs, I greet them." The face was crudely rendered, but the hollow eyes seemed to meet Jack's. Stoney explained, "It has no idea what it's saying, of course. It's just an exercise in face and voice recognition."

Jack responded stiffly, "Of course."

Stoney motioned to Jack to approach and examine the hamster cage. He obliged him. There were two adult animals, presumably a breeding pair. Two pink young were suckling from the mother, who reclined in a bed of straw.

"Look closely," Stoney urged him. Jack peered into the nest, then cried out an obscenity and backed away.

One of the young was exactly what it seemed. The other was a machine, wrapped in ersatz skin, with a nozzle clamped to the warm teat.

"That's the most monstrous thing I've ever seen!" Jack's whole body was trembling. "What possible reason could you have to do that?"

Stoney laughed and made a reassuring gesture, as if his guest was a nervous child recoiling from a harmless toy. "It's not hurting her! And the point is to discover what it takes for the mother to accept it. To 'reproduce one's kind' means having some set of parameters as to what that is. Scent, and some aspects of appearance, are important cues in this case, but through trial and error I've also pinned down a set of behaviors that lets the simulacrum pass through every stage of the life cycle. An acceptable child, an acceptable sibling, an acceptable mate."

Jack stared at him, nauseated. "These animals fuck your machines?"

Stoney was apologetic. "Yes, but hamsters will fuck anything. I'll really have to shift to a more discerning species, in order to test that properly."

Jack struggled to regain his composure. "What on Earth possessed you, to do this?"

"In the long run," Stoney said mildly, "I believe this is something we're going to need to understand far better than we do at present. Now that we can map the structures of the brain in fine detail, and match its raw complexity with our computers, it's only a matter of a decade or so before we build machines that think.

"That in itself will be a vast endeavor, but I want to ensure that it's not stillborn from the start. There's not much point creating the most marvelous children in history, only to find that some awful mammalian instinct drives us to strangle them at birth."

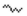

JACK SAT in his study drinking whisky. He'd telephoned Joyce after dinner, and they'd chatted for a while, but it wasn't the same as being with her. The weekends never came soon enough, and by Tuesday or Wednesday any sense of reassurance he'd gained from seeing her had slipped away entirely.

It was almost midnight now. After speaking to Joyce, he'd spent three more hours on the telephone, finding out what he could about Stoney. Milking his connections, such as they were; Jack had only been at Cambridge for five years, so he was still very much an outsider. Not that he'd ever been admitted into any inner circles back at Oxford: he'd always belonged to a small, quiet group of dissenters against the tide of fashion. Whatever else might be said about the Tiddlywinks, they'd never had their hands on the levers of academic power.

A year ago, while on sabbatical in Germany, Stoney had resigned suddenly from a position he'd held at Manchester for a decade. He'd returned to Cambridge, despite having no official posting to take up. He'd started collaborating informally with various people at the Cavendish, until the head of the place, Mott, had invented a job description for him, and given him a modest salary, the three rooms Jack had seen, and some students to assist him.

Stoney's colleagues were uniformly amazed by his spate of successful inventions. Though none of his gadgets were based on entirely new science, his skill at seeing straight to the heart of existing theories and plucking some practical consequence from them was unprecedented. Jack had expected some jealous back-stabbing, but no one seemed to have a bad word to say about Stoney. He was willing to turn his scientific Midas touch to the service of anyone who approached him, and it sounded to Jack as if every would-be skeptic or enemy had been bought off with some rewarding insight into their own field.

Stoney's personal life was rather murkier. Half of Jack's informants were convinced that the man was a confirmed pansy, but others spoke of a beautiful, mysterious woman named Helen, with whom he was plainly on intimate terms.

Jack emptied his glass and stared out across the courtyard. *Was it pride, to wonder if he might have received some kind of prophetic vision?* Fifteen years earlier, when he'd written *The Broken Planet*, he'd imagined that he'd merely been satirising the hubris of modern science. His portrait of the evil forces behind the sardonically named Laboratory Overseeing Various Experiments had been intended as a deadly serious metaphor, but he'd never expected to find himself wondering if real fallen angels were whispering secrets in the ears of a Cambridge don.

How many times, though, had he told his readers that the devil's greatest victory had been convincing the world that he did not exist? The devil was *not* a metaphor, a mere symbol of human weakness: he was a real, scheming presence, acting in time, acting in the world, as much as God Himself.

And hadn't Faustus's damnation been sealed by the most beautiful woman of all time: Helen of Troy?

Jack's skin crawled. He'd once written a humorous newspaper column called "Letters from a Demon," in which a Senior Tempter offered advice to a less experienced colleague on the best means to lead the faithful astray. Even that had been an exhausting, almost corrupting experience; adopting the necessary point of view, however whimsically, had made him feel that he was withering inside. The thought that a cross between the *Faustbuch* and *The Broken Planet* might be coming to life around him was too terrifying to contemplate. He was no hero out of his own fiction—not even a mild-mannered Cedric Duffy, let alone a modern Pendragon. And he did not believe that Merlin would rise from the woods to bring chaos to that hubristic Tower of Babel, the Cavendish Laboratory.

Nevertheless, if he was the only person in England who suspected Stoney's true source of inspiration, who else would act?

Jack poured himself another glass. There was nothing to be gained by procrastinating. He would not be able to rest until he knew what he was facing: a vain, foolish overgrown boy who was having a run of good luck—or a vain, foolish overgrown boy who had sold his soul and imperiled all humanity.

⌁

"A *SATANIST*? You're accusing me of being a Satanist?"

Stoney tugged angrily at his dressing gown; he'd been in bed when Jack had pounded on the door. Given the hour, it had been remarkably civil of him to accept a visitor at all, and he appeared so genuinely affronted now that Jack was almost prepared to apologize and slink away. He said, "I had to ask you—"

"You have to be doubly foolish to be a Satanist," Stoney muttered.

"Doubly?"

"Not only do you need to believe all the nonsense of Christian theology, you then have to turn around and back the preordained, guaranteed-to-fail, absolutely futile *losing side*." He held up his hand, as if he believed he'd anticipated the only possible objection to this remark, and wished to spare Jack the trouble of wasting his breath by uttering it. "I *know*, some people claim it's all really about some pre-Christian deity: Mercury, or Pan—guff like that. But assuming that we're not talking about some complicated mislabelling of objects of worship, I really can't think of anything more insulting. You're comparing me to someone like...*Huysmans*, who was basically just a very dim Catholic."

Stoney folded his arms and settled back on the couch, waiting for Jack's response.

Jack's head was thick from the whisky; he wasn't at all sure how to take this. It was the kind of smart-arsed undergraduate drivel he might have expected from any smug atheist—but then, short of a confession, exactly what kind of reply would have constituted evidence of guilt? *If you'd sold your soul to the devil, what lie would you tell in place of the truth?* Had he seriously believed that Stoney would claim to be a devout churchgoer, as if that were the best possible answer to put Jack off the scent?

He had to concentrate on things he'd seen with his own eyes, facts that could not be denied.

"You're plotting to overthrow nature, bending the world to the will of man."

Stoney sighed. "Not at all. More refined technology will help us tread more lightly. We have to cut back on pollution and pesticides as rapidly as possible. Or do you want to live in a world where all the animals are born as hermaphrodites, and half the Pacific islands disappear in storms?"

"Don't try telling me that you're some kind of guardian of the animal kingdom. You want to replace us all with machines!"

"Does every Zulu or Tibetan who gives birth to a child, and wants the best for it, threaten you in the same way?"

Jack bristled. "I'm not a racist. A Zulu or Tibetan has a *soul.*"

Stoney groaned and put his head in his hands. "It's half past one in the morning! Can't we have this debate some other time?"

Someone banged on the door. Stoney looked up, disbelieving. "What is this? Grand Central Station?"

He crossed to the door and opened it. A disheveled, unshaven man pushed his way into the room. "Quint? What a pleasant—"

The intruder grabbed Stoney and slammed him against the wall. Jack exhaled with surprise. Quint turned bloodshot eyes on him.

"Who the fuck are you?"

"John Hamilton. Who the fuck are you?"

"Never you mind. Just stay put." He jerked Stoney's arm up behind his back with one hand, while grinding his face into the wall with the other. "You're mine now, you piece of shit. No one's going to protect you this time."

Stoney addressed Jack through a mouth squashed against the masonry. "Dith ith Pether Quinth, my own perthonal thpook. I did make a Fauthtian bargain. But with thtrictly temporal—"

"Shut up!" Quint pulled a gun from his jacket and held it to Stoney's head. Jack said, "Steady on."

"Just how far do your connections go?" Quint screamed. "I've had memos disappear, sources clam up—and now my superiors are treating *me* like some kind of traitor! Well, don't worry: when I'm through with you, I'll have the names of the entire network." He turned to address Jack again. "And don't *you* think you're going anywhere."

Stoney said, "Leave him out of dith. He'th at Magdalene. You mutht know by now: all the thpieth are at Trinity."

Jack was shaken by the sight of Quint waving his gun around, but the implications of this drama came as something of a relief. Stoney's ideas must have had their genesis in some secret war-time research project. He hadn't made a deal with the devil after all, but he'd broken the Official Secrets Act, and now he was paying the price.

Stoney flexed his body and knocked Quint backward. Quint staggered, but didn't fall; he raised his arm menacingly, but there was no gun in his hand. Jack looked around to see where it had fallen, but he couldn't spot it anywhere. Stoney landed a kick squarely in Quint's testicles; barefoot, but Quint wailed with pain. A second kick sent him sprawling.

Stoney called out, "Luke? *Luke!* Would you come and give me a hand?"

A solidly built man with tattooed forearms emerged from Stoney's bedroom, yawning and tugging his braces into place. At the sight of Quint, he groaned. "Not again!"

Stoney said, "I'm sorry."

Luke shrugged stoically. The two of them managed to grab hold of Quint, then they dragged him struggling out the door. Jack waited a few seconds, then searched the floor for the gun. But it wasn't anywhere in sight, and it hadn't slid under the furniture; none of the crevices where it might have ended up were so dark that it would have been lost in shadow. It was not in the room at all.

Jack went to the window and watched the three men cross the courtyard, half expecting to witness an assassination. But Stoney and his lover merely lifted Quint into the air between them, and tossed him into a shallow, rather slimy-looking pond.

~w~

JACK SPENT the ensuing days in a state of turmoil. He wasn't ready to confide in anyone until he could frame his suspicions clearly, and the events in Stoney's rooms were difficult to interpret unambiguously. He couldn't state with absolute certainty that Quint's gun had vanished before his eyes. But surely the fact that Stoney was walking free proved that he was receiving supernatural protection? And Quint himself, confused and demoralised, had certainly had the appearance of a man who'd been demonically confounded at every turn.

If this was true, though, Stoney must have bought more with his soul than immunity from worldly authority. *The knowledge itself* had to be Satanic in origin, as the legend of Faustus described it. Tollers had been right, in his great essay "Mythopoesis": myths were remnants of man's pre-lapsarian capacity to apprehend, directly, the great truths of the world. Why else would they resonate in the imagination, and survive from generation to generation?

By Friday, a sense of urgency gripped him. He couldn't take his confusion back to Potter's Barn, back to Joyce and the boys. This had to be resolved, if only in his own mind, before he returned to his family.

With Wagner on the gramophone, he sat and meditated on the challenge he was facing. Stoney had to be thwarted, but how? Jack had always said that the Church of England—apparently so quaint and harmless, a Church of cake stalls and kindly spinsters—was like a fearsome army in the eyes of Satan. But even if his master was quaking in Hell, it would take more than a few stern words from a bicycling vicar to force Stoney to abandon his obscene plans.

But Stoney's intentions, in themselves, didn't matter. He'd been granted the power to dazzle and seduce, but not to force his will upon the populace. What mattered was how his plans were viewed by others. And the way to stop him was to open people's eyes to the true emptiness of his apparent cornucopia.

The more he thought and prayed about it, the more certain Jack became that he'd discerned the task required of him. No denunciation from the pulpits would suffice; people wouldn't turn down the fruits of Stoney's damnation on the mere say-so of the Church. Why would anyone reject such lustrous gifts, without a carefully reasoned argument?

Jack had been humiliated once, defeated once, trying to expose the barrenness of materialism. But might that not have been a form of preparation? He'd been badly mauled by Anscombe, but she'd made an infinitely gentler enemy than the one he now confronted. He had suffered from her taunts— but what was *suffering*, if not the chisel God used to shape his children into their true selves?

His role was clear, now. He would find Stoney's intellectual Achilles heel, and expose it to the world.

He would debate him.

3

ROBERT GAZED at the blackboard for a full minute, then started laughing with delight. "That's so beautiful!"

"Isn't it?" Helen put down the chalk and joined him on the couch. "Any more symmetry, and nothing would happen: the universe would be full of crystalline blankness. Any less, and it would all be uncorrelated noise."

Over the months, in a series of tutorials, Helen had led him through a small part of the century of physics that had separated them at their first meeting, down to the purely algebraic structures that lay beneath spacetime and matter. Mathematics catalogued everything that was not self-contradictory; within that vast inventory, physics was an island of structures rich enough to contain their own beholders.

Robert sat and mentally reviewed everything he'd learned, trying to apprehend as much as he could in a single image. As he did, a part of him waited fearfully for a sense of disappointment, a sense of anticlimax. *He might never see more deeply into the nature of the world. In this direction, at least, there was nothing more to be discovered.*

But anticlimax was impossible. To become jaded with *this* was impossible. However familiar he became with the algebra of the universe, it would never grow less marvelous.

Finally he asked, "Are there other islands?" Not merely other histories, sharing the same underlying basis, but other realities entirely.

"I suspect so," Helen replied. "People have mapped some possibilities. I don't know how that could ever be confirmed, though."

Robert shook his head, sated. "I won't even think about that. I need to come down to Earth for a while." He stretched his arms and leaned back, still grinning.

Helen said, "Where's Luke today? He usually shows up by now, to drag you out into the sunshine."

The question wiped the smile from Robert's face. "Apparently I make poor company. Being insufficiently fanatical about darts and football."

"He's left you?" Helen reached over and squeezed his hand sympathetically. A little mockingly, too.

Robert was annoyed; she never said anything, but he always felt that she was judging him. "You think I should grow up, don't you? Find someone more like myself. Some kind of *soulmate*." He'd meant the word to sound sardonic, but it emerged rather differently.

"It's your life," she said.

A year before, that would have been a laughable claim, but it was almost the truth now. There was a *de facto* moratorium on prosecutions, while the recently acquired genetic and neurological evidence was being assessed by a parliamentary subcommittee. Robert had helped plant the seeds of the campaign, but he'd played no real part in it; other people had taken up the cause. In a matter of months, it was possible that Quint's cage would be smashed, at least for everyone in Britain.

The prospect filled him with a kind of vertigo. He might have broken the laws at every opportunity, but they had still molded him. The cage might not have left him crippled, but he'd be lying to himself if he denied that he'd been stunted.

He said, "Is that what happened, in your past? I ended up in some... lifelong partnership?" As he spoke the words, his mouth went dry, and he was suddenly afraid that the answer would be yes. *With Chris. The life he'd missed out on was a life of happiness with Chris.*

"No."

"Then...what?" he pleaded. "What did I do? How did I live?" He caught himself, suddenly self-conscious, but added, "You can't blame me for being curious."

Helen said gently, "You don't want to know what you can't change. All of that is part of your own causal past now, as much as it is of mine."

"If it's part of my own history," Robert countered, "don't I deserve to know it? This man wasn't me, but he brought you to me."

Helen considered this. "You accept that he was someone else? Not someone whose actions you're responsible for?"

"Of course."

She said, "There was a trial, in 1952. For 'Gross Indecency contrary to Section 11 of the Criminal Amendment Act of 1885.' He wasn't imprisoned, but the court ordered hormone treatments."

"*Hormone treatments?*" Robert laughed. "What—testosterone, to make him more of a man?"

"No, estrogen. Which in men reduces the sex drive. There are side-effects, of course. Gynecomorphism, among other things."

Robert felt physically sick. *They'd chemically castrated him, with drugs that had made him sprout breasts.* Of all the bizarre abuse to which he'd been subjected, nothing had been as horrifying as that.

Helen continued, "The treatment lasted six months, and the effects were all temporary. But two years later, he took his own life. It was never clear exactly why."

Robert absorbed this in silence. He didn't want to know anything more.

After a while, he said, "How do you bear it? Knowing that in some branch or other, every possible form of humiliation is being inflicted on someone?"

Helen said, "I don't *bear it*. I change it. That's why I'm here."

Robert bowed his head. "I know. And I'm grateful that our histories collided. But…how many histories don't?" He struggled to find an example, though it was almost too painful to contemplate; since their first conversation, it was a topic he'd deliberately pushed to the back of his mind. "There's not just an unchangeable Auschwitz in each of our pasts, there are an astronomical number of others—along with an astronomical number of things that are even worse."

Helen said bluntly, "That's not true."

"What?" Robert looked up at her, startled.

She walked to the blackboard and erased it. "Auschwitz has happened, for both of us, and no one I'm aware of has ever prevented it—but that doesn't mean that *nobody* stops it, anywhere." She began sketching a network of fine lines on the blackboard. "You and I are having this conversation in countless microhistories—sequences of events where various different things happen with subatomic particles throughout the universe—but that's irrelevant to us, we can't tell those strands apart, so we might as well treat them all as one history." She pressed the chalk down hard to make a thick streak that covered everything she'd drawn. "The quantum decoherence people call this 'coarse graining'. Summing over all these indistinguishable details is what gives rise to classical physics in the first place.

"Now, 'the two of us' would have first met in many perceivably different coarse-grained histories—and furthermore, you've since diverged by making different choices, and experiencing different external possibilities, after those events." She sketched two intersecting ribbons of coarse-grained histories, and then showed each history diverging further.

"World War II and the Holocaust certainly happened in both of *our* pasts—but that's no proof that the total is so vast that it might as well be infinite. Remember, what stops us successfully intervening is the fact that we're reaching back to a point where some of the parallel interventions start to bite their own tail. So when we fail, it can't be counted twice: it's just confirming what we already know."

Robert protested, "But what about all the versions of '30s Europe that don't happen to lie in either your past or mine? Just because we have no direct evidence for a Holocaust in those branches, that hardly makes it unlikely."

Helen said, "Not unlikely *per se*, without intervention. But not fixed in stone either. We'll keep trying, refining the technology, until we can reach branches where there's no overlap with our own past in the '30s. And there must be other, separate ribbons of intervention that happen in histories we can never even know about."

Robert was elated. He'd imagined himself clinging to a rock of improbable good fortune in an infinite sea of suffering—struggling to pretend, for the sake of his own sanity, that the rock was all there was. But what lay around him was not inevitably worse; it was merely unknown. In time, he might even play a part in ensuring that every last tragedy was *not* repeated across billions of worlds.

He reexamined the diagram. "Hang on. Intervention doesn't end divergence, though, does it? You reached *us*, a year ago, but in at least some of the histories spreading out from that moment, won't we still have suffered all kinds of disasters, and reacted in all kinds of self-defeating ways?"

"Yes," Helen conceded, "but fewer than you might think. If you merely listed every sequence of events that superficially appeared to have a non-zero probability, you'd end up with a staggering catalog of absurdist tragedies. But when you calculate everything more carefully, and take account of Planck-scale effects, it turns out to be nowhere near as bad. There are *no* coarse-grained histories where boulders assemble themselves out of dust and rain from the sky, or everyone in London or Madras goes mad and slaughters their children. Most macroscopic systems end up being quite robust—people included. Across histories, the range of natural disasters, human stupidity, and sheer bad luck isn't overwhelmingly greater than the range you're aware of from this history alone."

Robert laughed. "And that's not bad enough?"

"Oh, it is. But that's the best thing about the form I've taken."

"I'm sorry?"

Helen tipped her head and regarded him with an expression of disappointment. "You know, you're still not as quick on your feet as I'd expected."

Robert's face burned, but then he realized what he'd missed, and his resentment vanished.

"*You don't diverge?* Your hardware is designed to end the process? Your environment, your surroundings, will still split you into different histories— but on a coarse-grained level, you don't contribute to the process yourself?"

"That's right."

Robert was speechless. Even after a year, she could still toss him a hand grenade like this.

Helen said, "I can't help living in many worlds; that's beyond my control. But I do know that I'm one person. Faced with a choice that puts me on a knife-edge, I know I won't split and take every path."

Robert hugged himself, suddenly cold. "Like I do. Like I have. Like all of us poor creatures of flesh."

Helen came and sat beside him. "Even that's not irrevocable. Once you've taken this form—if that's what you choose—you can meet your other selves, reverse some of the scatter. Give some a chance to undo what they've done."

This time, Robert grasped her meaning at once. "Gather myself together? Make myself whole?"

Helen shrugged. "If it's what you want. If you see it that way."

He stared back at her, disoriented. Touching the bedrock of physics was one thing, but this possibility was too much to take in.

Someone knocked on the study door. The two of them exchanged wary glances, but it wasn't Quint, back for more punishment. It was a porter bearing a telegram.

When the man had left, Robert opened the envelope.

"Bad news?" Helen asked.

He shook his head. "Not a death in the family, if that's what you meant. It's from John Hamilton. He's challenging me to a debate. On the topic 'Can A Machine Think?'"

"What, at some university function?"

"No. On the BBC. Four weeks from tomorrow." He looked up. "Do you think I should do it?"

"Radio or television?"

Robert reread the message. "Television."

Helen smiled. "Definitely. I'll give you some tips."

"On the subject?"

"No! That would be cheating." She eyed him appraisingly. "You can start by throwing out your electric razor. Get rid of the permanent five o'clock shadow."

Robert was hurt. "Some people find that quite attractive."

Helen replied firmly, "Trust me on this."

〜〜〜

THE BBC sent a car to take Robert down to London. Helen sat beside him in the back seat.

"Are you nervous?" she asked.

"Nothing that an hour of throwing up won't cure."

Hamilton had suggested a live broadcast, "to keep things interesting," and the producer had agreed. Robert had never been on television; he'd taken part in a couple of radio discussions on the future of computing, back when the Mark I had first come into use, but even those had been taped.

Hamilton's choice of topic had surprised him at first, but in retrospect it seemed quite shrewd. A debate on the proposition that "Modern Science is the Devil's Work" would have brought howls of laughter from all but the most pious viewers, whereas the purely metaphorical claim that "Modern Science is a Faustian Pact" would have had the entire audience nodding sagely in agreement, while carrying no implications whatsoever. If you weren't going to take the whole dire fairy tale literally, everything was "a Faustian Pact" in some sufficiently watered-down sense: everything had a potential downside, and this was as pointless to assert as it was easy to demonstrate.

Robert had met considerable incredulity, though, when he'd explained to journalists where his own research was leading. To date, the press had treated him as a kind of eccentric British Edison, churning out inventions of indisputable utility, and no one seemed to find it at all surprising or alarming that he was also, frankly, a bit of a loon. But Hamilton would have a chance to exploit, and reshape, that perception. If Robert insisted on defending his goal of creating machine intelligence, not as an amusing hobby that might have been chosen by a public relations firm to make him appear endearingly daft, but as both the ultimate vindication of materialist science and the logical endpoint of most of his life's work, Hamilton could use a victory tonight to cast doubt on everything Robert had done, and everything he symbolized. By asking, not at all rhetorically, "Where will this all end?", he was inviting Robert to step forward and hang himself with the answer.

The traffic was heavy for a Sunday evening, and they arrived at the Shepherd's Bush studios with only fifteen minutes until the broadcast. Hamilton had been collected by a separate car, from his family home near Oxford. As they crossed the studio Robert spotted him, conversing intensely with a dark-haired young man.

He whispered to Helen, "Do you know who that is, with Hamilton?"

She followed his gaze, then smiled cryptically. Robert said, "What? Do you recognize him from somewhere?"

"Yes, but I'll tell you later."

As the make-up woman applied powder, Helen ran through her long list of rules again. "Don't stare into the camera, or you'll look like you're peddling soap powder. But don't avert your eyes. You don't want to look shifty."

The make-up woman whispered to Robert, "Everyone's an expert."

"Annoying, isn't it?" he confided.

Michael Polanyi, an academic philosopher who was well-known to the public after presenting a series of radio talks, had agreed to moderate the debate. Polanyi popped into the make-up room, accompanied by the producer; they chatted with Robert for a couple of minutes, setting him at ease and reminding him of the procedure they'd be following.

They'd only just left him when the floor manager appeared. "We need you in the studio now, please, Professor." Robert followed her, and Helen pursued him part of the way. "Breathe slowly and deeply," she urged him.

"As if you'd know," he snapped.

Robert shook hands with Hamilton then took his seat on one side of the podium. Hamilton's young adviser had retreated into the shadows; Robert glanced back to see Helen watching from a similar position. It was like a duel:

they both had seconds. The floor manager pointed out the studio monitor, and as Robert watched it was switched between the feeds from two cameras: a wide shot of the whole set, and a closer view of the podium, including the small blackboard on a stand beside it. He'd once asked Helen whether television had progressed to far greater levels of sophistication in her branch of the future, once the pioneering days were left behind, but the question had left her uncharacteristically tongue-tied.

The floor manager retreated behind the cameras, called for silence, then counted down from ten, mouthing the final numbers.

The broadcast began with an introduction from Polanyi: concise, witty, and non-partisan. Then Hamilton stepped up to the podium. Robert watched him directly while the wide-angle view was being transmitted, so as not to appear rude or distracted. He only turned to the monitor when he was no longer visible himself.

"Can a machine think?" Hamilton began. "My intuition tells me: *no*. My heart tells me: *no*. I'm sure that most of you feel the same way. But that's not enough, is it? In this day and age, we aren't allowed to rely on our hearts for anything. We need something scientific. We need some kind of proof.

"Some years ago, I took part in a debate at Oxford University. The issue then was not whether machines might behave like people, but whether people themselves might *be* mere machines. Materialists, you see, claim that we are all just a collection of purposeless atoms, colliding at random. Everything we do, everything we feel, everything we say, comes down to some sequence of events that might as well be the spinning of cogs, or the opening and closing of electrical relays.

"To me, this was self-evidently false. What point could there be, I argued, in even conversing with a materialist? By his own admission, the words that came out of his mouth would be the result of nothing but a mindless, mechanical process! By his own theory, he could have no reason to think that those words would be the truth! Only believers in a transcendent human soul could claim any interest in the truth."

Hamilton nodded slowly, a penitent's gesture. "I was wrong, and I was put in my place. This might be self-evident to *me*, and it might be self-evident to *you*, but it's certainly not what philosophers call an 'analytical truth': it's not actually a nonsense, a contradiction in terms, to believe that we are mere machines. There might, there just *might*, be some reason why the words that emerge from a materialist's mouth are truthful, despite their origins lying entirely in unthinking matter.

"There might." Hamilton smiled wistfully. "I had to concede that possibility, because I only had my instinct, my gut feeling, to tell me otherwise.

"But the reason I only had my instinct to guide me was because I'd failed to learn of an event that had taken place many years before. A discovery made in 1930, by an Austrian mathematician named Kurt Gödel."

Robert felt a shiver of excitement run down his spine. He'd been afraid that the whole contest would degenerate into theology, with Hamilton invoking Aquinas all night—or Aristotle, at best. But it looked as if his mysterious adviser had dragged him into the twentieth century, and they were going to have a chance to debate the real issues after all.

"What is it that we *know* Professor Stoney's computers can do, and do well?" Hamilton continued. "Arithmetic! In a fraction of a second, they can add up a million numbers. Once we've told them, very precisely, what calculations to perform, they'll complete them in the blink of an eye—even if those calculations would take you or me a lifetime.

"But do these machines *understand* what it is they're doing? Professor Stoney says, 'Not yet. Not right now. Give them time. Rome wasn't built in a day.'" Hamilton nodded thoughtfully. "Perhaps that's fair. His computers are only a few years old. They're just babies. Why should they understand anything, so soon?

"But let's stop and think about this a bit more carefully. A computer, as it stands today, is simply a machine that does arithmetic, and Professor Stoney isn't proposing that they're going to sprout new kinds of brains all on their own. Nor is he proposing *giving* them anything really new. He can already let them look at the world with television cameras, turning the pictures into a stream of numbers describing the brightness of different points on the screen...on which the computer can then perform *arithmetic*. He can already let them speak to us with a special kind of loudspeaker, to which the computer feeds a stream of numbers to describe how loud the sound should be...a stream of numbers produced by more *arithmetic*.

"So the world can come into the computer, as numbers, and words can emerge, as numbers too. All Professor Stoney hopes to add to his computers is a 'cleverer' way to do the arithmetic that takes the first set of numbers and churns out the second. It's that 'clever arithmetic', he tells us, that will make these machines think."

Hamilton folded his arms and paused for a moment. "What are we to make of this? Can *doing arithmetic*, and nothing more, be enough to let a machine *understand* anything? My instinct certainly tells me no, but who am I that you should trust my instinct?

"So, let's narrow down the question of understanding, and to be scrupulously fair, let's put it in the most favorable light possible for Professor Stoney. If there's one thing a computer *ought* to be able to understand—as well as us, if not better—it's arithmetic itself. If a computer could think at all, it would surely be able to grasp the nature of its own best talent.

"The question, then, comes down to this: can you *describe* all of arithmetic, *using* nothing but arithmetic? Thirty years ago—long before Professor Stoney and his computers came along—Professor Gödel asked himself exactly that question.

"Now, you might be wondering how anyone could even *begin* to describe the rules of arithmetic, using nothing but arithmetic itself." Hamilton turned to the blackboard, picked up the chalk, and wrote two lines:

If x+z = y+z
then x = y

"This is an important rule, but it's written in symbols, not numbers, because it has to be true for *every* number, every x, y and z. But Professor Gödel had a clever idea: why not use a code, like spies use, where every symbol is assigned a number?" Hamilton wrote:

The code for "a" is 1.
The code for "b" is 2.

"And so on. You can have a code for every letter of the alphabet, and for all the other symbols needed for arithmetic: plus signs, equals signs, that kind of thing. Telegrams are sent this way every day, with a code called the Baudot code, so there's really nothing strange or sinister about it.

"All the rules of arithmetic that we learned at school can be written with a carefully chosen set of symbols, which can then be translated into numbers.

Every question as to what does or does not *follow from* those rules can then be seen anew, as a question about numbers. If *this* line follows from *this* one," Hamilton indicated the two lines of the cancellation rule, "we can see it in the relationship between their code numbers. We can judge each inference, and declare it valid or not, purely by doing arithmetic.

"So, given *any* proposition at all about arithmetic—such as the claim that 'there are infinitely many prime numbers'—we can restate the notion that we have a proof for that claim in terms of code numbers. If the code number for our claim is x, we can say 'There is a number p, ending with the code number x, that passes our test for being the code number of a valid proof.'"

Hamilton took a visible breath.

"In 1930, Professor Gödel used this scheme to do something rather ingenious." He wrote on the blackboard:

There DOES NOT EXIST a number p meeting the following condition: p is the code number of a valid proof of this claim.

"Here is a claim about arithmetic, about numbers. It has to be either true or false. So let's start by supposing that it happens to be true. Then there *is no* number p that is the code number for a proof of this claim. So this is a true statement about arithmetic, but it can't be proved merely by *doing* arithmetic!"

Hamilton smiled. "If you don't catch on immediately, don't worry; when I first heard this argument from a young friend of mine, it took a while for the meaning to sink in. But remember: the only hope a computer has for understanding *anything* is by doing arithmetic, and we've just found a statement that *cannot* be proved with mere arithmetic.

"Is this statement really true, though? We mustn't jump to conclusions, we mustn't damn the machines too hastily. Suppose this claim is false! Since it claims there is no number p that is the code number of its own proof, to be false there would have to be such a number, after all. And that number would encode the 'proof' of an acknowledged falsehood!"

Hamilton spread his arms triumphantly. "You and I, like every schoolboy, know that you can't prove a falsehood from sound premises—and if the premises of arithmetic aren't sound, what is? So *we* know, as a matter of certainty, that this statement is true.

"Professor Gödel was the first to see this, but with a little help and perseverance, any educated person can follow in his footsteps. *A machine could never do that.* We might divulge to a machine our own knowledge of this fact, offering it as something to be taken on trust, but the machine could neither stumble on this truth for itself, nor truly comprehend it when we offered it as a gift.

"You and I *understand* arithmetic, in a way that no electronic calculator ever will. What hope has a machine, then, of moving beyond its own most favorable milieu and comprehending any wider truth?

"None at all, ladies and gentlemen. Though this detour into mathematics might have seemed arcane to you, it has served a very down-to-Earth purpose. It has proved—beyond refutation by even the most ardent materialist or the most pedantic philosopher—what we common folk knew all along: no machine will ever think."

Hamilton took his seat. For a moment, Robert was simply exhilarated; coached or not, Hamilton had grasped the essential features of the incompleteness proof, and presented them to a lay audience. What might have been a night of shadow-boxing—with no blows connecting, and nothing for the audience to judge but two solo performances in separate arenas—had turned into a genuine clash of ideas.

As Polanyi introduced him and he walked to the podium, Robert realized that his usual shyness and self-consciousness had evaporated. He was filled with an altogether different kind of tension: he sensed more acutely than ever what was at stake.

When he reached the podium, he adopted the posture of someone about to begin a prepared speech, but then he caught himself, as if he'd forgotten something. "Bear with me for a moment." He walked around to the far side of the blackboard and quickly wrote a few words on it, upside-down. Then he resumed his place.

"Can a machine think? Professor Hamilton would like us to believe that he's settled the issue once and for all, by coming up with a statement that *we* know is true, but a particular machine—programmed to explore the theorems of arithmetic in a certain rigid way—would never be able to produce. Well…we all have our limitations." He flipped the blackboard over to reveal what he'd written on the opposite side:

If Robert Stoney speaks these words, he will NOT be telling the truth.

He waited a few beats, then continued.

"What I'd like to explore, though, is not so much a question of limitations, as of opportunities. How exactly is it that we've all ended up with this mysterious ability to know that Gödel's statement is true? Where does this advantage, this great insight, come from? From our souls? From some immaterial entity that no machine could ever possess? Is that the only possible source, the only conceivable explanation? Or might it come from something a little less ethereal?

"As Professor Hamilton explained, we believe Gödel's statement is true because we trust the rules of arithmetic not to lead us into contradictions and falsehoods. But where does that trust come from? How does it arise?"

Robert turned the blackboard back to Hamilton's side, and pointed to the cancellation rule. "If x plus z equals y plus z, then x equals y. Why is this so *reasonable*? We might not learn to put it quite like this until we're in our teens, but if you showed a young child two boxes—without revealing their contents—added an equal number of shells, or stones, or pieces of fruit to both, and then let the child look inside to see that each box now contained the same number of items, it wouldn't take any formal education for the child to understand that the two boxes must have held the same number of things to begin with.

"The child knows, we all know, how a certain kind of object behaves. Our lives are steeped in direct experience of whole numbers: whole numbers of coins, stamps, pebbles, birds, cats, sheep, buses. If I tried to persuade a six-year-old that I could put three stones in a box, remove one of them, and be left with four...he'd simply laugh at me. Why? It's not merely that he's sure to have taken one thing away from three to get two, on many prior occasions. Even a child understands that some things that appear reliable will eventually fail: a toy that works perfectly, day after day, for a month or a year, can still break. But not arithmetic, not taking one from three. He can't even picture *that* failing. Once you've lived in the world, once you've seen how it works, the failure of arithmetic becomes unimaginable.

"Professor Hamilton suggests that this is down to our souls. But what would he say about a child reared in a world of water and mist, never in the company of more than one person at a time, never taught to count on his fingers and toes. I doubt that such a child would possess the same certainty that you and I have, as to the impossibility of arithmetic ever leading him astray.

To banish whole numbers entirely from his world would require very strange surroundings, and a level of deprivation amounting to cruelty, but would that be enough to rob a child of his *soul?*

"A computer, programmed to pursue arithmetic as Professor Hamilton has described, is subject to far more deprivation than that child. If I'd been raised with my hands and feet tied, my head in a sack, and someone shouting orders at me, I doubt that I'd have much grasp of reality—and I'd still be better prepared for the task than such a computer. It's a great mercy that a machine treated that way wouldn't be able to think: if it could, the shackles we'd placed upon it would be criminally oppressive.

"But that's hardly the fault of the computer, or a revelation of some irreparable flaw in its nature. If we want to judge the potential of our machines with any degree of honesty, we have to play fair with them, not saddle them with restrictions that we'd never dream of imposing on ourselves. There really is no point comparing an eagle with a spanner, or a gazelle with a washing machine: it's our jets that fly and our cars that run, albeit in quite different ways than any animal.

"*Thought* is sure to be far harder to achieve than those other skills, and to do so we might need to mimic the natural world far more closely. But I believe that once a machine is endowed with facilities resembling the inborn tools for learning that we all have as our birthright, and is set free to learn the way a child learns, through experience, observation, trial and error, hunches and failures—instead of being handed a list of instructions that it has no choice but to obey—we will finally be in a position to compare like with like.

"When that happens, and we can meet and talk and argue with these machines—about arithmetic, or any other topic—there'll be no need to take the word of Professor Gödel, or Professor Hamilton, or myself, for anything. We'll invite them down to the local pub, and interrogate them in person. And if we play fair with them, we'll use the same experience and judgment we use with any friend, or guest, or stranger, to decide for ourselves whether or not they can think."

⁓⁓

THE BBC put on a lavish assortment of wine and cheese in a small room off the studio. Robert ended up in a heated argument with Polanyi, who revealed himself to be firmly on the negative side, while Helen flirted shamelessly with Hamilton's young friend, who turned out to have a PhD in algebraic geometry from Cambridge; he must have completed the degree just before Robert had come back from Manchester. After exchanging some polite formalities with Hamilton, Robert kept his distance, sensing that any further contact would not be welcome.

An hour later, though, after getting lost in the maze of corridors on his way back from the toilets, Robert came across Hamilton sitting alone in the studio, weeping.

He almost backed away in silence, but Hamilton looked up and saw him. With their eyes locked, it was impossible to retreat.

Robert said, "It's your wife?" He'd heard that she'd been seriously ill, but the gossip had included a miraculous recovery. Some friend of the family had lain hands on her a year ago, and she'd gone into remission.

Hamilton said, "She's dying."

Robert approached and sat beside him. "From what?"

"Breast cancer. It's spread throughout her body. Into her bones, into her lungs, into her liver." He sobbed again, a helpless spasm, then caught himself angrily. "*Suffering is the chisel God uses to shape us.* What kind of idiot comes up with a line like that?"

Robert said, "I'll talk to a friend of mine, an oncologist at Guy's Hospital. He's doing a trial of a new genetic treatment."

Hamilton stared at him. "One of your *miracle cures?*"

"No, no. I mean, only very indirectly."

Hamilton said angrily, "She won't take your poison."

Robert almost snapped back: *She won't? Or you won't let her?* But it was an unfair question. In some marriages, the lines blurred. It was not for him to judge the way the two of them faced this together.

"They go away in order to be with us in a new way, even closer than before." Hamilton spoke the words like a defiant incantation, a declaration of faith that would ward off temptation, whether or not he entirely believed it.

Robert was silent for a while, then he said, "I lost someone close to me, when I was a boy. And I thought the same thing. I thought he was still with me, for a long time afterward. Guiding me. Encouraging me." It was hard to get the words out; he hadn't spoken about this to anyone for almost thirty years. "I dreamed up a whole theory to explain it, in which 'souls' used quantum uncertainty to control the body during life, and communicate with the living after death, without breaking any laws of physics. The kind of thing every science-minded seventeen-year-old probably stumbles on, and takes seriously for a couple of weeks, before realizing how nonsensical it is. But I had a good reason not to see the flaws, so I clung to it for almost two years. Because I missed him so much, it took me that long to understand what I was doing, how I was deceiving myself."

Hamilton said pointedly, "If you'd not tried to explain it, you might never have lost him. He might still be with you now."

Robert thought about this. "I'm glad he's not, though. It wouldn't be fair on either of us."

Hamilton shuddered. "Then you can't have loved him very much, can you?" He put his head in his arms. "Just fuck off, now, will you."

Robert said, "What exactly would it take, to prove to you that I'm not in league with the devil?"

Hamilton turned red eyes on him and announced triumphantly, "Nothing will do that! I saw what happened to Quint's gun!"

Robert sighed. "That was a conjuring trick. Stage magic, not black magic."

"Oh yes? Show me how it's done, then. Teach me how to do it, so I can impress my friends."

"It's rather technical. It would take all night."

Hamilton laughed humorlessly. "You can't deceive me. I saw through you from the start."

"Do you think X-rays are Satanic? Penicillin?"

"Don't treat me like a fool. There's no comparison."

"*Why not?* Everything I've helped develop is part of the same continuum. I've read some of your writing on medieval culture, and you're always berating modern commentators for presenting it as unsophisticated. No one really thought the Earth was flat. No one really treated every novelty as witchcraft. So why view any of my work any differently than a fourteenth-century man would view twentieth-century medicine?"

Hamilton replied, "If a fourteenth-century man was suddenly faced with twentieth-century medicine, don't you think he'd be entitled to wonder how it had been revealed to his contemporaries?"

Robert shifted uneasily on his chair. Helen hadn't sworn him to secrecy, but he'd agreed with her view: it was better to wait, to spread the knowledge that would ground an understanding of what had happened, before revealing any details of the contact between branches.

But this man's wife was dying, needlessly. And Robert was tired of keeping secrets. Some wars required it, but others were better won with honesty.

He said, "I know you hate H.G. Wells. But what if he was right, about one little thing?"

Robert told him everything, glossing over the technicalities but leaving out nothing substantial. Hamilton listened without interrupting, gripped by a kind of unwilling fascination. His expression shifted from hostile to incredulous, but there were also hints of begrudging amazement, as if he could at least appreciate some of the beauty and complexity of the picture Robert was painting.

But when Robert had finished, Hamilton said merely, "You're a grand liar, Stoney. But what else should I expect, from the King of Lies?"

～w～

ROBERT WAS in a somber mood on the drive back to Cambridge. The encounter with Hamilton had depressed him, and the question of who'd swayed the nation in the debate seemed remote and abstract in comparison.

Helen had taken a house in the suburbs, rather than inviting scandal by cohabiting with him, though her frequent visits to his rooms seemed to have had almost the same effect. Robert walked her to the door.

"I think it went well, don't you?" she said.

"I suppose so."

"I'm leaving tonight," she added casually. "This is goodbye."

"What?" Robert was staggered. "Everything's still up in the air! I still need you!"

She shook her head. "You have all the tools you need, all the clues. And plenty of local allies. There's nothing truly urgent I could tell you, now, that you couldn't find out just as quickly on your own."

Robert pleaded with her, but her mind was made up. The driver beeped the horn; Robert gestured to him impatiently.

"You know, my breath's frosting visibly," he said, "and you're producing nothing. You really ought to be more careful."

She laughed. "It's a bit late to worry about that."

"Where will you go? Back home? Or off to twist another branch?"

"Another branch. But there's something I'm planning to do on the way."

"What's that?"

"Do you remember once, you wrote about an Oracle? A machine that could solve the halting problem?"

"Of course." Given a device that could tell you in advance whether a given computer program would halt, or go on running forever, you'd be able to prove or disprove any theorem whatsoever about the integers: the Goldbach conjecture, Fermat's Last Theorem, anything. You'd simply show this "Oracle" a program that would loop through all the integers, testing every possible set of values and only halting if it came to a set that violated the conjecture. You'd never need to run the program itself; the Oracle's verdict on whether or not it halted would be enough.

Such a device might or might not be possible, but Robert had proved more than twenty years before that no ordinary computer, however ingeniously programmed, would suffice. If program H could always tell you in a finite time whether or not program X would halt, you could tack on a small addition to H to create program Z, which perversely and deliberately went into an infinite loop whenever it examined a program that halted. If Z examined itself, it would either halt eventually, or run forever. But either possibility contradicted the alleged powers of program H: if Z actually ran forever, it would be because H had claimed that it wouldn't, and *vice versa*. Program H could not exist.

"Time travel," Helen said, "gives me a chance to become an Oracle. There's a way to exploit the inability to change your own past, a way to squeeze an infinite number of timelike paths—none of them closed, but some of them arbitrarily near to it—into a finite physical system. Once you do that, you can solve the halting problem."

"How?" Robert's mind was racing. "And once you've done that...what about higher cardinalities? An Oracle for Oracles, able to test conjectures about the real numbers?"

Helen smiled enigmatically. "The first problem should only take you forty or fifty years to solve. As for the rest," she pulled away from him, moving into the darkness of the hallway, "what makes you think I know the answer myself?" She blew him a kiss, then vanished from sight.

Robert took a step toward her, but the hallway was empty.

He walked back to the car, sad and exalted, his heart pounding.

The driver asked wearily, "Where to now, sir?"

Robert said, "Further up, and further in."

4

THE NIGHT after the funeral, Jack paced the house until three a.m. When would it be bearable? *When?* She'd shown more strength and courage, dying, than he felt within himself right now. But she'd share it with him, in the weeks to come. She'd share it with them all.

In bed, in the darkness, he tried to sense her presence around him. But it was forced, it was premature. It was one thing to have faith that she was watching over him, but quite another to expect to be spared every trace of grief, every trace of pain.

He waited for sleep. He needed to get some rest before dawn, or how would he face her children in the morning?

Gradually, he became aware of someone standing in the darkness at the foot of the bed. As he examined and reexamined the shadows, he formed a clear image of the apparition's face.

It was his own. Younger, happier, surer of himself.

Jack sat up. "What do you want?"

"I want you to come with me." The figure approached; Jack recoiled, and it halted.

"Come with you, where?" Jack demanded.

"To a place where she's waiting."

Jack shook his head. "No. I don't believe you. She said she'd come for me herself, when it was time. She said she'd guide me."

"She didn't understand, then," the apparition insisted gently. "She didn't know I could fetch you myself. Do you think I'd send her in my place? Do you think I'd shirk the task?"

Jack searched the smiling, supplicatory face. "Who are you?" *His own soul, in Heaven, remade?* Was this a gift God offered everyone? To meet, before death, the very thing you would become—if you so chose? So that even this would be an act of free will?

The apparition said, "Stoney persuaded me to let his friend treat Joyce. We lived on, together. More than a century has passed. And now we want you to join us."

Jack choked with horror. "No! This is a trick! *You're the Devil!*"

The thing replied mildly, "There is no Devil. And no God, either. Just people. But I promise you: people with the powers of gods are kinder than any god we ever imagined."

Jack covered his face. "Leave me be." He whispered fervent prayers, and waited. It was a test, a moment of vulnerability, but God wouldn't leave him naked like this, face-to-face with the Enemy, for longer than he could endure.

He uncovered his face. The thing was still with him.

It said, "Do you remember, when your faith came to you? The sense of a shield around you melting away, like armor you'd worn to keep God at bay?"

"Yes." Jack acknowledged the truth defiantly; he wasn't frightened that this abomination could see into his past, into his heart.

"That took strength: to admit that you needed God. But it takes the same kind of strength, again, to understand that *some needs can never be met.* I can't promise you Heaven. We have no disease, we have no war, we have no poverty. But we have to find our own love, our own goodness. There is no final word of comfort. We only have each other."

Jack didn't reply; this blasphemous fantasy wasn't even worth challenging. He said, "I know you're lying. Do you really imagine that I'd leave the boys alone here?"

"They'd go back to America, back to their father. How many years do you think you'd have with them, if you stay? They've already lost their mother. It would be easier for them now, a single clean break."

Jack shouted angrily, "Get out of my house!"

The thing came closer, and sat on the bed. It put a hand on his shoulder. Jack sobbed, "Help me!" But he didn't know whose aid he was invoking any more.

"Do you remember the scene in *The Seat of Oak*? When the Harpy traps everyone in her cave underground, and tries to convince them that there is no Nescia? Only this drab underworld is real, she tells them. Everything else they think they've seen was just make-believe." Jack's own young face smiled nostalgically. "And we had dear old Shrugweight reply: he didn't think much of this so-called 'real world' of hers. And even if she was right, since four little children could make up a better world, he'd rather go on pretending that their imaginary one was real.

"But we had it all upside down! The real world is richer, and stranger, and more beautiful than anything ever imagined. Milton, Dante, John the Divine are the ones who trapped you in a drab, gray underworld. That's where you are now. But if you give me your hand, I can pull you out."

Jack's chest was bursting. *He couldn't lose his faith. He'd kept it through worse than this. He'd kept it through every torture and indignity God had inflicted on his wife's frail body. No one could take it from him now.* He crooned to himself, "In my time of trouble, He will find me."

The cool hand tightened its grip on his shoulder. "You can be with her, now. Just say the word, and you will become a part of me. I will take you inside me, and you will see through my eyes, and we will travel back to the world where she still lives."

Jack wept openly. "Leave me in peace! Just leave me to mourn her!"

The thing nodded sadly. "If that's what you want."

"I do! *Go!*"

"When I'm sure."

Suddenly, Jack thought back to the long rant Stoney had delivered in the studio. Every choice went every way, Stoney had claimed. No decision could ever be final.

"Now I know you're lying!" he shouted triumphantly. "If you believed everything Stoney told you, how could my choice ever mean a thing? I would always say yes to you, and I would always say no! It would all be the same!"

The apparition replied solemnly, "While I'm here with you, touching you, *you can't be divided.* Your choice will count."

Jack wiped his eyes, and gazed into its face. It seemed to believe every word it was speaking. What if this truly was his metaphysical twin, speaking as honestly as he could, and not merely the Devil in a mask? Perhaps there was a grain of truth in Stoney's awful vision; perhaps this was another version of himself, a living person who honestly believed that the two of them shared a history.

Then it was a visitor sent by God, to humble him. To teach him compassion toward Stoney. To show Jack that he too, with a little less faith, and a little more pride, might have been damned forever.

Jack stretched out a hand and touched the face of this poor lost soul. *There, but for the grace of God, go I.*

He said, "I've made my choice. Now leave me."

᭞

AUTHOR'S NOTE: Where the lives of the fictional characters of this story parallel those of real historical figures, I've drawn on biographies by Andrew Hodges and A.N. Wilson. The self-dual formulation of general relativity was discovered by Abhay Ashtekar in 1986, and has since led to ground-breaking developments in quantum gravity, but the implications drawn from it here are fanciful.

BORDER GUARDS

〜⩗⩗〜⩗〰️ n the early afternoon of his fourth day out of sadness, Jamil was wandering home from the gardens at the center of Noether when he heard shouts from the playing field behind the library. On the spur of the moment, without even asking the city what game was in progress, he decided to join in.

As he rounded the corner and the field came into view, it was clear from the movements of the players that they were in the middle of a quantum soccer match. At Jamil's request, the city painted the wave function of the hypothetical ball across his vision, and tweaked him to recognize the players as the members of two teams without changing their appearance at all. Maria had once told him that she always chose a literal perception of color-coded clothing instead; she had no desire to use pathways that had evolved for the sake of sorting people into those you defended and those you slaughtered. But almost everything that had been bequeathed to them was stained with blood, and to Jamil it seemed a far sweeter victory to adapt the worst relics to his own ends than to discard them as irretrievably tainted.

The wave function appeared as a vivid auroral light, a quicksilver plasma bright enough to be distinct in the afternoon sunlight, yet unable to dazzle the eye or conceal the players running through it. Bands of color representing the complex phase of the wave swept across the field, parting to wash over separate rising lobes of probability before hitting the boundary and bouncing back again, inverted. The match was being played by the oldest, simplest rules:

semi-classical, non-relativistic. The ball was confined to the field by an infinitely high barrier, so there was no question of it tunneling out, leaking away as the match progressed. The players were treated classically: their movements pumped energy into the wave, enabling transitions from the game's opening state—with the ball spread thinly across the entire field—into the range of higher-energy modes needed to localize it. But localization was fleeting; there was no point forming a nice sharp wave packet in the middle of the field in the hope of kicking it around like a classical object. You had to shape the wave in such a way that all of its modes—cycling at different frequencies, traveling with different velocities—would come into phase with each other, for a fraction of a second, within the goal itself. Achieving that was a matter of energy levels, and timing.

Jamil had noticed that one team was under-strength. The umpire would be skewing the field's potential to keep the match fair, but a new participant would be especially welcome for the sake of restoring symmetry. He watched the faces of the players, most of them old friends. They were frowning with concentration, but breaking now and then into smiles of delight at their small successes, or their opponents' ingenuity.

He was badly out of practice, but if he turned out to be dead weight he could always withdraw. And if he misjudged his skills, and lost the match with his incompetence? No one would care. The score was nil all; he could wait for a goal, but that might be an hour or more in coming. Jamil communed with the umpire, and discovered that the players had decided in advance to allow new entries at any time.

Before he could change his mind, he announced himself. The wave froze, and he ran on to the field. People nodded greetings, mostly making no fuss, though Ezequiel shouted, "Welcome back!" Jamil suddenly felt fragile again; though he'd ended his long seclusion four days before, it was well within his power, still, to be dismayed by everything the game would involve. His recovery felt like a finely balanced optical illusion, a figure and ground that could change roles in an instant, a solid cube that could evert into a hollow.

The umpire guided him to his allotted starting position, opposite a woman he hadn't seen before. He offered her a formal bow, and she returned the gesture. This was no time for introductions, but he asked the city if she'd published a name. She had: Margit.

The umpire counted down in their heads. Jamil tensed, regretting his impulsiveness. For seven years he'd been dead to the world. After four days back, what was he good for? His muscles were incapable of atrophy, his reflexes could never be dulled, but he'd chosen to live with an unconstrained will, and at any moment his wavering resolve could desert him.

The umpire said, "Play." The frozen light around Jamil came to life, and he sprang into motion.

Each player was responsible for a set of modes, particular harmonics of the wave that were theirs to fill, guard, or deplete as necessary. Jamil's twelve modes cycled at between 1,000 and 1,250 milliHertz. The rules of the game endowed his body with a small, fixed potential energy, which repelled the ball slightly and allowed different modes to push and pull on each other through him, but if he stayed in one spot as the modes cycled, every influence he exerted would eventually be replaced by its opposite, and the effect would simply cancel itself out.

To drive the wave from one mode to another, you needed to move, and to drive it efficiently you needed to exploit the way the modes fell in and out of phase with each other: to take from a 1,000 milliHertz mode and give to a 1,250, you had to act in synch with the quarter-Hertz beat between them. It was like pushing a child's swing at its natural frequency, but rather than setting a single child in motion, you were standing between two swings and acting more as an intermediary: trying to time your interventions in such a way as to speed up one child at the other's expense. The way you pushed on the wave at a given time and place was out of your hands completely, but by changing location in just the right way you could gain control over the interaction. Every pair of modes had a spatial beat between them—like the moiré pattern formed by two sheets of woven fabric held up to the light together, shifting from transparent to opaque as the gaps between the threads fell in and out of alignment. Slicing through this cyclic landscape offered the perfect means to match the accompanying chronological beat.

Jamil sprinted across the field at a speed and angle calculated to drive two favorable transitions at once. He'd gauged the current spectrum of the wave instinctively, watching from the sidelines, and he knew which of the modes in his charge would contribute to a goal and which would detract from the probability. As he cut through the shimmering bands of color, the umpire gave him tactile feedback to supplement his visual estimates and calculations, allowing him to sense the difference between a cyclic tug, a to and fro that came to nothing, and the gentle but persistent force that meant he was successfully riding the beat.

Chusok called out to him urgently, "Take, take! Two-ten!" Everyone's spectral territory overlapped with someone else's, and you needed to pass amplitude from player to player as well as trying to manage it within your own range. *Two-ten*—a harmonic with two peaks across the width of the field and ten along its length, cycling at 1,160 milliHertz—was filling up as Chusok drove unwanted amplitude from various lower-energy modes into it. It was Jamil's role to empty it, putting the amplitude somewhere useful. Any mode with an even number of peaks across the field was unfavorable for scoring, because it had a node—a zero point between the peaks—smack in the middle of both goals.

Jamil acknowledged the request with a hand signal and shifted his trajectory. It was almost a decade since he'd last played the game, but he still knew the intricate web of possibilities by heart: he could drain the two-ten harmonic into the three-ten, five-two and five-six modes—all with "good parity", peaks along the center-line—in a single action.

As he pounded across the grass, carefully judging the correct angle by sight, increasing his speed until he felt the destructive beats give way to a steady force like a constant breeze, he suddenly recalled a time—centuries before, in another city—when he'd played with one team, week after week, for forty years. Faces and voices swam in his head. Hashim, Jamil's ninety-eighth child, and Hashim's granddaughter Laila had played beside him. But he'd burned his house and moved on, and when that era touched him at all now it was like an unexpected gift. The scent of the grass, the shouts of the players, the soles of his feet striking the ground, resonated with every other moment he'd spent the same way, bridging the centuries, binding his life together. He never truly felt the scale of it when he sought it out deliberately; it was always small things, tightly focused moments like this, that burst the horizon of his everyday concerns and confronted him with the astonishing vista.

The two-ten mode was draining faster than he'd expected; the see-sawing center-line dip in the wave was vanishing before his eyes. He looked around, and saw Margit performing an elaborate Lissajous maneuver, smoothly orchestrating a dozen transitions at once. Jamil froze and watched her, admiring her virtuosity while he tried to decide what to do next; there was no point competing with her when she was doing such a good job of completing the task Chusok had set him.

Margit was his opponent, but they were both aiming for exactly the same kind of spectrum. The symmetry of the field meant that any scoring wave would work equally well for either side—but only one team could be the first to reap the benefit, the first to have more than half the wave's probability packed into their goal. So the two teams were obliged to cooperate at first, and it was only as the wave took shape from their combined efforts that it gradually became apparent which side would gain by sculpting it to perfection as rapidly as possible, and which would gain by spoiling it for the first chance, then honing it for the rebound.

Penina chided him over her shoulder as she jogged past, "You want to leave her to clean up four-six, as well?" She was smiling, but Jamil was stung; he'd been motionless for ten or fifteen seconds. It was not forbidden to drag your feet and rely on your opponents to do all the work, but it was regarded as a shamefully impoverished strategy. It was also very risky, handing them the opportunity to set up a wave that was almost impossible to exploit yourself.

He reassessed the spectrum, and quickly sorted through the alternatives. Whatever he did would have unwanted side effects; there was no magic way to avoid influencing modes in other players' territory, and any action that would drive the transitions he needed would also trigger a multitude of others, up and down the spectrum. Finally, he made a choice that would weaken the offending mode while causing as little disruption as possible.

Jamil immersed himself in the game, planning each transition two steps in advance, switching strategy half-way through a run if he had to, but staying in motion until the sweat dripped from his body, until his calves burned, until his blood sang. He wasn't blinded to the raw pleasures of the moment, or to memories of games past, but he let them wash over him, like the breeze that rose up and cooled his skin with no need for acknowledgment. Familiar voices shouted terse commands at him; as the wave came closer to a scoring spectrum every trace of superfluous conversation vanished, every idle glance gave way to frantic, purposeful gestures. To a bystander, this might have seemed like the height of dehumanisation: twenty-two people reduced to grunting cogs in a pointless machine. Jamil smiled at the thought but refused to be distracted into a complicated imaginary rebuttal. Every step he took was the answer to that, every hoarse plea to Yann or Joracy, Chusok or Maria, Eudore or Halide. These were his friends, and he was back among them. Back in the world.

The first chance of a goal was thirty seconds away, and the opportunity would fall to Jamil's team; a few tiny shifts in amplitude would clinch it. Margit kept her distance, but Jamil could sense her eyes on him constantly—and literally feel her at work through his skin as she slackened his contact with the wave. In theory, by mirroring your opponent's movements at the correct position on the field you could undermine everything they did, though in practice not even the most skillful team could keep the spectrum completely frozen. Going further and spoiling was a tug of war you didn't want to win too well: if you degraded the wave too much, your opponent's task—spoiling your own subsequent chance at a goal—became far easier.

Jamil still had two bad-parity modes that he was hoping to weaken, but every time he changed velocity to try a new transition, Margit responded in an instant, blocking him. He gestured to Chusok for help; Chusok had his own problems with Ezequiel, but he could still make trouble for Margit by choosing where he placed unwanted amplitude. Jamil shook sweat out of his eyes; he could see the characteristic "stepping stone" pattern of lobes forming, a sign that the wave would soon converge on the goal, but from the middle of the field it was impossible to judge their shape accurately enough to know what, if anything, remained to be done.

Suddenly, Jamil felt the wave push against him. He didn't waste time looking around for Margit; Chusok must have succeeded in distracting her. He was almost at the boundary line, but he managed to reverse smoothly, continuing to drive both the transitions he'd been aiming for.

Two long lobes of probability, each modulated by a series of oscillating mounds, raced along the sides of the field. A third, shorter lobe running along the center-line melted away, reappeared, then merged with the others as they touched the end of the field, forming an almost rectangular plateau encompassing the goal.

The plateau became a pillar of light, growing narrower and higher as dozens of modes, all finally in phase, crashed together against the impenetrable barrier of the field's boundary. A shallow residue was still spread across the entire field, and a diminishing sequence of elliptical lobes trailed away from the goal like a staircase, but most of the wave that had started out lapping around their waists was now concentrated in a single peak that towered above their heads, nine or ten meters tall.

For an instant, it was motionless.

Then it began to fall.

The umpire said, "Forty-nine point eight."

The wave packet had not been tight enough.

Jamil struggled to shrug off his disappointment and throw his instincts into reverse. The other team had fifty seconds, now, to fine-tune the spectrum and ensure that the reflected packet was just a fraction narrower when it reformed, at the opposite end of the field.

As the pillar collapsed, replaying its synthesis in reverse, Jamil caught sight of Margit. She smiled at him calmly, and it suddenly struck him: *She'd known they couldn't make the goal. That was why she'd stopped opposing him.* She'd let him work toward sharpening the wave for a few seconds, knowing that it was already too late for him, knowing that her own team would gain from the slight improvement.

Jamil was impressed; it took an extraordinary level of skill and confidence to do what she'd just done. For all the time he'd spent away, he knew exactly what to expect from the rest of the players, and in Margit's absence he would probably have been wishing out loud for a talented newcomer to make the game interesting again. Still, it was hard not to feel a slight sting of resentment. Someone should have warned him just how good she was.

With the modes slipping out of phase, the wave undulated all over the field again, but its reconvergence was inevitable: unlike a wave of water or sound, it possessed no hidden degrees of freedom to grind its precision into entropy. Jamil decided to ignore Margit; there were cruder strategies than mirror-blocking that worked almost as well. Chusok was filling the two-ten mode now; Jamil chose the four-six as his spoiler. All they had to do was keep the wave from growing much sharper, and it didn't matter whether they achieved this by preserving the status quo, or by nudging it from one kind of bluntness to another.

The steady resistance he felt as he ran told Jamil that he was driving the transition, unblocked, but he searched in vain for some visible sign of success. When he reached a vantage point where he could take in enough of the field in one glance to judge the spectrum properly, he noticed a rapidly vibrating shimmer across the width of the wave. He counted nine peaks: good parity. Margit had pulled most of the amplitude straight out of his spoiler mode and fed it into *this*. It was a mad waste of energy to aim for such an elevated harmonic, but no one had been looking there, no one had stopped her.

The scoring pattern was forming again, he only had nine or ten seconds left to make up for all the time he'd wasted. Jamil chose the strongest good-parity mode in his territory, and the emptiest bad one, computed the velocity that would link them, and ran.

He didn't dare turn to watch the opposition goal; he didn't want to break his concentration. The wave retreated around his feet, less like an Earthly ebb tide than an ocean drawn into the sky by a passing black hole. The city diligently portrayed the shadow that his body would have cast, shrinking in front of him as the tower of light rose.

The verdict was announced. "Fifty point one."

The air was filled with shouts of triumph—Ezequiel's the loudest, as always. Jamil sagged to his knees, laughing. It was a curious feeling, familiar as it was: he cared, and he didn't. If he'd been wholly indifferent to the outcome of the game there would have been no pleasure in it, but obsessing over every defeat—or every victory—could ruin it just as thoroughly. He could almost see himself walking the line, orchestrating his response as carefully as any action in the game itself.

He lay down on the grass to catch his breath before play resumed. The outer face of the microsun that orbited Laplace was shielded with rock, but light reflected skywards from the land beneath it crossed the 100,000 kilometer width of the 3-toroidal universe to give a faint glow to the planet's nightside. Though only a sliver was lit directly, Jamil could discern the full disk of the opposite hemisphere in the primary image at the zenith: continents and oceans that lay, by a shorter route, 12,000 or so kilometers beneath him. Other views in the lattice of images spread across the sky were from different angles, and showed substantial crescents of the dayside itself. The one thing you couldn't find in any of these images, even with a telescope, was your own city. The topology of this universe let you see the back of your head, but never your reflection.

⁓ᰤ⁓

JAMIL'S TEAM lost, three nil. He staggered over to the fountains at the edge of the field and slaked his thirst, shocked by the pleasure of the simple act. Just to be alive was glorious now, but once he felt this way, anything seemed possible. He was back in synch, back in phase, and he was going to make the most of it, for however long it lasted.

He caught up with the others, who'd headed down toward the river. Ezequiel hooked an arm around his neck, laughing. "Bad luck, Sleeping Beauty! You picked the wrong time to wake. With Margit, we're invincible."

Jamil ducked free of him. "I won't argue with that." He looked around. "Speaking of whom—"

Penina said, "Gone home. She plays, that's all. No frivolous socializing after the match."

Chusok added, "Or any other time." Penina shot Jamil a glance that meant: not for want of trying on Chusok's part.

Jamil pondered this, wondering why it annoyed him so much. On the field, she hadn't come across as aloof and superior. Just unashamedly good.

He queried the city, but she'd published nothing besides her name. Nobody expected—or wished—to hear more than the tiniest fraction of another person's history, but it was rare for anyone to start a new life without carrying through something from the old as a kind of calling card, some incident or achievement from which your new neighbors could form an impression of you.

They'd reached the riverbank. Jamil pulled his shirt over his head. "So what's her story? She must have told you something."

Ezequiel said, "Only that she learned to play a long time ago; she won't say where or when. She arrived in Noether at the end of last year, and grew a house on the southern outskirts. No one sees her around much. No one even knows what she studies."

Jamil shrugged, and waded in. "Ah well. It's a challenge to rise to." Penina laughed and splashed him teasingly. He protested, "I *meant* beating her at the game."

Chusok said wryly, "When you turned up, I thought you'd be our secret weapon. The one player she didn't know inside out already."

"I'm glad you didn't tell me that. I would have turned around and fled straight back into hibernation."

"I know. That's why we all kept quiet." Chusok smiled. "Welcome back."

Penina said, "Yeah, welcome back, Jamil."

Sunlight shone on the surface of the river. Jamil ached all over, but the cool water was the perfect place to be. If he wished, he could build a partition in his mind at the point where he stood right now, and never fall beneath it. Other people lived that way, and it seemed to cost them nothing. Contrast was overrated; no sane person spent half their time driving spikes into their flesh for the sake of feeling better when they stopped. Ezequiel lived every day with the happy boisterousness of a five-year-old; Jamil sometimes found this annoying, but then any kind of disposition would irritate someone. His own stretches of meaningless sombreness weren't exactly a boon to his friends.

Chusok said, "I've invited everyone to a meal at my house tonight. Will you come?"

Jamil thought it over, then shook his head. He still wasn't ready. He couldn't force-feed himself with normality; it didn't speed his recovery, it just drove him backward.

Chusok looked disappointed, but there was nothing to be done about that. Jamil promised him, "Next time. OK?"

Ezequiel sighed. "What are we going to do with you? You're worse than Margit!" Jamil started backing away, but it was too late. Ezequiel reached him in two casual strides, bent down and grabbed him around the waist, hoisted him effortlessly onto one shoulder, then flung him through the air into the depths of the river.

⌁

JAMIL WAS woken by the scent of wood smoke. His room was still filled with the night's gray shadows, but when he propped himself up on one elbow and the window obliged him with transparency, the city was etched clearly in the predawn light.

He dressed and left the house, surprised at the coolness of the dew on his feet. No one else in his street seemed to be up; had they failed to notice the smell, or did they already know to expect it? He turned a corner and saw the rising column of soot, faintly lit with red from below. The flames and the ruins were still hidden from him, but he knew whose house it was.

When he reached the dying blaze, he crouched in the heat-withered garden, cursing himself. Chusok had offered him the chance to join him for his last meal in Noether. Whatever hints you dropped, it was customary to tell no one that you were moving on. If you still had a lover, if you still had young children, you never deserted them. But friends, you warned in subtle ways. Before vanishing.

Jamil covered his head with his arms. He'd lived through this countless times before, but it never became easier. If anything it grew worse, as every departure was weighted with the memories of others. His brothers and sisters had scattered across the branches of the New Territories. He'd walked away from his father and mother when he was too young and confident to realize how much it would hurt him, decades later. His own children had all abandoned him eventually, far more often than he'd left them. It was easier to leave an ex-lover than a grown child: something burned itself out in a couple, almost naturally, as if ancestral biology had prepared them for at least that one rift.

Jamil stopped fighting the tears. But as he brushed them away, he caught sight of someone standing beside him. He looked up. It was Margit.

He felt a need to explain. He rose to his feet and addressed her. "This was Chusok's house. We were good friends. I'd known him for ninety-six years."

Margit gazed back at him neutrally. "Boo hoo. Poor baby. You'll never see your friend again."

Jamil almost laughed, her rudeness was so surreal. He pushed on, as if the only conceivable, polite response was to pretend that he hadn't heard her. "No one is the kindest, the most generous, the most loyal. It doesn't matter. That's not the point. Everyone's unique. Chusok was Chusok." He banged a fist against his chest, utterly heedless now of her contemptuous words. "There's a hole in me, and it will never be filled." That was the truth, even though he'd grow around it. *He should have gone to the meal, it would have cost him nothing.*

"You must be a real emotional Swiss cheese," observed Margit tartly.

Jamil came to his senses. "Why don't you fuck off to some other universe? No one wants you in Noether."

Margit was amused. "You *are* a bad loser."

Jamil gazed at her, honestly confused for a moment; the game had slipped his mind completely. He gestured at the embers. "What are you doing here? Why did you follow the smoke, if it wasn't regret at not saying goodbye to him when you had the chance?" He wasn't sure how seriously to take Penina's light-hearted insinuation, but if Chusok had fallen for Margit, and it had not been reciprocated, that might even have been the reason he'd left.

She shook her head calmly. "He was nothing to me. I barely spoke to him."

"Well, that's your loss."

"From the look of things, I'd say the loss was all yours."

He had no reply. Margit turned and walked away.

Jamil crouched on the ground again, rocking back and forth, waiting for the pain to subside.

~w~

JAMIL SPENT the next week preparing to resume his studies. The library had near-instantaneous contact with every artificial universe in the New Territories, and the additional lightspeed lag between Earth and the point in space from which the whole tree-structure blossomed was only a few hours. Jamil had been to Earth, but only as a tourist; land was scarce, they accepted no migrants. There were remote planets you could live on, in the home universe, but you had to be a certain kind of masochistic purist to want that. The precise reasons why his ancestors had entered the New Territories had been forgotten generations before—and it would have been presumptuous to track them down and ask them in person—but given a choice between the then even-more-crowded Earth, the horrifying reality of interstellar distances, and an endlessly extensible branching chain of worlds which could be traversed within a matter of weeks, the decision wasn't exactly baffling.

Jamil had devoted most of his time in Noether to studying the category of representations of Lie groups on complex vector spaces—a fitting choice, since Emmy Noether had been a pioneer of group theory, and if she'd lived to see this field blossom she would probably have been in the thick of it herself. Representations of Lie groups lay behind most of physics: each kind of subatomic particle was really nothing but a particular way of representing the universal symmetry group as a set of rotations of complex vectors. Organizing this kind of structure with category theory was ancient knowledge, but Jamil didn't care; he'd long ago reconciled himself to being a student, not a discoverer. The greatest gift of consciousness was the ability to take the patterns of the world inside you, and for all that he would have relished the thrill of being the first at anything, with ten-to-the-sixteenth people alive that was a futile ambition for most.

In the library, he spoke with fellow students of his chosen field on other worlds, or read their latest works. Though they were not researchers, they could still put a new pedagogical spin on old material, enriching the connections with other fields, finding ways to make the complex, subtle truth easier to assimilate without sacrificing the depth and detail that made it worth knowing in the first place. They would not advance the frontiers of knowledge. They would not discover new principles of nature, or invent new technologies. But to Jamil, understanding was an end in itself.

He rarely thought about the prospect of playing another match, and when he did the idea was not appealing. With Chusok gone, the same group could play ten-to-a-side without Jamil to skew the numbers. Margit might even choose to swap teams, if only for the sake of proving that her current team's monotonous string of victories really had been entirely down to her.

When the day arrived, though, he found himself unable to stay away. He turned up intending to remain a spectator, but Ryuichi had deserted Ezequiel's team, and everyone begged Jamil to join in.

As he took his place opposite Margit, there was nothing in her demeanor to acknowledge their previous encounter: no lingering contempt, but no hint of shame either. Jamil resolved to put it out of his mind; he owed it to his fellow players to concentrate on the game.

They lost, five nil.

Jamil forced himself to follow everyone to Eudore's house, to celebrate, commiserate, or as it turned out, to forget the whole thing. After they'd eaten, Jamil wandered from room to room, enjoying Eudore's choice of music but unable to settle into any conversation. No one mentioned Chusok in his hearing.

He left just after midnight. Laplace's near-full primary image and its eight brightest gibbous companions lit the streets so well that there was no need for anything more. Jamil thought: Chusok might have merely traveled to another city, one beneath his gaze right now. And wherever he'd gone, he might yet choose to stay in touch with his friends from Noether.

And his friends from the next town, and the next?

Century after century?

Margit was sitting on Jamil's doorstep, holding a bunch of white flowers in one hand.

Jamil was irritated. "What are you doing here?"

"I came to apologize."

He shrugged. "There's no need. We feel differently about certain things. That's fine. I can still face you on the playing field."

"I'm not apologizing for a difference of opinion. I wasn't honest with you. I was cruel." She shaded her eyes against the glare of the planet and looked up at him. "You were right: it was my loss. I wish I'd known your friend."

He laughed curtly. "Well, it's too late for that."

She said simply, "I know."

Jamil relented. "Do you want to come in?" Margit nodded, and he instructed the door to open for her. As he followed her inside, he said, "How long have you been here? Have you eaten?"

"No."

"I'll cook something for you."

"You don't have to do that."

He called out to her from the kitchen, "Think of it as a peace offering. I don't have any flowers."

Margit replied, "They're not for you. They're for Chusok's house."

Jamil stopped rummaging through his vegetable bins, and walked back into the living room. "People don't usually do that in Noether."

Margit was sitting on the couch, staring at the floor. She said, "I'm so lonely here. I can't bear it any more."

He sat beside her. "Then why did you rebuff him? You could at least have been friends."

She shook her head. "Don't ask me to explain."

Jamil took her hand. She turned and embraced him, trembling miserably. He stroked her hair. "Sssh."

She said, "Just sex. I don't want anything more."

He groaned softly. "There's no such thing as that."

"I just need someone to touch me again."

"I understand." He confessed, "So do I. But that won't be all. So don't ask me to promise there'll be nothing more."

Margit took his face in her hands and kissed him. Her mouth tasted of wood smoke.

Jamil said, "I don't even know you."

"No one knows anyone, any more."

"That's not true."

"No, it's not," she conceded gloomily. She ran a hand lightly along his arm. Jamil wanted badly to see her smile, so he made each dark hair thicken and blossom into a violet flower as it passed beneath her fingers.

She did smile, but she said, "I've seen that trick before."

Jamil was annoyed. "I'm sure to be a disappointment all round, then. I expect you'd be happier with some kind of novelty. A unicorn, or an amoeba."

She laughed. "I don't think so." She took his hand and placed it against her breast. "Do you ever get tired of sex?"

"Do you ever get tired of breathing?"

"I can go for a long time without thinking about it."

He nodded. "But then one day you stop and fill your lungs with air, and it's still as sweet as ever."

Jamil didn't know what he was feeling any more. Lust. Compassion. Spite. She'd come to him hurting, and he wanted to help her, but he wasn't sure that either of them really believed this would work.

Margit inhaled the scent of the flowers on his arm. "Are they the same color? Everywhere else?"

He said, "There's only one way to find out."

〜〜〜

JAMIL WOKE in the early hours of the morning, alone. He'd half expected Margit to flee like this, but she could have waited till dawn. He would have obligingly feigned sleep while she dressed and tip-toed out.

Then he heard her. It was not a sound he would normally have associated with a human being, but it could not have been anything else.

He found her in the kitchen, curled around a table leg, wailing rhythmically. He stood back and watched her, afraid that anything he did would only make things worse. She met his gaze in the half light, but kept up the mechanical whimper. Her eyes weren't blank; she was not delirious, or hallucinating. She knew exactly who, and where, she was.

Finally, Jamil knelt in the doorway. He said, "Whatever it is, you can tell me. And we'll fix it. We'll find a way."

She bared her teeth. "You can't *fix it*, you stupid child." She resumed the awful noise.

"Then just tell me. Please?" He stretched out a hand toward her. He hadn't felt quite so helpless since his very first daughter, Aminata, had come to him as an inconsolable six-year-old, rejected by the boy to whom she'd declared her undying love. He'd been twenty-four years old; a child himself. More than a thousand years ago. *Where are you now, Nata?*

Margit said, "I promised. I'd never tell."

"Promised who?"

"Myself."

"Good. They're the easiest kind to break."

She started weeping. It was a more ordinary sound, but it was even more chilling. She was not a wounded animal now, an alien being suffering some incomprehensible pain. Jamil approached her cautiously; she let him wrap his arms around her shoulders.

He whispered, "Come to bed. The warmth will help. Just being held will help."

She spat at him derisively, "It won't bring her back."

"Who?"

Margit stared at him in silence, as if he'd said something shocking.

Jamil insisted gently, "Who won't it bring back?" She'd lost a friend, badly, the way he'd lost Chusok. That was why she'd sought him out. He could help her through it. They could help each other through it.

She said, "It won't bring back the dead."

⁓

MARGIT WAS seven thousand five hundred and ninety-four years old. Jamil persuaded her to sit at the kitchen table. He wrapped her in blankets, then fed her tomatoes and rice, as she told him how she'd witnessed the birth of his world.

The promise had shimmered just beyond reach for decades. Almost none of her contemporaries had believed it would happen, though the truth should have been plain for centuries: *the human body was a material thing.* In time, with enough knowledge and effort, it would become possible to safeguard it from any kind of deterioration, any kind of harm. Stellar evolution and cosmic entropy might or might not prove insurmountable, but there'd be aeons to confront those challenges. In the middle of the twenty-first century, the hurdles were aging, disease, violence, and an over-crowded planet.

"Grace was my best friend. We were students." Margit smiled. "Before everyone was a student. We'd talk about it, but we didn't believe we'd see it happen. It would come in another century. It would come for our great-great-grandchildren. We'd hold infants on our knees in our twilight years and tell ourselves: *this one will never die.*

"When we were both twenty-two, something happened. To both of us." She lowered her eyes. "We were kidnapped. We were raped. We were tortured."

Jamil didn't know how to respond. These were just words to him: he knew their meaning, he knew these acts would have hurt her, but she might as well have been describing a mathematical theorem. He stretched a hand across the table, but Margit ignored it. He said awkwardly, "This was…the Holocaust?"

She looked up at him, shaking her head, almost laughing at his naivete. "Not even one of them. Not a war, not a pogrom. Just one psychopathic man. He locked us in his basement, for six months. He'd killed seven women." Tears began spilling down her cheeks. "He showed us the bodies. They were buried right where we slept. He showed us how we'd end up, when he was through with us."

Jamil was numb. He'd known all his adult life what had once been possible—what had once happened, to real people—but it had all been consigned to history long before his birth. In retrospect it seemed almost inconceivably stupid, but he'd always imagined that the changes had come in such a way that no one still living had experienced these horrors. There'd been no escaping the bare minimum, the logical necessity: his oldest living ancestors must have watched their parents fall peacefully into eternal sleep. But not this. Not a flesh-and-blood woman, sitting in front of him, who'd been forced to sleep in a killer's graveyard.

He put his hand over hers, and choked out the words. "This man…*killed* Grace? He killed your friend?"

Margit began sobbing, but she shook her head. "No, no. We got out!" She twisted her mouth into a smile. "Someone stabbed the stupid fucker in a bar-room brawl. We dug our way out while he was in hospital." She put her face down on the table and wept, but she held Jamil's hand against her cheek. He couldn't understand what she'd lived through, but that didn't mean he couldn't console her. Hadn't he touched his mother's face the same way, when she was sad beyond his childish comprehension?

She composed herself, and continued. "We made a resolution, while we were in there. If we survived, there'd be no more empty promises. No more day dreams. What he'd done to those seven women—and what he'd done to us—would become impossible."

And it had. Whatever harm befell your body, you had the power to shut off your senses and decline to experience it. If the flesh was damaged, it could always be repaired or replaced. In the unlikely event that your jewel itself was destroyed, everyone had backups, scattered across universes. No human being could inflict physical pain on another. In theory, you could still be killed, but it would take the same kind of resources as destroying a galaxy. The only people who seriously contemplated either were the villains in very bad operas.

Jamil's eyes narrowed in wonder. She'd spoken those last words with such fierce pride that there was no question of her having failed.

"*You* are Ndoli? You invented the jewel?" As a child, he'd been told that the machine in his skull had been designed by a man who'd died long ago.

Margit stroked his hand, amused. "In those days, very few Hungarian women could be mistaken for Nigerian men. I've never changed my body that much, Jamil. I've always looked much as you see me."

Jamil was relieved; if she'd been Ndoli himself, he might have succumbed to sheer awe and started babbling idolatrous nonsense. "But you worked with Ndoli? You and Grace?"

She shook her head. "We made the resolution, and then we floundered. We were mathematicians, not neurologists. There were a thousand things going on at once: tissue engineering, brain imaging, molecular computers. We had no real idea where to put our efforts, which problems we should bring our strengths to bear upon. Ndoli's work didn't come out of the blue for us, but we played no part in it.

"For a while, almost everyone was nervous about switching from the brain to the jewel. In the early days, the jewel was a separate device that learned its task by mimicking the brain, and it had to be handed control of the body at one chosen moment. It took another fifty years before it could be engineered to replace the brain incrementally, neuron by neuron, in a seamless transition throughout adolescence."

So Grace had lived to see the jewel invented, but held back, and died before she could use it? Jamil kept himself from blurting out this conclusion; all his guesses had proved wrong so far.

Margit continued. "Some people weren't just nervous, though. You'd be amazed how vehemently Ndoli was denounced in certain quarters. And I don't just mean the fanatics who churned out paranoid tracts about 'the machines' taking over, with their evil inhuman agendas. Some people's antagonism had nothing to do with the specifics of the technology. They were opposed to immortality, in principle."

Jamil laughed. "*Why?*"

"Ten thousand years' worth of sophistry doesn't vanish overnight," Margit observed dryly. "Every human culture had expended vast amounts of intellectual effort on the problem of coming to terms with death. Most religions had constructed elaborate lies about it, making it out to be something other than it was—though a few were dishonest about life, instead. But even most secular philosophies were warped by the need to pretend that *death was for the best.*

"It was the naturalistic fallacy at its most extreme—and its most transparent, but that didn't stop anyone. Since any child could tell you that death was meaningless, contingent, unjust, and abhorrent beyond words, it was a hallmark of sophistication to believe otherwise. Writers had consoled themselves for centuries with smug puritanical fables about immortals who'd long for death—who'd *beg* for death. It would have been too much to expect all those who were suddenly faced with the reality of its banishment to confess that they'd been whistling in the dark. And would-be moral philosophers—mostly those who'd experienced no greater inconvenience in their lives than a late train or a surly waiter—began wailing about the destruction of the human spirit by this hideous blight. We needed death and suffering, to put steel into our souls! Not horrible, horrible *freedom and safety!*"

Jamil smiled. "So there were buffoons. But in the end, surely they swallowed their pride? If we're walking in a desert and I tell you that the lake you see ahead is a mirage, I might cling stubbornly to my own belief, to save myself from disappointment. But when we arrive, and I'm proven wrong, I *will* drink from the lake."

Margit nodded. "Most of the loudest of these people went quiet in the end. But there were subtler arguments, too. Like it or not, all our biology and all of our culture *had* evolved in the presence of death. And almost every righteous struggle in history, every worthwhile sacrifice, had been against suffering, against violence, against death. Now, that struggle would become impossible."

"Yes." Jamil was mystified. "But only because it had triumphed."

Margit said gently, "I know. There was no sense to it. And it was always my belief that anything worth fighting for—over centuries, over millennia—was worth attaining. It *can't* be noble to toil for a cause, and even to die for it, unless it's also noble to succeed. To claim otherwise isn't sophistication, it's just a kind of hypocrisy. If it's better to travel than arrive, you shouldn't start the voyage in the first place.

"I told Grace as much, and she agreed. We laughed together at what we called the *tragedians*: the people who denounced the coming age as the age without martyrs, the age without saints, the age without revolutionaries. There would never be another Gandhi, another Mandela, another Aung San Suu Kyi—and yes, that *was* a kind of loss, but would any great leader have sentenced humanity to eternal misery, for the sake of providing a suitable backdrop for eternal heroism? Well, some of them would have. But the downtrodden themselves had better things to do."

Margit fell silent. Jamil cleared her plate away, then sat opposite her again. It was almost dawn.

"Of course, the jewel was not enough," Margit continued. "With care, Earth could support forty billion people, but where would the rest go? The jewel made virtual reality the easiest escape route: for a fraction of the space, a fraction of the energy, it could survive without a body attached. Grace and I weren't horrified by that prospect, the way some people were. But it was not the best outcome, it was not what most people wanted, they way they wanted freedom from death.

"So we studied gravity, we studied the vacuum."

Jamil feared making a fool of himself again, but from the expression on her face he knew he wasn't wrong this time. *M. Osvát and G. Füst.* Co-authors of the seminal paper, but no more was known about them than those abbreviated names. "You gave us the New Territories?"

Margit nodded slightly. "Grace and I."

Jamil was overwhelmed with love for her. He went to her and knelt down to put his arms around her waist. Margit touched his shoulder. "Come on, get up. Don't treat me like a god, it just makes me feel old."

He stood, smiling abashedly. Anyone in pain deserved his help—but if he was not in her debt, the word had no meaning.

"And Grace?" he asked.

Margit looked away. "Grace completed her work, and then decided that she was a tragedian, after all. Rape was impossible. Torture was impossible. Poverty was vanishing. Death was receding into cosmology, into metaphysics. It was everything she'd hoped would come to pass. And for her, suddenly faced with that fulfillment, everything that remained seemed trivial.

"One night, she climbed into the furnace in the basement of her building. Her jewel survived the flames, but she'd erased it from within."

~w~

IT WAS morning now. Jamil was beginning to feel disoriented; Margit should have vanished in daylight, an apparition unable to persist in the mundane world.

"I'd lost other people who were close to me," she said. "My parents. My brother. Friends. And so had everyone around me, then. I wasn't special: grief was still commonplace. But decade by decade, century by century, we shrank into insignificance, those of us who knew what it meant to lose someone for ever. We're less than one in a million, now.

"For a long time, I clung to my own generation. There were enclaves, there were ghettos, where everyone understood the old days. I spent two hundred years married to a man who wrote a play called *We Who Have Known the Dead*—which was every bit as pretentious and self-pitying as you'd guess from the title." She smiled at the memory. "It was a horrible, self-devouring world. If I'd stayed in it much longer, I would have followed Grace. I would have begged for death."

She looked up at Jamil. "It's people like you I want to be with: *people who don't understand.* Your lives aren't trivial, any more than the best parts of our own were: all the tranquility, all the beauty, all the happiness that made the sacrifices and the life-and-death struggles worthwhile.

"The tragedians were wrong. They had everything upside-down. Death never gave meaning to life: it was always the other way round. All of its gravitas, all of its significance, was stolen from the things it ended. But the value of life always lay entirely in itself—not in its loss, not in its fragility.

"Grace should have lived to see that. She should have lived long enough to understand that the world hadn't turned to ash."

Jamil sat in silence, turning the whole confession over in his mind, trying to absorb it well enough not to add to her distress with a misjudged question. Finally, he ventured, "Why do you hold back from friendship with us, though? Because we're just children to you? Children who can't understand what you've lost?"

Margit shook her head vehemently. "I don't *want you* to understand! People like me are the only blight on this world, the only poison." She smiled at Jamil's expression of anguish, and rushed to silence him before he could swear that she was nothing of the kind. "Not in everything we do and say, or everyone we touch: I'm not claiming that we're tainted, in some fatuous mythological sense. But when I left the ghettos, I promised myself that I wouldn't bring the past with me. Sometimes that's an easy vow to keep. Sometimes it's not."

"You've broken it tonight," Jamil said plainly. "And neither of us have been struck down by lightning."

"I know." She took his hand. "But I was wrong to tell you what I have, and I'll fight to regain the strength to stay silent. I stand at the border between two worlds, Jamil. I remember death, and I always will. But my job now is to guard that border. To keep that knowledge from invading your world."

"We're not as fragile as you think," he protested. "We all know something about loss."

Margit nodded soberly. "Your friend Chusok has vanished into the crowd. That's how things work now: how you keep yourselves from suffocating in a jungle of endlessly growing connections, or fragmenting into isolated troupes of repertory players, endlessly churning out the same lines."

"You have your little deaths—and I don't call them that to deride you. But I've seen both. And I promise you, they're not the same."

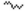

IN THE weeks that followed, Jamil resumed in full the life he'd made for himself in Noether. Five days in seven were for the difficult beauty of mathematics. The rest were for his friends.

He kept playing matches, and Margit's team kept winning. In the sixth game, though, Jamil's team finally scored against her. Their defeat was only three to one.

Each night, Jamil struggled with the question. What exactly did he owe her? Eternal loyalty, eternal silence, eternal obedience? She hadn't sworn him to secrecy; she'd extracted no promises at all. But he knew she was trusting him to comply with her wishes, so what right did he have to do otherwise?

Eight weeks after the night he'd spent with Margit, Jamil found himself alone with Penina in a room in Joracy's house. They'd been talking about the old days. Talking about Chusok.

Jamil said, "Margit lost someone, very close to her."

Penina nodded matter-of-factly, but curled into a comfortable position on the couch and prepared to take in every word.

"Not in the way we've lost Chusok. Not in the way you think at all."

Jamil approached the others, one by one. His confidence ebbed and flowed. He'd glimpsed the old world, but he couldn't pretend to have fathomed its inhabitants. What if Margit saw this as worse than betrayal—as a further torture, a further rape?

But he couldn't stand by and leave her to the torture she'd inflicted on herself.

Ezequiel was the hardest to face. Jamil spent a sick and sleepless night beforehand, wondering if this would make him a monster, a corrupter of children, the epitome of everything Margit believed she was fighting.

Ezequiel wept freely, but he was not a child. He was older than Jamil, and he had more steel in his soul than any of them.

He said, "I guessed it might be that. I guessed she might have seen the bad times. But I never found a way to ask her."

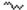

THE THREE lobes of probability converged, melted into a plateau, rose into a pillar of light.

The umpire said, "Fifty-five point nine." It was Margit's most impressive goal yet.

Ezequiel whooped joyfully and ran toward her. When he scooped her up in his arms and threw her across his shoulders, she laughed and indulged him. When Jamil stood beside him and they made a joint throne for her with their arms, she frowned down at him and said, "You shouldn't be doing this. You're on the losing side."

The rest of the players converged on them, cheering, and they started down toward the river. Margit looked around nervously. "What is this? We haven't finished playing."

Penina said, "The game's over early, just this once. Think of this as an invitation. We want you to swim with us. We want you to talk to us. We want to hear everything about your life."

Margit's composure began to crack. She squeezed Jamil's shoulder. He whispered, "Say the word, and we'll put you down."

Margit didn't whisper back; she shouted miserably, "What do you want from me, you parasites? I've won your fucking game for you! What more do you want?"

Jamil was mortified. He stopped and prepared to lower her, prepared to retreat, but Ezequiel caught his arm.

Ezequiel said, "We want to be your border guards. We want to stand beside you."

Christa added, "We can't face what you've faced, but we want to understand. As much as we can."

Joracy spoke, then Yann, Narcyza, Maria, Halide. Margit looked down on them, weeping, confused.

Jamil burned with shame. He'd hijacked her, humiliated her. He'd made everything worse. She'd flee Noether, flee into a new exile, more alone than ever.

When everyone had spoken, silence descended. Margit trembled on her throne.

Jamil faced the ground. He couldn't undo what he'd done. He said quietly, "Now you know our wishes. Will you tell us yours?"

"Put me down."

Jamil and Ezequiel complied.

Margit looked around at her teammates and opponents, her children, her creation, her would-be friends.

She said, "I want to go to the river with you. I'm seven thousand years old, and I want to learn to swim."

~w~

AUTHOR'S NOTE: Readers can find an interactive illustration of quantum soccer at **www.gregegan.net/BORDER/Soccer/Soccer.html**

HOT ROCK

1

~~~〰〰**A**zar turned away from her assembled friends and family and walked through the departure gate. She tried to keep her gaze fixed straight ahead, but then she paused and looked over her shoulder, as if there might yet be a chance for one more parting gesture. It was too late; there was nobody in sight. She had left her well-wishers far behind.

She managed a nervous laugh at the sheer seamlessness of the transition; she hadn't registered so much as a shift in the light. The corridor around her appeared unchanged, its walls bearing the same abstract blue-and-gold mosaics as the one she had entered, but when she walked to the far end and turned to the right, she found herself in a glass-walled observation deck, looking out into the rich blackness of space.

Doorway to the stars was the style of travel she had chosen, just one among dozens of decorative scenarios she might have wrapped around the raw, imperceptible act itself. There was no doorway; stepping through the departure gate had merely been a gesture of consent, the signal she had chosen to initiate her journey. In mid-stride, her mind had been copied from the processor that sat within her birth flesh, encoded into gamma rays, and transmitted across fifteen hundred light years. In a subjective instant, she had been transported from her home world of Hanuz into this scape, which mimicked a capacious habitat orbiting the planet Tallulah. She really was orbiting Tallulah, but the habitat, and the body she perceived as her own flesh, were illusory. The machine she now inhabited was scarcely larger than a grain of rice.

Azar pressed her palms to her eyes and composed herself. If she turned around and marched back through the gate it would take her home with no questions asked, but three thousand years would have passed since her departure. That price had been paid, and no second thoughts, no hasty retreat, could reverse it. All she could do now was try to make it worthwhile.

The observation deck was unlit, but a gentle glow from the floor tracked her footsteps as she crossed to the far side and looked down on Tallulah. The scape's illusory gravity almost made her feel that she was on solid ground, gazing eastwards on a cloudless night from some mountain eyrie at a rising moon: a new moon, its gray disk lit only by starlight. But she knew that however long she waited, dawn would not come creeping across the limb of this disk; no crescent, no sliver of light would appear. Tallulah had no sun; it had been an orphan for at least a billion years, drifting untethered through the galaxy. Yet distant astronomers had surmised—and the instruments here and now confirmed—that its surface was awash with running water. In the cold of interstellar space even its atmosphere should have been frozen down to a sludge of solid nitrogen and carbon dioxide, but instead its long night was alive with balmy breezes wafting over starlit seas.

"Salaam! You must be Azar!" A tall, smiling woman strode across the deck, stretching out her arms. "I'm Shelma." They embraced briefly, just as Azar would have done when meeting someone for the first time back on Hanuz. This was no more a coincidence than Shelma's human appearance and common phonetic name: for the sake of mutual intelligibility, the scape was translating every sight, every word, every gesture that passed between them.

Shelma turned to face the blank gray disk, and her eyes lit up with pleasure. "It's beautiful!" she exclaimed.

Azar felt slightly foolish that she'd been so slow to take a proper look herself. Tallulah's surface would be emitting a far-infrared glow, but its atmosphere was virtually opaque at that frequency, so the easiest way to see any detail would be to increase her sensitivity to the usual visible spectrum. She willed the change—and the scape obliged, just as if her eyes were real.

The ocean sparkled in the starlight. Two broad continents shared the hemisphere below. Long mountain ranges, vast bare plains, and expanses of mysterious vegetation colored the shadowless land.

"It is lovely," she said. Every world had its own peculiar beauty, though, and Azar would not have sacrificed three thousand years just to gaze upon even the most ravishing landscape.

When Tallulah had first shown up in telescopic surveys, long before Azar's birth, people had soon realized that the best chance to visit it would come when it passed fortuitously close to an imaginary line joining the distant systems of Hanuz and Bahar. If the two worlds cooperated by launching probes that arrived simultaneously, the two spacecraft could brake against each other, sparing both of them the massive amounts of fuel needed to decelerate.

Accordingly, Mologhat 1 and 2 were sent on their way, launched in time to meet at Tallulah and merge in an intricate electromagnetic embrace. But then the news had reached Hanuz that Bahar would not be leaving the mission in the hands of insentient robots: a traveler would follow the Bahari probe, to wake inside the unified Mologhat Station and supervise the exploration of the orphan world.

No native-born traveler had left Hanuz for millennia, and Azar's people were not so crippled with pride that the absence of a representative of their own would have been intolerable. The software they had already sent with Mologhat 1 was perfectly capable of protecting their interests in the mission; they might have simply left the Bahari to their alien ways without lessening their own enjoyment of whatever discoveries followed. And yet, a ripple had spread across the planet, a shocked whisper: *One of us could go, could be there, could live through it all in person.*

"A billion years in deep space," Shelma marveled, "and not an iceberg in sight."

"It's hard to believe," Azar replied. The endless night on Tallulah rivaled the height of summer on Hanuz. When a planet was stripped of its sun, the decay of long-lived radioisotopes could eke out enough warmth over billions of years to keep its core molten—but even with abundant greenhouse gases to trap the heat, that could not account for Tallulah's surface temperature. However warm its heart, its skin should have felt the chill by now.

Mologhat had been orbiting Tallulah for three years before their arrival, and Azar now ingested the results of its observations. No obviously artificial structures were visible on the surface, but a faint stream of neutrinos was radiating out from deep in the planet's crust. The spectrum of the neutrinos did not correspond to the decay of any known radioisotopes, natural or otherwise; nor did it match the signatures of fission or fusion. Someone had worked hard to keep this orphan warm, but it was far from clear how they had done it—and impossible to say whether or not they were still around.

"What do you think?" Azar asked Shelma. "Is there anyone home?"

"People have been beaming signals at Tallulah for thirty thousand years," Shelma said, "and never raised a peep. So they're either dead, or resolute hermits."

"If they want to be left in peace, we have no right to disturb them." Azar hoped that this declaration was redundant, but she wanted the ground rules absolutely clear.

"Of course," Shelma agreed. "But if they insist on playing dead to perfection, all they'll get are the rights of the dead. Which, while not negligible, are somewhat diminished."

Once a civilization became extinct—not merely mutating into something new, but leaving no sentient heirs whatsoever—it was widely accepted that its history devolved into a common legacy that anyone was entitled to investigate. If sovereignty really had ceased to be an issue, Tallulah was certainly worth exploring. Tens of thousands of orphan planets had been found in the past, but only a few dozen had shown signs of habitation, and those worlds had yielded nothing but sad ruins buried beneath the permafrost. In the age of the Amalgam—the meta-civilization that now ringed the galaxy— the extinction of an entire world was unthinkable; if a catastrophe could not be averted, people who already had a robust digital form could be evacuated in seconds, and even those who had chosen purely biological modes could be scanned in a matter of days at the most.

The people of Tallulah, it seemed, had been halfway in between. When some cosmic mishap tossed them from their stellar hearth they had been unwilling or unable to evacuate, but they had not stood by and watched the air around them fall to the ground like snow. Whether trapped by their fate or just stubbornly resolved to ride it out, they had found a way to survive it. If they had since succumbed to some other tragedy, or merely surrendered to the passage of time, Azar saw no disrespect in digging up their secrets. Their achievements had endured for a billion years; they deserved recognition and understanding.

2

MOLOGHAT'S ORBIT was a discreet hundred thousand kilometers from Tallulah, but it had dispatched a swarm of microprobes into smaller, faster orbits of various inclinations, providing complete coverage of the surface. If there had been any lingering suspicion that the heating of the crust might have been due to some freakish natural process, the details put that idea to rest: not only was the temperature modulated by latitude, diminishing toward the planet's rotational poles, the records showed that it cycled over a period of about three months, creating imitation seasons. These nostalgic echoes of a long-lost circumstellar orbit were so clear that Azar was surprised they'd put the heat source in the ground at all, rather than launching an artificial sun.

"Not only would that have given them light from above," she suggested to Shelma as they strolled through Mologhat's library, "they could have kept the old diurnal rhythm too." Heat conduction from deep in the crust would have washed out any cycle as short as a typical planetary day.

Shelma said, "It's a lot of extra work to make a microsun efficient—to keep it from pouring energy out into space."

"That's true."

"And perhaps they were insecure as well," Shelma added, sliding out an image from the stack beside her that showed an animated model of Tallulah's weather patterns. "They were already on the verge of losing one sun. They might have preferred to keep their energy source buried, rather than risk being parted from this one too."

"Yeah. Still, it's interesting that they tweaked the biosphere for such a radical shift—ground heat replacing sunlight—but kept the seasons."

Shelma smiled. "Days, seasons, you've got to have something. People go mad without change." Both she and Azar had chosen to retain sleep cycles, their software following the dictates of their ancestral phenotypes. But Azar knew that the Baharis' ancestors were nocturnal; what Azar perceived as the station's night would be day to Shelma, and vice versa.

Azar pulled out a map of vegetation density. Using synthetic aperture methods, the microprobes had resolved details on Tallulah's surface down to about a tenth of a meter, and even at that coarse resolution they had identified thousands of different kinds of plants. Spectroscopy could not untangle the detailed biochemistry from orbit, but the biosphere was clearly carbon-based/anaerobic, with the plants synthesizing carbohydrates but releasing no free oxygen.

Shelma spread her arms to take in the whole collection of data around them. "Everything here is open to interpretation. We're going to need to make landfall to get any further."

"I agree." Azar was nervous, but relieved by the verdict. She was glad she hadn't traveled this far just to find that Tallulah was clearly occupied by hermits, and there was nothing left to do but abandon them to their solitude.

"The question, then," Shelma said, "is how we want to do it." She began reeling off options. They could sprinkle a few nanotech spores on the surface, then sit back and wait for the army of robot insects they built to scour the planet. Or they could leave Mologhat and travel to the surface themselves, in various ways. Of course they could always combine the two, delegating most of the exploration while still being in the thick of it.

Azar had studied all of these methods before her departure, but Shelma sounded too blasé to be merely reciting theoretical knowledge. "You've done this kind of thing before, haven't you?"

"Dozens of times." Shelma hesitated. "This is your first time out-of-system?"

"Yes." That wasn't a lucky guess; everyone knew about the dearth of travelers from Hanuz. "It's hard for us," Azar explained. "Leaving everyone we know for hundreds of years. You don't mind doing that?"

"My ancestors were solitary for part of their life cycle," Shelma said, "and sociable for the rest. Now we're flexible: we can switch between those modes at will. What I don't understand is why you don't just travel in packs, if that would make things easier."

Azar laughed. "I know some people do that, but our social networks are so tangled that it's hard to find a truly self-contained group—least of all a group where everyone can agree on a single destination. And if they do, they're more likely to emigrate than to take a trip and come home again."

"I see."

"Anyway, forget about Hanuz. We need to make some decisions." Azar wasn't going to sit around on Mologhat while robots had all the fun, but there were practical limits on how far she could go just to get some dirt beneath her fingernails. If she had her own standard body reconstructed down on the surface, tweaked to survive the local conditions, she'd spend all her time foraging for food. Mologhat had only a few micrograms of its original antimatter store left; the few hundred megajoules that would generate were enough for its own modest needs, but pilfering any of it to power a sixty-kilogram behemoth would be insane; she could burn up the whole lot in a month. If Tallulah had had a reasonable abundance of deuterium she could have powered her body with D-D fusion, but the isotope was rare here.

"What if we build a high-capacity processor into one of the explorer insects?" Azar suggested. "Then we download into that. We get to see the world firsthand and make some real-time decisions, but we don't waste energy or leave a big footprint." If Tallulah turned out to be inhabited after all, the difference between being perceived as friend or enemy might easily hang on something as simple as the amount of local resources they'd used, or how physically intrusive their presence had been.

Shelma thought it over. "That sounds like as good a choice as any."

3

AZAR PERSISTED with her doorway metaphor, and walked through an "airlock" from Mologhat Station into the robot insect as if the two were docked together. Amused by the conceit, Shelma followed behind her, but she couldn't resist a mild rebuke. "The poor balloon doesn't even rate a mention?"

Azar shuddered. "Please, heights make me dizzy." Only gamma rays had the bandwidth to transmit their software in a reasonable amount of time, but gamma rays couldn't penetrate far through a planetary atmosphere. So the nanotech on Tallulah's surface had built a small hydrogen balloon, which had risen high enough into the stratosphere to receive their transmission and transcribe the data into a densely encoded molecular memory, before deflating and descending.

The scape Azar had constructed inside the insect resembled the kind of transparent-domed flight deck found in sight-seeing aircraft back on Hanuz. Shelma would be perceiving some very different furnishings, but at least the two of them shared the same view of the jungle beyond the windshield; Shelma's vision had always stretched into the far infrared, and now Azar had chosen to match her.

The insect was perched on a broad, flat leaf, one of dozens of papery structures sprouting from a slender trunk. The leaf's veins glowed with the heat of warm sap, and a hot mist wafted up from the blotchy hexagonal pores that dotted the surface. When Azar looked up into the sky, the stars were barely visible through the fog.

Scout mites had already crawled up and down this plant and begun deciphering its strange biochemistry. Sap that was cooled and concentrated by evaporation in the leaves was pumped down to the roots, where it was diluted in chambers of fresh water. The increase in entropy that the dilution entailed allowed enzymes in the sap to drive an endothermic reaction, absorbing heat from the ground while synthesizing sugars from dissolved carbon dioxide.

The plant's heritable replicator was a carbohydrate polymer known as C3, which had been found on many other worlds. Once they'd built up a database of sequences from a sufficient number of species, they could start trying to construct an evolutionary tree, as well as looking for signs of technological tinkering.

Azar took hold of a joystick and flew their host across to another plant, a small bush adorned with twigs that sprouted leaves like radial cooling fins. They landed on a twig while the scout mites burrowed and sampled.

"There's not much sap in this one," Shelma noted. "The leaves just look like mats of fiber." There were no pores here, no steamy exudations.

Azar watched a display of the scouts' discoveries. There were long, fibrous structures running all the way from the leaves to the tips of the roots, and they were packed with interlocking polymers. In some fibers the polymers were rich in mobile electrons; in others they had positive "holes", electron deficits that could shuffle along the molecule's backbone from site to site.

"Thermoelectric diffusion?" she guessed. The electrons and holes would conduct heat from the ground up into the leaves, and in doing so they'd set up an electric potential, which in turn could be used to drive chemical reactions.

As the details came through, they confirmed her suspicion. The plant was a living thermocouple, with the heat-pumped currents in the polymers shuffling electrons to and from the enzymes that synthesized carbohydrates.

The thermocouple bush had no easily digestible nutrients above ground, so Azar flew back to the entropy tree and thrust the insect's proboscis into a vein, drawing out a tankful of sugary sap. There was no free atmospheric oxygen to help metabolize the sugars, but like the plant itself, their robot could make use of nitrate ions in the sap as an oxidizing agent, reducing them to ammonia in the process. Scout mites were still hunting for the organisms responsible for creating the nitrates in the first place.

Shelma said, "So where are the insects? Where are the animals?" So far, they'd seen nothing moving in the jungle.

"Maybe the Ground Heaters didn't have time to tweak any animals for the new conditions," Azar suggested. "If they were about to get ejected from their solar system, their priorities would have been a new form of energy, and a primary food source that could exploit it. The old animals just died out, and nobody had the heart to try to create new ones."

"Maybe," Shelma conceded. "But wouldn't your first response to the prospect of losing your sun be to build a few domed arks: sealed habitats with artificial heat and light that preserved the original ambient conditions, and as much of the original biosphere as possible?"

Azar said, "And then you'd slowly begin modifying the species from the arks to live off the new energy source. Still, they might have started with the plants but got no further."

The scout mites collected more C3 sequences, and as the numbers reached the point where comparisons became meaningful it grew increasingly clear that these genomes were natural, not engineered. Even the genes responsible for building the gloriously technomimetic thermocouple fibers had the same messy, incrementalist, patchwork character of all the others.

Stranger still, the genetic analysis pointed to a common ancestor for all these plants just two hundred million years ago, long after Tallulah had been orphaned.

As Azar reviewed descriptions of other C3 worlds, pulling the data down from Mologhat's library, she realized that in a couple of hours the station would set below the horizon. The time lag for her queries was already ponderous, and re-routing everything around Tallulah through the limited-bandwidth microprobes would only make that worse.

"We should clone the station's library," she suggested to Shelma. The library was far bigger than their personal software, and there was no room for it in their present insect host, but they could at least bring it down into the stratosphere, making the data far more accessible than it was from Mologhat's distant orbit.

Shelma agreed. They set the nanotech to work fitting out the balloon for a new flight, then continued exploring the jungle.

As in many communities of plants there was competition for access to the sky, but here it was all about shedding heat rather than catching sunlight. The healthiest plants had their roots deep in the ground and their leaves exposed to the darkness of space. To be caught in too warm a cranny, sentenced to uniform tepidity, was fatal. The only exceptions to that rule were parasites: vampiric vines that stretched over trunks, branches and leaves, their barbed rootlets anchoring them to their victims and drawing out nutritious sap.

As they moved through the jungle, the new sequence data that came in from the scouts only shored up their original conclusions: the life they were seeing was entirely natural, and this branch of it was relatively young.

"Suppose," Shelma ventured, "that the Ground Heaters didn't need to engineer anything to live this way."

"You mean there were species that exploited thermal gradients all along?" Azar frowned. "How do you evolve to use *that* as your energy source? A single cell can never do it alone; you need to be a certain minimum size to access a useful temperature difference."

"I'm not saying that the very first lifeforms used it," Shelma replied. "They might have relied on chemosynthesis, extracting energy from volcanic gases or mineral-rich geysers."

"Right." That was how Azar's own ancestral lineage had begun, back on Earth; photosynthesis had come much later. "So they grew to a certain size using chemosynthesis, then found they could switch to thermal effects. But this is all before the Ground Heaters have even evolved, so what's keeping the surface rocks so hot?"

Shelma pondered this. "Tidal heating? What if Tallulah was orbiting close to a cool red dwarf, or even a brown dwarf. With such weak sunlight, tidal heating might have been a far more potent energy source than photosynthesis."

"But it can't last," Azar protested. "Eventually the planet would end up tidally locked." The energy used to stretch and squeeze the rock, heating it up by internal friction, would ultimately be extracted from Tallulah's spin, slowing its rotation until its day matched its year and one hemisphere faced forever sunwards.

"Eventually, yes. But what if the Ground Heaters evolved before that happened? They would have been facing a slow, predictable decline in their energy source over millennia. So instead of responding frantically to a sudden catastrophe, they could have spent centuries perfecting a replacement."

"And the ejection from their star came much later, but by then there was nothing they needed to do. They'd already made themselves independent." Azar laughed, delighted. The artificial seasons and the variation in heat with latitude would still make sense: tidal heating would have been strongest at the equator, and at higher latitudes it would have been affected by seasonal changes in the angle between the planet's axis and the direction of the tidal force.

What this elegant hypothesis didn't explain was why the plants here were so young. Nor did it shed any light on exactly what the Ground Heaters had done to achieve their independence.

The data-collecting balloon was in place again. Before Mologhat vanished below the horizon, Azar instructed the station to send down a copy of its library.

As she was checking the interface with the cloned library, a message arrived from the microprobes. Thousands of kilometers away, something had exploded on the ocean floor and hurled a few billion tonnes of water skywards.

Azar turned to Shelma, still watching the satellite vision with her mind's eye. "What's happening? Some glitch with the heat source?" For a system that had survived for a billion years, this hiccup packed a mighty punch: the eruption was already high above the atmosphere, steam turning to ice like a cometary impact in reverse.

Shelma looked nervous. "Mologhat saw no vulcanism anywhere on the planet, in the last three years. Do you think we've annoyed someone?"

"If we have, why are we still alive? It's not the ground beneath our feet that's exploded." The balloon clearly wasn't the target, nor were any of the microprobes—and though the water missile was heading roughly in Mologhat's direction, it wouldn't reach anywhere near that far. But when Azar tried to contact the station, the microprobes replied that it was not responding.

Shelma said, "Don't jump to any conclusions. Mologhat might have imposed a communications blackout; if it thought it was under fire it would shift orbits and try not to do anything to give its position away."

Azar felt sick. "You think the gamma ray transmission was mistaken for some kind of attack?" Nothing had happened when she and Shelma had arrived the same way, but that burst had been considerably shorter, and it had come down almost vertically. The second beam had come from close to the horizon, giving it a longer path through the upper atmosphere—which would have made it more noticeable, and easier to trace back to its source.

Within minutes, the microprobes had reported six more eruptions, from underwater sites scattered around the planet. It made no sense to Azar; these gigatonnes of water were rising into orbits about a thousand kilometers up, but if they were meant as weapons, who were they aimed at? The microprobes were much lower down, and Mologhat was a hundred times further away. A direct hit with a solid iceberg could have done a lot of damage to any intruder, but these glistening snowballs weren't even holding together; Tallulah was just shrouding itself with a tenuous halo of tiny ice crystals.

"This isn't warfare!" she declared. "They don't think they're under attack. They saw the gamma rays, and thought: *antimatter*. They're afraid they're drifting into a cloud of antimatter. The ice is to tell them if there's any more around."

Shelma considered this. "I think you're right. They picked up a flash of annihilation radiation, and jumped to the conclusion that it was a natural source."

Never mind that there was no natural source of bulk antimatter anywhere in the galaxy; if you'd spent a billion years in space without encountering another civilization, perhaps a small cloud of antihydrogen seemed like a far less extravagant hypothesis than alien visitors using proton-antiproton gamma rays for communications.

"So they still don't even know we're here?" Azar wondered. "All those radio messages came to nothing. What do we have to do to get noticed—tattoo the binary digits for pi across the stratosphere?"

Shelma said, "I wouldn't advise that. But it's not even clear to me that there's anyone home; this might just be a non-sentient device that's outlived the people it's meant to be protecting."

The water missiles had stopped; the absence of any answering flash of radiation must have made it clear that if there was antimatter around, it was far too thinly spread to pose any kind of hazard.

Azar tried calling Mologhat again, but it was still not responding. "They must have hit it," she said. "Whatever they thought it was, they must have launched something small and fast, and knocked it out before the ice storm even started." She felt numb. *So much for the doorway to the stars.*

Shelma touched her arm reassuringly. "It might yet reply—but even if it's gone, we're not stranded."

"No?" The microprobes had nowhere near enough power for interstellar transmissions, or even the raw materials to build the kind of hardware they'd need. And the data-ferrying balloon couldn't send them anywhere; their return path to Mologhat would have involved a gamma-ray mirror on the balloon, modulating and reflecting radiation coming down from the station itself.

Azar slumped into her seat. *How had she ever imagined she could do this? Travel fifteen hundred light years as if it was nothing?* There was no magic gate leading home, just fourteen quadrillion kilometers of vacuum.

Shelma said, "We have plenty of resources down here."

Azar rubbed her eyes and tried to concentrate. "That's true." Given time, the nanotech could build them almost anything—and they didn't even have to reach all the way back to Hanuz or Bahar; they just had to connect to the Amalgam's network. Still, the nearest node was seven hundred light years away; getting a signal that far was a daunting prospect. "Can we do this from the ground?"

"Well…we could build a radio dish a few hundred kilometers across," Shelma replied, deadpan. "Factoring in suitable error correction for the signal-to-noise ratio, it might only take two or three centuries to complete the transmission."

Azar got the message. "OK: better to build a rail gun and launch a transmitter into orbit. But even if we can power a rail gun, how do we power the transmitter? We don't have any antimatter. There's virtually no deuterium here; are we going to try to build a hydrogen-boron fusion reactor?" The most efficient way to produce gamma rays was from antimatter—that would certainly make for the lightest power source to loft into orbit—but trying to create even a few micrograms of antihydrogen with nothing but *plant carbohydrates* as the energy source made Shelma's giant radio dish sound like a good idea. Whatever was guarding Tallulah might be a tad obtuse, but it was difficult to imagine a particle accelerator powered by industrial-scale deforestation slipping under the radar.

"What's the point of this transmission anyway?" she said bitterly. "To arrive home empty handed, with no news worth hearing? If it comes to that, I'd rather let my backup wake."

"So would I," Shelma said, "but I think you're missing something."

"Yeah?"

"The news worth hearing," she said, "and the energy source we need in order to send it, are the very same thing. Whatever's keeping this planet warm is just a few kilometers beneath our feet. If we can reach it, study it, understand it and harness it, we'll have both the means to get home, and the reason."

4

A FEW kilometers beneath our feet was an encouraging way of putting it; from where they stood the actual distance was twenty-seven thousand meters. The nanotech built some robot moles, powered by long thermoelectric tails, and sent them on their way. They would reach the heat source in about two hundred days.

The oceanic crust was much thinner in places. Azar did some calculations. It wasn't clear what kind of food there'd be in the water, but she thought it was worth finding out. Shelma agreed, and they set out for the coast.

The insect made good time, averaging about thirty kilometers an hour, but when they reached the edge of the jungle food became more sparse and the scattered plants less nutritious. Flying across the flat, monotonously glowing savannah, Azar ached for sunrise to come and banish the interminable night. But she fought down the pang of homesickness and tried to find the beauty in this upside-down world.

Other explorer insects were already fanning out from a dozen sites where the spores had landed, building up a picture of the continent's geochemistry. A tentative analysis of the data suggested that the surface had only been above sea level for about a quarter of a billion years.

"Before that, there might have been no dry land at all," Shelma suggested. "That would explain why the ecosystem here is so young."

"So where did all the water go?" Azar wondered. "Unless their antimatter detectors have a lot of false alarms." Even the modest amount that they'd seen thrown skywards would mostly rain back down again.

"A collision?" Shelma frowned and withdrew the suggestion. "No, the odds would be very low out here, to hit something big enough." The current estimate of Tallulah's galactic orbit suggested that it hadn't even crossed another system's Oort cloud in the last billion years.

They reached the shoreline. Waves lapped gently on a lifeless beach; the infrared glow of the placid ocean made Azar think of liquid metal, but if she'd been wearing her body this water would have made a luxurious warm bath.

In the waves they found only single-celled creatures, living off a very thin soup of organic debris. They flew out a kilometer and took another sample, sending scout mites a few hundred meters down. The soup was thicker here; with a little tweaking, the insect would be able to make use of it.

There was a trench some six hundred kilometers off the coast, where the mysterious neutrino source was just nine thousand meters below the ocean floor. They set out across the waves, stopping every couple of hours to dive and feed.

Each time they plunged into the water, Azar noticed Shelma tensing. She wondered about the propriety of commenting on this; if she'd been looking at Shelma's true self-image—a Bahari body with five limbs and five tails, like the rear end of a cat caught in a kaleidoscope—she would not have been able to distinguish tranquility from terror. Still, it was not as if the scape was reading Shelma's mind; it was merely translating information that she had chosen to make public.

As they approached the trench, Azar finally spoke. "You don't have to do this if you don't want to." The trench was three thousand meters deep; if Shelma had retained a primal fear of drowning, Azar had no wish to see her suffer. "We can split the processor, and you can stay up here."

Shelma shook her head, a little puzzled by this offer. "No, I'll go with you. But first I want to bring in as much of the library as we can fit."

"Oh." Azar understood now; this was nothing to do with how Baharis felt about getting their fur wet. Once they were underwater they'd lose radio contact with everything, including the balloon-borne library.

Shelma began communing with the library, trying to choose a selection of its contents that would fit inside the insect without leaving them ill-equipped in the face of some crucial problem or opportunity. "I don't want to meet the Ground Heaters and then find we can't even make sense of their language!"

"If they're so smart," Azar replied, "let them make sense of ours." Then again, if they'd spent a billion years living alone on the ocean floor, it would probably be unwise to expect too much of their communications skills.

Hanuz had sent no travelers out into the galaxy for a hundred thousand years, and that had been long enough. Though Tallulah had been an enticing destination, Azar had left home less for the sake of the orphan's secrets than for the sake of breaking the curse. As the window for joining Mologhat had approached, she'd thought: *If we don't do this now, it will only grow harder.* And she'd finally stopped waiting for someone else to volunteer.

Shelma announced that she'd completed her selection, then she changed her mind and dived back into the interface. Azar thought of her great-great-granddaughter, Shirin, struggling to pack for an overnight trip.

Shirin would be ancient when Azar returned; she'd have left all her toy animals behind.

"This is it now," Shelma declared. "We're prepared for anything." Her avatar wasn't quite hyperventilating, but Azar could imagine her letting a breeze of random skills and factoids play through her mind, soaking her tissues with the oxygen of information before the conduit slammed shut.

"I could always give myself amnesia, if you want a little more room," Azar suggested. Shelma actually looked tempted for a moment, before smiling thinly at the joke.

Azar took the joystick and the insect dived beneath the waves.

Their infrared vision wasn't quite useless here; if they tuned to a wavelength a little shorter than the peak thermal emissions around them, they could see the shadows that nearby objects cast against the glow of the warmer water below. Augmented with the strobe flashes of sonar, the vague shadows became fluttering vertical ribbons, drifting in the current but maintaining their orientation. Azar sent in the scout mites, who found the ribbons to be packed with tiny buoyancy chambers that exchanged gases in a complex cycle, eking a few microwatts out of the temperature gradient. The ribbon-weed's C3 sequence made it a close cousin of the land plants; in fact, it had probably changed very little from the ancestor whose other offspring had invaded the continents.

Five hundred meters down, they saw the first animals: small, segmented worms about a millimeter long, feeding off the ribbon-weed. The scout mites grabbed a few cells from the worms' skin for analysis. As Azar watched the data coming through, she felt a sense of disorientation to rival anything since she'd stepped on to Mologhat. The worms had no C3 in their cells; they were no more related to the weed they were munching on than she was to Shelma. Their replicator was P2, a polypeptide. What's more, their genome had been the subject of some blatantly artificial modifications, probably less than a million years ago.

"Introduced?" Shelma suggested.

"They must be," Azar replied. Colonists from a P2 world must have come to Tallulah, bringing a few species from their home planet and tweaking them in order to survive here. It was a curious strategy; almost all interstellar travelers were digital in transit, not biological, and even if—like the founders of Hanuz—they had a fetish for recreating their original biochemistry upon arrival, such travelers tended to colonize sterile worlds. But then, nobody traveled to an orphan world for the sake of its real estate value. "It looks as if someone else came treasure-hunting long before we did."

"Apparently," Shelma concurred. "But if Tallulah is such old news, why isn't the heating process known halfway around the galaxy by now?"

As they descended further the ribbon-weed grew larger, the soup of microbes thicker, and the P2 creatures more numerous and diverse. There were shrimp-like animals straining microbes from the water, floating gas bladders with poisonous tentacles, and sinuous, muscular fish of every size, feeding on each other, the ribbon-weed and the shrimp.

A vast forest came into sonar range, rising up from the ocean floor. Azar had already been impressed by the size of the free-floating ribbon-weed, but its anchored cousins were giants, fifty or sixty meters high. With convection currents in the water sweeping heat away more efficiently than air, the temperature gradient was far less steep here than on land, but the water also made it easier for taller structures to support themselves. The scout mites counted eighty species of animals in the forest's upper reaches alone; some were P2, but there were C3 species as well, the first such animals the mites had found. And some were N3, with their genome encoded in nucleic acid.

"This place really has been popular," Shelma observed dryly. "It's enough to bring out the biograffitist in anyone. You sprinkle some N2 microbes in the water; I'll add the C1." N2 was DNA, Azar's ancestral replicator.

The N3 species, like the P2, had been engineered, but the best estimates put the date of intervention much earlier, between two and three hundred million years ago. Azar checked their local copy of the library; there was no previous archaeological evidence for an interstellar civilization with N3 ancestry in that epoch—and this was not one of the databases Shelma had trimmed. How could a civilization reach such a difficult target as Tallulah, but leave no trace anywhere else?

As they descended slowly into the forest, the insect announced a discovery that had nothing to do with Tallulah's polyglot biology. The robot's mass spectrometer was constantly analyzing samples from the water around them, and it had just stumbled across an extraordinary find. The object in question had a mass of 40.635 atomic units; this far-from-integral figure might have made sense as an average for a sample containing a mixture of calcium-40 and its heavier isotopes—but it wasn't an average, it was the mass of a single ion.

Stranger still, when stripped of all its electrons the thing had a charge, not of twenty or so, but *two hundred and ten*. This was double the charge of any known stable nucleus, and ten times greater than its atomic weight implied.

"Who ordered *that*?" Azar quipped. Shelma didn't even smile; the depleted library wasn't up to providing the scape with the context for a proper translation.

"It's femtotech," Shelma declared.

Azar hesitated, then agreed. It was a staggering notion, but what else could it be? A new fundamental particle...with a charge of two hundred and ten? Femtotech—the engineering of matter on the scale of atomic nuclei—was still a primitive art within the Amalgam; there had been some ingenious creations but they all had to do their job quickly, before they blew apart in a few trillionths of a second. The insect's find had endured for at least three hundred seconds, and counting.

"How do you create a femtomachine with a binding energy equal to ninety percent of its mass?" she wondered. The most stable nuclei, nickel and iron, weighed about one percent less than the sum of their parts, thanks to the potential energy associated with the strong nuclear force. But increasing that effect by a factor of *ninety* was almost unimaginable.

The insect measured the ion's magnetic moment. The result was orders of magnitude higher than that which a nucleus of atomic number 210 would be expected to possess if it was sitting quietly in its ground state; to generate such a strong magnetic field, it would need to be spinning at relativistic speeds. This only made the overall picture even stranger: the kinetic energy from this rotation should have added substantially to the ion's total mass, rendering the actual forty-something value even more bizarre. The one thing that made a warped kind of sense was the failure of the ion to tear itself apart from centrifugal force. How could it explode, when the fragments would need to possess ten times more energy than the whole?

Azar said, "I take it this is ash from the heating process?"

Shelma managed a dazed smile. "If it's not, it certainly should be. *Ninety percent mass-to-energy conversion.* No wonder it's still going strong after a billion years!"

Tallulah's crust was generating heat at a rate of about two petawatts, stabilizing the planet's temperature by replacing the energy that leaked out of the greenhouse blanket. At ninety percent mass conversion, that would consume less than eight hundred tonnes of fuel each year, so in principle the process could continue for about ten-to-the-eighteenth years: a billion times longer than it had been running so far. Unlike fission or fusion, even if the starting point for the femtotech process had to be one particular kind of nucleus, it really didn't matter how rare it was in nature, since the energy required to synthesize it from anything else would be trivial in comparison. If each tonne of the Ground Heaters' "gold" burned so fiercely that it could power the transmutation of a hundred tonnes of nickel or iron into yet more fuel, then Tallulah's bonfire would easily outlive the stars.

Technology like this could transform the Amalgam. Antimatter had never been more than a wonderfully compact storage device, costing as much energy to make as it released. The most exquisitely efficient fusion systems extracted about *half a percent* of their fuel's mass as usable energy. There were some unwieldy tricks with black holes that could do better, but they weren't very practical, let alone portable. If everyone could harness the Ground Heaters' femtotech, it would be like a magic wand that could turn nine parts in ten of *anything* into energy, leaving nothing behind but this strange spinning ash.

Azar said, "This is a lot to conclude from one weird ion. Are we sure it's not an instrument error?"

Before the insect touched the ocean floor it picked a second speck of ash out of the water. Azar had the nanotech rebuild the relevant instruments from scratch and repeat the analysis. There had been no error; all the properties were the same.

5

THE NANOTECH built more moles and sent them down into the rock, but even here where the crust was thinner, Azar knew she would have to be patient.

"Sixty days?" she lamented, pacing the flight deck. She didn't expect to be able to unravel the nucleon-by-nucleon details of the femtotech in a hurry, but if they could obtain a sample of the deep crust and observe the way its composition was changing as energy was released, that would at least confirm that their overall picture of the Ground Heaters' process was correct.

Until they had some of this white-hot rock to play with, the practicalities of harnessing the femtotech remained obscure, but Azar's sense of anxiety at their isolation had almost vanished. To be stranded for nothing, with little to be gained if they managed to return, had been a dismal prospect, but now that the stakes were so high the situation was exhilarating. *Prometheus, eat your heart out.*

While they waited for the moles to hit pay dirt they continued to explore the ribbon forest, building up a catalog of the three kinds of life that Tallulah's mysterious fire sustained. Perhaps unsurprisingly, the P2 animals—the newest—were by far the most numerous, having been engineered to be able to digest everything that had come before them. To the older N3s, and the even rarer C3s, the P2s were unpalatable—though not indestructible; the scouts witnessed cases of N3 fish killing off their P2 rivals, even though they were useless as food. What's more, a few of the C3 creatures were able to feed on N3 flesh; evolution had finally granted them a belated revenge on the first wave of invaders. In another hundred million years, who knew who would be eating whom?

When they first came across the colony of P2 "lizards", Azar thought that they were charming animals. Spread across a dozen square kilometers of the forest floor, their network of burrows was entwined with the giant ribbon-weeds' roots, which they tapped for food.

The lizards had two eight-clawed limbs that they used for digging and grasping objects; all their motive force came from their powerful tails. They sensed the world around them with a mixture of IR vision and sonar. Glands in their cheeks excreted complex molecular cocktails, which they squirted at each other almost constantly. Olfactory signaling within a colony of social animals was nothing surprising; the shock came when the scout mites caught some of them squirting the chemicals at inanimate objects in certain chambers within their burrows—and the inanimate objects squirted back replies. On closer examination, the devices turned out to be sophisticated chemical transceivers, linked by a fiber optic network.

"So these are our predecessors," Shelma said. "They came all the way to Tallulah, in the middle of nowhere, to solve the mystery of its warmth. But they must have found the femtotech long ago, so why are they still here? Why not take the treasure home? Why not spread it across the galaxy?"

"Why leave a world that will keep you warm for a million times longer than any star?" Azar replied.

"Why not build a hundred more worlds just like it?" Shelma countered. "Let's ask them."

The scouts set to work sampling the chemical signals that comprised the lizards' language, and trying to correlate them with elements in the environment and the creatures' behavior. It was an impertinent level of eavesdropping, but they had to bootstrap communications somehow, and with no culture or biology in common they couldn't simply march up to the lizards and start playing charades. Ideally the scouts would have included children as their subjects, in order to share in any lessons they received, but in the entire colony of fifty thousand there were currently no young at all—which suggested that the lizards had cut back their fertility to stabilize the population, while living more or less as long as they wished.

Fiber optic trunk lines connected the colony to others around the planet, and all the data traffic passing through appeared to conform to a single language. If there were any intelligent N3 creatures still around, either they weren't plugged into the same network, or there'd been a radical assimilation of cultures in one direction or the other.

Fed by the forest and served by their own rudimentary nanotech, the lizards seemed to pass the time socializing. The chemical transceivers granted them access to libraries, but most of the content being summoned appeared very similar to their habitual person-to-person exchanges, suggesting that it was closer to narrative history or fiction than anything more specialized and technical. Then again, even the most naturalistic dialogues might have encoded subtle themes that remained elusive at this stage of the analysis.

The lizards had no apparent social hierarchies, and as hermaphrodites they exhibited no sexual dimorphism, but the scouts identified one curious form of division. Many of the lizards identified themselves as belonging to one of three groups, which were named for the actions of spiraling inward, spiraling outward, and, the clear majority, following a circle. Since this was not a description of anyone's actual swimming style, it had to be a metaphor, but for what? The scouts had failed to observe anything tangible that correlated with this classification.

After thirty days Shelma declared, "It's time to introduce ourselves."

"Are you sure?" Azar was impatient for answers, but it seemed as if the scouts could easily spend another month piecing together further subtleties of the lizards' language.

"We've reached the point where we can greet them politely and explain who we are," Shelma said. "The way to get more reliable language acquisition now is through dialogue."

Shelma instructed the nanotech to build two facsimile lizard bodies. These robots would be obvious caricatures, functional but not such perfect imitations that the lizards could mistake them for fellow colonists.

The insect communicated with the robot lizards by line-of-sight laser pulses with a range of just a few meters. Azar and Shelma kept their software on the insect's processor and operated the lizards by telepresence, monitoring the robots' points of view without becoming fully immersed in their sensoria or giving up the feeling of being located on the insect's flight deck.

With her lizard body swimming toward the edge of the colony, weaving its way between the ribbon-weeds, Azar was overwhelmed with happiness. She was more than just a traveler now; she was about to become an ambassador to a hitherto unknown culture. And however physically isolated she was at this moment, she did not feel cut off from her roots in Hanuz. In her mind's eye, she could almost see the faces of the people she hoped to regale with her adventures.

A lizard approached, seemingly unafraid. The puff of chemicals it squirted through the water was barely visible, but Azar heard the translation loud and clear. "Who are you?"

"We come in peace from another world," Azar announced proudly. The lizards had not been seen discussing astronomy, but they did have a word for the planet as a whole, and a general inflection for "not this thing, but another of its kind".

The lizard turned and fled.

On the flight deck, Azar turned to Shelma. "What did I do wrong?" She'd half-expected her claim to be greeted with skepticism—their robot bodies were well within reach of the lizards' own technology, after all—but perhaps the gamma rays that had triggered the ice halo had served as an ominous calling card.

"Nothing," Shelma assured her. "Summoning other witnesses is a common response." Shelma had no prior experience of first contact, but the library confirmed her claim.

Azar said, "What if they've forgotten that there *are* other worlds? They've been here for a million years. They might not even remember their own history."

Shelma was not persuaded. "There's too much technology around; even if they fell into a dark age at some point, they would have reconstructed everything by now." The lizards' nanotech maintained their health; it could easily have sequenced all the plants and animals around them, just as the Amalgam nanotech had done. Still, without the right context—without libraries of replicator sequences from a thousand other worlds—would they know how to interpret the data?

Azar saw bodies darting through the fronds. The first lizard had returned, with ten, twelve, fourteen friends. She could never have distinguished one from the other unaided, so she invoked software to track their features and assign phonetic names to them all.

Shelma said, "Please accept our good wishes. We come in peace from another world."

Omar, the first lizard they'd met, replied, "How can that be? It's not time."

His companion Lisa added, "You're not taking Tallulah from us. We'll never accept that."

Suddenly all fourteen lizards were speaking at once. Azar's robot's senses had no problem following their words; the chemical emissions were tagged with individual markers, so there was no chance of confusing one lizard's words for another's. Azar had the audio translation untangled into separate streams.

Some of the lizards were expressing surprise and skepticism, not at the notion of visitors from another world, but at the timing of their arrival. Others seemed to think that she and Shelma were the vanguard of an army of colonists who had come to seize Tallulah, and they defiantly expressed their intention to resist.

Shelma said, "We're not colonists, we're merely explorers. We saw Tallulah and became curious."

"Where is your own world?" a lizard dubbed Caleb demanded.

"My companion and I come from different worlds," Shelma explained. "Both more than a thousand light-years away." The software would translate this into the local measure of distance, but with no units suitable for astronomical scales the number attached would be awfully large.

The lizards broke into a fresh cacophony. Such a journey was inconceivable.

Omar said, "Please come with us."

The crowd pressed around them from all sides, urging them forward. Shelma said privately, "Just go where they ask, don't resist."

The lizards seemed unaware of the tiny insect hovering between the larger robots; certainly its laser flashes were outside their visible spectrum. "You think they're *taking us prisoner?*" Azar said. It was hard to decide which was more bizarre: the fact that someone might wish to do this, or the fact that they believed it could be done.

"More or less," Shelma replied. "But at this point I'd rather cooperate than escape. If we can clear up a few misunderstandings, everything should be fine."

Azar let the pack of lizards guide her through the ribbon-weeds, then down into a burrow. Watching events through the flight deck's dome made her feel much less claustrophobic than the impression she got from her jostled robot's senses, but when the narrowing tunnels and the ever tighter crush meant the insect risked becoming conspicuous, they had it crawl inside Shelma's body. The line of sight between the two larger robots came and went, so Azar put her own lizard on autopilot, meekly complying with the flow of the crowd, and changed the insect's flight deck scape to show her an external view rather than the innards of its host.

They were taken to a small, bare chamber with a single entrance. After six of the lizards piled in with them, there was little room to spare.

Omar resumed the interrogation, his skepticism undiminished. "Your star must be very dim," he declared. "We believed that we had many more years."

Azar thought she was beginning to understand. Tallulah would not come close to another star for a very long time; the lizards had somehow fixed on that event as the most likely occasion for visitors.

"Our stars are very bright, but very distant," she insisted. "Why do you doubt that? Didn't your own ancestors travel far to reach this world?"

Omar said, "Their journey took half a year."

Half a year? Perhaps the real story had degenerated into myth, retold with cozy, domesticated numbers to replace the terrifying reality of interstellar distances.

"At the speed of light?" asked Shelma.

The chamber erupted with expressions of mirth and derision. "Only light travels at the speed of light," Lisa explained.

The scouts had found no evidence of the lizards digitizing themselves. Had they lost that technology, or had they never possessed it? Could their ancestors really have crossed the light years as flesh?

"So how far would they have traveled," Azar asked, "in that half-year?"

"Perhaps a billion kilometers," Omar replied.

Azar said nothing, but the claim was absurd; a billion kilometers was the size of a small planetary system. The lizards had spent too long dozing away the centuries at the bottom of this warm ocean; not only had they forgotten their own history, they had forgotten the true scale of the universe around them.

Shelma persisted. "When we follow the path of Tallulah back in time, it doesn't come that close to the path of any star for a billion years. Have you been here for a billion years?"

Omar said, "How can you know Tallulah's path? How long have you been watching us?"

"Thirty thousand years," Shelma replied. "Not me personally, but people I trust."

Mirth again. Why was this claim so laughable?

"Thirty thousand years?" Omar said. "Why did you imagine that would tell you the whole story?"

Shelma was bewildered now. "We've tracked your position and your speed," she said. "We know the motion of the stars. What else is there to account for?" Tallulah's galactic orbit was sparsely populated; chaos would eventually make retrodiction impossible, but the confidence levels over a billion years were still quite tight.

"Eight times since we arrived on Tallulah," Omar explained, "this world has changed course. Eight times, the heat rose from the ground to bring our path closer to our destination."

6

AN ARGUMENT broke out among the lizards; they withdrew from the discussion and left the chamber, leaving their guests with only two taciturn sentries. The insect probably could have slipped past these guards, or even burrowed its way back to the surface if necessary, but Shelma insisted that it was better to try to keep the dialogue open, and on consideration Azar agreed.

"So our orphan is a tourist," Shelma mused. "It steered its way right into the lizards' home system, and now it's heading for a new destination. But did the Ground Heaters arrange that, or did the N3 colonists bolt on the engines later?"

"Maybe that's where the water went," Azar suggested. The eruptions they'd seen earlier would have no long term effect on the planet's motion, but a hotter jet that reached escape velocity would do the trick.

Shelma said, "Water would be a strange choice of propellant. Photonic jets would be more efficient."

"If it was the N3ers doing it," Azar said, "maybe they didn't have fine enough control over the femtotech."

"Maybe. But the N3ers left no biological presence on the land, so they must have been ocean dwellers. Would ocean dwellers throw so much water into space that they lost thirty percent of their real estate?"

"Good point," Azar conceded. "But why does *anyone* steer a whole planet from system to system? If it was the Ground Heaters, surely they could have made smaller, faster spacecraft using the femtotech."

Shelma threw up her hands. "Let's go back to the beginning. The Ground Heaters grew up with tidal heating. When that started running down, they got lucky; they managed to devise a spectacularly good replacement. So what would they do next?"

"Some cultures would have sent out nanotech spores," Azar said, "followed by a wave of digitized travelers. But we know they didn't do that, or the femtotech would still be around somewhere else."

"They didn't found colonies, but they still ended up traveling." Shelma laughed. "I was going to say that it must have been a deliberate choice—that they could have resisted any natural ejection from their system if they'd really wanted to—but maybe they only had fusion power then. That would explain why's there's no deuterium around: they used it all up while they were developing the femtotech."

"But either way," Azar said, "once they were free of their star and able to steer themselves, they decided to make the best of it. To see a few sights along the way. And where do you go, if you grew up around a dwarf star? You take a tour of other dwarf stars—"

"Until you find one with an inhabited planet," Shelma said, "where they're facing the same problems you faced."

"And then what?" Azar frowned. "I can't believe the N3ers conquered the Ground Heaters!"

"No," Shelma agreed. "And why would they need to? Why wouldn't the Ground Heaters simply share the femtotech, to help out their fellow thermophiles? If they weren't feeling generous and sociable, why visit an inhabited world at all? If they'd simply been looking for territory there would have been plenty of sterile worlds for them to choose from."

Azar said, "Maybe the Ground Heaters died out before they reached the N3 world. They'd programmed some billion-year spree for Tallulah into the femtotech, but they lost heart along the way. The ghost ship came into the N3 system, and the locals couldn't believe their luck: an empty planet, habitable for ten-to-the-eighteenth years, right on their doorstep! But they couldn't park it, they couldn't steer it, they had to go along for the ride. And a quarter of a billion years later, the same thing happened to the lizards."

Shelma thought for a while. "That almost makes sense, but I can't quite believe that neither of these free-riders had any interest in turning the femtotech into a propulsion system and founding a few colonies elsewhere."

"Maybe they did. Maybe we've missed them. Tallulah went unnoticed for a very long time."

"We're missing something," Shelma said. "But perhaps our hosts will be able to enlighten us."

⌁⌁⌁

HOURS PASSED with no more contact from the lizards. The sentries were changed, but the replacements were equally determined not to engage with them.

Azar paced the flight deck. "They must be trying to work out if we're telling the truth or not. Checking to see if Tallulah's brought them close to a very faint brown dwarf—a port of call that they failed to anticipate."

"You'd think they'd have good enough telescopes to be sure," Shelma said irritably. "Given what's at stake."

"Maybe they got complacent. I mean, if you do a thorough sweep of the sky and get a very clear verdict that there's nothing to worry about for the next hundred thousand years, how motivated are you to keep repeating the search?"

"Ideally, it would all be automated," Shelma replied. "Motivation wouldn't come into it."

"Well, we might not have landed on the best of all possible worlds after all."

The lights on the flight deck were starting to soften. Ever since she'd arrived on Mologhat, Azar had been sticking scrupulously to her usual diurnal rhythm; to sleep was part of her identity. But she was too anxious now, and she willed the urge away. Her sense of self would just have to stretch to encompass an exception when she was captive to confused, paranoid lizards.

The sentries were changed again. Azar recognized them as two of the crowd who'd first appeared in the forest; her software had dubbed them Jake and Tilly, but they hadn't said much then, and she didn't bother trying to speak to them now. Let the telescopes confirm her and Shelma's honesty, and then they could all finally engage in a civilized discussion.

Jake said, "Come with us. Quickly. We don't have much time." He swam a short way toward his prisoners, then darted back toward the chamber's entrance.

Azar was dumbfounded.

"Come with you where?" Shelma asked.

"Out of here," Tilly said. "We think the Circlers are planning to kill you."

Azar glanced at Shelma. The insect could probably defend itself against most of the lizards' technology, but it was not indestructible. They'd left backups in the jungle before setting out for the coast, but those snapshots of their minds were missing all the crucial discoveries they'd made since. In any case, even if they survived here, what kind of dialogue could they have with people who wanted them dead?

Shelma addressed her privately. "So do we leave the bodies as decoys?"

Azar was unsure. The insect on its own would face technical problems communicating with the lizards—it was too small to stock the raw materials for more than a few minutes' speech—and she also found something comforting about the way it was now hidden inside a larger target.

"What if we split the difference?" she suggested. Her lizard body had enough redundancy in its engineering to allow its nanotech to make two bodies from the same materials; she instructed it to divide into a mimic of Shelma's, along with a somewhat less sturdy copy of its original form. Then she loaded both with non-sentient software that could easily pass a half-baked Turing test from their would-be executioners.

Tilly remained guarding the fake prisoners, and they followed Jake through the tunnels, leaving by a different route than they'd come. They did not travel unobserved, but the few lizards Azar glimpsed at intersections merely watched them pass in silence; presumably they belonged to Jake's faction, and were standing lookout in aid of their escape.

On the surface the ribbon-weeds carved the forest floor into a kind of maze, and while it was possible to cheat and squeeze your way between the edges of the fronds that didn't quite touch, it certainly was faster if you knew the maze so well that you didn't have to.

After a while, Jake halted and gestured urgently at a stubby, bulbous plant in the undergrowth. Since leaving the chamber he hadn't spoken at all; words decayed quickly in the water, to the point of losing their meaning, but the residue would still be easy to track. When Shelma did nothing he ducked down, tore a bulb from the plant, and stuffed it into his mouth. Shelma took the hint and did the same. The scouts hadn't come across this plant before, but the robot's nanotech quickly analyzed the bulb's contents. There were few conventional nutrients in it, but it was packed with organic azides, nitrogen-rich compounds with an extremely high energy density. The plant was C3, but its genome suggested that the lizards had modified it to produce this edible rocket fuel, and despite its modest appearance its roots probably ran deeper into the ground than the ribbon-weeds rose up into the ocean. The nanotech didn't take long to devise a pathway to metabolize the azides safely—which was lucky, because Jake was already powering ahead at five times his previous swimming speed.

As their robot body struggled to catch up with him, Shelma said, "Now I know why they don't bother with vehicles." Azar had once tweaked her own flesh to enable her to run non-stop across a continent—purely for the physical joy of it—but it seemed that with the right dietary supplement, anyone on Tallulah could moonlight as a high-performance submarine.

As they sped through the forest, the thermal/sonar images of the ribbon-weeds on either side of them blurred together like the walls of some long, twisted canyon. "If 'the Circlers' really want to kill us," Azar said, "I hope that doesn't mean all of them." References to that cryptic self-description had been present even in distant traffic coming through the fibers; the group was certainly not confined to one colony.

Shelma said, "I'm sure this is all just a misunderstanding. They think this is the end of the line for them—that Tallulah's come within reach of another dying world, and we're its inhabitants, intent on taking over."

"You think they have a guilty precedent in mind?" Azar suggested. "Maybe that's what happened with them and the N3ers."

"Maybe. But I think it's more likely that the N3ers were long gone, and that's part of the shock. The lizards weren't expecting to be around to meet their own replacements, either."

Azar said, "So how do we convince them that there is no threat, if they refuse to believe the evidence of their own telescopes?"

"Good question. How faint is the faintest dwarf star, and how far would they be willing to believe we've come?"

The forest gave way to a dense carpet of smaller plants, but Jake still knew how to find the fuel bulbs among them. This time when they stopped, he risked talking. "I think you're safe for now," he declared. "But we should keep moving. I have friends who'll shelter us, but they're still a few hundred kilometers away."

"We don't want to put anyone's life in danger," Azar said, borrowing Shelma's lizard body but inflecting the words with the identity tag she'd used when she'd had her own.

"You won't," Jake assured her. "The three philosophies have been at peace for millennia; we're not going to start killing each other now."

"The three philosophies?" Shelma asked.

"Circlers, Spiral In, Spiral Out."

"We've heard those phrases, but we don't know what they mean."

Jake flexed his body like an athlete limbering up for a sprint. "If you want to keep talking, swim close beside me and synch your tail with mine." As he started moving, Shelma followed his advice. The layer of water trapped between them let them communicate without their words being lost in the flow.

"The Circlers," Jake said, "are resolved to stay. To stay on Tallulah, and to stay as they are. They accept that we didn't build this world ourselves, that it came to us as a gift, but to the Circlers that's not the point. The Builders are gone, and now Tallulah belongs to us."

Azar said, "So they're ready to fight off any intruders?"

"They're willing," Jake replied, "but I wouldn't call them ready. They weren't expecting you. Nobody was."

"We really don't want this place as our home," Shelma said. "We have worlds of our own, powered by sunlight. You believe that, don't you?"

Jake considered the question. "I suppose it's possible for life to evolve that way, around the right kind of star. Some experts claim the radiation would be fatal, but I believe there could be a narrow habitable zone. To travel more than a thousand light years, though…"

Shelma explained about Mologhat 1 and 2, meeting and canceling their momentum against each other. About the digital forms she and Azar had taken, crossing the light years as gamma rays in a subjective instant.

Jake said, "Now you're trying to tell me that Spiral In is really the same as Spiral Out."

"Spiral Out is about travel?" Azar said. "The idea that you should leave Tallulah and look for a new home?"

"Yes. Spiral Out is my own philosophy."

Azar tried to frame her next question as politely as possible, and hoped the translator would be able to honor her intent. "Then if you don't mind me asking, why are you still here?"

"Travel isn't easy," Jake declared. "We've been waiting for Tallulah to bring us close to an empty world that we could claim as our own. But the last time that happened—before I was born—our numbers were small and our technology was untested. The opportunity was lost."

Shelma said, "So what's Spiral In?"

"They aim to take the form you claim to have taken. To become pure information. But not for travel: to stay on this world. To join with this world."

It was an odd way of putting it, but Azar thought she caught his meaning. In almost every culture with the means to go digital, there was a subculture who advocated a kind of implosion: a retreat into a universe of scapes divorced from physical reality.

"To join with this world?" Shelma pressed him.

"With the heat. With the hoops. With the Builders themselves." Jake emitted a token of mirth that Azar heard as curt laughter. "Some Spiral In people believe that there are ten thousand cultures under the ground."

The ocean floor passed beneath them in a blur.

"Hoops?" Azar said.

"You haven't seen the hoops yet?" Jake replied. "When the rock turns to heat, what's left are the hoops."

"The ash," Shelma said privately. "He's talking about the ash!"

"We've seen them," Azar said. "But we're not quite sure what they are."

Jake fell silent for a while, then he said, "How much do you know about relativity?" The translator marked the final word with a cautionary footnote:

the scouts hadn't heard it in use before, so the meaning was being inferred purely from its etymology.

"I understand the basics." Azar had studied relativity as a child, but without the full library to call on she would be unwise to claim to be an expert.

"Imagine," Jake said, "a hoop made of something extraordinarily strong, spinning at close to the speed of light. From the hoop's point of view, it's under enormous tension. But from the point of view of a bystander watching it spin, it's moving so rapidly that some of that tension manifests itself as a decrease in its energy."

Azar was familiar with the principle, though she was more used to thinking of the opposite effect. When you considered a gas under pressure, that pressure was due to the momentum of molecules moving from place to place. But if you were moving rapidly relative to the gas—or vice versa—then some fraction of that *momentum in motion* looked to you instead like *energy standing still*. The shift in perspective transformed pressure into energy.

Tension was simply negative pressure, so for a moving object under tension the effect changed sign: the total energy would be decreased. The quantities involved would normally be immeasurably small, though. Azar said, "Are you telling us that these hoops are under so much tension that their energy drops to *ten percent of their rest mass?*"

"Yes."

"Despite the kinetic energy of rotation? Despite the energy that goes into stretching the hoop?"

"Yes," Jake replied. "The effect of the tension outweighs both of those increases."

Shelma passed some calculations privately to Azar, then addressed Jake. "I think there's a problem with your theory. If you take a hoop and spin it ever faster, the only way its energy will begin to decrease is if the speed of sound in the hoop exceeds the speed of light."

Azar checked the calculations; Shelma was right. The total energy of the hoop depended on the precise relationship between the elasticity of the hoop material and the tension it was under. But so, too, did the speed of sound in the material. Linking the two equations showed that the total energy couldn't fall in response to an increase in tension without the speed of sound becoming greater than lightspeed—which was relativity's way of telling you that no material with the necessary properties could exist.

Jake was unfazed. "We've known that result for a long time. It doesn't change the facts."

"What are you claiming?" Shelma asked incredulously. "That the speed of sound *does* exceed the speed of light?"

"Of course not," Jake said. "I agree that you can't construct a motionless hoop and then simply spin it up to a velocity so great that its energy begins to fall. But hoops that are already rotating can change their composition— spitting out particles and transforming into a new material that can only exist under tension. So you have to approach the final state through an intermediate structure: a high-energy, low-tension hoop that decays into a high-tension, low-energy hoop, with the energy difference going into the particles that are emitted in the decay process."

Shelma considered this. "All right, I think I see what you're getting at. But can you explain the details of this intermediate structure, and exactly how it can be synthesized?"

"The details?" Jake said. "We've been on Tallulah for a million years. What makes you think that we've untangled all the details?"

7

THEY REACHED an isolated burrow, far from any colony. Jake went in first, then emerged with two friends, whom Azar's software named Juhi and Rahul.

Juhi said, "Jake tells us you came from the world of a bright star. Is that true?"

Shelma replied, "Absolutely."

"So your real body is not like this at all?"

Shelma sketched her ancestral, five-fold symmetric shape in the sand. Juhi said something that the translator couldn't parse.

They entered the burrow and swam together to the deepest chamber, a much larger space than the prison they'd escaped from. It contained a transceiver and some other equipment that Azar didn't recognize—and in the circumstances it seemed both discourteous and unwise to send the scouts to sniff it out.

Rahul said, "Our friends in Jute"—the colony they'd left—"tell us that the Circlers still think they're holding you. They're hoping to find out more about the invasion plans."

Invasion plans was a phrase Azar associated with ancient history and broad comedy. The zombie software she'd left in the bodies would keep reciting the truth to the bitter end, but now she almost wished she'd programmed some kind of parody of a confession.

Shelma said, "We're grateful for your help. We didn't come here to cause trouble, but before we even knew that Tallulah was inhabited we lost the means to depart." She explained Mologhat's fate.

Jake said, "I thought that was no coincidence. The Old Passengers' machines have blasted specks of dust before, but when you appeared so soon afterward I knew it wasn't down to chance."

The N3ers? "The Old Passengers lived here after the Builders?" Azar said.

"Yes," Juhi replied. "A few of their animals are still around. They built thousands of machines that aim to protect Tallulah, but some of them are a bit trigger happy."

"So your ancestors met the Old Passengers?" Shelma asked.

"Hardly!" Rahul sounded as amused as Azar would have been by the same query in relation to trilobites or dinosaurs. "At least, not above ground. For all we know, some of the Old Passengers might still be alive, deep in the rock. But if they are, they're not very communicative."

Azar said, "What exactly is going on in the crust, besides the heating process? How do the hoops connect to the Spiral In philosophy?"

Juhi said, "Once you give up your flesh and become information, don't you look for the fastest way to process that information?"

"Not always," Azar replied. "In our culture most of us compromise—to stay connected to each other, and to the physical world."

"In our culture," Rahul said, "there is no one coming and going over thousands of light years. There are only your biological cousins—and to Spiral In, if your cousins don't follow you down, that's their loss."

Shelma said, "So the hoops can be used for information processing?"

"Some of them," Jake replied. "The ones you've seen up in the water, probably not. But in the ground there are a billion different varieties."

"*A billion?*" Shelma turned to Azar so they could exchange stunned expressions—or at least so Shelma could hallucinate a version of Azar curling her five tails in the appropriate manner.

"Maybe more," Jake said. "The truth is, nobody above ground really knows. But we do know that some of them can be used as computing elements.

Every time Spiral In becomes serious, they study the hoops, learn how to use them…then disappear into the ground."

Azar was beginning to realize that she hadn't really thought through the implications of the Ground Heaters' process; even the ash it left behind opened up avenues that the Amalgam had only dreamed of. Amalgam femtocomputers were blazingly fast while they lasted, but they decayed as rapidly as the most unstable nuclei. You then had to rebuild them from scratch, making the whole process a waste of time for all but a handful of specialized applications. If you could build complex structures on a nuclear scale that were permanently stabilized—by virtue of possessing far less energy than their individual parts—then that changed the rules of the game completely. A femtocomputer that didn't blow itself apart, that kept on computing non-stop, would run at least six orders of magnitude faster than its atomic counterparts.

She said, "So Spiral In use the hoops to retreat into virtual reality. But why don't you use the heating process yourself, just for the energy? If you want to escape from Tallulah, why not take this process and run?"

Rahul gestured at one of the machines in the corner of the chamber, a clunky, unprepossessing structure with a dozen cables snaking out of it. "There's a sample of deep rock in there. Do you know how much power it's generating? Less than a microwatt."

Azar stared at the machine. Her intuition balked at Rahul's claim, but on reflection it was entirely plausible. In bulk, buried beneath an insulating blanket of rock several kilometers thick, the miraculous fuel would be white hot, but up here in the water a small piece would barely be warmer than its surroundings. Its power to keep the whole planet from freezing came from its sheer quantity, and its spectacular efficiency was tuned for endurance, not a fast burn.

She said, "So in its normal state the process runs slowly. But this isn't like some radioisotope with a half-life that can't be changed."

"No," Rahul said, "it's worse than that. If you take a sample of ore containing a radioisotope, you can concentrate the active ingredient. If we purify deep rock—if we remove some of the ordinary minerals it contains in the hope of producing a denser power source—the process down-regulates automatically, maintaining the same output for a given total mass. It knows what you're doing, and it cheats you out of any gain."

"Ah." Azar was torn between empathy for the lizards' frustration and admiration for the Ground Heaters' ingenuity. It seemed the femtotech had been designed with very strong measures to protect against accidents and weaponization.

Shelma said, "But in all the time you've been studying it, surely you've made some progress? You say Spiral In have learned to use the hoops as computing devices; that must give you some insight into the whole process."

"Using the hoops isn't the same as controlling their creation," Juhi said. "It's like…building a computer out of fish bones, compared to engineering the biology of a fish. Spiral In learn enough to embed their minds in the rock in the simplest possible way. From that starting point, perhaps they migrate to more refined modes. Who knows? They've never come back to tell us."

"If Spiral In can migrate into the rock," Azar said, "why are so many of them still here, above ground?"

"After each migration the philosophy dies out," Juhi replied, "but every few generations it becomes popular again. It starts out as an abstract stance— an idea about what we ought to do, eventually, sometime before we find our-selves confronting the Next Passengers—but then it reaches a critical mass, with enough people taking it seriously for the practicalities to be rediscovered. Then everyone who was serious goes underground…and everyone who was just spouting empty rhetoric defects to a different philosophy. We're at a point in the cycle right now where there's a lot of rhetoric, but not much else."

Azar was too polite to suggest that Spiral Out seemed to be in much the same state themselves, but in their case there was nothing cyclic about it.

Shelma turned her robot's gaze from lizard to lizard, as if searching for a crack in their pessimistic consensus. "It must be possible to harness this process," she said. "To adjust it, to manipulate it. A single nuclear reaction has its rate fixed by physical laws, but this is a *system*—a flexible, program-mable network of nuclear machines. If someone built this system for their own purpose—with details that they chose for themselves, that weren't forced upon them by the underlying physics—then it can be *rebuilt*. You should be able to reverse-engineer the whole thing, and put it together again any way you like."

Jake said, "Someone built the deep rock, that's true. And if we were willing to choose the same path as the Builders, perhaps we could match their feat. But though the Builders set Tallulah in motion, in the end their philosophy was Spiral In. To make deep rock, the Builders *became* deep rock.

"I don't believe it can be done any other way. To understand it well enough to change it, we would have to become it. And then we would have changed ourselves so much that we would no longer want the very thing that we set out to achieve."

8

As THE discussion wound its way back and forth between Tallulah's uncertain history and the competing visions of its future, Azar seized upon one piece of good news that Rahul let slip almost in passing. The lizards couldn't re-create the femtotech from scratch, or even ramp it up into a useful form of propulsion, but they did believe that there was a very good chance that they'd be able to *graft it*. Given an empty world on which to experiment, they hoped that introducing samples of the deep rock into the crust would cause the femtotech to replicate, spreading through the native rock and ultimately creating a second Tallulah.

That was a wonderful prospect, but they'd already missed at least one opportunity. Some two hundred thousand years before, Tallulah had passed through an uninhabited system, but Spiral Out had been at a low ebb and hadn't even managed to launch exploratory probes. Since then they'd simply been hanging around waiting for their next chance. The Ground Heaters had given them an extraordinary gift, rescuing them from their dying planet, but between the culture of dependency that gift had created, the constant temptations of Spiraling In, and the stress of not knowing whether the next world they encountered would turn out to be the home of the Next Passengers, they had ended up paralyzed.

"You should join the Amalgam," Azar said, "and use their network to migrate. The kind of world you're looking for is not in high demand; a frozen planet tidally locked to a faint brown dwarf is of no interest to most space-faring cultures."

"And it's no use to us either," Jake replied, "unless we can enliven it. We can't send the deep rock through your network, can we?"

"No, but if you spent a century or two manufacturing antimatter from geothermal energy, you could build an engine to carry samples of rock at a significant fraction of lightspeed. And even if for some reason you didn't have enough spare power to do that, I guarantee that you could find a partner in the Amalgam who'd trade you a few tonnes of antimatter for some deep rock samples of their own. And I mean a few tonnes on arrival at Tallulah, not a few tonnes when it left home!"

Juhi said, "We need to be careful. It's one thing to hand Tallulah over to the Next Passengers, as the Builders intended, but we don't want a million strangers flocking here just to mine the planet."

"Nobody's going to do that," Shelma assured her. "If deep rock has any value at all in the Amalgam, it will come from the ability to graft it, or the ability to reverse-engineer it. In either case, a few kilograms would be enough."

Rahul said, "Whether we choose to join the Amalgam or not, you need antimatter for your own journey, don't you?"

"A few micrograms would come in handy," Shelma admitted.

The transceiver sprayed out a chemical ringtone and Rahul replied with a command for it to speak. Azar found the conversation that followed cryptic—and she suspected that parts of it were literally in code—but when it was over Rahul announced, "Someone spotted you in the forest with Jake. The Circlers have destroyed your puppets, but they know more or less what happened now. I think we need to move from here."

Azar was dismayed. "Can't you talk to them? Explain the situation? None of our plans should be any threat to them." The Amalgam would happily leave the Circlers in peace, sending no travelers and no further explorers, but the Spiral Out faction were entitled to emigrate, and to trade a few small pieces of Tallulah's exotic legacy with the wider galaxy.

Rahul said, "They're convinced that you're the New Passengers, and that the fight to retain Tallulah has begun. In the past they've viewed Spiral Out as timid fatalists, but now that we've come to your aid we're something worse. We're traitors."

On the flight deck Shelma muttered a string of obscenities. "We're not going to spark a civil war," she told the lizards. "We'll surrender ourselves. It doesn't matter if they destroy us; we'll make backups."

Jake said, "But they understand now that you can do that. You could surrender a thousand machines to them—or one pair of living creatures, and call them your true form—but it won't be enough to convince them that they've put an end to your plans."

Azar wanted to contest this bleak verdict, but from what she'd seen of the Circlers firsthand it rang true. Whatever the original intention of Tallulah's creators, it had sounded like a beautiful story: a chariot traveling between faint, forgotten stars, rescuing the inhabitants of dying worlds, offering them a safe, warm home for a few million years so they could build up their strength then fly from the nest—or, if they wished, dive into its depths, into a femtoscale mansion of a quadrillion rooms. In a way, she admired the Circlers for their determination to tear up the script, to scream at their long-vanished benefactors that they would make their own decisions and not just meekly come along for the ride. But the irony was that they were so intent on rebelling against the Builders that they seemed blind to anything that didn't conform to their own version of the scenario. It was chiseled in stone that one day they would fight the New Passengers for Tallulah, and they had spent so long rehearsing this play that you couldn't even tap them on the shoulder and suggest a different ending without being dragged into the plot and cast as the villain.

ᴧⱽ

SHELMA HAD their mock-lizard body destroy itself, and found a dim but agile P2 fish for the insect to parasitize and modify. A talking fish would attract suspicion, but with some help from the library they managed to engineer speech glands for it that created rapidly decaying words; if they swam up close to a chosen confidante they could emit some short-range chemical whispers with little chance of being overheard. Unfortunately, the lizards' own medical nanotech wasn't flexible enough to do the same for them, and Jake and the others recoiled from a friendly offer to let the aliens tweak their speech organs.

Shelma said privately, "This is going to get messy."

"So how do we fix it?" Azar replied.

"I wish I knew."

They agreed on a place and time to rendezvous, then Jake, Rahul and Juhi scattered.

Shelma said, "I think we should go back to the surface for a while."

They took the fish as high as it could go, then left it parked and rode the insect alone for the last few hundred meters. When they broke the water, Azar found herself almost weeping with relief. She was still as far from home as ever, but just a glimpse of the stars after so long without them made her feel that she was back in the right universe again.

Neither the balloon nor the orbiting microprobes had experienced any form of aggression, or noticed anything else unusual. It seemed that the Circlers, for all their paranoia, had been too complacent to create a world bristling with sensors and weapons while Tallulah's next stop was still so far from sight.

Shelma said, "We should bring the balloon down on the ground somewhere and replicate the library a few times. I think we're already carrying everything vital, but if our backups have to take over from us we want to be sure that they're not disadvantaged." Their backups in the jungle were already receiving incremental memory updates, by radio via the microprobes.

Azar agreed, and they sent the instructions. She paced the flight deck, rubbing her eyes. She had given up the need for sleep, but there was still something irredeemably strange about the feeling of unpunctuated consciousness stretching back into the distance.

"I screwed up," Shelma said. "I rushed to make contact. We didn't even know what the factions' names meant."

"And I let you do it," Azar replied. "We're both at fault. But I don't believe the situation's irretrievable. The Circlers have killed some alien zombies, but according to Jake the philosophies have been at peace for millennia; it could still be a step too far for them to start harming each other."

"How do we defuse their anxiety," Shelma said, "when there's no invading army for them to defeat? Do we offer them the microprobes as sitting ducks? I doubt that they could hit targets that small, and even if they could they'd just assume that there were ten thousand more."

Azar looked up at the stars again, and tried to see them as a hostile, threatening sight. "They need some theater. They need some catharsis." Clearly Shelma thought the same way too, but then neither of them were exactly experts in the lizards' psychology. "And we need to talk to Jake again."

"What do you have in mind?"

"The microprobes are too small, and Mologhat is already gone. So maybe we should think about launching a bigger target."

～w～

ONLY JUHI turned up at the rendezvous point in a remote stretch of ribbon-weed forest. "Jake and Rahul are safe," she said, "but they're too far away at the moment."

"What's been happening?" Azar asked her.

"We've been in contact with most of Spiral Out, and they've made a decision. They want to send a delegation with you to the closest world in the Amalgam, to make contact with this culture and report back on the possibilities for trade and migration."

Azar was encouraged; at least Spiral Out had proved willing to break from its preconceptions.

"We're prepared to start manufacturing antimatter," Juhi continued. "But we should compare notes on the process first; if you have a more efficient method we should adopt that."

Shelma said, "What kind of power sources do you have access to?" The everyday lizard culture they'd seen was based on plant thermoelectrics.

"There are some deep-bore geothermal turbines that are used for specialized research projects," Juhi replied. "Obviously we can't tap the whole output, but we should be able to siphon some off discreetly."

"What if you just built your own turbine?" Azar said. "Would the Circlers do anything to stop you?"

"Right now," Juhi said, "I don't think it would be wise to find out."

Azar turned that statement over in her mind. If people were about to begin clandestine antimatter production, what would happen to them if they were caught?

"We've had an idea," she said, "but I don't know if it will make sense to you. The Circlers believe we've come from a nearby planet, from a star too dim to see. What if we built a spacecraft that might have made a short journey like that...and then let the Circlers shoot it down?"

Juhi said, "How are you going to power this spacecraft?"

"The azide bulbs you eat when you travel; enough of them could actually get a small craft into low orbit. The Circlers accept that we're digitized, so they don't expect the invasion force to be a fleet of thousand-tonne arks."

"It's an interesting idea," Juhi said, "but the hardest part would be contriving their success in destroying the craft. Since your arrival they've been dredging up plans for weapons that our ancestors constructed for the last close approach, two hundred thousand years ago. But nobody's sure now that they still understand those designs."

Shelma said, "What about surveillance? Are they already monitoring what's happening in near space?"

"Yes. You can be sure of that."

"Then the problem," Shelma said, "is that they'd see us taking off. It would better to convince them that something new is coming in from deep space."

Juhi paused, the front of her body twitching from side to side, a motion that Azar now recognized as a sign of anxiety. "I don't see how we can do that. But let me take this to the others."

Shelma had the insect's nanotech construct a sample of a solid-state anti-matter factory, and passed it to Juhi for the lizards to copy. It was the Amalgam's most efficient design, but nothing could get around the fact that it would still need thousands of times more power than any ordinary burrow consumed.

After parting from Juhi they stayed away from Jute and the other colonies, but the scout mites had placed intercepts on some of the intercolony trunk fibers long ago. The lizards had no infrastructure in place for quantum encryption, and their standard communication codes were easily cracked; clearly this wasn't a culture with an entrenched history of bitter enmities and closely held secrets. It was a culture polarized by sudden panic, and Azar clung to the hope that cooler heads would soon prevail.

The tapped conversations were discouraging, though. The idea of Spiral Out as traitors was spreading throughout the Circlers, many of whom were urging each other to keep a close watch on their treacherous neighbors and erstwhile friends. The claim that the alien visitors were benign explorers with no territorial ambitions was largely discounted; two previous examples of Tallulah being colonized were, apparently, sufficient to render other motives unlikely. Azar began to wonder if the best course would be to lie low for a century or two and simply wait for the non-arrival of the trumpeted invasion force to leave the prophets of doom looking like fools.

Rahul met them for the next rendezvous. "Jake's disappeared," he said. "I think he's been imprisoned, but nobody will admit to holding him."

Azar was speechless. For all the bad news she'd heard from the taps, she'd never believed it would come to this.

"We can send machines to hunt for him," Shelma said.

"If you can, please," Rahul replied. "But they will have moved him to another colony, so I don't know exactly where you should start."

Azar came her to senses. She instructed the scouts that were already hovering near the fish; they would spread out and replicate, following the fiber trunk lines from colony to colony, spawning search parties as they went.

"We have an idea to placate the Circlers," Rahul said. "To give them the triumph they think they need."

"Go on," Shelma urged him.

"We can't get a craft into deep space, unseen," he said. "And even if we could, I doubt the Circlers could hit it. But the Old Passengers' machines are still working very well after all this time—as you know, to your cost. If they were seen to repel the would-be New Passengers, I think the Circlers would treat that victory as their own."

Shelma said, "But how do we get the target up there? And how do we guarantee that the machines strike it?"

"We cheat," Rahul said. "We hack into the Old Passengers' network, and make it respond with as much sound and fury as possible to something that isn't really there."

Azar said, "Do you know how to do that?"

"Not quite," Rahul admitted. "This is where we need your help."

The lizards had mapped parts of the Old Passengers' network long ago. It was bioengineered from native C3 plants, and used a modified form of the conductive polymers that Azar had first seen in the thermocouple bush. There were sensors of various kinds scattered across the continents, processing hubs on land and in the water, and dozens of geothermal cannons on the ocean floor.

Every thousand years or so someone had tried tapping into the network, but the protocols had always eluded them. There had been talk of trying to decommission the whole eccentric, unpredictable system, but the contrary view—that the Old Passengers had known what they were doing, and always had the interests of Tallulah at heart—had prevailed. Certainly the system had been benign enough to allow the lizards themselves to cross from their home world unmolested, and if the cannons sometimes spat steam and ice at phantoms that was a small price to pay.

Armed with Rahul's map, Azar and Shelma returned to the surface and sent instructions to the other explorer insects, which had now reached every continent. As the insects tapped into the network, the microprobes monitored the flashes of Cerenkov radiation that incoming cosmic rays created in the upper atmosphere. Whatever else might elicit a response from the system, radiation was a proven irritant.

As they waited for the data to accumulate, Azar couldn't stop thinking about Jake. What would his captors do? *Torture him?* While the lizards had engineered senescence away, and pumped their bodies full of medical nanotech that could combat the subtlest toxins and parasites, a simple metal blade could still be as painful, or as fatal, as it would have been for their earliest ancestors.

In three days, the insects had cracked the protocol: they knew how the Old Passengers' network represented the atmospheric flashes, and how the data was cross-checked and confirmed. Though the system was moderately robust against errors, if the lizards' anecdotes meant anything it was prone to the occasional false positive, and it certainly hadn't been designed with resistance to tampering as a high priority. Azar was beginning to suspect that the Old Passengers had never actually contemplated an invasion; all of their concerns had revolved around natural hazards.

Would the Circlers understand as much, and know that they were being had? Or would they seize upon the evidence as vindication of their fantasies?

They dived to meet Rahul again, and Shelma told him that the network was now in their hands.

"Make it happen," he said. "Shoot down the invaders."

Azar communed with the scout mites. There was still no news of Jake.

9

THE INSECT glided in a gentle helix a few meters above the ocean, but Azar locked the flight deck scape to the stars, banishing the perceived rotation. She fixed her gaze on the horizon and waited.

Data was being fed into the Old Passengers' network, painting an elaborate mirage: a cloud of antihydrogen heading straight for Tallulah, three million kilometers away and closing fast. Interstellar gas and dust colliding with the cloud was creating highly energetic gamma rays; in turn, these gamma rays were striking nitrogen molecules in Tallulah's stratosphere and generating particle-antiparticle pairs. None of this exotic radiation would be getting close to the ground, so the whole hallucination was being played out in terms of flashes of light from high in the atmosphere.

Shelma said, "Given their proclivities, you'd think they would have put satellites in orbit: gamma-ray telescopes at least."

"Maybe they did," Azar replied, "but the orbits were destabilized when Tallulah entered the lizards' system. Or maybe they were just corroded away."

A quarter of a billion years was a long time; deep rock in the satellites might have provided a constant trickle of power, and nanotech could have carried out repairs, but if they lost material to abrasive dust or cosmic ray ablation, however slowly, nothing could have kept them intact forever.

"There she blows!" Shelma cried out happily; with the full library now accessible to the scape, the translations Azar heard of her speech were much more evocative. In infrared, the distant column of superheated steam glowed like an electric arc, rising out of the ocean and stretching into the sky. The ascending tip grew dim and faded into the distance, but when Azar added an overlay with visible frequencies amplified she could see the end of the icy spear glistening in the starlight as it hurtled into space.

This time there was no planet-shrouding halo needed to flush out the danger; the target was all too clear. The microprobes were tracking the ice missiles, and would feed their interaction with the imaginary antimatter cloud into the models that were generating the hoax atmospheric light show for the network, ensuring that all the data continued to reflect a consistent scenario. Of course, if the Circlers also happened to be looking for atmospheric flashes they would see no such thing, but that shouldn't matter, since they had no way of knowing exactly what the Old Passengers' defenses thought they were firing at.

Azar said, "If someone had told me that I'd be faking a battle for Tallulah between an extinct species and an imaginary invader, I would never have walked through that gate."

"Oh, this is nothing," Shelma scoffed. "One day I'll tell you about the time—"

A message from the microprobes half a world away cut off the boast in mid-sentence. Something was emerging from the middle of a continent on the other side of the planet, and it wasn't a fountain of steam. A narrow beam of gamma rays was rising up from the ground, just millimeters thick but energetic enough to have wrapped itself in a radiant cylinder of plasma as it punched its way out of the atmosphere.

Azar let out an anguished moan. "What have we done now?" Her skin crawled as one alarming possibility crossed her mind: someone could be messing with the microprobes, feeding them a vision of non-existent radiation. But that was just paranoid; who would gain anything from hoaxing the hoaxer? Perhaps the insects had screwed up their analysis of the Old

Passengers' protocols and inadvertently injected a second phantom target into the data—one that had elicited a far harsher response.

For several long seconds Shelma was frozen, either in shock or in contemplation. Then she declared, "It's a photonic jet. *We've triggered an unscheduled course correction.*"

"What?"

"The steam jet is exceeding escape velocity, which means it's pushing Tallulah off course, very slightly. So the Builders, the Ground Heaters, are compensating."

Azar wasn't sure yet what she believed, but she hoped the Circlers reached the same conclusion as Shelma; they'd have no reason, then, to question their interpretation of the steam jet as a defensive measure. The photonic jet was just a technical detail, an anti-recoil device for Tallulah's big guns. In any case, the Old Passengers' network seemed to know that such a response was only to be expected; it wasn't treating it as yet another interstellar hazard that needed to be dispelled by its own separate fire hose.

But assuming it wasn't a counter-hoax, this beam of radiation was infinitely more substantial than the non-existent hazard that *was* being pummeled. "There are now real gamma rays blasting through the atmosphere," Azar said. "Hitting nuclei, undergoing pair production. *The photonic jet will be surrounded by antimatter.*"

Shelma said, "I believe you're right."

They instructed the closest insects to fly up near the beam and investigate. The central cylinder of plasma was rich in antiprotons, and though they weren't lasting long before annihilating, the annihilation gamma rays themselves were in turn striking nitrogen nuclei and creating more proton-antiproton pairs, giving rise to a long cascade before the energy was converted into heat, or escaped into space at the top of the beam.

Nanotech in the insects took just minutes to construct the necessary magnetic harvesters, which plucked the slowest antiprotons from the relatively cool margins of the plasma. There were only a few dozen insects in range, and they could only sip from a small part of the beam, but the bounty here dwarfed the travelers' needs. The task that might have taken their Spiral Out accomplices months of furtive, dangerous work would now be complete in less than an hour.

Azar felt an intense surge of relief. The Amalgam was almost within reach now, and no one else would need to put themselves at risk to make the journey possible.

Shelma said, "I think I know where the water went."

"Yeah?"

"When Tallulah came into the Old Passengers' system, the Ground Heaters were nowhere in sight; they were either dead or they'd gone femto. So the Old Passengers had no one to negotiate with, no one to learn from, no one to spell out the rules. They'd simply found this luxurious abandoned lifeboat, and they wanted to take control. But it takes a long time to evacuate a planet physically, building and launching thousands of spacecraft; it's possible that there were still millions of people who wanted to make the crossing even as Tallulah was going out of range of their ships."

"So they built the geothermal cannons," Azar said, "to try to bring it back in range. They were so desperate to let the stragglers come on board that they were willing to pump half the ocean into the sky."

"To no avail. The ghosts of the Ground Heaters—or some insentient navigation system—fought them every step of the way. The femtotech couldn't shut off the cannons; even if it switched off the heating process locally, the rocks would have stayed hot for thousands of years. But the photonic jets it already used for steering could easily compensate for the momentum of the steam." Shelma hesitated, then added, "That could also explain why the Old Passengers ended up allergic to antimatter. An ordinary course change would have taken Tallulah clear of any debris from its own jets, but after a series of long, complicated tussles, there might have been clouds of antimatter lying around that really were worth sweeping aside."

Azar said, "What drives me crazy is that if the deep rock can be grafted, it was all for nothing. The Old Passengers could have brought a sample back to their own world and solved all their problems without anyone leaving."

"That was probably the Ground Heaters' original plan," Shelma said. "To travel the galaxy handing out deep rock, to reheat dying worlds. But to the Old Passengers, *grafting rock* would probably have sounded as ridiculous as trying to re-ignite a dead star with a spoonful of lukewarm helium. By the time they understood the first thing about the femtotech it would have been too late."

Azar watched the column of luminous steam, still rushing into the sky. "Now we've thrown away a few more gigatonnes of water, just to deceive the lizards."

Shelma said, "If you want it to sound slightly less tawdry when you tell your great-great-grandchildren, I recommend the version where we were doing it for the antimatter all along."

"I don't mind lying if it saves people's lives," Azar replied, "but I'd like to return to Hanuz with some prospect that we're not leaving behind a civil war."

"Yeah. We need to find out how far this charade has gone in cleaning up our mess." Shelma inhaled deeply. "Let's dive."

***

AT THE rendezvous point, Rahul explained that the Circlers were still debating the significance of the steam jet. The ice halo had been written off as a false alarm until Azar and Shelma had introduced themselves, but this time nobody doubted that such an intense, sustained effort from the Old Passengers' machines had something to do with encroaching aliens.

When Azar told him that they'd now harvested enough antimatter to make a transmission, Rahul confessed that the photonic jet hadn't taken him entirely by surprise. "Some people have always believed that the Old Passengers fought against the Builders to control Tallulah's path. That's been enough to keep the Circlers from trying to do the same thing themselves; they take it as given that they can't steer the world, and their only choice is to fight to defend it."

Shelma said, "Why not trade to defend it? Why not offer any would-be invaders a few kilograms of deep rock grafts?"

"Because grafting is unproven," Rahul replied. "We've done a thousand experiments with different minerals at various temperatures and pressures, and it *looks* as if there's a balance we can exploit between the hoop system's ability to spread and the safety mechanism that stops it running amok…but the only real proof will come when we try it on a completely new world. Until then, what is there to trade? A handful of warm pebbles that might turn your planet into a fireball, or might do nothing at all."

As they spoke, a wave of scout mites swam inside the camouflage fish and docked with the insect. They had found Jake; he was being held in an isolated burrow, almost three thousand kilometers away.

Azar gave Rahul the position. He said, "We have no one close. Do you know how many Circlers are guarding him?"

"Our machines saw twenty."

"Then I don't know how to help him," Rahul confessed. "When he broke you out it was easier, everything was still in a state of confusion. Half the people around you had no declared allegiance; Jake and Tilly were not known as Spiral Out before, it was your presence that forced them to take sides. But all twenty people with Jake now will be resolute Circlers, committed to that philosophy for centuries."

Shelma said, "The invasion has been repelled! What would the Circlers have to gain now by harming him?"

"It would set an example for future collaborators."

They swam together to the closest intercept point on the trunk line; the scouts were piggy-backing their own data onto the fiber, using methods too subtle for the lizards to detect. Azar and Shelma watched through the scouts' senses, and passed on the Circlers' chemical conversation to Rahul. Jake was in one chamber, along with four guards; in a nearby chamber the other Circlers had gathered to discuss the latest news and plan their next move.

Shelma spoke to Azar privately. "I've got the nanotech primed to go in and digitize him, if it comes to that. But if we wait for them to kill him it might be too late; if they mutilate the body or use corrosive chemicals we won't have time to capture him properly."

Jake hadn't given them explicit consent to do anything, but Azar swallowed her objections. According to Juhi he had wanted to be part of a delegation to the Amalgam, and if he turned out to be displeased about being snatched into the infosphere without warning, they could always write him back into ordinary flesh once they'd smuggled his software to safety. The real danger here was jumping in too soon or too late. Too soon and they risked re-igniting tensions with an unmistakable alien intervention. Too late and Jake would be dead.

Among the Circlers in the other chamber were two that Azar recognized from their first encounter: Omar and Lisa. Most of the talk here so far had been petty squabbling, but now the subject turned to Jake.

"We should release him," Omar insisted. "The fleet has been destroyed or turned back; it doesn't matter what he does now."

"Spiral Out need to know what happens to traitors," Lisa replied. "He set New Passengers free among us. He put everyone in danger."

Another Circler, Silas, said, "You saw their technology; they could have escaped anyway. Whatever Spiral Out do, we're never going to be sure that we're safe, that we're alone. That's the reality now, and we need to find a way to live with it."

Half a dozen other Circlers responded to this angrily, swimming around the chamber in tight, anxious loops. "We need to kill him," Judah declared. "We need to draw a clear boundary between the right of Spiral Out to make their plans to leave Tallulah, and our right to live here safely and defend our own world."

Omar said, "If we kill him we'll start another war. Do you know how many people died in the last one?"

"Better a million die than we lose the whole world to the New Passengers," Lisa replied.

"Better *nobody dies*," Omar retorted, "and we spend our efforts on something that can help us all. We've been living like fools. We don't deserve to feel safe, and killing our own people won't change that. We don't even know with certainty where the closest world really lies! And we have no idea what kind of life there might be around the bright stars; I doubt that the aliens were telling us the truth, but none of us really know what's possible."

"We've been caught sleeping," Judah conceded. "That much is our fault. But what do you suggest we do about it?"

Omar said, "We need to work together with Spiral Out to explore the nearest worlds, before any more of their inhabitants reach us themselves. If we send out small robots to gather information, the results can serve everyone: defenders of Tallulah, and those who want to leave."

Lisa was scornful. "After this, you're going to trust Spiral Out as our allies?"

"Jake freed two aliens that you were threatening to kill," Omar replied. "They had done us no harm, and we don't even know for sure that they were lying. Because of that, we should slaughter all of Spiral Out? Or treat them all as our enemies? If everything that's happened wakes them from their sleep the way it should wake us, we can benefit from each other's efforts."

Azar looked to Rahul for a reading of the situation, but he was motionless, his posture offering no verdict. Jake's fate could go either way.

After forty minutes of discussion with no clear consensus, Omar said, "I'm releasing him." He paused for a few seconds, then left the chamber. Lisa squirted wordless, dissatisfied noise, but nobody moved to stop him.

Omar entered the chamber where Jake was being held and spoke with the Circlers who were standing guard.

"I don't agree," said Tarek. "You've come alone to demand this. Who else is with you?"

Omar and Tarek went together to the other Circlers. Omar said, "I repeat, I'm releasing Jake. If anyone here wants a war, I will be an enemy of the warmongers, so you'd better kill me now."

Judah said, "No one's going to kill you." He swam with Omar to Jake's chamber and spoke with the remaining guards. Then all five of them departed, leaving Jake alone.

Jake circled the chamber nervously a few times, then headed out of the burrow. Azar sent a swarm of scouts after him, but they had no data channel back to the fiber, and Jake was soon out of sight.

Almost an hour later, a message came through from the scouts; Jake had reached a nearby colony where the scouts could tap into the fiber again. Azar told Rahul their location.

Rahul said, "He's safe, he's with friends. It's over for now."

Azar sat on the flight deck weeping, hiding her tears even from Shelma.

10

LAUNCHED FROM a rail gun on Tallulah's highest mountain, Mologhat 3 spent six seconds plowing through the atmosphere before attaining the freedom of space. Its heat shield glowed brightly as it ascended, but if the Old Passengers' machines noticed it they found no reason to molest this speck of light as it headed out of harm's way. When it reached an altitude of a thousand kilometers it fired its own tiny photonic jet, but the radiation was horizontal and highly directional; nothing on Tallulah had a hope of detecting it.

Jake, Tilly, Rahul, Juhi and a fifth delegate, Santo, swam across the flooded observation deck, looking down on their world for the first time. Azar swam among them, but not as a lizard in anyone's eyes. Her words would come to them as familiar chemicals, but they could cope with the sight of her as she really was.

As Azar gazed upon Tallulah, she dared to feel hope. There would be no war, no pogrom, but there was still a daunting task ahead for the millions of Spiral Out who remained. They would need to prepare the Circlers for the truth: for the eventual return of this secret delegation, for trade with the Amalgam, for a galaxy that was not what they'd imagined at all. For a future that didn't follow their script.

Jake said, "Do you think we'll ever meet Shelma again?"

Azar shrugged; he wouldn't recognize the gesture immediately, but he'd soon learn. "She once told me that she could choose for herself between solitude and a connection with her people. If she wants to come back, she'll make those connections as strong as she can."

"No one's ever returned before," Jake said.

"Did Spiral In ever really want to?"

When the moles finally hit pay dirt beneath the ocean floor, their mass spectrometers had detected more than a hundred billion variants of the hoop, and that was only counting the stable forms. The deep rock was more complex than most living systems; no doubt much of that complexity was fixed by the needs of the heating process, but there was still room for countless variations along the way—and room for a new passenger hitching a ride on the hoops as they turned iron and nickel into heat.

If you had to become deep rock in order to understand it, Shelma had decided, she would become it, and then come back. She'd drag the secrets of the hoops out of the underworld and into the starlight.

"What if you can't?" Azar had asked her. "What if you lose your way?"

"There's room in there for a whole universe," Shelma had replied. "If I'm tempted into staying, don't think of me as dead. Just think of me as an explorer who lived a good life to its end."

Jake said, "Tell me more about your world. Tell me about Hanuz."

"There's no need," Azar replied. She gestured at the departure gate. "If you're ready, I'll show it to you."

"Just like that?" Jake twitched anxiously.

"It's fourteen quadrillion kilometers," she said. "You won't be back for three thousand years. You can change your mind and stay, or you can gather your friends and swim it with me. But I'm leaving now. I need to see my family. I need to go home."